Marnie Riches grew up on a rough estate in Manchester, aptly within sight of the dreaming spires of Strangeways prison. Able to speak five different languages, she gained a Masters degree in Modern & Medieval Dutch and German from Cambridge University. She has been a punk, a trainee rock star, a pretend artist, a property developer and professional fundraiser. In her spare time, she likes to run, mainly to offset the wine and fine food she consumes with great enthusiasm.

Having authored the first six books of HarperCollins Children's Time-Hunters series, she now writes crime thrillers for adults. She is the author of the bestselling George McKenzie series, and her first novel in the Manchester series, *Born Bad*, was published in 2017.

By the same author:

George McKenzie eBook series
The Girl Who Wouldn't Die
The Girl Who Broke the Rules
The Girl Who Walked in the Shadows
The Girl Who Had No Fear

Manchester series
Born Bad

Praise for Marnie Riches:

'Gritty and gripping'   **Kimberley Chambers**

'A leading light in the field of Mancunian noir' *Guardian*

'Drags you down the mean streets of Manchester with verve
and authenticity. You can almost smell the blood and rain'
Simon Toyne

'Riches' storytelling is blistering, vivid and super-pacy. It's
also very funny, even at its darkest'   **Helen Cadbury**

'Fast-paced, enthralling and heartrending; I couldn't put it
down'   **C. L. Taylor**

'A strong, edgy debut that deserves to do well'
Clare Mackintosh

'Fast, furious, fantastic . . . One killer thriller!'
Mark Edwards

What the reviewers said:

'Absolutely brilliant, kept me on my toes from the start to the final page!'

'A great gritty story. Plenty of drama with the Manchester underworld!'

'Breathtakingly brilliant'

'More please – and soon!'

'Truly outstanding'

'An intricate, fast-paced and utterly compelling thriller'

The Cover Up

MARNIE RICHES

Avon
A division of HarperCollins*Publishers*
1 London Bridge Street
London SE1 9GF
www.harpercollins.co.uk

A Paperback Original 2018
1
Copyright © Marnie Riches 2018

Marnie Riches asserts the moral right to
be identified as the author of this work.

A catalogue record for this book is
available from the British Library

ISBN 978-0-00-820396-2

Typeset in Minion by Palimpsest Book Production Ltd, Falkirk, Stirlingshire
Printed and bound by CPI Group (UK) Ltd, Croydon CR0 4YY

MIX
Paper from
responsible sources
FSC
www.fsc.org   FSC C007454

This book is produced from independently certified FSC™ paper
to ensure responsible forest management.

For more information visit: www.harpercollins.co.uk/green

For my grandparents,
Margaret, Ida and Harry:
three of Manchester's finest.

Though they're gone, I owe my fat knees and terrific boobies
to Margaret – a beautiful woman and the kindest of souls,
who knew how to rock a leopard-skin dress. I owe my love
of a good rummage for a bargain to Ida, the inimitable
Jumble Queen of Manchester whose carbon footprint in
her long, long lifetime was lightly trodden. I owe my love
of cars to Harry, who drove a black cab by night and a
burgundy Wolseley by day – potless, maybe, but never less
than stylish. They were all terrible cooks but I loved them
for other reasons.

Chapter 1

Sheila

Turns out, marking your territory wasn't the sole preserve of spraying tom cats with big balls. Sheila smiled at the thought as she prowled around the basement bar of M1 House in her Louboutins.

'I'd like you to rearrange the seating down here,' she told Frank, describing the space in the bowels of the super-club with a wave of her arm. Her Tiffany bangles jangled merrily, audible above the thub, thub, thub of the bass from upstairs, as the DJ and sound engineers performed the soundcheck ahead of an evening of revelry.

Frank was nodding like one of those toy dogs you got in the rear window of crappy cars. Jumpy, as usual. Her brother-in-law had never been anything but.

'Yeah. Yeah, Sheila, love. Mint. But what do you mean?'

'Get one of the staff to move the furniture, Frank. Set up single tables and two chairs.' Visualising how the space would ideally work in this debut foray into the world of speed-dating, Sheila stalked over to one of the tables in the subterranean bar, recently redubbed, 'Jack's bar'. On the wall hung a neon sign, styled from a lyric her nephew had apparently written on one of the toilet doors.

1

In the beginning, there was Jack.

She glanced momentarily at it. Reminded of how much Frank had lost. Grabbing the sleeve of Frank's baggy top – an old James long-sleeved T from the band's *Gold Mother* heyday – she changed tack. 'Are you eating?' Through the cotton fabric, worn soft and thin with use, she could feel that his forearms, always wiry at the best of times, were mere bone and sinew now, covered with skin.

Frank cocked his head to one side. Entirely grey-white, though he'd always boasted the best head of hair out of the two O'Brien brothers. Paddy had had only a ring of shorn fluff around a shining freckled pate, by the end. The fiery ginger of his youth had dulled in later years to a dirty strawberry blond. But Frank had inherited different genes entirely. And not just follically. 'Course,' he said. 'I had a lovely kebab on Tuesday. It had sauce and everything.'

'That's two days ago. Have you eaten since?' Sheila asked, pondering the shadows that the basement bar's mood-lighting cast along the gaunt furrows either side of his mouth.

He grinned at her. Narrowed his eyes. Wagging his finger, as if he'd just sussed some sister-in-lawly subterfuge. 'I see what you're doing. You're checking up on me, aren't you?' He pulled his sleeve gently out of reach, ramming his hands into the pockets of his jeans. 'It's nice of you but—'

'Come round for dinner with me and Conks tonight. I'll make a curry.' Sheila knew what an overgrown boy like Frank needed. Mothering. Perhaps she could find him a woman through her speed-dating venture.

'Aw, She. I'm busy actually. I've got this—'

'Now. Tables and chairs,' Sheila said, assuming that the dinner was a done deal and turning her attention to the layout of the bar area. 'Me and Gloria went to another speed-dating night, run as a franchise by some big company that covers the north. They had the same set-up. A number on each table. You ring the bell. The men move round after three minutes to sit with a new woman. So the seating's really important.'

Scratching at his ear, Frank frowned. 'Sheila, I hope you don't think I'm a cheeky sod, but you're the head of the O'Briens, now. You're the boss-lady. What the hell are you doing, messing around with lonely hearts crap?'

Sheila moved over to the bar where she had left her laptop in its bag. Beckoned Frank to follow her. She could barely contain her excitement as it effervesced like Cristal champagne inside her. Several months ago, Paddy would have popped those bubbles for her with a verbal put-down or a physical slap.

'This is my latest entrepreneurial vision, Frank. And you're helping me do it. Come and look.'

Opening the laptop on the bar, she brought up a brightly coloured website. Photo after photo of beaming, attractive, wholesome-looking couples holding hands, kissing, embracing . . . 'Online dating.'

Slack-jawed, Frank stared at the web page's masthead. *True Love Dates.*

'It's a play on words,' Sheila said. 'True Love Dates instead of True Love Waits. Get it?'

Frank nodded, clearly not getting it at all.

'It's me and Gloria's new venture. We're gonna do speed-dating to draw people in, and I've just had this website designed. There's millions of subscribers to some of the bigger online-dating sites. We get their credit card details and bam! You slap on an admin charge and you're making a fortune from sod all. Algorithms do the work. And once

I've got a stack of subscribers, I'm going to do a big phishing scam that can't be traced. I've got this speccy computer geek from UMIST reckons he can cream millions off the top, straight into an offshore account.'

'I don't get it.'

'It's the darknet, or some shit, Frank,' she said, savouring the thrill of her racing pulse and the endorphins that momentarily almost snuffed out the stress of Ellis James and the tax and annoying CCTV cameras that saw everything. 'This is the future. It's so good, because it's almost legal!' She tapped her nail extensions on the gleaming reinforced glass bar for emphasis. 'And sophisticated. The set-up costs are sod all. And me and Gloria get to spread a little love into the bargain. We've already got fifty sign-ups for tomorrow night's speed-dating and a couple of thousand on this dating website.'

'Doesn't sound like much,' Frank said, leaning over the bar to pour himself half a lager from the tap. His T-shirt riding up to reveal an emaciated, concave stomach.

Sheila looked away abruptly, stroking the web page that glowed lovingly out at her from the laptop's screen. 'Give it a couple of months and it will,' she said, somewhat irritated that her enthusiasm wasn't as contagious as she'd hoped. Remembering the way Paddy had ridiculed her idea to start up a cleaning agency all those years ago. Bastard. But now he was dead, and the cleaning agency, staffed by women they'd rescued from scumbag traffickers, had a turnover of a couple of million a year and was growing month on month. Income she could spend, however circuitously it made its way to her current account . . . unlike Paddy's dirty cash that sat in rubble sacks beneath the tiled floor of her guest en-suite. 'I know what I'm doing, you know. Same as you knew what you were doing when you bought this place, Frank.'

'I've had nothing but aggro since I bought this club,' Frank said, opening an old-fashioned pill box and dropping a small tablet into his drink. 'My son was murdered on my dance floor, and then, that twat, the Fish Man killed a load of kids. Our Jack's dead. My reputation's hanging by a thread. Some savvy businessman I am.'

'But that was all down to Paddy,' Sheila said, rubbing Frank's bony shoulder as a gesture of solidarity, though he shrugged away from her touch. 'And he's gone. You've done well to get this place open again. Sod that bullying arsehole. He's just a memory. To hell with the past, Frank. You own one of the country's biggest super-clubs and you do it well. All the outrage in the papers from worried middle-class parents made kids who were desperate for a walk on the wild side wanna come back! M1 House is edgy and cool. *You're* cool! Have faith in yourself, chuck.'

Sighing heavily, the crow's feet around Frank's eyes seemed to deepen. The shadows on his face seemed to lengthen. The Adam's apple bobbed up and down, sticking out of his scrawny neck as though a malign spirit had taken up residence in his throat and was trying to punch its way out.

'I'm not so sure,' he said. 'Just when I got the Boddlingtons off my back, and I'm getting back on my feet with the club, there's been a few new faces around. I've got a bad feeling about it.'

Sheila snapped the lid of the laptop shut. 'New faces? How do you mean?' She studied Frank's face for signs of drug-fuelled paranoia and hippy bullshit.

'You got new lads working for you? Dealing in here?'

'A couple of temporary workers, doing a bit of this and that. We're struggling to find the staff since Paddy got stabbed. A couple of the lads got caught in the crossfire when the Boddlingtons did over the cannabis farm. Quite a few have just lost their nerve and said they were going straight. I can't exactly stop them. Or blame them.'

'Paddy would have had them killed before he'd let them go,' Frank said, running a thin finger around and around the rim of his half-pint glass.

'I'm not Paddy,' Sheila said, pressing her lips together tightly. Stifling an outburst. 'And that's precisely why I'm trying to build up me and Gloria's cleaning business and do these new start-ups. White-collar crime, Frank. It's less risky. It's more forward-thinking. It's how the rich get richer. All that gun-toting bad-boy crap is Paddy's legacy. I've got a functioning brain and a beating heart, Frank. I can't fill my days, sitting on my backside, sewing a fine seam like some merry widow. My Amy and Dahlia have grown up and flown the nest. One at uni. One a lawyer in the City. I need something more than nail bars and chardonnay and I *don't* want my daughters having their inheritance seized by the coppers and dying of shame if I go down. Now, who were these new faces? You got any security footage of them?'

Taking her laptop bag with her, Sheila followed Frank up the winding staircase to the echoing vastness of the main club. Here, the house music that the DJ played reverberated off the empty, gleaming dance floor – sanded down and refinished not once, but twice, to remove the life's blood of those who had fallen at the hand of that slippery eel of a Fish Man, the Boddlington gang enforcer, Asaf Smolensky. Glancing at the DJ booth, she expected to see her nephew standing there, all muscles and bronzed-Adonis-handsome, with his cans pressed to his ear. Young Jack, Manchester's golden boy, waving at his Aunty Sheila. In his stead, there was just some young, trendy-looking black guy she didn't recognise – up from London no doubt – and the chubby, middle-aged sound engineer, perched behind a mixing console on the other side of the club.

As Frank disappeared through to the backstage area, Sheila noticed the tanned man in overalls, marking a spot on the wall with a pencil. He wore a baseball cap at a ridiculous angle for a middle-aged man. Wielded a measuring tape with clean hands that looked out of place on a manual labourer. The thought that he was somewhat familiar drifted in and out of her head so rapidly that it left no trace whatsoever. Her brother-in-law was always having work done to a building that was now tantamount to a memorial to Jack.

'Here we go,' Frank said in his office, pulling several sheets of paper out of his desk drawer. 'I had Otis, the security feller, come up with these. Pictures from the footage.' He pushed them across the desk towards Sheila. Tapped on the heads of two men – one black with dreads, one white with a crew cut, both man-mountains – who, even given the poor quality of the CCTV stills, clearly stuck out as far older interlopers among the firm, lithe bodies of the partying youngsters.

Sheila noted a shiftiness to the men's eyes – perhaps imagined, given how grainy the images were. But the tense way that they held their bodies gave them away as dealers, not dancers. And who the hell wore quilted bomber jackets on a sweaty dance floor?

'They're not any of my temps,' she said, digging at the back of her molars with her tongue, feeling some kale left behind from the badly blended smoothie that Conky had made her. A for effort. C for execution. 'Give them to me. I'll see what Conks thinks. He knows everyone. If it's a rival crew, he'll be on it like flies on dog shit.'

Click-clacking her way across the dance floor, clutching

her fur gilet close around her slender body against the cold air of the vast unheated super-club, Sheila pondered how she might offload the responsibility of the dirtier side to the business elsewhere. Heading into the triple-height vestibule, she contemplated the meeting she had yet to attend that day at the head office of a commercial airline. Ably assisted by Gloria, she would deliver a pitch to the airline's board members for the contract to clean European-bound aircraft at several airports in the north. She imagined speaking authoritatively, dressed just on the business side of provocatively. She would use a breathy, sexy, irresistible voice. She was sure that flashing a little titty, in addition to their competitive rates and immaculate reputation, would land the lucrative deal.

In fact, Sheila was so caught up in her fantasies of success and the residual enthusiasm over her speed-dating venture that she only barely registered the white van parked outside M1 House. Nor did she realise that the man in the overalls with the stupid baseball cap was following her onto the street. And when her phone rang out with the full-bodied Pop Queen warble of Adele, Sheila was so baffled by the Brummie accent of the unfamiliar caller at the other end, she failed to notice that the man in the overalls, who did in fact own the white van, was standing right behind her.

Chapter 2

Gloria

'Is he looking?' Gloria asked Winnie, who, as usual, was sitting to her right at the end of the pew. No response. She elbowed the old woman gently. Whispering loud enough so that a couple of the elderly men in front turned around and grimaced at her disapprovingly. 'Is he looking?'

'No, dear.' Winnie shook her head, tickling Gloria's ears with a flurry of petrol-coloured feathers. Waving a lace fan slowly up and down in the stuffy place.

It was a wonder she could see anything from under that hat. 'Are you sure?'

'I'm old, dear. Not blind. Hush! Pastor's speaking.'

Irritated that her studied cool and feigned disinterest wasn't working, Gloria faced forward again. Trying desperately to catch the pastor's eye once more by pushing out her chest and batting her eyelashes.

No response.

The fine man standing in the pulpit, preaching to the swollen ranks of the congregation with vim, vigour and pleasantly developed triceps when he raised his hands to praise Jesus, had not cast so much as a glance her way since the start of the Sunday morning service. And there was

Kitty Fried Chicken, still sitting at the front in the spousal hot-seat, wearing a beret, looking like some cross between Jabba the Hut and a black Che Guevara in BHS' best. Still clinging on to that fine man of God like the oniony stink of sweat clinging to that ghastly polyester ensemble she was wearing.

Smoothing down her own pure silk Hobbs dress, Gloria wondered what had gone wrong in her grand plan. The pastor, by rights, should have been hers now. She'd been giving it her best shot for years, praying to the good Lord that fate would finally bring her the true love with this wonderful man that she so needed and deserved. But despite her best efforts, his marriage to a woman who smelled of four-day-old chicken was no closer to disintegration, and Gloria was no closer to the union of holy souls with the pastor that she desired.

'Praise Jesus!' the congregation intoned. 'Praise him. Oh yes!'

Amid much fervour and hubbub, singing started up. 'Father Can You Hear Me?' Naturally, Kitty Fried Chicken was out of her seat, clutching a microphone, her chins wobbling and a sweat breaking out on her forehead as she worked her way up from a delicate soulful whisper to a growling fever pitch. Belting the hymn out, with the choir answering her every worshipful stanza in glorious harmony; the band playing along with enough skilful dynamism to usher a host of angels into the church. The hall was thrumming with love for the Lord Jesus Christ, but Gloria felt only cold and loneliness and bitterness inside, for she saw the truth.

At that moment, the adoration visibly poured out of the pastor, directed not at Gloria but at his dumpy, fugly wife who sang better than any soprano in the Royal Opera

House, and who had more soul than any two-bit R&B singer on the television. Gloria realised the game was up.

'I'm wasting my time,' she told Winnie.

Winnie popped a mint on the end of her tongue and fanned herself nonchalantly. 'You give it a good go,' she said, squeezing Gloria's arm, like the mother she wished she'd had. 'But it *is* time to move on, love.'

'But she stinks of stale chicken, Win.' Gloria could feel tears prick the backs of her eyes. 'I smell of Christian Dior.'

'Some men just don't have a very good sense of smell, darling.' There was sympathy in the milky-ringed irises of Winnie's brown eyes. 'He might have blocked sinuses.'

'But she's boring!'

Winnie offered her a mint. Speaking the quiet wisdom of the elderly, just audible above the jubilant singing, she said: 'The only difference between her and you, Gloria, is that she got there first. And he obviously needs his eyes testing, because Kitty has got a face like tripe and beans gone wrong. Or maybe she's got a diamond-encrusted tutu hidden in those big knickers of hers. Who knows? You can do better, love. Honestly. Pastor's not all that. He had bad breath last Sunday.'

With the service over, Gloria's heart thumped insistently inside her ribcage. Time to get face-to-face with the pastor and see for certain, now that the filter of hope had been removed from her sight, if there was any longing for Gloria Bell in his eyes. Just one last double-check. Maybe she could even whisper in his ear that she loved him, just in case he was too stupid to have sussed it after all these years. She knew men were often slow on the uptake like that. But the realisation that her dream was dying settled in her stomach like an accumulation of heavy metal, rendering her optimism nothing more than a giant, unwanted malignancy.

Gloria filed out into the cold vestibule with the other worshippers, buffeted along by her ever-thankful trafficked workers, looking like jewel-coloured parrots in their Nigerian wraps and skirts.

'Hello, Aunty Gloria! Blessings to you!'

'Coming for cake, Aunty G?'

'Loving your dress, Mrs Gloria!'

Kind words from her cleaners. At least somebody loved her, even if their love had been bought by offering them slave labour and free cramped living conditions as an alternative to prostitution in Benin City or destitution in the DRC.

'Greetings and blessings, ladies!' Gloria could hear that her voice was tremulous. It didn't do to appear weak in front of her employees. She opted not to say anything more.

But her legs almost buckled with adrenalin as she caught sight of the pastor's handsome face in amongst the crowd. Clyde, who owned the soul food takeout, was shaking his hand by the large, arched doorway. Was Pastor alone? No. Clyde stepped aside to reveal the short, squat Kitty Fried Chicken by the pastor's side. Fleetingly, Gloria wondered if there was a passage in the Bible that would excuse ramming a ricin patty into Kitty's fat face at the next church mingle.

She muttered under her breath. *'Beat your plowshares into swords and your pruning hooks into spears; let the weak say, "I am a warrior!"* If it's good enough for Joel, it's good enough for me.'

By the time Gloria had reached the vestibule to be thanked by the pastor, her anger had started to morph into sadness. She could see the lumpy bad skin of Kitty's cheeks, yet still the pastor had his arm around her. Rubbing her shoulder encouragingly, as the churchgoers heaped praise on her for her soulful singing.

Stepping forwards, Gloria held her hand out to the hand-some man who had taken up residence in her heart with his flirtation and mixed messages. My, how he looked like Luther Vandross in his thin days. Even now, he caused the butterflies in her stomach to take flight. But as this heavenly man reached out to reciprocate her greeting, Gloria realised the pastor was not looking into her eyes at all. His radiant smile was not for her. She followed his gaze, glancing over her shoulder, whereupon it dawned on her that he was ogling fresh meat. Pat Nicholas' girl, Kendra. Wearing a miniskirt and stilettos, though she couldn't have been more than seventeen.

Gloria gripped the pastor's hand so tightly, he had no option but to make eye contact with her, finally. In a strong voice, she said, '*I have fought the good fight, I have finished the race, I have kept the faith* – 2 Timothy 4:7,' and walked briskly out onto the street, before he had chance to see her first tear fall.

Making haste along the high street of Parson's Croft before the affable gang of illicit cleaners had the chance to sweep her up into their ranks and into the cake shop, as was the usual post-church arrangement, Gloria eventually came to a halt outside the Western Union money shop. She looked around the busy, scruffy street through blurred, watery eyes. Disoriented by the traffic that whipped past and the group of youths that were pushing by her, five abreast, one doing wheelies on his mountain bike on the pavement. Ordinarily, she'd have shouted after him to get on the road where he belonged. But now . . .

'Are you okay, Mrs Bell?' one of the boys asked her. 'Are you crying?'

Gloria shook her head vociferously, treating the lad to a hard stare. Who was he? She didn't recognise him. He looked like a younger Leviticus. She didn't need sympathy from a little toerag like him. 'Conjunctivitis,' she said, aggressively wiping the tears away with the back of her hand. Clutching her coat close and her handbag closer. 'And tell your mate to get off his bike. Pavements are for pedestrians.'

Where had she left her Mazda? There it was, on Samuel Street. Had she had any breakfast? She couldn't remember. *Get yourself together, Gloria Bell,* she chided herself. *Right, where am I going? Where are my car keys?* She turned over the engine. *Why has Jesus forsaken me and made a barren wasteland of my heart yet again?*

Driving away from the city, she found herself bypassing the quiet cul-de-sac on which she was living with her son and grandson. She continued on through the shower of falling golden leaves to Bramshott. Pulled up outside the high gates of Sheila's sprawling house, where she spotted the dogged detective, Ellis James, ensconced on the opposite side of the road in his foetid Ford – a sinner's vehicle, if ever there was one. He was clearly staking out the place. She paid no heed to the white van that was parked yet again outside the neighbour's pile.

'Let me in,' she shouted through the intercom through tears that simply wouldn't let up.

'Hey! Hey! What's all this for?' Sheila asked, ushering her through to the kitchen, draping a comforting arm around her shoulders.

Unable to stem the flow of heartbreak, Gloria sobbed openly, stumbling across the marble floor and throwing herself onto a bar stool.

'I'll put the kettle on and rustle up some cheese toasties,' Conky said, donning an apron as though he wasn't a murdering henchman at all but rather some Northern Irish alternative to Paul Hollywood. He wasn't wearing his hairpiece or sunglasses today. If anything, his kindness made Gloria sob harder. 'Let you ladies talk. Don't mind me.' He chuckled.

Five minutes and half a kitchen roll later, the tears were replaced by hiccoughs and fatigue. Running her work-worn fingers along the gleaming granite worktop of the island, Gloria sighed heavily. Turned to Sheila. 'I give up, Sheila. The pastor, I mean. He's a cad. Nothing but a broken, unhappy man with bad breath and an eye for the ladies.'

Sheila's carefully plucked brows furrowed. She squeezed Gloria's hand in solidarity. 'You'll get over it. Honest.'

Conky set a coffee down before her on a coaster, leaning in to offer her the dubious wisdom and sincerity behind those bulbous thyroid eyes. 'You've got to find someone new, Gloria. Someone better. Sure, I don't know what you saw in some attention-seeking Bible-basher anyway!'

'*Man shall not live by bread alone*, Conky, *but by every word that comes from the mouth of God* – Matthew 4:4.' She tried to treat him to a disapproving scowl but hadn't the energy to screw her features into the correct shape.

'Aye. Oh, well,' he simply said. 'Some things just aren't meant to be.'

Feeling her resolve weaken and her lip tremble, Gloria whispered. 'He was the love of my life. I'll never be able to rid myself of these feelings. I know it.'

'Bullshit!' Sheila said, smiling encouragingly. Glancing at the clock. Clearly, her sisterly support was on a time limit. How very Sheila. 'You're a fighter and a survivor, Gloria Bell. A successful entrepreneur! You're worth more.'

Conky set a plate full of perfect golden cheese toasties onto the worktop. Fidgeting at their side, as though he were waiting to hatch some nugget of manly advice. Sure enough . . .

'You have to push your feelings aside for this eejit and

start again, Gloria,' he said, waving a well-meaning spatula in her direction. 'Don't make a fool of yourself over a man that has the glad eye for every bit of skirt that comes his way.'

At her side, Sheila suddenly started to clap her hands like an excited seal. She encircled Gloria's wrist in a cage made from those shellac talons. 'You, my dear, are going speed-dating!'

'What?' Gloria said, biting into a triangle of toastie. Noticing Sheila's plate remained empty.

'You'll be a guinea pig for our first speed-dating night!'

'Beezer!' Conky said, grinning. 'Sure, you'll find yourself a nice man that way. An emotionally available man, for a start.'

'I am *not* going speed-dating!' Gloria slapped her snack onto her plate in disgust.

'Yes you bloody well are,' Sheila said. All smiles. Eye on the clock. 'Now, get your skates on with that cuppa because I've got a meeting with a Brummie who reckons he's got the answer to all my problems.'

Chapter 3

Conky

'Whereabouts are we meeting this Nigel Bancroft?' Conky asked, shoving his handgun further into his waistband, turning his back to the grey-faced shoppers in the Lowry Centre's multi-storey car park so that they couldn't see what he was about. The cold metal dug uncomfortably into the overhang of his burgeoning belly. Sheila's cooking was too good. He prayed he wouldn't inadvertently shoot his own testicles off.

'Near the bridge,' Sheila said, slamming the car door. 'Just by the water's edge. He didn't want anyone earwigging.' She examined her reflection in the Panamera's gleaming tinted window. Smoothed the tresses of her hair. Bared her white teeth at him across the roof of the car. 'Have I got lipstick on my teeth?'

Peering over his Ray-Bans, Conky smiled. Continually surprised that Sheila should ever question her own beauty.
Those cherries fairly do enclose
Of orient pearl a double row,
Which when her lovely laughter shows,
They look like rosebuds fill'd with snow.'
He finished his recital with a grin, ignoring the sniggers

from two teenaged girls who passed by on their way to the lifts.

Sheila frowned at him uncertainly. Touching her incisors with her index finger. 'What?'

'It's a poem from the seventeenth century.'

'So, have I got lippy on my teeth?'

'No, darling. You're grand.' He touched his own carefully arranged hair ensemble, hoping that the wind wouldn't be blowing stiffly along the waterway. It wouldn't do to show weakness to a man like Nigel Bancroft.

Silence in the lift with the genuine punters hoping to nab a bargain in the M&S clearance section. Conky reached out in the squash of the stuffed metal box for Sheila's hand but was disappointed. Her stern expression was all business. She clutched her Hermès handbag, holding it against her stomach as though it provided a force field protecting her from the unwashed mortals and whatever was to come.

He noticed people staring up at him as the lift travelled downwards; turning away abruptly as they suspected they had just made eye contact with the ominous-looking wall of man, clad all in black like a funeral director. They were lucky he was wearing sunglasses. Poor wee bastards would have a heart attack if he treated them to The Eyes.

'Come on. We're late,' Sheila said, dragging him through the depressing upper mall of the shopping centre, where half the units were still unoccupied, post-recession.

She took a step onto the escalator down, checking her watch again. Her shoulders were so hunched up inside her cashmere coat, Conky was tempted to reach down and smooth them out.

'He can fuck away off. Make him wait!' he said, catching the reflection of the two of them standing together in a shopfront window. Still disbelieving that this doll was his lover. Paddy O'Brien would be spinning in his grave. But he now knew the truth of how Paddy had treated his wife behind closed doors. Screw him, the wife-beating bastard.

'Tell me again what you found out about this Bancroft?' She fixed him with those cobalt blue eyes, the crow's feet crinkling around them like an elegant, ageing frame around crisp, perfectly composed photography.

Marching past the brightly lit shops to the exit, he explained. 'Nigel Bancroft runs Birmingham, basically. He's big in commercial property. He owns a chain of restaurants – tapas, burgers, Tex-Mex: places where you can eat and drink. Backs small business start-ups. But naturally, that's all bullshit.'

Outside in the gusting wind, Sheila click-clacked ahead of him to the stone stairs that led down to the Lowry Theatre. The giant silver structure, comprising several bold shapes lumped together, always put Conky in mind of the old metal storage tins that knocked around the kitchen of his childhood home, into which his Mammy had stashed food and cash for the bills, lest his father fritter it away down the bookies.

Today, as with most other days in Manchester, the cloud cover was heavy, lending the deserted paved plaza and the hulking grey structure that sat beside it an oppressive Soviet air.

Sheila was struggling on the steps in those shoes.

'Give me your hand?' he offered.

'I'm fine. I'm not a cripple.'

She shooed him away, but even after months as a couple, it felt more like he'd taken a hefty right hook.

Approaching the bridge by the dull grey-brown snake of the River Irwell, he spotted an average-sized man, standing by the rail. Expensively dressed, the man wore a camel overcoat with a grey suit underneath. A big bruiser with close-cropped hair, standing some ten feet away, clad in dark jeans and a leather donkey jacket. Muscle. More muscle – a big black guy with dreads, wearing a parka – standing further down. The well-dressed man glanced towards them, smiling expansively at Sheila. Conky was careful to make a show of touching the place where the gun bulged, not quite hidden beneath the fabric of his coat.

'Wait here,' Sheila said, squeezing his arm but not taking her eyes from the man.

'No. I'm coming with you. You're exposed.'

Sheila shot him a narrow-eyed glance. Lips thinned to a line. 'You're not the only one who's packing, Conky. I'm not an amateur.' Her features softened. 'At least hang back a bit. Give us a bit of distance, yeah?'

Conky halted. Exhaled heavily, chewing over his lover's stubborn streak like a piece of unpalatable gristle.

'Nigel?' Sheila asked, marching forwards with her hand held out.

'Sheila O'Brien,' Bancroft said, flashing a dazzling dentist's-dream smile that almost lit up the dank quayside scene. He clasped Sheila's hand between his, leaning attentively in for an air kiss on both cheeks, which Sheila reciprocated.

Bastard. Couldn't have been more than thirty-five, unless he'd had work done. Conky mused that he had the kind of face you saw on tired catalogue models. Starting to go at the jawline and underneath the eyes. A vain man, for sure with that fecking hair gel in his hair. A wedding ring on his finger though. Not that that ever stopped men like Nigel Bancroft. His words were being whipped away by a fickle breeze. What was he saying, with that grin plastered all over his nipped-and-tucked bake? There sure as hell was a lot of laughing going on.

Conky moved a little closer so that he was within earshot of the two once more.

'You're even more beautiful than they say,' Bancroft said in that Brummie accent of his.

'Who says that then?' There was a sceptical edge to Sheila's voice, despite the coquettish giggle.

'The great and the good of the criminal underworld, Sheila. You and I mix in the same esteemed circles, after all.'

It sounded like the prick had rehearsed his lines. *Ma gavte la nata*, Conky said to himself, musing on the classic line delivered by Jacopo Belbo in *Foucault's Pendulum*. Take the cork out of his arse and let some of that hot air out. Prick.

The two started to walk towards the footbridge that spanned the river. Conky followed, straining to catch their conversation.

'I can tell you now,' Bancroft said, 'when it's just between lads, the hardest nuts from Portsmouth to Glasgow all say they admire your assets, and I'm not just talking what you've inherited from Paddy.' Wink.

Sheila came to a halt, clutching her bag close. 'Flattery's all very well, Nigel, but I can't bank it, and there's more to me than a pair of tits, *son*.' The mirth had evaporated from her voice, leaving only a sour residue behind, Conky noted with some satisfaction. 'Now what did you come up here to say?'

'I hear you're looking to offload your traditional business interests to a third party.'

'Who the bloody hell told you that?' Sheila raised an eyebrow. 'I certainly never told anyone that.'

21

Bancroft's men had moved from their positions by the river's guardrail and were now also trailing the couple. Conky studied them surreptitiously through the dark lenses of his Ray-Bans, checking for sudden movements. These tossers had been at Paddy's funeral. Casting his mind back to some of the lesser-known mourners gathered at the back of the throng, he recalled the black feller. Those dreadlocks, tied in a fat ponytail and that acne scarring that covered his forehead and cheeks were a dead giveaway. He had been standing at the side of your Man-at-Burton Bancroft. And now they were in Manchester, thinking they could simply swoop down and pick over the O'Brien empire's carcass.

'Let's just say, I've got my sources of reliable information,' Bancroft told Sheila. 'News travels fast in our world, and I can help you get on with the things that are more in your comfort zone.'

Conky noticed that the veins on the backs of Sheila's hands were standing proud. She appeared taut from her feet to her face, like a gymnast holding her body before executing a finale on the beam.

She poked Bancroft in the shoulder. 'You can take that shit-eating grin off your face for a start, mister.' Taking a step towards him. Matching his height in those heels. 'Now, first, I want to know which double-crossing little shit you've got working for me, earwigging and then mouthing off about my business. And second, cut the flirtatious crap and tell me what you're proposing. South Manchester's mine. All mine. I'm a businesswoman, Nigel. Not a bleeding hobbyist or the show pony you seem to be mistaking me for.'

Bancroft's muscle marched towards her, puffing themselves up like peacocks, squaring for a fight over a hen.

Conky withdrew his weapon, pointing it at them but still keeping it for the most part concealed up his overcoat

22

sleeve. 'Back off, gentlemen,' he said. 'Or you'll have more holes in you than Emmental cheese, before you can shout croque-fucking-monsieur.'

The Midlander muscle looked to their boss for a signal. Holding his hand aloft, Bancroft's smile no longer reached his eyes. 'Easy, lads. We're just talking shop here, aren't we, Sheila?' He glanced at Conky's gun, blinking too hard and fast. 'No need for any nastiness. Call your dog off, will you?' He turned his attention back to Sheila. His puffed-up ego seemed to have deflated somewhat, making that camel coat look a size too big.

'Dog?' Conky took a step towards him. 'Catch yourself on, you cheeky wee bastard. You call me a dog again, I'll show you the ferocity of my bite.' He caught sight of Sheila's steely glare and flinching jaw. Took a step back again and put the gun away. Satisfied that he had set his stall out for this posing ponce.

'Now. Stop wasting my time, Mr Bancroft,' Sheila said, checking her watch as though she had some more pressing engagement to attend. 'I wanna know who fed you information about me and I want to hear your proposal. No dicking around.'

'I'm not giving you my sources,' Bancroft said, grinning like a bloody eejit again. 'But I will say this: I'll run your drugs, protection racket, any girls, gambling . . . whatever. All the tough stuff, I'll run and give you fifteen per cent. I take all the risk. You just sit back and take the money.' He opened his arms, raising them up as though he had just announced he had found a cure for cancer to a hospital ward full of the dying.

'Fifteen?!' Conky said, hoping the arsehole could hear the derision in his voice.

Sheila stalked towards Bancroft, pushing her face right

up against his. 'You're taking the piss. Shall I tell you what you can do with your fifteen lousy per cent?'

Sheila dipped her slender hand into the handbag. Bancroft's eyes widened as she pressed her gun into his gut.

Conky held his breath. Would she shoot?

'You can stick your offer right up your jacksy,' she said, seeming to grow even more in stature. 'You've wasted my time. Getting me down here, just so you can wave your dick at me before you try to shaft me for my business?'

'No, I haven't!' Bancroft said. 'The offer's in good faith.'

'Feel that?' Sheila said, pushing the snub nose down towards his abdomen. Still out of the eyeline of Bancroft's henchmen, who hung back, too far away to hear this exchange, Conky calculated. 'That's *my* dick you can feel.' She raised her eyebrows and widened her eyes like an excited child, boarding a ride at a fairground. 'If you want me to shoot my load, carry on with the insults, pal. Because you're insulting me right now, and my dick feels a romance explosion coming on that won't end well for you.'

'Twenty per cent, then,' Bancroft's skin had paled to a sickly yellow now. His eyes darted to and fro, as though he was desperate to alert his boys to the danger he faced.

Conky could see Sheila click the safety off. 'There you go again with the insults. How about you tell me the name of the grassing little shit who seems to think my business is his business?'

'Twenty-five. There. That's my best offer, Sheila. Twenty-five per cent to run your drugs and protection and that.'

'Raise your hands where I can see them,' she said. 'Any last words?'

'All right! All right!' Bancroft did as asked, shaking his head vociferously at his two men, as they moved in towards him, guns drawn, aimed at Sheila and Conky. 'Just mull it over, will you? It's good business sense, and you know it. Please.'

Appraising the scene with the swift eyes of a militia man, Conky noted the innocent passers-by some hundred metres away. Made a split-second decision as to whether he could take out these two lumps and their bossman before the situation got out of hand. The specially manufactured prisms in the lenses of his Ray-Bans boosted his weak thyroid-eyes back to better than twenty-twenty vision. He could take them out, all right.

'Put your guns away, lads,' Bancroft said. A sheen of sweat glistened on his forehead. 'Sheila here is just being cautious, aren't you? It's understandable.'

'She's taking the piss, Nige,' the black guy said.

'Stand down, Steve. And you, Trev. It's okay. We're all good. Sheila's just going to chew over my offer, aren't you, love?'

Conky could almost taste the adrenalin in the air. Blood rushed and roared in his ears. Here was the crux of the meet.

'Love? Don't you, "love" me, you presumptuous bastard,' Sheila said, taking an all-important step away from Bancroft, though she still clutched the pistol in her hand.

Bancroft lowered his arms uncertainly. Gestured for his men to back down.

A young woman, clutching the hands of two small children, had started to cross the footbridge. She was moving closer by the second to the shores of the Lowry Theatre. Conky estimated that they had thirty seconds tops in which to negotiate a peaceful conclusion to the ill-fated proceedings. He was relieved to see the black guy shove his weapon back inside his coat pocket.

'This meeting's over,' Sheila said, clumsily opening her

25

handbag with the hand that clutched her gun. 'Now, piss off back down the M6 with your proposition.'

But the white man-mountain in the leather donkey jacket was still aiming his gun at Sheila's head. His colour was high. His eyes were glazed. Conky knew a man who had lost control when he saw one. The woman with the two small children was upon him, looking askance at the spectacle of a giant clutching a gun. When she screamed, Conky knew he'd left it too long to react.

Chapter 4

Paddy

'Another pint, Marcus, kind sir!' Paddy thrust his glass out towards the craggy-faced landlord, brandishing it beneath the short man's nose as if it were a broken bottle. His words were slurring – he could hear that much. Had been for the last hour. But with every pint of bitter he drank, the reality of Kenneth Wainwright's sad, shitty, low-rent world became more blissfully blurred around the edges; the ache of the scar where his body had been opened up with a boning knife by that little arsehole Leviticus Bell, posing as Asaf Smolensky, had dulled . . . just for a booze-numbed while.

'You've had enough, Ken,' the landlord said, grabbing Paddy's wrist with an unforgiving hand. Stronger than he looked. 'Go home and sleep it off, mate.'

Swaying slightly, Paddy calculated whether he should accept the rejection or square up to this pint-sized hard nut. He slapped several pound coins onto the sticky bar with his free hand. 'My money not good enough for you?'

The landlord released his wrist. Looked down at the money. 'Go home. Sleep it off. Come back later. Then I'll serve you.' His face softened only slightly, revealing a smile that was like a tight fissure in his bark-like skin. 'Come on,

Ken. You're not worth much to me as a regular if you get knocked down on the way home cos you're too pissed to see straight.'

Feeling his pulse thunder with adrenalin, the Paddy of old relished the invincible feeling of The Rage taking over his battered body. But the part of Paddy that was still just about sober dimly acknowledged that he was – for now – no longer the boss of South Manchester. He was not the King. At the insistence of Katrina – the almighty Sister Benedicta – he had taken on the threadbare mantel of Kenneth Wainwright willingly and for a reason. *Lie low, Pad. Gather your strength. Sting those plotting, lying bastards when they least expect it. Destroy every last one of them. Tariq, Jonny, Conky, Lev, Gloria and Sheila. Sheila . . . bring that bitch to heel and reclaim her as your wife.* His intentions, not Katrina's. His sister had hoped he'd use the fresh start to make a new life for himself. But hadn't she always played the controlling older sibling? Paddy, despite his new-found vulnerability, was in no mood to be ruled by another.

His sluggish, internal debate was interrupted by his phone ringing loudly. Buzzing its way across the beer-splattered mahogany, where it butted up against a washed-out bar towel. Katrina's name on the display, of course.

'Oh, bloody hell. Here we go.'

On the other end of the crackling line, Katrina's voice sounded edged with hellfire and damnation. 'Patrick! I got your message. You sounded drunk. Please tell me you haven't burned through your week's money already. And please tell me you're not in that crumbling den of iniquity, The Feckless Oik's Arms again.'

In the background, he could hear the noises of the nursing home that she ran with military bombast – the beeping of residents' alarms; the monotonous verbal ramblings of old

Rose, who tottered up and down the corridors all day long on her zimmer, repeating the same demented shit about needing the toilet, though she wore an inconti-pad so big that it barely fit inside her gusset. Swaying slightly on his bar stool, he imagined he could still smell the stale cabbage and cloying stink of soiled underwear.

He belched down the phone. 'I can't live on peanuts, Kat. Drop us hundred quid round, will you? Just til Giro day.'

There was a muffled noise on the other end – his sister, putting her well-scrubbed hand over the mouthpiece, perhaps, to stop the other nuns from eavesdropping. 'I didn't commit fraud to get you a new identity just so you could wash your chance of a new life into a barman's swill bucket, Patrick O'Brien.'

Paddy tugged absently at the wadding that spilled out of the vinyl seat cover. 'Piss off, Kat. You don't have the first bloody idea what it's like for a rich man to need state hand-outs. Do you know how little a sad bastard like Wainwright—' In amongst the beer fumes, he realised he had slipped up. Eyed Mark the landlord furtively. 'I mean, a man like *me* gets in disability benefit? I spent more on my aftershave than I get to live on for a week now.' Damn. Another slip-up. Putting his mouth into gear before his brain was switched on. That's what his Mammy would have said.

'Patrick!' The agitation in her voice was clear. Paddy had called the shots for decades. Now, suddenly, the jackboot was on the other foot. 'I am not giving you extra money out of the nursing home's coffers to fund death by cirrhosis of the liver. You're turning into Dad.'

'Thanks a bundle. Is that a no, then?'

The line went dead. Paddy smashed his phone onto the bar top, cracking the screen.

'Right!' the landlord shouted. 'That's it, Ken. Out!'

Surprised to find himself deftly manhandled by the land-lord towards the door, Paddy pointed confusedly at him. 'How did you get over the bar? Fucking . . . Spiderman!'

The other drinkers barely looked up from their pints, sitting as they were, in silence around three or four old tables that were dark-stained with ages-old stout spillage and nicotine from a bygone era. Cracked and dirty single-glazed windows barely shed light on the dump, with its swirling brown and lime carpet.

'Shithole!' Paddy shouted, shrugging the landlord off. Searching for words that came only reluctantly through the hoppy fog of beer-thoughts. 'Shitty carpet.'

'See you later, Ken,' the landlord said, pushing him gently onto the street. 'Go home and eat something.' The door was closed firmly behind him.

Stumbling into the street, Paddy clutched at his stomach. Even now, after six pints, he could feel the ache of a body healing reluctantly.

A horn honked, loud and long. Then, an angry voice.

'Get out of the way, wanker!'

Paddy jerked himself backwards onto the kerb, surprised that he had veered into the road and the path of a white van without realising. The driver had stopped abruptly, his passenger hanging out of the cab window, screaming at him with an angry red face, peeping out from a plaster-en-crusted beany.

Not registering the words but understanding their senti-ment, Paddy stuck his middle finger up at the man. 'Shove it up your arse!'

The passenger opened the van door and got out. He was tall too, seeming larger in a hi-vis donkey jacket with baggy plaster-spattered cargo trousers and elephantine steel-toecap workmen's boots.

'Come on, you big bastard,' Paddy slurred, holding his fists aloft. Squaring up to the far younger man. Couldn't have been more than thirty. But even in his early sixties, Paddy was certain he was more than a match for this prick. He swung a punch. Missed.

The enraged plasterer, now accompanied by the van's driver – a giant of a man who looked like a brickie, judging by his physique – raised his fist.

'Leave him be! He's an invalid! Leave it, lads. No harm done, right?'

A woman's voice to Paddy's left. He felt someone link him and drag him across the road. With sluggish eyes, he registered that it was Brenda. He grinned.

'Hiya, Brenda, love! I thought you was at work.' Lunging for her, he planted a wet kiss on her cheek and squeezed her breast through her bright green liveried work fleece. 'C'mere gorgeous. Give Pad— Kenny a kiss.'

Brenda giggled girlishly and blushed. Swiped his hand away delicately. 'Not in public, Kenneth. Come on. I'll walk you home. I'm not due back off my dinner for half an hour. I'll microwave you something to soak up the booze. Have you got anything in?'

Paddy grabbed at his crotch. 'I've always got something in for you, Brenda!' The polar opposite of Sheila, he thought, eyeing up this new easy lay that he'd met during the pub's quiz night. All pillowy breasts and a nice big fat arse. He had never thought that would be his thing, but Brenda – recently abandoned by her ex and desperately needing a man to bestow her womanly love on – was comforting and obliging. She made good stew and cleaned his house for him. A man like him shouldn't go without.

Sturdy, reliable Brenda steered him along the road towards the purgatorial two-up, two-down that he had rented in Kenneth Wainwright's name. Rent paid by the dole. Furnished sparsely with MDF shit from the catalogue.

'Right, let's get you a nice, strong cup of tea,' Brenda said, rummaging in his trouser pocket and finding his keys.

Paddy stumbled through the door, making a beeline for the old-fashioned sofa – a British Heart Foundation shop classic in threadbare wine jacquard. The cig burns were all his. As the institutional magnolia-painted walls spun around him, he took out his phone. Realised Brenda was otherwise occupied, clattering around in the kitchen – no doubt looking for something edible among the empties and the mouldy takeout leftovers. He dialled the number that appeared most frequently in his call log, apart from Katrina's and Brenda's.

The familiar gravelly voice at the other end: 'All right, Paddy? How's it going?'

'Don't use my bleeding name!' he said, checking over his shoulder. No sign of Brenda. The room continued to spin. He drowned out the profuse apologies with his reason for calling. 'What have you found out? Anything?'

There was a brief pause. Squeaking – perhaps the sound of a window being wound up on a vehicle. 'That detective has been sat outside your old house day and night, from what I can tell,' his oldest school friend and now paid ally said. 'It's hard to say without getting inside the property. I followed her into town this morning though. She took a big sack of something into a safety deposit facility.'

'And? Have you seen her with any men?'

There was another pause. The sound of a cigarette being lit, inhaled, exhaled. 'The only one she knocks around with is Conky McFadden. I've seen them together in her car, coming out of her drive.'

Paddy scratched at his four-day-old stubble, mulling over

the news. Was it unreasonable that Sheila would have retained Conky's services? No. And it was highly unlikely that she'd be shagging the big, ugly bastard. Not after she'd had Paddy O'Brien giving it to her for all those years like a proper man.

'Try to get closer,' he said. 'Keep an eye on that cow, Gloria Bell, too. And I want to know where she lives. I've got a bone to pick with that lump of shit she calls a son.'

'The black woman? She's a crafty bastard, that one. Slippery, like. I can never keep tabs on her. I've tried following her, like you asked, but she always does a bloody Houdini.'

'Try harder, then,' Paddy said, thinking of Sheila and reaching into his jogging bottoms to grab his erect penis. He started to massage himself rhythmically. 'That's what I'm paying you for, isn't it? I want information, not a damned sightseeing tour!'

Ending the call, he withdrew his hand from his jogging bottoms and hurled the phone onto the sofa. Hauled himself to his feet, swaying slightly, watching the scuffed skirting board move upwards, upwards, downwards, rising and falling in waves like a heat shimmer created from alcohol fumes. Brenda.

Weaving his way to the kitchen at the back of the terrace, he found his humble, willing shelf-stacker checking on the progress of a pie through the greasy oven door. He started to yank his jogging bottoms and underpants down, eyeing Brenda's ample bottom as she knelt down.

'Brenda, love,' he said. 'Grab the worktop. I've got something to give you.'

Glancing over her shoulder with a watery smile on her unadorned lips, she stood up, and turning, caught sight of Paddy's erection. Baulked.

'Oh, Kenneth. I've got to be back in work in five minutes.' She pointed to the clock. 'I'm already running late. I'll get told off by the manager.'

But Paddy wasn't interested in Brenda's work concerns or tardiness. He wanted what he wanted.

'Don't come all coy with me,' he said, advancing towards her. Grabbing her around her stout middle and pressing her large breasts against him. Grinding his penis into her stomach. 'You love giving me the runaround, don't you?' He reached behind her and hitched up her frowsy skirt. Yanked at her knickers and stuck his finger inside her, enjoying the feel of her struggling against him.

'I'm going to be late, Ken!' She giggled nervously, clearly unsure as to whether she should be flattered or affronted. 'We can do this properly later when you've slept the booze off. You're hurting me! The drawer handle's digging in my bum.'

'I'm going to fuck you through to the other side of Christmas,' he said. 'Your arse will be hurting from more than a frigging handle when I've finished with you.'

She tried to push him away. 'No, Ken! I need the work!'

'My chunky monkey.' He could feel she was dry and unyielding. It didn't matter. In fact, that was better. Made him feel like a triumphant Viking, claiming his spoils.

The fingernails digging in his neck and the knee in his inner thigh, however, were unexpected.

'No, Ken! *No!*' Anger contorted Brenda's smooth moon-face into something unfamiliar and unwelcome.

When he brought his fist down on her defiant face, he was pleased to see that it knocked the rebellion and fire out of her immediately.

He stood back to admire his work. completely unaware of Brenda's teenaged son, Kyle, who should have been at school but who had bunked off straight after chemistry, following his mother to her boyfriend's house. Now, stealthy, keen-eyed Kyle was lurking in the doorway, watching this domestic noir unfold.

Deciding the thump was assault enough, Paddy put his deflating penis – unreliable thanks to the alcohol slopping around inside him – back inside his pants.

Brenda cowered before him, sobbing, with hurt in her eyes that he found almost delicious. She pulled her skirt back down. 'Your pie's ready.' She wiped her tears away with the sleeve of her supermarket fleece.

Paddy said the words he knew would be balm for the bruise. They worked every time on women like her. 'You know I love you, don't you, Bren?'

Chapter 5

Youssuf

'Ah. There you are! At last,' Youssuf said in Urdu as his son Tariq marched towards him, wearing a concerned look on his face.

Grabbing his walking stick optimistically, contemplating hoisting himself off the leather sofa that was positioned against the wall near Tariq's office, Youssuf opened his mouth to ask again if he was ready to drive him over to the old people's day centre.

But Tariq had already disappeared into his office. And Youssuf's words were swallowed by Mohammed, the book-keeper, who breezed past with his own demands, clutching at a sheaf of paperwork.

'Tariq! What do you want me to do about this faulty order?' Mohammed asked, pausing at the threshold to the office. Fingering the brass plate telling everyone that a Director occupied the sacred space beyond the door, with its big, oak desk and only slightly worn brown carpet tiles. 'You know? For the *other* site.'

Tariq reappeared in the doorway, thumbing his beard contemplatively. Youssuf waved frantically at him, hoping to catch his attention, but his son's focus was reserved solely for Mohammed.

'Get the supplier on the phone. I'll speak to them.' He dropped his voice to a whisper, though Youssuf could hear well enough. 'I can't sell poorly recorded porn films as the latest from Leo DiCaprio. They've got a cheek. This is Jonny's contact, isn't it?' He tutted. Finally, Tariq glanced towards his father. Scratched at the beard, clearly distracted. Turned back to Mohammed. 'Not out here.' He held his hand up to Youssuf, fingers splayed. 'Five minutes, Dad. I promise.' Slammed the door to the office.

Except Youssuf had been promised five minutes at least forty minutes ago and his bottom had gone numb.

'This is nonsense,' Youssuf muttered, rubbing his stomach that growled audibly, even beneath the layers of his tunic, cardigan and overcoat. He checked his watch, barely able to see the time clearly as his hand trembled with ill health and low blood sugar. It was almost midday. He'd spent too long with too many tablets in his system and nothing to eat beyond the toast that his daughter-in-law, Anjum, had given him for breakfast. The prospect of missing out on lunch at the day centre was a grim one. That stuck-up old idiot, Ibrahim, was sure to snaffle all the bhajis as was his wont if he didn't get there soon. It wasn't that great a distance to walk. Not if he paced himself.

With a grunt, he rose from the low sofa, donned his karakul hat and made his way downstairs. The staff of T&J Trading smiled benignly at him. Even the girl on the desk bade him a friendly, 'Morning, Mr Khan!' But nobody stopped him.

Outside, the air was fresh. Too fresh. Youssuf had never been a fan of the Mancunian cold and damp that crept into his bones a little more with every year that passed. He buttoned his coat, glanced up at the offices on the first floor and made a disgruntled harrumphing noise.

'Treats me like a child,' he said, making his way towards Derby Street where he would quickly blend in with the hustle and bustle of men going about their business. Here, among the poorly parked vans and mess of discarded cardboard packaging that was whipped around on the stiff wind like abandoned kites gone rogue, he could be just another brown man in an area full of industrious brown men. No longer somebody's ailing father or liability.

'Youssuf!' A voice called after him on the other side of the street.

He looked beyond the black Volkswagen van that was hugging the kerb on the opposite side of the road, crawling along at a walking pace. Squinted, peering at the small old fellow in the smart navy suit. 'Amir!' Wheezed with laughter as his sprightly chum from the Asian elderly people's day centre crossed the road with a spring in his septuagenarian step.

They embraced.

'I've escaped,' Youssuf said, nudging Amir. 'That boy of mine was driving me insane. Five times he promised me a lift to the centre; I gave up in the end.'

'Ah, the price you pay for having a child who's a big shot.' When Amir spoke, his false teeth clacked slightly. He smoothed his thinning, Brylcreemed hair, making sure Youssuf saw the gold watch his own son had bought him for his last birthday. The same trick, every time they met. 'I just dropped a packed lunch in to *my* boy. He didn't give me the time of day either. Come on! We don't need them.'

Together, they ambled towards Cheetham Hill Road, engaging in a well-intentioned game of one-upmanship on their son's behalves. Tariq was buying and selling this gadget from the Far East and that sought-after skincare from Paris. Making a packet, of course. Amir's son, Rashid, was importing that specialist model of Mercedes from Germany and exporting this must-have toy to America. Sitting on a fortune, naturally. In this game of vicarious career-tennis, Youssuf knew he could volley for hours with Amir and happily neither win nor lose. Old men loved to boast about their sons. This much he acknowledged.

As they neared the sprawling plot of the hand car wash on the corner of Derby Street and the deafening din of Cheetham Hill Road with its wholesalers and Asian fast-food takeouts and kebab shops, Amir stopped suddenly and looked askance at the black Volkswagen van.

'Are we being followed?' he said, tugging at Youssuf's sleeve.

Youssuf leaned on his stick, panting from the exertion of having walked some two hundred metres in sandals. 'What am I looking at, here?'

'The black man in the van.' Amir pointed, though Youssuf instinctively pulled his friend's arm down. 'Is he staring at you?'

'Keep walking,' Youssuf said, almost tripping as he sped up. He'd seen enough. The driver of the van had indeed locked eyes with him. He had dreadlocks, untidily stuffed beneath a knitted hat of some description. Though Youssuf had never seen the fellow before, the hairs on his arms were standing to attention and his bladder was throbbing as if in protest. 'If he's following us, he'll have to turn onto Cheetham Hill Road. Not so easy with all those buses.'

'Let's cut through the car wash,' Amir suggested. There was excitement in his voice as if this was some big adventure.

But Youssuf knew the line of business Tariq was actually in – beneath the shining entrepreneur-of-the-year veneer. And the dreadlocked stranger's face didn't fit round here, in the tight-knit business district that nestled in the long shadows cast by Strangeways Prison.

They shuffled onto the forecourt of the car wash. Youssuf stole a glance over his shoulder. All thoughts of steaming hot bhajis and of bagsying the massage chair in the day centre were gone. The driver was speaking on a phone. Nodding. But eyes still on them.

'Go through the car wash bit itself,' he told Amir. 'He'll lose sight of us in there. We'll just sidle past the cleaners.'

But the van's idling engine thrummed swiftly into overdrive. With squealing tyres, it hung a sharp right, bouncing onto the forecourt of the car wash, coming to an abrupt halt only inches from Youssuf and Amir. They were hemmed in between the unforgiving front end of the van and the rear of a large saloon in front, awaiting its turn beneath the spray.

The dreadlocked driver hopped out, a rash of acne scarring across his forehead and cheeks.

'Ya-allah, what's going on?' Amir cried. 'Help!'

Youssuf had swung around to face his assailant and was now gripping his walking stick like a baton. Ignoring the pains in his chest and the crippling icy pangs of fear that prodded his tired, old body. Trying to gauge the situation.

'Get in the fucking van, granddad,' the driver said in an accent that Youssuf wasn't immediately familiar with. The man slid the side door open to reveal a cargo hold that was empty, save for a burly white man with shorn fair hair, crouched in the shadows. 'Don't give us no trouble and you won't come to no harm.' Birmingham. Maybe that was the sing-song accent. Same as his cousin in Solihull.

Chatting animatedly in some central Asian dialect behind him, Youssuf spotted the car cleaners in his peripheral vision. Would they step up to defend two defenceless Pakistani old codgers? But as the driver grabbed at Youssuf's shoulder, he realised that, just for once, he didn't want young men leaping to his aid, emasculating him.

He trod heavily on the driver's trainer-clad foot, grinding the man's toes beneath the sole of his unyielding chunky leather sandal. Somehow shook loose from his grip. Brought the walking stick down on his forearm with a satisfying crack.

'Ow, you fucking old psycho!' he yelled, clutching at his arm. 'Who do you think you are? Paki Rambo? Sort this bastard out, Trev!'

Youssuf raised his stick, preparing to hit him again, when the giant white man clambered out of the van.

'Oi! You can pack that in,' Trev said, trying to wrench the stick from Youssuf's determined grasp. 'Don't play no hero with us. Get in the fucking van, old man.' His voice was gruff but tinged with amusement.

'You think I'm some kind of joke?' Youssuf shouted, steadfastly clinging to the stick. The incandescent fury that burned within him gave him courage. He aimed another hefty kick, this time at Trev's private parts. Missed. Watched with irritation as his sandal flew off, skittering like a frightened rat beneath the van.

Suddenly Youssuf gasped as an icy deluge of water hit the side of his head, knocking his hat off. The jet bypassed him, becoming stronger and more directional as two of the car cleaners advanced towards Dreadlocks and Trev, training the spray on them. Shouting in pidgin English that these interlopers should get the hell off their forecourt.

Amir grasped at Youssuf's arm, trying to drag him out

from between the vehicles and away from the claustro-phobic jet-wash enclosure.

'Let's get out of here!' he said in Urdu.

Finding himself rooted to the spot, Youssuf was only dimly aware that the sock that covered his one bare foot was now ringing wet.

'Come *on*!' Amir yelled.

Youssuf snatched up his hat but still couldn't move. Amir let go of his coat, slowly starting to back away from the scene.

Suddenly, Youssuf was standing alone, caught in the middle of a fight of fists and high-intensity hoses between out-of-towners, hell-bent on kidnap, and outraged Uzbeks. But the hoses started to fail. The flow of water slowed. Soon, there was nothing more than a trickle dribbling from the ends. The car-cleaners looked quizzically at their equip-ment, shouting to the kiosk in which their boss lurked. When the pressure didn't return, they too started to retreat in haste.

'Get Khan, and let's go!' shouted Dreadlocks.

Paralysed, feeling the adrenalin drain away rapidly from his ailing body as though someone had pulled a plug in his bunioned feet, Youssuf was aware of being grabbed from behind. Strong-armed towards the open door of the van. He shouted for help. He prayed to God that he might be saved. He thought of Tariq and his grandchildren, little Shazia and Zahid, whom he might never see again.

'No! No! I'm not getting in!' he cried, kicking against the side of the van, though the man-mountain hoisted him aloft like a doll.

'Put my father down!' A familiar voice sliced through the pandemonium. Tariq.

To his right, Youssuf caught sight of his son's henchman,

Asaf Smolensky, sprinting towards the kidnapping Midlanders. Clad in his usual Hassidic garb of a full-length black overcoat and an oversized felt Homburg hat, his ringletted sidelocks jiggling atop his shoulders, it was an unexpected sight to see him move with the pace of a panther. He was wielding a machete.

Dreadlocks baulked. 'Shit! It's the Fish Man. Leg it, Trev!'

Trev released Youssuf from his grip instantly, leaving him to stagger back against the enclosure's damp walls.

'I'm gonna kill you!' Tariq shouted, throwing himself onto the man-mountain.

As Dreadlocks scrambled into the van to escape the blade of a Fish Man with human harvest on his mind, Youssuf watched Trev square up to his only son. The difference in height between them was at least ten inches. Tariq's slender build didn't help. It was like David facing down Goliath.

'I'd like to see you try,' Trev said, swinging a punch at Tariq.

But Tariq was quick on his feet and deft with his hands. Years of aikido and judo lessons as a youth had stood him in good stead. Within three easy moves, he had thrown his outsized opponent to the ground and sat astride him now, clutching the man-mountain's bull neck with the manicured hand of a gentleman.

Overwhelmed by a fresh surge of outrage, Youssuf whacked at his felled attacker's legs with his walking stick, hurling insults at him in Urdu.

'Leave it, Dad!' Tariq said, calmly. Turned to the vanquished man, ignoring the van's revving engine and the hacking sound of the Fish Man slashing at the vehicle's tyres. Hissing, as the air in the back tyre escaped. One down ... 'Now, who do you work for? And what do you want with my dad?'

'No one,' Trev said, spitting in Tariq's face.

'Donkey!' Youssuf yelled, swiping at his ankles.

Tariq wiped the spit calmly from his face, though Youssuf knew his fastidious son must have been cringing inside. 'You work for the O'Brien crew?'

'Fuck you, man!'

'Smolensky!' Tariq shouted. He looked over to the Fish Man who had just punctured another of the van's tyres. Inside the vehicle, Dreadlocks was screaming something unintelligible through the closed window to his associate. 'Come here! Our friend needs a little encouragement.'

The tall, thin henchman stalked towards Tariq, holding the machete in his right hand. But he blanched suddenly, his gaze fixed on something on the far side of the road.

'Ellis James!' Smolensky's machete miraculously disappeared up into the sleeve of his coat. He slipped out of sight behind a parked van.

Like a startled goat, Tariq descended the man-mountain, disappearing swiftly into the shadows of the jet-wash enclosure, dragging Youssuf with him. He pressed his index finger to his lips, pushing his father out towards the kiosk on the far side of the car wash, where they could not be seen by whoever this Ellis James might be.

The Volkswagen van sped off on its wobbling, clack-clacking flats in the direction of Cheetham Hill Road, disappearing along with its kidnapping driver and passenger into the streets beyond the neighbouring Chapatti Corner and Gurdwara temple.

Youssuf staggered over to the low wall and slumped against it. Amir popped up from behind.

'Have they gone?' Amir asked. 'Have you called the police?'

Tariq nodded, putting his arm around his father. 'They're gone. You both okay?'

Youssuf shrugged him off, though he was now shaking with cold. Light-headed. He felt like he might vomit onto his wet feet at any moment. 'What a disgrace.'

'What were you two thinking, wandering these busy streets on your own?'

'Show some respect, Tariq!' Youssuf said, glancing over at Amir for moral support. 'We're not children, are we? We're grown men.' He picked up his walking stick and shook it. 'You think me and Amir can't see off a couple of amateur pick-pockets?'

When Amir muttered an insult about the younger generation in Urdu, agreeing with him, Youssuf silently hoped his friend had bought the story that the aspiring kidnappers were nothing more than thieving opportunists. It wouldn't do for an elder of the Asian community to click onto the sort of nefarious dealings Tariq was involved with on the side. To realise that those men had come for him – Youssuf Khan. What a dreadful situation to find himself in! Lying to his respectable buddy to protect his fool of a son!

'Didn't we decide that you weren't going to leave my offices until I drove you to the day centre, Dad?' Tariq tried again to put his arm around Youssuf, encouraging him to stand.

'Don't be so patronising!' he said, taking his karakul hat out of his coat pocket. Agitated to see that it was sodden. He manoeuvred himself from the ground, using his stick. Wincing and grunting at the effort and stiffness in his knees. 'If I have to spend another morning sitting around, waiting for you to drive me quarter of a mile down the road, like I'm some kind of deranged, drooling halfwit, I'm going to get on the first plane back to Karachi and I'm never coming back.'

Amir laughed. 'And because the ladies love me, your

45

dad's taking me with him, aren't you, Youssuf?' More cackling. 'Wait 'til Ibrahim hears about *this*! Ha. Me and Youssuf. Fighting off criminals. That will knock the stuffing out of the stuck-up—'

'Dad,' Tariq said, making another attempt to grab him by the elbow. Scanning the street. 'It's not safe. Come back with me. Both of you! I'll drive you both to the day centre once we've got Dad some dry socks and found his sandal.'

But Youssuf could barely articulate his mounting frustration. 'No! I don't want your help. Because it's the *wrong kind*, Tariq! I need that kind of help like I need a prostate check from a doctor with fat fingers.'

'I'll make my own way, thanks all the same,' Amir said, smoothing his suit down, starting to make his way across the forecourt. 'I don't need a babysitter.'

'Wait for me!' Youssuf called after his friend.

'Look, Dad. If you come with me now, I'll take you to Mecca for Hajj next year.' Tariq held his hand out, his eyes softening at the edges. 'How about that? We'll fly first-class on Emirates.'

Youssuf inhaled deeply and raised an eyebrow. Ignoring the hand. 'Really? You'd do that for me?'

But Tariq's face fell. A short, chubby white man clad in a beige raincoat had just got out of a grey Mondeo and was walking towards them. Ellis James, no doubt.

'We've got to go, Dad. *Now!*'

Too late.

'Well, well, well,' the man said, a twitch of a smile breaking the thin line of his lips. 'Tariq Khan.'

The confrontation in the middle of Derby Street was short and civil but, Youssuf noticed, with a clear edge of hostility to every word uttered by both young men. Tariq insisted that nothing whatsoever had come to pass at the car wash – Ellis James could feel free to question the workers – *if* their English was good enough. Ellis James insisted that he was watching Tariq and was in possession of some interesting information about the Boddlington Gang that he would soon be acting upon. Youssuf knew to keep quiet.

When he got back to T&J Trading, stomach still rumbling, Youssuf rummaged in his coat pocket to see if there was perhaps a boiled sweet, hidden beneath the now sodden tissues and the container for his false teeth. His fingers picked out something smooth and dry with sharp, stiff edges. He withdrew a business card that had certainly not been there before. Took out his reading glasses to study the wording.

Detective Ellis James, GMP.

Beneath the name and number was a neat handwritten note.

Call me when the truth becomes too heavy to bear, Mr Khan.

Chapter 6

Gloria

'You be careful,' Leviticus said, cleaning Jay's hands with a wet wipe before the child could shampoo the mashed banana into his hair entirely. 'You wanna watch your back, Mam.'

Gloria eyed her son and grandson disdainfully. 'I'd be more worried about him getting that banana on the carpets, if I were you. Don't expect me to cover the cost of a lost deposit because you let him paint the floor with his pudding.' She turned back to applying her lip liner in the make-up mirror that she'd set up on the kitchen windowsill. The remainder of the autumn daylight was best in there in the evenings. The last thing she needed was poorly applied lip liner. Her lips were her best feature, and first impressions counted.

'Mam! Seriously. The farm's on red alert. One of the lads spotted a van staking the place out the other day. And M1 House is definitely a target after that meeting between Sheila and Bancroft went tits up.'

'Language, young man! I'm going to an elegant reception for grown-ups in Jack's Bar. I'm sure nothing untoward will happen whatsoever. You're being melodramatic.'

'You're being daft.'

'Shouldn't a child as little as my Jay be in bed by now?'
Her remark was pointed, she knew. It was an easy non-confrontational way to respond to her son's flagrant impudence. Gloria was determined to have a nice evening and neither the perceived threat of Midland-based gangsters nor her cynical, paranoid son would rain on her parade. Speed-dating beckoned. Old Gloria felt like a hussy for even contemplating it; couldn't stop thinking of how her heart had been smashed into smithereens by that scoundrel, Leviticus' father and then, more recently, the pastor. New Gloria had relished every second of donning her most flattering Windsmoor dress and couldn't wait to slip into the fancy matching heels that she could just about squeeze her only slightly swollen feet into. Water retention was a pig, but even that wouldn't spoil her evening.

Climbing out of the taxi a while later, she felt a pang of apprehension at ever having agreed to this nonsense. The emotionally daring Gloria of old had been supplanted yet again by the heartbreak-fearing church elder.

'Don't do anything I wouldn't, love!' the taxi driver shouted after her as she approached the bouncers. 'You tight old cow.'

She wondered if the fifty-pence tip had been adequate. Decided it had been, given the taxi had stunk of stale sick. Beastly.

To her delight, Frank's bouncers stood to attention, opening the doors for her with some ceremony.

'I'm here for the *speed-dating*.' She spoke her intention with an air of secrecy, mouthing the words in exaggerated fashion as though she was hard of hearing. Checking over her shoulder to see she hadn't been overheard or spotted by anybody she knew who might conceivably be walking around an industrial area at 8 p.m.

Toying with the strap of her Sunday-best handbag, wishing she hadn't worn a dress with such a plunging neck-line – because she had *no* intention of meeting anyone anyway – she crossed the lofty main space of the night club. Conscious of the click-clack of her heels on the parquet dance floor. Was she stepping over the spot where Jack O'Brien had breathed his last? She shuddered, suddenly tempted to about-turn and head for home.

'All right, Glo!' Frank loomed before her like a well-meaning, underfed spectre.

'Hello, Francis,' she said, her smile faltering as she saw the sign for 'Speed-dating this way.'

'Come to find a nice feller to keep you warm at night?' Frank asked, draping his arm over her shoulder in a gesture of friendship that was far too familiar for her liking. 'Well you've come to the right place, then. Love is all you need, right?'

She shrugged him off, shuddering at the prospect of being judged by strange men. 'Sheila talked me into it, and I agreed, in a moment of lunacy.'

'Get a drink down you, Glo,' Frank said, nudging her and winking. 'Bit of Dutch courage, eh? You'll be sorted. It's on the house.'

As she descended into the basement bar, she was both thrilled and horrified to see so many others of her age, milling around with drinks in their hands. The women were all dolled up to the nines, of course – the smell of their perfume and hairspray rose up to greet her in a heady fug of optimism and trying too hard. Far too much cleavage and leg on show. But the men . . . Scanning the men, it was immediately apparent that not a single one of them bore any resemblance to the pastor. In fact, the only black man in the room was at least twenty-five stone in weight and, judging by his leper-like complexion, needed the curing hand of Jesus Christ and a better diet far more than a three-minute mini-date.

Somewhat crestfallen, realising that the notably absent Sheila had cleverly dumped the responsibility for their inaugural speed-dating event onto her by nagging her to take part, she grabbed a flute of prosecco from the bar. Took a sip, followed by a deep breath. The bell rang. *Here we go.*

Seated at her own numbered table, as were the other women, Gloria felt like livestock at an auction as the men moved around the room, one by one, to vet her. But even as she nodded politely while being spoken at by Steve, the forty-year-old man from Widnes, whose strange, rubbery face looked as though it had been partially melted by a blowtorch, she felt as though she was being watched. *You wanna watch your back, Mam.* Lev's words buzzed in her head like unwanted tinnitus.

'Well, I'd always been interested in ice cream,' Steve told her breasts. 'I like the whippy stuff, me. My vans sell a *lot* of Flake 99s.' He wiped the sweat from his brow with the napkin from beneath his tumbler of whisky, staining the charcoal tissue black. Gloria noticed then that he had a bogey, suspended on the hairs in his right nostril. 'I make a packet at the football after a match. Even in winter.'

'Is visible snot considered acceptable in ice cream retail circles, Steven?' Gloria asked, pointing to his nose. Irritated. Every pore in her skin and every tiny hair on her body became super-sensitive to her environment. She grabbed the number eight sign in the middle of the table, an anchor to her seat, as anxiety whipped the composure from under her feet.

As Steve poked at his nose with the bitten fingernail of his chubby index finger, wearing a bemused expression,

Gloria took the opportunity to scan the room. Everyone was deep in stilted, hopeful conversation, wiping their sweaty hands on their knees beneath the table. Everyone, except the man at the next table to her – an orange man with perfect, gelled white hair, plucked eyebrows and a very smooth face. Though the blonde at his table was speaking, waving her manicured hands animatedly as if what she had to say was *hyst-er-i-cal,* the man's bright blue eyes were on Gloria and Gloria alone. He smiled.

The connection sent a shiver down her spine that was not entirely pleasant. She was certain she recognised this over-groomed dandy from somewhere.

The bell rang. No time to scroll through her recent memories in a bid to place him. Gloria's heartbeat escalated to a thunderous pace as Steve, the ice-cream magnate left and her mystery man moved towards her. He held his hand out and remained standing, expecting her to get out of her seat, clearly.

She stood, shook his hand formally and was surprised when he pulled her into him for a full-on peck on not one but two cheeks.

'I like to *faire les bises,*' he said, pronouncing the French like Spanish, spoken with a Lancashire accent.

'How sophisticated,' Gloria said, taking her seat carefully and hooking her hair behind her ear. Coquettishly smiling down at the table-top.

'My name's Bob,' he said, pointing to the name-sticker on his shiny pin-stitched jacket. He peered at her sticker, positioned near her shoulder. 'Pleased to meet you, Gloria.'

Studying his face, Gloria was transfixed by those piercing blue eyes. She took a sip from her prosecco, then a gulp. Felt a Bible quote about to push its way out of her mouth but inexplicably held back this time. Feeling like this Bob was the best of a bad bunch and that there was some peculiar chemistry between them, Gloria forced herself to delve deep into her long-term memory, to the time of The Wastrel, when talking to men had been easy. The time in her life when she had learned to please men professionally. Young Gloria had been hot stuff. Young Gloria had forgotten most of the Bible quotes drummed into her as a child. She would channel young Gloria now. Just for fun. Jesus could take an evening off.

'Pleased to meet you, Bob. My, what arresting eyes you have.'

'You've got me banged to rights. I can't take them off you, love.' He held his hands up, as if in surrender. 'I'm under your spell.'

Gloria ran her finger around the rim of her prosecco glass. 'Are you implying I'm wicked?' She batted her mascaraed eyelashes. The thrill of flirting after decades of the utilitarian exchange of facts with Sheila or spouting of religious platitudes at church was intoxicating. She felt like an old, neglected engine that was being cleaned of a lifetime's sludge and lubricated by fresh oil. She bit her lip. Felt the alcohol loosening up her muscles and short-circuiting her inhibitions.

Bob grinned. He had small, clean teeth that shone blue beneath the bar's lights. His white hair was dazzling. Wondering how it felt, Gloria wanted to reach out and touch it.

'I think you've got a naughty lickle twinkle in your eye, Gloria,' he said, leaning into her. 'What do you do?'

'Me? Oh, I bewitch men with my womanly assets and sparkling conversation.' She threw back her head and laughed, aware that in doing so, her ample bosom would be more noticeable. The pastor's handsome face loomed large in her mind's eye, castigating her for acting like a wanton hussy with a smooth-faced, strange man called Bob, who couldn't enunciate 'little' properly. But then, prosecco-fuelled Gloria of old reminded her that the pastor thought nothing of sizing up a teenaged girl's lower portions whilst pressing the older flesh of his adoring congregation and his devoted fat wife. 'And you?'

Bob laughed, running his clean fingers along the edge of the table. 'When I'm not property-developing, I'm making conversation with beautiful coloured ladies.'

Coloured. Aye, there was the rub.

The Gloria that was a capable entrepreneur and an elder at the Good Life Baptist Church was just about to castigate him for his outdated and racist terminology when she became aware of a ruckus, audible above the distant thump-thump-thump of the sound system in the club's main area.

Girls, screaming. Shouts for help. The sound of breaking glass.

Watch your back, Mam.

Chapter 7

Frank

'Keep an eye out for unfamiliar dealers.' Sheila's words of warning. 'Call Conky *straight away* if you spot anything iffy.'

When Frank had gazed out at the sea of gyrating young people in M1 House from the vantage point of the DJ booth, he had considered the difference between the time when Paddy had ruled and his widow's fledgling reign.

'One, two, three . . . four.' He had inhaled sharply, counting on his fingers; drinking in the smell of sweat, dry ice and alcohol that had come from the writhing mass on the dance floor. 'Ten, eleven.' Ignoring the disapproving looks of the DJ whose concentration he had been interrupting, he'd turned to Degsy, who had been standing just beyond the threshold in the corridor. 'Eleven. And those are just the ones I can see. I bet there's more.' Shaking his head, he had wiped the moisture from his upper lip with a quaking hand. Feeling doubly jittery, thanks to the speed he had taken earlier.

"This would never have happened when Paddy was still alive,' Degsy had said.

He'd voiced Frank's niggling doubts over the new head

of the O'Brien empire, but Frank wasn't about to show disloyalty to Sheila in front of a foot-soldier. And he certainly wasn't prepared to eulogise over Paddy.

'My son died thanks to that bastard.' Stepping down from the DJ booth into the corridor, Frank had slammed a fist into Degsy's shoulder. 'Now get out there and earn your money, you useless dick!'

'What do you mean?' Hurt in Degsy's spotty, junkie-thin face.

Frank had reached up and had grabbed him by the collar of his Lacoste shirt, pulling him close. Without Paddy around as the unassailable enforcer, he'd had no option but to play the alpha with the likes of Degsy. Stepping up had been hard, but he'd done it. 'I mean, Sheila's paying you to run the drugs in my club. You'd have been well sacked by now if it wasn't for the run on shifty arseholes, thanks to the war with the Boddlingtons. I wasn't keen to have any drugs in here at all after what went on, but I said yous could still deal in M1 out of family loyalty. So, don't be pissing my sister-in-law about.'

'Hey! No need to slag us off, Frank. I run a tight ship, me.'

'Oh yeah? Then who the hell are them dickheads out there? It's not the first time I've seen them. There's two black fellers – one with dreads, one's wearing a red T-shirt. Asian lad in a denim jacket. Three or four white guys with tramlines cut in their heads. Dealers, Degsy. And not Sheila's fucking dealers.'

'I don't know who you mean.' Degsy's small, bloodshot eyes, with their pin-prick pupils that said he consumed as much gear as he sold, had darted towards the dark corridor of the backstage area, as if he had been hoping for some way out of this awkward confrontation. He'd picked at one of the scabs around his mouth. All receding gums, when he spoke, and teeth that looked like he gargled in strong urine. That much had been visible, even in the crappy light. 'I'm telling you Frank. I swear on my nan's life. I haven't seen nowt. It's just O'Brien lads working the club. As far as I know.'

'You don't know your arse from your elbow, you!' Frank had let go of Degsy's collar, contemplating his next move. He hadn't wanted to call Conky for backup. Not again. Every time he'd dialled the henchman's number, he had felt like one of his balls had been snipped loose. 'Get them dealers out of my club. Get the bouncers to help you. Find out who they're working for. Report back to me. Right?'

'Chill out, man.'

'Don't *chill out, man* me, you twat. Get out there and earn your cash. Or would you prefer to explain this to the Loss Adjuster? Don't make me call Conky.'

Degsy had held his hands up. 'All right, all right. Keep your wig on.'

As he'd accompanied the hapless Degsy to the edge of the dance floor, the reverberation of the bass and beat had felt like warning tremors beneath Frank's feet, heralding a seismic shift of the club's karma in the wrong direction. The atmosphere in M1 House that Saturday night was distinctly off.

He'd grabbed Degsy by his shoulder. 'Be careful. Right? You're not packing are you? I said no more guns or knives.'

The memory of his son, Jack, already growing cold and bleeding out on an empty dance floor, had hovered like an unwelcome spectre above the reality of hot, hedonistic youngsters having the time of their lives. It had been joined by the recollection of Asaf Smolensky, creeping in through the open back door, bearing a Bren gun and the bloodlusty intentions of criminal-insanity-on-the-payroll. For a peace-loving temple to dance and music, M1 House had seen more than its fair share of violent death back in the spring. Frank had been keen not to let the grim reaper defile his altar to the beat ever again.

The crowd had parted reluctantly to absorb Degsy. Frank had watched as the other O'Brien muscle had appeared from the sidelines, all given the order. The spotlights had shone on the bouncers' bald pates as they too merged with the revellers from front of house.

'I can't see a bleeding thing,' Frank had muttered, wringing his hands.

He'd shooed some kids off a sofa in one of the seating areas then, scrambling onto the sticky leatherette seating to see what was going on.

Degsy had made for the black guys. The entry-fee-paying clubbers had scattered around them, sensing danger like a herd of antelope at the water's edge where hyenas lurk in the tall reeds. The bouncers had rounded on the white guys.

It had started with a scuffle. A little pushing and a testos-terone-fuelled hokey-cokey where neither had conceded ground to the other.

'No guns,' Frank had prayed quietly to a God that never seemed to listen. 'Please don't let them have sodding guns.'

The transition from minor altercation to full-on fisticuffs had taken less than a minute. Otis, his burliest bouncer, had taken a right hook from one of the guys with dreads that had sent him flying backwards into a podium like an ungainly clown.

Now, Degsy had pulled a gun to best the Asian lad's knife in an underworld rendition of rock, paper, scissors. Shit, shit, shit. The lying, lanky arsehole was armed to the teeth. Should he stop the music? Should he call Conks, after all?

Frank withdrew a baggie of coke from the pocket of his

jeans. Took a hefty pinch of the white powder and deposited it on the back of his sinewy hand. Snorted what he could. Rubbed the rest around his gums. The effect was instant. Pharmaceutical Columbian courage followed soon after.

'Right, you bastards,' he said to himself, pulling the sleeves of his old James T up in some deluded act of strong-arm bravado. 'Nobody messes with an O'Brien.'

Ignoring his racing pulse and the feeling that his legs were liquefying, he crossed the club, heading towards the scrum. No need for that big Northern Irish bollocks. Not tonight. *Remember Jack. Don't make this all for nowt.* He approached one of the white rogue dealers from behind.

'Get out my sodding club!' he screamed in the man's ear, grabbing him tightly by the scruff of his neck. Turning his collar into a garrotte. Kneeing him in the sweet spot on the backs of his legs so that they buckled.

Frank was a warrior, now, posthumously defending his son's honour. Heard his own voice, hoarse and venomous above the music.

'Who's your boss? Tell me or I'll rip your bleeding head off.' Fingers in the man's kidneys.

'Fuck you!' the dealer shouted, elbowing Frank in the stomach.

There was a flash of metal as the Asian lad stabbed one of the bouncers. Fists flew. It was carnage.

'Back off, or I'm gonna blow you all into next Wednesday!' Degsy yelled, waving his piece at the interlopers.

But the guy with the dreads and bad acne scarring was suddenly upon Degsy, waving a semi-automatic. 'Drop the gun, Manc twat, or I'll put a bullet in your ugly head!' His death threats were levelled in a sing-song accent like some nightmarish nursery rhyme.

Degsy and Dreads both clicked their safeties off. A stand-off. Not good.

Frank was dimly aware of the shrieking of the clubbers on the fringes of his ill-fated dance floor and of the speed-daters who were clattering up the iron staircase from Jack's Bar below, fleeing the scene. Gloria Bell's face in among them, somewhere. An overwhelming sense of déjà vu and fear that his club-owning days were finished bore down on him. But his melancholy musings were interrupted by the unmistakeable growl of Conky McFadden, striding through the phalanx of onlookers.

'Hands in the air, you scabby wee turds or I'll take the lot of yous out!'

Who the hell had called the Loss Adjuster? The bouncers, almost certainly.

Upon them now and casting a long shadow over the interlopers like an avenging dark angel, Conky held a SIG Sauer before him. The music had stopped, as if to pay respectful tribute to the fabled Loss Adjuster's appearance on the charged scene.

'Do you remember me?' he bellowed, bearing down on dreads-with-a-gun. Striding right up to him, as though his opponent clutched a child's toy weapon. Pressing the nose of his gun right into the dealer's jaw. With his free leather-gloved hand, he removed his shades with a flourish. His bulging eyes shone with obvious professional glee. 'Do you know who I am?'

Dreads dropped his pistol. Held his hands up. Swallowed visibly. 'Yeah.'

'Get out of this club and get on a train back to Birmingham, like the yokels you are,' Conky said, encasing Dreads' throat in a large hand. 'Tell your eejit boss Nigel Bancroft that if any of you set foot in South Manchester again, you'll be going home in Tupperware stacking boxes. And you make sure he understands fully that if I see his ponce's bake in O'Brien territory again, I'll shoot some fucking wrinkles in him that Botox will never remove.'

Realising that he had been holding his breath all the while that Conky had been speaking, Frank straightened himself up. Inhaled. Exhaled. He acknowledged with some bitterness that he'd been unable to control what went on in his own environment. He felt the humiliation neutralise the bravado in his body. But his pulse thundered on apace and for a moment, as pain travelled up his left arm and encased his tired heart in pure, uncut agony, he wondered if he too would be going home in a wooden overcoat.

'Frank. Are you okay?' Conky's voice, close by.

Clutching his arm, Frank dropped to his knees. *I'm coming, Jack. I'm coming.*

Chapter 8

Tariq

'I'm not coming in,' Jonny said. His voice was gruff and thick with sleep.

Tariq imagined his business partner lounging in bed or, perhaps, sprawled on the sofa in his den. Par for the course, these days.

'Aw, come on, Jon. For God's sake! You've been in work twice in a fortnight. When you do come in, you hole yourself up in your office with the Fish Man.' Tariq held his phone in one hand, pouring muesli into a bowl with the other. He could feel Anjum's eyes on him, scanning his every move for signs of subterfuge. The kitchen felt several degrees colder with every second that she scrutinised him. He lowered his voice, turning his back to her, hoping the sound of her mashing egg mayo for the children's packed lunches would be enough to drown out the finer points of his conversation. 'Plotting. That's all you do. Plotting revenge. Like that's going to bring Mia back!'

Screwing down the plastic muesli sack deftly, he replaced the box inside the cereals cupboard. Irritated that the flaps wouldn't quite fold shut, destroying the neat line of the cereal packets. Taking the muesli out again, he jostled the phone in one hand and rummaged for the sellotape in the stationery drawer with the other.

'Hold on,' he said, exasperated. Setting the phone down, he detached a length of tape with his teeth and strapped the wayward flaps shut – the way he liked it. At least he could impose order on a cardboard box, if on no other area of his life. 'Now. What was I saying?' Eyeing his wife as she smoothed the eggs onto bread for Shazia and Zahid and buttered toast for his father, he imagined agitation, rising in waves from the top of her hair. She wore a chignon today – styled tightly against her skull, mirroring the tight expression on her unmade-up face. Only animosity between them now that she finally knew how he and Jonny really made their handsome living. 'So, you're staying at home. Again?'

'Yeah. I'll be in tomorrow.'

'I won't hold my breath.'

Tariq was just about to hang up when he remembered the point of the call. 'Wait! Before you go . . . You ever seen a black guy with dreadlocks and a big white guy with a dirty blond crop working for the O'Briens?'

There was silence, followed by a yawn. 'No.'

Glancing at the finance pages of the newspaper, laid out on the breakfast bar, Tariq yet again scanned the article that reported on multi millionaire Nigel Bancroft's expansion into corporate property, north of Birmingham. He tapped the photo of the bland-faced playboy in his collarless, pin-tucked dress-shirt and jazzy leather-trimmed evening jacket, posing for a professional shot at some postpolo-match charity ball. 'What do you know about Nigel Bancroft?'

On the other end of the phone, Jonny smacked his lips. A rustling sound as he rolled over in bed, perhaps, preparing himself for nothing more taxing than spending yet another day obsessing over the possible Margulies blood on Leviticus Bell's hands while Tariq did all the work.

'Runs the Midlands, doesn't he?'

'Yep.' Tariq walked to the fridge. Scowled at the selection of milk in the door, staring in disbelief at the almond milk. Sweetened! He took out the carton, shaking it at Anjum with a questioning look on his face.

There was a hint of mischief in his wife's eyes. A smile, playing at the corners of her mouth. Had she deliberately bought him the sweetened milk, knowing he wouldn't drink it? Knowing that if he resorted to using the wrong milk, it would set him on edge for the rest of the day?

'Look. I don't know any more than you about Nigel-whatever-his-name-is,' Jonny said. He hung up then, leaving Tariq staring at the word 'sweetened' with a bad taste in his mouth.

Had the men who had tried to snatch his father from the car wash forecourt been Sheila's soldiers? Or had they heralded the arrival in Manchester of a sortie that had been despatched on a reconnaissance mission by an enemy force from beyond the Staffordshire hills?

He set the phone down. Held the almond milk out gingerly, as if it contained plutonium. 'Darling, what's with this?' he asked Anjum. 'You know I've cut out processed carbs.'

She slammed the plate of toast onto the butcher's block counter in front of Youssuf with some force, sending the toast scudding onto the wooden surface. 'You know where Tesco's is, *darling.*'

With a bemused expression, Youssuf looked from Anjum to him, then to Shazia and Zahid. His father smiled at his grandchildren with a shrug and a wink, though Tariq could see the discomfiture behind those milky eyes. The children merely giggled in response, thinking their old Daada funny; not for an instant picking up on the bitter acrimony between their parents in that kitchen.

Sighing, Tariq poured the wrong milk onto his muesli, wincing inwardly as the sickly-sweet taste registered on his discerning palate as a culinary affront. Damned if he was going to give his wife the satisfaction of not drinking it.

'What have you got on the cards today, my love?' he asked, willing her to make nice for the sake of the kids.

She peered at him through her Prada glasses, narrowing her eyes. 'Oh, you know . . . preparing asylum cases for trafficked girls . . .' She raised her voice. There was an edge to it. Even the children fell silent. 'Who have been forced into slave labour by morally bankrupt, money-grubbing hypocrites and subjected to systematic abuse by men who see them as nothing more than commodities made from flesh.' Anjum sat down primly at the breakfast bar and took a violent bite of her apple, gnashing her molars together without moving her laser-like gaze from him.

Tariq felt a twinge of corresponding pain in his groin. He swallowed hard, wishing that time-travel back to the winter – the time when his secret had still been safe – were feasible, or that if parallel worlds were really a possibility, another Tariq Khan existed, still living a harmonious family life with a wife who still believed he was nothing more than a respectable, hard-working businessman. He pushed away the bowl of unpalatable muesli, realising that Anjum would never unsee the trafficked Slovakian girl in her offices or unhear the story of her enslavement at the hands of the Boddlington bosses.

In spite of the comforting sound of the children jabbering away excitedly in the back, the journey to school was agony.

At his side, his father sat in silence, clutching his karakul hat on his lap and sighing repeatedly.

'Give it a rest, will you, Dad?'

The old man threw his hands up. 'What? You have a go at me for talking while you drive. If I sit quietly, minding my own business, you're still not happy. I can't win.'

'Daddy! Daddy!' Shazia shouted.

With mounting frustration, Tariq glanced at his daughter in the rear-view mirror. 'What is it, sweetie?'

'Is Mummy picking us up?'

'No darling. Daddy is. Mummy's in court today.'

The traffic came to an abrupt standstill. A black van pulled alongside his Mercedes at the lights. Tariq held his breath, feeling suddenly over-exposed on that school run. He strained to see who was behind the vehicle's wheel. Exhaled when he realised it was an elderly white guy. Behind him, a white van was too close to his bumper. He edged forward, annoyed when the van driver closed the gap.

'Change, damn it!' he muttered under his breath.

In every car, on every bus, on every motorbike and, above all, in every van, Tariq saw the enemy, poised to snatch the light from his children's eyes or to tear his father from the car's passenger seat.

Standing at the school gates, Tariq still felt watched. Checking behind him, he looked for dreadlocked inter-lopers among the yummy mummies and the odd stay-at-home dad. He appraised the site's security measures and judged them insufficient. Made a mental note to call the head teacher of the exclusive preparatory school as soon as he was behind his desk. He was paying enough in astronomical termly fees, after all. The least they could do was install some sturdier gates and stick an extra security guard on the door. Old-fashioned striped blazers and the novelty of kids wearing straw hats suddenly didn't seem enough bang for his buck. Tariq wanted his family to be bullet-proof, and highly rated teaching staff couldn't promise that.

As he kissed Shazia and Zahid goodbye with a guilty lump in his throat, it suddenly occurred to him that the same white van that had hogged his rear bumper at the lights had parked up, two cars down from where his father was now sitting, glum-faced in the CLS. He cast his mind back to the driver, who had worn a baseball cap at a ridiculous angle. Was it feasible such a man was a parent of a kid at a private prep where solicitors and surgeons sent their kids?

You're being paranoid, he told himself, waving at the kids; sprinting back to the parking bays to see if the van was still there.

When he got back to his own car, the van had gone. *Get a grip, for God's sake. You can't turn into Jonny, dwelling on the pitfalls of this crazy path in life you've chosen.*

Pulling away from the kerb, he thumped his steering wheel in frustration.

'What's got into you?' his father asked, stroking the brain-like folds of fur on his hat.

'I'm a failure. I can't protect any of you.'

His father coughed – a deep, rasping rattle. Spat some phlegm into a snow-white handkerchief. 'You know the answer to that, son.'

'Look, when I drop you at the day centre, do me a favour. Don't go walkabout.'

He shot a sideways glance at the old man, noticing to his chagrin that he had trimmed one side of his white beard for him higher than the other. He was losing his touch.

'Red light!' Youssuf shouted.

Tariq faced forward abruptly, slamming on his brake. He yelped as somebody ploughed into the back of the Mercedes, sending him lurching over the stop line into the path of a heavy goods vehicle.

Chapter 9

Sheila

'We've got a grass,' Sheila said, pounding away at the Stairmaster as though she was wreaking vengeance on the little shit that had been leaking her business to Nigel Bancroft. She pumped the handles up and down, raining imaginary blows on his or her head. 'And now you're telling me that M1 House is overrun with Brummies? You idiot!'

In her brightly lit home-gym in the subterranean spa of the Bramshott mansion, she stared past Frank, fixated by their reflection in the ceiling-to-floor mirrors, repeated in infinite regress: an athletic, middle-aged woman in her prime, clad in pink Lycra, powered by long-suppressed ambition, bawling out a stooped, grey-faced middle-aged man, dressed like a youth, who looked as though the gravity of this harsh world had finally all but flattened him. It was a scene of the strong bullying the weak. And she didn't like it one bit.

'Sorry,' she said, stepping off the Stairmaster. 'I should be asking you how you are, not having a pop at you.'

The dimpling in Frank's chin abated. He offered her a weak smile by way of a truce and sat down onto the seat pad of her lateral pull-down machine. He waggled his head from side to side uncertainly. 'I'm all right, me. Ta for asking. I ended up in A&E thinking I was having a heart attack like our Pad. Turns out it was only bloody indigestion! I'd taken too much gear on an empty stomach and a load of painkillers a few hours earlier. Buggered me guts up, didn't it?'

Sheila dried her sweaty hands on a towel and squeezed Frank's shoulder in sympathy. 'That's lucky.'

'The doc kicked us out with a warning about watching what I eat and stress and that. But is it any wonder I'm strung out? Them Brummies are taking the piss. The last thing I need is another shooting in the club. It was close, She. Bloody close.'

Sheila shook her head. Inhaled deeply, conjuring the memory of Nigel Bancroft's easy, cheesy smile. It was like Paddy all over again. A man, trying to bully her when she didn't do as she was told, like a good little girl. She ground her molars together until they squeaked. 'I'm gonna sort this,' she said. 'Bancroft seemed to know I was mulling over selling the drugs and protection or farming it out as a franchise. The only time I've ever discussed that outside of my house has been at the weed farm. We've got a leak. I'm gonna find it. And we need more O'Brien men at the club.' She pointed at her brother-in-law like an accusing schoolmarm. 'You need to sort out your bouncers. They're the gatekeepers and they're not doing their jobs.'

'Sorry, She.'

Taking a hearty swig from her water bottle, Sheila said, 'Bancroft's muscle nearly blew holes in some woman with a kid in a trolley outside the Lowry. Only reason they stood down was coppers showed up. If they hadn't been doing a routine patrol, we all could have ended up in the cells or body bags. And Paddy surrounded himself with incompe-

70

tents, apart from Conky.' Glancing down, she noted the hurt in Frank's haunted, bloodshot eyes. 'And you, obviously.' No. The hurt was still there. Frank wasn't that easily fooled or flattered. Much of his child-like lack of cynicism had been buried along with his son. 'Leave it with me, chuck.'

'Chuck', at least, put a half-hearted smile back on her brother-in-law's woebegone face.

With Frank gone, Sheila pushed herself to put in twenty lengths in the glittering turquoise pool. Swimming on her back, she followed the line of the bricks in the spotlit, vaulted ceiling, savouring the notion that all this contemporary opulence was hers and hers alone, now. She was a woman of independent means with hundreds of staff on the payroll, no longer Paddy's pushover trophy-wife and punchbag. She realised that it was time to step into the big boss' shoes in earnest.

'I've had enough of this,' she told the lapping water, clinging to the side and wiping her face. 'It's time to get tough.'

Dressing for success in skin-tight leather trousers and her favourite Burberry leather biker jacket, she threw her highest-heeled boots into her Chanel tote and drove the Rolls Royce to Gloria's house. Knocked smartly on the door to the rented semi, clutching the hard case in her right hand. Her freshly worked-out biceps protested at the weight.

When she answered, Gloria was already wearing her coat and shoes. Her best dress that she wore to most meetings was visible beneath the three-quarter-length coat. She looked like a formidable Latin mistress on a weekend off. 'About time.' Gloria thrust her watch-clad wrist towards

Sheila, raising an eyebrow in the sort of disapproval that only the overtly religious mastered. 'You're late!'

Sheila thrust the case into Gloria's hands. 'I want a quick word,' she said, waving her business partner back into the house.

'What's with the leather and the Roller? Who you trying to impress?' Gloria asked, kicking off her chunky-heeled shoes and padding in her stockinged feet towards the kitchen. The straps had left an indent in her swollen ankles. 'Take your trainers off, She! If the no-shoes rule's good enough for you, it's darn well good enough for me.' She peered up the stairs towards the landing. 'Leviticus! Shake a leg! You'd better be dressed and baby Jay better be ready to roll. *Whoever is slack in his work is a brother to him who destroys* – Proverbs 18:9!'

Her words were met with a groan and something muffled in the long-suffering tone normally used by teenagers. Sheila stifled a smile. Remembered that she was here on business.

'What's in this case?' Gloria asked, grunting as she heaved it onto the laminated surface of the kitchen worktop. 'Your make-up?'

Ignoring the comment, Sheila strode over and clicked the locks open, revealing the contents of the red velvet interior.

'A shotgun?' Gloria took a step back, clasping her work-worn hand to her chest.

As Sheila waited for the surprise to sink in, Gloria approached the case again, gingerly lifting the box of cartridges from its recess. Frowning, holding the box at a distance, as though it might explode in her face.

'It's for you,' Sheila said. 'A gift.'

Her business partner turned to her, shaking her head in

protest but surreptitiously stretching an arm back to run her fingers over the beautiful polished wood of the stock. 'I'm a practising Christian, Sheila O'Brien. Why on earth would you give me an implement of violence?'

'What do you think they fought the Crusades with?' Sheila asked. 'Charm? B.O.?'

'The power of the Lord!' Gloria said.

'And weapons.' Sheila marched up to the case, pushing Gloria aside. She lifted the shotgun out. Presented it to Jesus' favourite sunbeam. 'Hold it. See how it feels.'

Shaking her head yet again, Gloria took her gift. A glimmer of a smile and a hint of mischief in her eyes. 'It's very heavy.' She dropped and raised the gun like barbells, hoisted it to her shoulder and peered down the barrel at Sheila. 'Ka-pow!'

Steeling herself not to flinch, Sheila prayed that Gloria would play ball. 'I need you, Glo. Paddy sent a load of boys in to do a woman's job. I've got junkies pretending to run a drugs enterprise that's worth millions a year. They're hopeless and smoke most of the product. They wouldn't know discipline or staffing structures if they came along and shagged them up the arse with a flip chart.'

'Oh, Sheila! Language! If you please!' Gloria winced.

Keep going, She. She's buckling. 'Your Lev is the most intelligent out of all of them put together. They're not trustworthy. Someone's shooting their mouth off to a rival gang in Birmingham. Frank's overrun with them in the club. And now I think about it, I'm not queuing up to give eighty per cent of my hard-earned cash to some out-of-towner who thinks I should step aside, just because I've got a vagina instead of a shrivelled little cock.' She wiggled her little finger for emphasis.

'Sheila O'Brien! You're *terrible!*' Gloria snorted. 'Why

should I get involved with that side, though? We don't have any agreement about Paddy's old affairs. That's sinners' business.'

'Ten percent if you take the job as my manager. If Christians weren't supposed to earn money, Jesus wouldn't have put zeros in "holy" and "godly".'

'That makes no sense. Fifteen.'

'Done.' Sheila grinned broadly. Knew she would get reliable old Gloria onside in the end. Even a Bible-basher like her had a price. Everyone had a price and Gloria's was significantly cheaper than Bancroft's.

'What did you say about rivals in Birmingham?' A man's voice.

Sheila looked over to the threshold of the kitchen and saw Lev leaning against the door frame with Jay on his hip. The child still had a bandaged head after the brain surgeon in Baltimore had removed his tumour. Size of an orange, Gloria had said. But now he was smiling and poking at the lightning bolt shaved into Lev's stubbled scalp. His honey-coloured skin was lighter than Lev's mixed-race-mocha, thanks to his white mother, Tiffany. But the little boy's beautiful, symmetrical features and the promise of high cheekbones once the baby-chub had gone were surely down to his father. Small wonder that Mia Margulies had had the hots for Leviticus Bell, Sheila mused. 'I've got trouble with Brummies and there's an internal leak. You seen anything out of place at the cannabis farm?'

Lev nodded, advancing into the kitchen. Ignoring his mother, who was rummaging in a broom cupboard for something or other. Gazing suspiciously at the shotgun on the worktop. 'That's not loaded, is it? I can't be having no guns in the house with my boy.' Little Jay stretched out towards the weapon but Lev pulled him gently back to hold him close against his body. 'Not for Jay-Jay,' he told the child. 'Dangerous.'

Sheila was touched by the fatherly love she could see in his concerned frown and ensuing smile. She wondered if Gloria had ever shown Lev that much affection. Couldn't remember her having done so when she had brought him to her house as a boy during the school holidays. 'It's your mam's. She's your new boss.' The smile slid from Lev's face. 'My manager. She's going to whip those little pillocks into shape. And I'm expecting you to be behind her every step of the way. None of that Boddlington crap. Your loyalty now is to the O'Briens. And I'm watching you, Leviticus Bell.'

Scowling now, Lev yanked open a cupboard and took out some biscuits. Bit on one angrily and gave one to Jay to chew on. Slammed the cupboard door shut with some force. 'I couldn't work for Tariq and Jonny if I wanted, thanks to you and all the bullshit you stoked up.'

'Need I remind you why your son's on the mend?' She knew it was a low comment but Sheila realised she was done for, the moment she allowed insubordination to creep in.

Lev blinked hard, a mouth full of biscuit. He chewed noisily, as if contemplating her sucker punch. Mouth open. Not so hot.

'Degsy's got a lad from Birmingham working in the weed farm,' he said, shoving his tongue beneath his top lip.

'You what?'

'Yeah. Kevin. Brummie Kev. We both used to work for Scots Mavis, twocking cars for her cut-and-shut business. He's been knocking around Manchester for years, has Kev. On and off, like.'

'What's he doing, working for me?'

Lev shrugged. 'Ask Degsy. He's the one give him a job. Said he was short-staffed after all what went on in the spring.'

Sheila narrowed her eyes. Took a step towards Lev and scrutinised his blemish-free face. 'What's he like, this Kevin? Do you trust him?'

Laughing, Lev threw his head back and closed his eyes. The thick cords of muscle in his neck bulged. 'You're having a laugh, aren't you? He's a fucking criminal. He'd steal the pennies off a dead man's eyes! And he's got no loyalty to you.'

'You think he's the grass?'

'What do you think? You're getting grief off some arsehole in Birmingham. Kev's not called Brummie Kev for nowt and he's a shifty little prick. Always was. He still owes us a tenner from 2007.'

'How can I trust a word that comes out of your mouth?' she asked.

'I give up everything for you, didn't I?'

'Don't come that shit. You gave up everything for money.'

Locking eyes, the two were caught in a silent battle of wills. Sheila could see that Lev had the same strength of character as his mother. But more than that . . . He had integrity.

There was a clatter from the broom cupboard, accompanied by a celebratory, 'Da-daaaa!' Gloria emerged, wheeling a tartan shopping wagon across the kitchen.

'What the hell is that?' Sheila asked, smiling with bemusement. 'You going to Alty market for spuds? Or are you moving into Sunrise Rest Home?'

'Don't be so quick to mock, Sheila,' Gloria said. 'This is the sheath for my righteous sword.' She started to sing lines from some hymn or other that Sheila vaguely remembered from Paddy's funeral. 'Jerusalem', maybe. 'Bring me my bow of burning gold. Bring me my arrows of desire!' Then, the words seemed to evade her. 'La di di deee, da-dum-de-dum. Bring me my chariot of fire.' She wheeled the shopping wagon round at speed and holstered the shotgun inside it with a flourish. 'This is my chariot of fire, She.' Rolling it back and forth, back and forth. Withdrawing the shotgun at speed and pointing it at the cooker.

'Jesus, Mam,' Lev cried. 'Put it away! Not in front of Jay.'

Ignoring his protest, Gloria swung the shotgun over her shoulder, as though its mere presence had transformed her into Jules from *Pulp Fiction*. 'Don't be embarrassed by it on my behalf, young man.' Clearly misunderstanding Lev's complaint as a slur against the tartan atrocity. 'This fine shopping wagon will save the rheumatism in your mother's poor hands. Years of having my hands in water, that is! I'm crippled when it's damp. And my back's not up to much either.'

'Pulp Friction,' Lev muttered under his breath, as though he had read Sheila's thoughts.

Chapter 10

Paddy

Staring at the flickering computer screen, Paddy considered what he might write next to Ellis James. He took a swig from his can of extra-strength lager, glad that he had managed to stave off another lunchtime hangover by continuing to drink steadily throughout the afternoon. Relieved that Brenda had taken pity on him and let him hang around at hers, where he could crank the heating up at her expense and raid her fridge. Kyle's laptop was infinitely superior to the piece of shit he had at his place. Kyle's bedroom was the only decent room in the dump, though the thirteen-year-old was way too old for the brightly coloured kiddy cars and trains that covered the wall, now partly concealed beneath posters of some dickhead band called *Twenty-One Pilots*.

Back to the screen. What to say today?

'If you want to know where Maureen Kaplan keeps bent accounting records,' he said out loud as he typed slowly with two fingers, 'check out *Bella's Afro Hair Supplies* in Crumpsall before end of month.' He signed the email off as 'Shadow Hunter', using the moniker of one of those YouTubing twats that Kyle followed. Pressed send and slurped at the beer. Waited for the response. And waited.

Paddy pressed F5 repeatedly, wondering when the hell the berk of a detective would get back to him. He scratched at his groin. Maybe he ought to shower more regularly. Kenneth Wainwright's shower in that tired two-up, two-down rental was shite. The water either came through scalding hot or freezing cold. The pressure was almost non-existent from the cheap electric shower rig-up that had been poorly screwed onto the tiled wall by the private landlord. Brenda's was no better.

Showering. Who would have thought that one of the things he missed most about being a wealthy man was daily access to a good power shower in a clean bathroom?

But Paddy was jolted out of his musings on personal hygiene and poor man's water pressure by the arrival of a response from his least favourite dogged detective.

Re: Maureen Kaplan tip-off
James, Ellis <ellis.r.james4@hotmail.co.uk>
To: Shadow Hunter (shadow.hunter@gmail.com)

Hi SH,
How do you know about Maureen Kaplan? Where are you getting your intel from? Can we meet? What can you tell me about Jonny Margulies and Tariq Khan?
Regards
E.J.

Paddy smiled at the screen. Ellis James was more than intrigued. He was well and truly on the hook, and Paddy would enjoy reeling him in slowly. All those years he'd spent trying to pull the thorn from his side that was the detective and his Rottweiler of a tax-inspecting sidekick,

Ruth Darley, and now, here James was: the instrument of Paddy's revenge.

'Don't worry where I got info from,' he wrote. 'It's good.'

He contemplated his link to the outside world – Hank the Wank had had a busy week of it, installing hi-tech sound-recording equipment in the offices of Maureen Kaplan when she was out at meetings. His oldest school friend was proving to be the perfect choice for a spy. Loyal as they came. No criminal record. Blended in everywhere, because who gave a workman in overalls a second thought if he went about his business with a merry whistle and an air of confidence? Endlessly excited by the novelty of subterfuge, and inexperienced enough not to have a clue what his skills were really worth on the black market. So far, Hank was working for peanuts and considered it a small fortune. So far, Katrina was indulging Paddy in sticking him an extra few hundred here and there to assist his transition back to normal life.

By the time the money runs out, Paddy thought, staring at the blinking cursor, *I'll have ruined the lot of them scheming bastards.* He rubbed his hands together. *Then, Kenneth Wainwright can shove it up his sad, dole-ite arse, because Paddy Big-Bollocks is coming back, baby!*

With his index fingers hovering over the keyboard, Paddy contemplated what else to feed the detective with.

'Did you know the Boddlingtons have brothels on Trafford Street and Grove Close in Sweeney Hall?' He clicked send.

The main focus for Paddy's anger was, of course, Sheila, since the lousy cow had sought to end him. Beyond that, he would not rest until Leviticus Bell was dead. Memories of that fateful poolside scene where he'd been sliced open and left for dead only months earlier were blurry, but he was certain that Lev Bell's face had been hiding beneath a false beard and those stupid bloody sidelocks – an imitation Shylock, coming for his pound of flesh, trying to pin it on Asaf Smolensky. Very damned clever. Not clever enough to dupe him – the mighty Paddy O'Brien, however. But the Boddlingtons . . .? Why the hell should they evade the strong arm of the law? It would be easier to take his empire back with the enemy already weakened.

Waiting for Ellis James to respond, he jumped when a thin voice behind him said, 'What the fuck you doing in my room on my laptop?'

Paddy turned around to find Kyle standing over him. A thin streak of piss with a sour expression on his malnourished face. The kid reeked of poverty – stale hand-me-down clothes that were too big on him, a whiff of unwashed boy, lard, school sports-hall changing rooms and the pervasive smell of mildew from living in a permanently damp Victorian terrace. Paddy hated the smell because he remembered smelling exactly like it as a child.

'Your Mam said I could,' Paddy lied, irritated that he had been caught in the act.

'Well, you can't. It's mine and I've got private stuff on there.'

Kyle reached out to snatch the laptop away but Paddy swung it out of his reach. 'Easy, tiger.'

'Give it back, Ken! It's mine! Mam bought it for me as a treat when my dad—'

'How long you been stood there?' He eyed the boy warily, keeping a firm grip on the laptop but snapping the lid shut. What had he seen?

'Long enough,' Kyle said, scratching at the florid rash of spots on his forehead.

The kid looked nothing like his mother. His eyes were

small and too close together. Paddy found it odd that there were no photos of the father around the house whatsoever, as if he had never existed. Perhaps Brenda had never forgiven him for simply disappearing one day. But with a creep of a son like Kyle, who could blame the guy?

'I was googling my ailments,' Paddy said, pre-empting any confrontation. Who knew how much the kid had seen? 'And they're confidential, right? None of your fucking business, nosey hole.' Had Paddy been thinking aloud while his back had been turned to the doorway? Conky used to frequently pull him up for that sort of thing. It would be no good if Kyle had worked out he'd been talking to a cop. The kid didn't seem entirely daft. Unlike his dimbo of a mother. 'Shouldn't you be at school?'

Kyle's gaze was unwavering. His attentions were focused on the laptop. With a jolt of realisation, it was clear to Paddy that the kid wasn't suspicious of him at all! *He* had something to hide. And there was only one thing thirteen-year-old lads might be doing on a computer that they didn't want a grown-up to know about.

'I won't tell her,' Paddy said. 'About the porn, I mean.'

Suddenly, the kid's stern face cracked, offering Paddy a wry, knowing smile. Was this the start of some kind of truce? Was Kyle going to stop being a miserable little sod just because Paddy was poking his mother?

'Ta,' Kyle simply said, pulling the sleeves of his hoodie over his bony hands. That half-smile had turned to a grin, lighting up his cadaverous ugly face. Maybe the kid was relieved.

In truth, Paddy wouldn't have the first idea on how to check someone's browser history, but he wasn't about to tell the little dipshit that. 'Sling your hook, son, while I finish up here. Okay?' He held his can of lager out to the boy. 'You wanna swig? Is that what you're waiting for?'

Shaking his head, Kyle sloped off back downstairs, still wearing a lopsided smile as though he was the only one in on some big secret. Creepy little smartarse.

Opening the laptop's lid, Paddy refreshed the screen to see if Ellis James had responded. Sure enough, he had.

Re: Maureen Kaplan tip-off
James, Ellis <ellis.r.james4@hotmail.co.uk>
To: Shadow Hunter (shadow.hunter@gmail.com)

Have you got addresses for those brothels and also the place in Crumpsall? We'll treat this information very seriously. I'd really like to meet you face-to-face, Shadow Hunter. Can I take you for lunch? I want to get to know you and let you know how GMP can help you, if you'd like to testify against the O'Brien crew or the Boddlington Gang.
Regards
E.J.
PS: What do you know about the main criminal firm in Birmingham? Have you ever heard of Nigel Bancroft before? If so, what can you tell me about him? I've attached a photo.

Paddy clicked on the attachment and studied what looked like a professionally shot corporate portrait of Bancroft. With his blow-dried hair and bone-white teeth, he put Paddy in mind of some male model off a Just for Men hair-dye packet. He'd heard of him, all right, but the ponce had never dared set foot in Manchester while Paddy had been king. If Ellis James was trying to pump him for information on Bancroft, that meant Sheila – and possibly the Boddlingtons too – were getting the heat. With Paddy gone, why wouldn't a man like Bancroft have a pop at annexing a destabilised Manchester as Midland turf? It was the sort of stunt Paddy would certainly have pulled. A calculated business risk, well worth taking.

He thought about the prospect of that dozy show pony, Sheila, trying to defend herself against the likes of Nigel Bancroft: organised, established, semi-legal and experienced as hell. Threw back his head and laughed so hard, he began to wheeze.

'What a bleeding joke!'

Sheila was just a woman. If the Brummies were after the O'Brien empire, she didn't stand a hope in hell. Maybe Bancroft would do the job of bringing down his treacherous widow for him.

Chapter 11

Sheila

Sheila was surprised that her breath wasn't steaming on the air in the office perched high above the warehouse floor of the cannabis farm. Despite the hot, moist, tropical climes artificially created in the vast industrial area below to keep the crops lush, she shivered in that claustrophobic crow's nest of a room. The stiletto boots she had pulled on before leaving the car were causing her feet to spasm. Or maybe she was just tense as hell at the prospect of what was to come.

'I don't think this is a good idea,' Conky said, perched on the dated 1970s desk that still bore the splintered bullet-holes from the Boddlingtons' attack back in the spring. He removed his glasses with a flourish and fixed Gloria with The Eyes. 'You don't have any experience of dealing with these eejits. Colin Chang just about managed because he had the technical nous. But you're an ex-cleaner, not a pharmacist, so you haven't even got that, have you? Having a gun in your shopping trolley won't give you any of the gravitas needed to run the O'Brien business interests.'

'Who says?' Gloria asked, folding her arms tightly across her chest. Bitterness audible in her clipped consonants. 'I manage over a hundred women. And you could do with one of our girls in here. Look at the state of it! Has this place ever seen a duster?'

Conky sighed, rubbing The Eyes like a despairing parent. He looked to Sheila for support, but Sheila focused on Lev, who was rolling Jay's pushchair to and fro along the wrinkled, threadbare old office carpet.

Seize control before Conky steam-rollers over you, Sheila O'Brien, she counselled herself. *Draw your sodding boundaries.* 'Gloria's taking over from that prick, Degsy, and that's my final decision.' Sheila turned back to her lover and noticed the dejected expression on his craggy face. Right then, Conky put her in mind of a chastised dog. 'I want him demoted so he's just running errands. I'm not having him mismanaging staff, leaving us open to attack and losing me money because he can't organise a piss-up at a brewery. We either pull him into line or he gets booted out on his arse completely.' She turned to Gloria. 'That's your first task, Glo.'

Patting her shopping trolley, Gloria nodded. '*Be strong and courageous. Do not fear or be in dread of them, for it is the Lord your God who goes with you.* Deuteronomy 31:6.' She beamed widely, sticking her tongue through the gap in her otherwise perfect teeth.

'And now, I want you to bring that Kevin up here,' Sheila said, catching Lev's eye.

'Me?' He continued to roll the pushchair. Daddy Day Care with tattoos.

'Leave the sodding pushchair, will you? You're making me seasick. You shouldn't be bringing your son to work with you. Hasn't he got a mother, for Christ's sake?'

Lev looked down at his high-top trainers. The muscles in his jaw flinched. 'His mam's a dyed-in-the-wool bitch. She's still drawing down his child allowance, no questions asked, but she doesn't actually give a shit about our Jay. I can't let her near him. I wouldn't leave that junkie slag in charge of beans on toast. I'm suing for custody.'

'Nursery?'

'I didn't save my son's life to pay some other bastard to bring him up, thanks. And I never asked for this job. *Actually.*' He shot an accusatory glance over to his own mother. 'Mam blackmailed me into it.'

'I'm not having you sponging off me, Leviticus,' Gloria said, wagging her finger at her son in admonition. 'You've got to pay your way if you want to live under my roof.'

'Oh, excuse me!' Lev said, a look of disbelief on his face. '*Your* bloody roof? You mean the rented house Sheila's stumping for because we're on the run from the Fish Man?'

Feeling irritation bristle along her cold, clammy spine, Sheila snatched the handle of the pushchair from him. 'Get that grassing arsehole Kevin up here. Now!'

When Lev had left the office, she strutted to the window, aware of the effect that her swaying hips had on Conky, even though he now shared her bed. She peered out of the office window that faced internally onto the cannabis farm below, making her feel as though she were suspended above a forest canopy. Queen of all she surveyed. 'I need you to send a message to Bancroft, Conks. Something that will make him think twice before he starts with me or mine again.'

'Aye,' Conky said. He stood with the grunt of a stiff, ageing man. But dwarfing both women with his height and bulk. Turned to Gloria. 'You'd better get your wee grandson out of here. This is not going to be pretty.'

Gloria looked to Sheila for approval.

Swallowing hard, secretly wondering what form 'not pretty' would take, she nodded. 'Best to take him back to the car.' She threw Gloria her car keys. 'Put the engine on if it's cold. There'll be plenty of time for you to show this lot who's in charge, but now's probably not ideal, what with Jay and all . . .'

Kevin appeared at the door to the office as Gloria was leaving. He stepped aside to allow the pushchair through. Looked like he might throw up at any moment on his shoes.

'Get in here,' Sheila said, praying there was some ferocity in her voice, though she felt anything but ferocious.

Lev pushed the imposter into the middle of the office.

'I didn't do it!' Kevin said, holding his hands high. 'I didn't grass.'

Sheila rounded on him, slapping his pasty face hard. He was slightly shorter than her, given she was wearing stilettos. Didn't look more than twenty-five. *Save the motherly love for your own kids*, she chided herself.

'Who else would be shooting his mouth off to the man who owns Birmingham but a Brummie? Come on, Kevin. I wasn't born yesterday. And don't you dare take me for a berk just because I'm a woman.'

Kevin clutched at his cheek, already reddening from the slap. 'I'm not. I swear. I don't even know Nigel.' His voice had risen an octave. He kept glancing towards Lev, as though his former ally would somehow pull him out of the mire. Those piggy eyes of his, glassy with fear, were darting towards Conky, who was approaching with menacing, almost glacial slowness, taking what appeared to be a garrotte out of his coat pocket. Kevin grinned and chuckled the nervous, mirthless grin and chuckle of a man who realised he was about to be dealt with by the Loss Adjuster. 'Come on, Conky. You know my rep is good.'

Sheila baulked as Conky stretched the garrotte taut.

'How do you know he's called Nigel?' Conky asked.

'He's the big boss back home. Everyone knows his name.' The sheen of sweat on his top lip glistened even in the dim light of the office. His eyes were everywhere except on Conky.

'You're a liar.'

He walked behind Kevin. Nimble like a ballet dancer for such a large man. Sheila wasn't sure she wanted to see any of this. She had always found Conky's physical might a turn-on, but now that she was faced with the reality of what Loss Adjusting really meant, she wasn't sure she'd ever be able find Conky attractive again.

'I've just been reading an interesting book about the Roman Army,' Conky said in that breezy, enthusiastic tone of voice he always used when he spoke about his reading habits. As though he were merely enjoying an espresso in her kitchen. 'Do you know what form the punishment took for lying in the Roman army, Kevin?'

Kevin glanced behind at Conky, but Conky clamped his head between his giant palms and forced him to face front.

He whispered in the dealer's ear. 'They called it "fustarium". The lying soldiers would be cudgelled to death. But I haven't got a cudgel handy. So we'll have to use this nice cheese wire.' In one swift movement, he released Kevin's head and wrapped the garrotte around his throat, pulling tightly. 'Don't worry. I'll send your head to Mr Bancroft so he can say his goodbyes properly.'

Lifting Kevin from the ground, Conky seemed to find

the act of choking the life out of a man almost effortless. Kevin, on the other hand, writhed and kicked out, trying to free himself.

Sheila couldn't bear to watch. *Please die quickly. Please die quickly.* She stared out of the internal window at the farm below, watching the Vietnamese children tend the lush green plants with great care. At that moment, feeling queasy and faint, she regretted more than anything that she had turned Nigel Bancroft down. It would have been so easy to relinquish this vile Man's Business and carry on with her own cleaning company and the online-dating-cum-phishing scam. Soft-end criminality that would allow her a good night's sleep. Not this. Could she have insisted Conky only half-choke the grass and then let him go? No. She would forever more have been known as a soft touch and Bancroft would be back, asking for a higher percentage.

'It's done,' Conky said. There was a thunk as he dropped Kevin's body to the floor. 'Get me a machete from one of the kids,' he told Lev.

'Jesus, Conky!' Sheila said, deliberately looking anywhere but at the dead man. The odour of death made her gag. 'Just leave it at that, will you. Send Bancroft a bloody photo or something.'

But Conky wasn't listening. 'There's only one way to send a message that will stick.'

When a trembling, reluctant Lev was despatched on a borrowed motorbike, carrying a fried-chicken delivery bucket containing Kevin's head with Conky's order that he 'hot-foot it to Nice Nigel's office in Birmingham to say the O'Briens have sent him a little food for thought', Sheila left the blood-splattered office choking back her tears.

As she joined Gloria and Jay in the Rolls Royce, she barely registered the sight of the man in the white van, watching from his vantage point some fifty yards from the apparently derelict warehouse.

Chapter 12

Tariq

Pulling into the parking space of the hospital, Tariq killed the engine of his Mercedes CLS. Pushed his father's disabled permit into the windscreen. Sighed.

'I can't stand this place,' he said, staring up at the tall Victorian houses that overlooked the disabled bays. 'Always a scrum to get parked. You're stressed out before you even get in there.' A light sweat had broken out beneath his clothes. This occasion was having more of an effect on him than he had anticipated.

His father laid a gnarled hand on his arm. 'It's me going for the consultation,' he said in Urdu. The lines at the corners of the old man's milky eyes crinkled up. 'You're just the chauffer. So, let me do the worrying. We've been lucky this week. We survived a near miss with that truck you nearly crashed into. Maybe it's a sign that things are going our way. Insha-Allah, everything will have stayed the same.' He readjusted his karakul hat and fastened the top button of his coat, his arthritic fingers shaking slightly.

'Come on. You'll miss your appointment.' Scanning the scene in his mirrors, Tariq kept the doors of the car locked until he was certain there were no faces out of keeping with the entrance to the Christie hospital. Only people bent double and shuffling through ill health, walking slowly because the chemo had bloated them up, or latching onto their chaperones for dear life. No sign of Conky – Roy Orbison on steroids – or of those scumbags in the black Volkswagen van. Surely they had been Sheila's men. The woman had more metal than he had given her credit for, not to mention new staff.

Tariq felt momentarily light-headed. Realised he had been holding his breath again.

'You need to calm down, Tariq,' his father said, pressing the button to unlock the car. He opened his door expectantly. 'Stress is a killer. You don't want to end up in here like your old Dad.'

Tariq fixed his father with a look of disbelief. Wiped the old man's spittle from the dashboard with the special Dad-Spit-Cloth in one automatic movement, trying to calm himself. 'I'm sorry,' he said in Urdu, blinking hard. 'But didn't two lunatics try to bundle you into a van last week in broad daylight?'

His father took hold of the stick he had been gripping between his knees. Brandished it and grinned. 'I gave them what for, though, didn't I? Nobody messes with Youssuf Khan!'

Back to English. 'Yeah. Right. Course you did.' He determined silently not to point out that the only reason the two wannabe kidnappers had got back in their van and driven away to whatever hole in Parsons Croft they'd presumably scuttled out from had been the mutual sighting of Ellis James, sitting in his unmarked Mondeo, parked a mere ten yards away. Watching. Waiting for some errant behaviour that would warrant arrest. 'You're a hero, Dad. But don't forget the line of work I'm in. It pays to be cautious.'

'You can talk! You nearly drove us into the path of a truck the other day. How about *you* exercise a little caution?'

Together, they began the sluggish advance to radiology, his father refusing to be pushed in a wheelchair. The corridors thronged with swiftly marching young doctors, cleaners pushing wheeled buckets and mops slowly along, and patients – some walking briskly, ready to ring the bell that signified the end of their treatment. Most were in the crawler lane like them, stooped with regret at the poor diet they'd spent a shortened lifetime enjoying, the cigarettes they'd chugged on defiantly or the daily ten pints they'd chosen to self-medicate with, which had turned out not to be quite so medicinal after all.

'What's that noise?' his father asked, frowning down at the pockets of Tariq's coat. 'You sound like a respirator.'

In his pocket, Tariq's phone pinged and buzzed constantly. He itched to know what was being sent through. Today was payday. Had the count from the brothels been correct? Had the take from the drugs been healthy? Had there been any more hassle from Sheila O'Brien's lot? Was Jonny acting up, ably assisted by the unpredictable Asaf Smolensky? Or perhaps, more worryingly, had there been any further threatening communication from that cow, Ruth Darley at HMRC or her shitty, shabby boyfriend, Detective Ellis James?

'Nothing.' Tariq's fingers itched to retrieve the phone but his sense of duty towards his father had to take precedence, at least until the old man was carted off to the scanner.

Advancing towards radiology, the pinging and buzzing grew more insistent. He helped his father to undress and don the hospital robe inside a changing cubicle that was too small for the two of them. He folded his father's tunic and trousers accurately, placing them in the plastic basket on the floor. Peeled the thermal underwear off the old man's frail body, wondering what on earth the scan would find this time. As if the heart surgery hadn't been trial enough.

'You need to speak to Anjum,' his father said unexpectedly, sitting down heavily onto the bench as Tariq slid his sandals back onto his now-bare feet. His breath whistled in and out through the broken bellows of his lungs. 'She's your wife, Tariq! It's been months. You shouldn't still be sleeping in the guest room. She knows about you, doesn't she? She found out what you really do for a living.'

'Grab my arm,' Tariq said. 'I think they're calling you through.'

'Youssuf Khan!'

The unfamiliar, perky voice that came from beyond the cubicle curtain felt like a buoy to which Tariq was only too happy to cling.

'Here he is!' Tariq said, smiling at the young male radiology nurse. 'You can have him, but I want him back.' He hoisted his father from the bench, gladly steering him towards the friendly, no-nonsense capability that the nursing staff offered. 'Don't let him get into any mischief!'

His father took his wire-framed glasses off and thrust them at Tariq. Narrowed those eyes that, for all their cataract-haze and high cholesterol white rings, seemed to see right into his soul. They always had. 'Show some respect!' In English, as some show of authority for the benefit of the nurse. Then, in Urdu. 'And don't think we've finished that conversation.'

Sitting alone in the waiting area, Tariq took out his phone. The perspiration rolled down his back, as if his limbic system already knew what dire news awaited him.

A semi-literate text from Little Jimmy: Shud I giv £ 2 Fish Man?

Tariq allowed himself an easy breath. The drugs money

95

was in, at least. Ordinarily, only he or Jonny took cash proceeds, so that the money could be quickly counted and concealed in the safe, the whereabouts of which only the two of them knew. But Jonny wasn't himself. And if cash was found on Smolensky, the repercussions for all of them didn't bear thinking about. He thumbed back a response.

Give it to Mohammed in accounts.

Next, a flurry of texts regarding the brothels, manned of late by a skeleton staff of remedial idiots, thanks to Degsy and that cow, Maggie, having blown half of the Boddlington foot-soldiers away in the war that had started with Jack O'Brien's murder.

There was one from Nasim: Coppers dun raid on Traf St n Grove Cl. Lads in nick. Girls gone.

He leaned forwards and wiped his face with his clammy palms. 'Oh, God.'

The patients, quietly sipping their iodine drinks, waiting in their robes to be called through for their CT scans, stared at him with selfless concern etched onto their already harried faces.

'Gets to you, doesn't it?' one of the men said, smiling sympathetically. Varicose-veined legs peeped out beneath his gown. He was almost certainly around Tariq's age, though his hair had thinned to a few lonely strands, making him seem decades older.

Tariq nodded. Non-committal. 'Just worried about my dad.' Avoided eye contact. Focussed on his phone. He didn't need to engage in polite chit-chat in this hellhole. He had more pressing matters – raids on Trafford Street and Grove Close. Sweeney Hall's finest low-rent brothels, both under Boddlington ownership. That meant he and Jonny were another six staff down. And where had the girls *gone*, exactly? Had they been taken into custody? Would any of them grass, revealing that they'd been trafficked to Manchester to order from Eastern Europe and Africa by people-smugglers who subcontracted for the Boddlington gang? Shit.

He thumbed out a text to Leviticus Bell yet again.

Please call me. There's a job here if you want it. T.

Lev had been good. Mildly dyslexic but reliable. Bright. Trustworthy. He was worth three of that big beefy dimwit, Nasim. Second cousin or no second cousin, Nasim couldn't be relied upon, even though he'd been under Smolensky's tutelage for almost a year now. He was just muscle. There had to be some way Tariq could overrule Jonny, with his misplaced need for retribution. Lev was worth a damn sight more back on the payroll as a Boddlington man than as a scapegoat for the murder of Jonny's daughter.

He dialled Jonny's number. When his partner picked up, his speech was heavy and sluggish with anti-depressant medication and sleep.

'You still in bed?' Tariq asked, careful to keep his voice low.

'And? Are you my mother?'

'Hasn't your phone been going mental? We've got problems, bro.'

'I know.' Jonny coughed at the other end of the phone. It was crackling and phlegmy. 'I told Smolensky to go round and see what's what.'

Irritation prickled beneath Tariq's skin. The tick beneath his eye started up. 'The Fish Man's not cut out to deal with staffing problems and lawyers, Jonny.'

The sound of Jonny lighting up. Exhaling heavily. 'So, *you* get onto the solicitors and get the lads bailed out.'

'I'm at the hospital with my dad, I can't. It's family.'

'And I don't have a family? Does my family – what's left

of it – count for nothing?' Bitterness curdled his consonants. 'You'll have to deal with it. I've got other fish to fry.'

The call ended abruptly before Tariq could even discuss the likelihood of the police having gathered damning evidence against them over time or them possibly having an informant among their number.

In yet another waiting area, crowded with optimistic patients and fidgeting relatives – petrified or bored, depending on how far along the treatment process they were – Tariq poured his father a plastic cup of water from the water cooler. The old man was sitting grim-faced, clutching his stick between his knees.

'Drink this, Dad. You don't want to get dehydrated.'

His father pushed the drink away. 'Ya-allah. I don't want water. I want coffee.'

Tariq sighed. 'The doctor said you're not to drink too much caffeine. It's bad for your heart. Drink the water.'

He proffered the cup to his father once more but the old man grabbed the cup, rose from his seat and shuffled over to the water cooler. He placed the full cup on top of the machine. Shuffled off to the café, returning moments later with a coffee clutched in a shaking hand.

'Remember who the father is here, young man.' He sipped the steaming drink, narrowing those milky eyes.

When the oncologist called them through, his stony expression revealed nothing of the scan results. As Tariq put a comforting hand on the old man's back, that light-headed feeling almost overwhelmed him yet again. Try as he might to listen to the oncologist's explanation of the CT scan, as he scrolled through the cross sections of his father's cancerous body that appeared on the computer's monitor, explaining each image in turn, all Tariq could think of was the brothels. Had they been sealed off with POLICE LINE DO NOT CROSS tape? Had the cops discovered anything at the scenes that might secure a conviction against Jonny and him in court?

'So, good news, Mr Khan,' the oncologist finished, at last, allowing himself a satisfied smile. 'You're officially in partial remission.'

At Tariq's side, his father clapped his hands together. Raised his face and looked up at the strip light on the ceiling. 'Allahu Akbar,' he said softly. 'God is great,' he explained to the oncologist with a chuckle.

'Perhaps, Mr Khan.' There was that tight smile again on the professional's face. 'But, personally, I prefer to say medical science is great.' A cheeky wink that Tariq knew his father wouldn't appreciate.

In the car, heading north along Princess Parkway, Tariq put his foot down. Eager to get out of O'Brien territory fast and get halfway down Deansgate to where the Boddlington turf began. But the car journey was proving intolerable, beset as he was by a mixture of incoming messages on his phone and his father's pronouncements.

'I've been given a clean bill of health, Tariq,' the old man said, waving to every pedestrian who looked his way, as if they too knew of his reprieve. The shoppers who milled around outside Kendals seemed indifferent to his near-euphoria. 'So there's going to be some changes between me and you, son.' He poked Tariq in the shoulder. 'I'm sick of being bossed around.'

'I don't want you overdoing it, Dad.'

'And I want you to stop all this illegal nonsense. Whatever it is you're up to.' He held his hands in the air. Closed his eyes. 'I don't want to know the details. But I want you to give it up and make amends. Sort your marriage out. Talk

Anjum round. I need to be able to hold my head up amongst the other elders at the masjid, Tariq.'

Tariq could feel his father's accusatory eyes on him. His beard itched. 'Don't get yourself excited, Dad. Think about your heart.' He hung a left into Blackfriars Street, which led down to the bowels of the city and the border with Salford, heading out to the ring road. The absolute safety of Lower Boddlington was not far now.

'Take me to the pharmacist's!' his father said. 'It's just down there.' He pointed to a quiet side street.

'No, Dad. I've got to go into work after I've dropped you off. I've got a lot on.'

'No?!' There was a strength to his father's voice now. 'I'm not asking for the earth, Tariq. I just want to see if Colin Chang is back. He's my friend.'

'He's just an acquaintance, Dad.'

'Colin's my friend! *He* listens to me. He's been missing for months, and if he's back, I want to see him.'

The old man had had his death sentence repealed and owned the moral high ground. That much, Tariq appreciated. Tutting, he took the short detour and pulled up outside the shuttered shopfront.

'It's closed.'

'There's a notice on the shutter. See what it says.' Pointing, pointing – the old man wouldn't take no for an answer.

Tariq got out of the car. Read the smudged ink on the fluttering piece of paper. Returned to the driver's seat. 'It's reopening in two weeks,' he said. 'Mystery solved. Your precious pharmacist must have just gone on one of his trips to Hong Kong.'

With the old man safely installed at home, Tariq paused to wedge one of Anjum's samosas into his mouth, snatched a bottle of Diet Coke from the fridge and drove over to the

Trafford Street brothel in Sweeney Hall. He was careful to park in an adjacent alleyway, feeling confident that no local scuzzball would dare touch the wheels of a Boddlington boss. But it wouldn't do him any good if the police were hanging around and saw his car parked up outside the brothel they had just raided.

Tariq scanned the litter-strewn street for unwelcome faces, then glanced up at the cracked and dirty windows of the terraced houses, checking for snooping eyes of grasses and local do-gooders. Trafford Street was empty of cops, but that dreaded police tape was indeed draped over the splintered remnants of the front door. Surreptitiously, he slid around the back and entered the property through the yard with his master key. The place smelled rank – of stale sex, overly floral air-freshener and rising damp. The accoutrements of breakfast had been abandoned, half-eaten, on the kitchen table. Upstairs, the beds looked as though they had been hastily tumbled out of, with crumpled sheets spilling onto the threadbare carpet. Every drawer had been emptied. Every cushion on the waiting room sofa had been removed. The place had been searched.

Tariq forced a hand into the thicket of his hair. 'Jesus. This is bad.' Couldn't shake off the feeling that he was being watched.

Walking to the front of the house, where they had turned the old living room into a bedroom, Tariq stepped gingerly over the sex toys and handcuffs that had been scattered on the floor during the police search. Grey dust from finger-printing covered every surface. He was careful to touch nothing. Using his knuckle to pull the grey-yellow nico-tine-stained net aside, he peered through the window onto the street.

'Everyone knows what this place is,' he whispered to

himself. 'But they know better than to grass. They're not daft.'

And then, as the trajectory of his appraising scan of the street took his focus upwards, he saw it. A small, discreet, black shining dome hanging down from a lamp post, not twenty feet away on the opposite side. State-of-the-art CCTV. Newly installed, by the looks.

'Shit!'

He let the curtain slip back and retreated to the kitchen, sweating freely beneath his pristine clothes.

When his phone pinged shrilly, he jumped. Peered at the display, wondering what nightmarish scenario could now possibly befall him. The text was from Anjum and in a morning of mixed fortunes, it was by far the worst thing he had heard that day.

I want a divorce. Give it me, or I'll go to the police.

Chapter 13

Lev

'Get off the sofa and go to work,' Gloria shouted. She flung a pair of his dirty socks at him, almost hitting Jay in the face. 'And tidy up after yourself!'

Lev stared at her open-mouthed, holding a protective hand over his son's bandages. 'Did you just throw shit at Jay's head? Are you having a fucking laugh with me?'

'*The soul of the sluggard craves and gets nothing, while the soul of the diligent is richly supplied.* Proverbs 13:4,' his mother said, shoving that sodding shotgun into the shopping wagon again. Flinging in a box of cartridges after it, as though her new-found status made her the god of all things, including hypocrisy and nagging.

Closing his eyes, Lev exhaled heavily. The memory of Conky's brutality was still freshly replaying itself behind his eyelids like a nasty GIF. 'I can't face it, Mam. I've got a migraine.' He touched his eyelids with thumb and index finger. Opened them to find Gloria mimicking him. Clutching her forehead dramatically. Moving her mouth with blah, blah, blah derision.

'You've got the same work ethic as your father, you lazy tripe-hound,' she said.

Too much. Lev snapped, setting Jay down in the playpen to be watched over by the eternally happy Teletubbies on the TV. 'Just get out, will you? And leave me alone to look after my son!'

He shooed his mother to the front door with that ridiculous tartan crutch for her ego. His heart was pounding too fast. Breath coming in ragged bursts as the harsh daylight of the quiet cul-de-sac poured in.

Get her off your case. Get back inside before the outside gets you.

Slamming the door behind her, he was aware of the film of cold sweat that coated his skin. Now he had the beginnings of a headache for real, not helped by the stinging knots of tension in his shoulders and the ache in his lower back from spending over an hour on a motorbike, negotiating rush hour on the M6 with a severed head in the top-box.

'Delivery for Mr Bancroft,' he had told the receptionist in the sleek lobby – the gateway to Bancroft's legitimate corporate kingdom. Speaking through the black-tinted visor of his crash helmet.

He had plonked the chicken family-bucket onto the shining wooden counter and had sprinted back out to the motorbike, almost ploughing into automatic glazed doors that were too slow to open. Barely able to kick-start the stolen Suzuki with legs that felt like jelly. He had imagined he could hear the receptionist's scream as the beast finally sprang to life beneath him. Inadvertently, he had wheelied his way out of the car park, barely in control of anything, let alone his imagination.

The cops are coming. I'll get done for murder or accessory to murder. I'll never get away from this nightmare life. If I'm lucky, I'll just crash into a juggernaut and the pain will be over.

His head had been full of foul noise on the short journey to the rendezvous point, where Conky had been due to meet him with a stolen car, engine already running: the sound of mucus inside Brummie Kev's gullet, gurgling as he had pointlessly fought strangulation at the iron hand of the Loss Adjuster; the dull, squelching sound as Conky had hacked away at the poor bastard's slippery, unyielding head with one of the cannabis-farmer's machetes.

I wish I was dead. I just want it all to end.

Tears had streamed down Lev's face inside the purpose-built prison of that tightly fitting helmet, steaming up the visor and wetting the padding that had covered his jaw and chin. If he had collided into something doing fifty, would his head have been ripped off too, still clad in that helmet? Would instant decapitation have hurt? But in the midst of those dark thoughts, Lev had remembered his boy. Jay. If nothing else represented hope in Lev's godforsaken life, his son did.

Get through this. Get back to Jay. He needs you. If you give up, there's only the witches to look after him and he deserves better than loony Gloria and shitty Tiffany.

They had made it back to the safety of Manchester with the message duly delivered that Nigel Bancroft and his Birmingham boys should piss off back behind their city line or face a bloody war. Lev had been paid a cool thou in cash for his time and trouble. But the money meant nothing. So far, he had successfully hidden from the Fish Man's boning knives and he'd evaded arrest for a cornucopia of criminal offences that would put him in a Category A prison with a double-digit sentence. But he couldn't escape his conscience.

Trudging back into the living room, he picked Jay out of the playpen and rocked the boy gently to the rhythm of the theme tune to *Postman Pat*. Wept hot tears over his son.

'You're daddy's best boy, you know.'

'Dad. Dad. Dad.' With a tiny, dribbly finger, Jay carefully traced the outline of the lightning bolt shaved into Lev's stubbled scalp, following the silvered line of an old scar. 'Kiss.' He smacked his little rosebud lips together – free of snotty crust now that Tiff was no longer looking after him. His green eyes shone with curiosity and love. A different boy from before.

'When Jay's a big boy, Daddy's gonna take him some-where hot and lovely. Like Florida! That's it! We'll go to Disneyland to see Mickey Mouse. Would you like that?'

He considered his time spent in Baltimore, during which he had eked out the agonising weeks, waiting for Jay to recover sufficiently post-surgery to travel home. The brain surgeon had done that non-committal thing of thinning his lips and cocking his head to one side when Lev had asked him if Jay had been cured.

'Mr Bell, I removed the tumour, which was a doozy,' he had said. 'But we'll just have to see how it goes over the coming months and hopefully years. It was benign, so that's a plus.'

Not the conclusively happy ending he had been hoping for.

Lev looked down at Jay's head. Carefully unwound the bandages – minimal now, after months of healing. Eyed the livid, Frankenstein-esque scar that ran across the boy's head. How could such a beautiful child hide such a terrible secret beneath those regrowing curls? And what if a second tumour had reappeared inside that little delicate dome, somehow hiding from all the gadgetry and the specialist's scrutiny? Who knew? Maybe all those scans would cause something new to take root. Radiation, wasn't it? Lev knew that shit was bad for kids.

He started to gasp for breath again. Jay looked at him quizzically. 'I'm all right,' he told the boy. 'Daddy's just feeling a bit weird.'

His phone pinged. A text. Could this be yet another death threat from Jonny Margulies? Lev swallowed hard, running a shaking hand over his top lip. Anticipating unwelcome words, heralding the start of his own personal end of days. But it wasn't from Jonny.

We need to talk. Please call. I've got work for you. Tariq.

Another love letter from Tariq Khan. Was it a trap? Was it even possible that one Boddlington boss should be courting him while the other wanted him dead?

Lev scrolled down his texts to read the last missive from Jonny. Sent only two weeks earlier.

I won't rest til Fish Man brings me your heart, cos you broke mine.

'They'll never forget,' he said aloud, squeezing his eyes shut. 'Neither of them! And Tariq's gotta be in cahoots.' He peered down at the phone's display. 'Leave me alone, for Christ's sake!'

There was the sound of a car pulling up. *Shit, shit, shit.* Right outside. And he was expecting nobody, so that definitely meant bad news. Didn't it?

Lev ran through all the emergency evacuation procedures he'd rehearsed in his head, time after time. Out the back door. Out the back gate. Down the cut-through onto the main road. Seek refuge under the bright lights and busy aisles of the local supermarket.

'Daddy might have to run somewhere very fast with you, Jay-Jay. Ready for some fun?'

Swinging Jay onto his hip, he peered through the half-

107

open shutters. The sunlight streaming through felt like it might burn him. The open space of the cul-de-sac felt like it might swallow him whole. The street was too empty of potential witnesses. The only thing of note in the street was the car. Its driver was peering into the living room window.

'Who the hell's this?' Lev muttered, trying to place a familiar face.

He observed the driver through the half-closed shutters. 'Anjum Khan?!'

He watched the Boddlington boss's wife get out of her Audi and walk up to the front door of the house. All business in her trouser suit for this detour to the wrong side of town.

'Ding dong!' Jay said when the bell chimed.

Lev stepped backwards into the living room, wondering what to do. Should he answer the door to the respected Dr Anjum Khan? Director of the asylum seekers' advocacy place in Cheetham Hill, she was one of life's good guys, for sure. This wasn't Tariq. But it *was* Tariq's wife. Was she friend or foe?

He shushed Jay, who merely nodded and smiled coyly. The bell rang again. Lev made the decision to dive behind the sofa too late. Anjum's sharp brown eyes were peering in at them both through the shuttered window. She knocked on the glass.

'I can see you're in there, Leviticus!'

'I'm not. Go away!' he shouted.

'Let me in. I need to talk to you. It's about Tariq. And Irina.'

Irina. The poor, pregnant trafficked cow from Estonia or Latvia or some far-flung dump. Almost gunned down by that prize dick, Degsy, in some tit-for-tat bullshit surrounding Jack O'Brien's murder.

'How did you find me?' he asked, holding the front door ajar.

Anjum looked tired, verging on haggard. She pushed past him into the living room, patting Jay affectionately on the cheek. 'I see he's had the surgery,' she said. 'He looks a lot better than last time I saw the little mite.'

'Yeah, well.'

'I think "thanks" is the word you're looking for.' She stood uncertainly by the playpen. Hands clasped before her, then dropping to her sides. Touching her long hair, which was hanging loose over her shoulders today.

'Ta. Does Tariq know where I'm living? Does he know I'm staying with my mam? Because I had no option. Jonny's gone mental on me, and my slag of a babymother's—'

Anjum shook her head. 'I'm not here on Tariq's dirty business, Leviticus.' She bit her lip tentatively. 'I'm divorcing him. I'm here to ask for your help to put him away. I want to take every last one of these scumbags down. But the police need reliable, willing witnesses.'

Was this some kind of a test of his loyalty to the Boddlingtons? He scrutinised her face for signs of shiftiness in amongst the scant crow's feet. Sniffed the air. He smelled not bullshit, but expensive perfume. 'You want me to grass?'

'Can you think of a better way to escape this life?'

'There isn't no escaping this life.'

Anjum took a step towards him. Another step. She reached out to stroke Jay's chin. 'I saw you in that hole where they torture people who don't toe the line. I saw the desperation in your face.' She looked deep into his eyes, and Lev felt certain that she saw his soul in terrifying, complex detail. 'You wanted out. Your son was dying. You brought Irina to me, when you could have left her for dead or taken her back to Tariq.' Glancing down at the boy, she smiled widely and with the warmth of a good mother. 'I know you're not like them.' She took her voice an octave up, doing that thing that women always did around cute kids. 'Daddy wants you to grow up to be a nice man, doesn't he? Yes.' Nodding. 'He doesn't want to end up in a body bag and with you caught in the crossfire, does he?' Shaking her head. 'No! Daddy's got morals.'

'Who are you talking to at the cop shop?' Lev asked, feeling her manipulative words yank at his heartstrings like the fingers of a skilled puppeteer.

'Ellis James,' she said.

Lev gasped. 'Oh, you're kidding me. Everybody hates that scruffy little arsehole. You dob your old man into him and chances are you're gonna wind up in a body bag anyhow. We all will, soon enough.'

'Think about it, Lev,' Anjum said, stroking Jay's cheek. 'The chance of a fresh start for you and your son. Come with me to the police. What do you say?'

Chapter 14

Gloria

'Get fucked, you silly black bitch!' the landlord said, barely giving her a second glance whilst he polished a pint glass badly with a greasy-looking bar towel. There was mockery in his voice and the suggestion of a chuckle.

Generalised hurt was a rough blanket, smothering her fire and gnawing at her skin. Gloria processed the insult, taking it apart, one unpleasant thread at a time. This unwashed oik had used foul language. He'd insulted her intelligence, her ethnicity and her gender. This was the sixth time she'd been verbally abused this way in the last fortnight. Sixth. And yet, the barman's words still stung. No immunity quite yet. *Toughen up, Gloria Bell! You've a job to do, and that Mazda's not going to replace itself with a nice little Audi TT.*

Gloria took a step towards the bar, pulling her shopping wagon along behind her. 'You're late with your payment, Glen Armstrong. This is an O'Brien pub and you enjoy O'Brien privileges. But not for free. Paddy wasn't running a charity, and neither is Sheila.' She treated him to a curt smile, silently saying a prayer under her breath.

The landlord slammed the pint pot down onto the wood.

Pulled a baseball bat out from behind the bar and slapped it repeatedly in the palm of his rather grubby-looking hand. An eyebrow raised, which was the only interesting feature in a blob of a face that Gloria thought resembled putty with unpleasant bits stuck to it.

'Opening time's not for two hours, so piss off out my pub,' he said in a guttural Parsons Croft accent. He pointed the baseball bat towards her. 'Cos if you don't, I'm gonna smash your gappy teeth down your throat and ram this up your cunt, you uppity slag.'

'Charming,' Gloria said, drawing on the power of the Lord Jesus Christ that she felt bubbling up from deep within her. Or was it pure fury? She couldn't be certain. *'You have heard that it was said, "You shall love your neighbour and hate your enemy."'* She unzipped the top of the shopping trolley, delving inside. Never took her eyes from the landlord. *'But I say to you, Love your enemies and pray for those who persecute you, so that you may be sons of your Father who is in heaven.'* She pulled out the shotgun and pointed it at the man's head, speaking from the bottom of her diaphragm, projecting as though she were in the church pulpit. She smiled, imagining the pastor. Then remembered the pastor was a philandering hypocrite who liked young girls. The smile transformed into a scowl. She savoured the wrath that had been kindled inside her. Took two swift and sure strides to the bar. *'For he makes his sun rise on the evil and on the good, and sends rain on the just and on the unjust.* Matthew 5:43-45. Give me a reason to pull the trigger, Mr Armstrong.'

Blob-faced Glen Armstrong neither smashed her teeth in nor inserted his baseball bat into her intimate parts. He merely dropped the bat onto the floor with a clatter and held his hands up. 'You're bleeding tapped.' A sheen of sweat

112

on his suet-pie-crust of a forehead revealed the full extent of his bravado. 'Who do you think you are? Samuel L. sodding Jackson?'

'No. I've got bigger balls and better taste in hats than him.' She made a show of peering along the sights at her target. 'You owe back-pay from March. I want to see big piles of Her Majesty's face. Now!'

Wheeling her shopping trolley, stuffed with the shotgun, cartridges and wads of used twenty- and fifty-pound notes from that morning's three successful collections, Gloria trotted along Parsons Croft High Road. Every part of her, from her ankles to the tips of her hair felt like it was buzzing from the adrenalin. Her stomach was in turmoil. Her heartbeat, more of a clatter – almost loud enough for the outside world to hear. Her senses were alight, and Jesus hadn't even been responsible for the strange feeling of abject fear, mingled with euphoria.

Glancing back over her shoulder to check that the odious landlord had not followed her out with that bat, she couldn't help but giggle. *Keep walking. Put some distance between you and that den of iniquity. Take this seriously!* The eminently sensible side to Gloria was appalled by the responsibilities she had agreed to take on and the levity with which she was dealing with these bottom-feeders. But new Gloria – the born-again young woman in a middle-aged church elder's body – simply told the old Gloria to shut the heck up and keep her fusty opinions to herself.

'Praise the Lord. Hallelujah!'

She started to strut down the street as if she owned that place, realising that in some ways, she did – at least, fifteen per cent of it. Yanked her shopping trolley over the cracked, chewing-gum-spattered paving stones as if it were a wheeled

Louis Vuitton trunk full of champagne; threw her head back and laughed aloud, attracting the bewildered looks of an old man who was waiting, barely sheltered by the semi-shattered glass, at the bus stop for the bus into town.

'Blessings, brother!' she shouted at the old man. '*Do not neglect to do good and to share what you have, for such sacrifices are pleasing to God.* Hebrews 13:16.' She stuffed a fifty-pound note into his dry, leathery hand, which was met with initial bafflement followed by the poor-man's Hollywood smile of a double-denture grin. 'Treat yourself to a cab.'

Buoyed by her success, she relocated her Mazda and popped the boot. Decanted the money into the recess where her spare tyre had been. Drove on to the next job with rousing hymns sung by her favourite gospel choir, blaring from her sound-system. Yes, Gloria Bell was doing good work, collecting tithes from the faithless. Channelling the spirit of the Lord. She had never felt better.

When she arrived at the Tanner's Arms in Whitcroft Street, her jubilant mood remained undimmed, even when she walked through from the front of the seemingly ordinary, grotty lounge of the pub to the back, where the sound of barking, howling and men's jeering warned her of the illegal dog fight that was underway.

'Oh, here we go,' the barman said, elbowing the landlady. He nodded towards Gloria. 'Pulp Friction's back.' He stepped out from behind the bar, blatantly flouting the smoking ban with his stinking lit cigarette. 'Where's your beret and your kilt, love?' Winking. Guffawing, as if Gloria hadn't heard this in every single pub, club, restaurant, wine bar and café that fell under O'Brien jurisdiction, from the southern end of the town centre right up to Bramshott Village. Two weeks of the same gag. Where on earth had they got such an outlandish comparison from?

'Ha . . . ha . . . ha,' Gloria said, locking eyes with her ferrety verbal abuser, ensuring he knew she wasn't intimidated by him in the slightest. She whipped the shotgun out of the trolley with the speed and deftness of an apocalyptic horseman. 'It's payday.'

She peered down the barrel at his legs. Barely registering the weight of the thing as her body flooded with the glorious endorphins of the newly power-crazed, she swung the weapon over to the landlady's head, then back to the barman's knees. Utterly fearless because she knew that her fine Christian soul was pure and prepared for heaven and, perhaps most importantly, that she was the one with the weapon.

Never taking her eyes from the barman, she raised her voice. Imagined she was preaching to a church hall full of repentant sinners – loud enough that the foul and pestilent dog-fanciers in the back might hear the words of James 2:26.

'For as the body apart from the spirit is dead, so also faith apart from works is dead. And legs apart from the knees will put you in a wheelchair, mister, so, put the cash on the bar, and I might let you keep your kneecaps.'

'What's wrong with your face, Leviticus?' she said, returning to their rented semi late in the afternoon to find that her son was sitting on the sofa in his pants, yet again. Dimpled chin and downturned mouth. Red-rimmed around the eyes as though he had been crying.

'Her dog died. It was dead sad.'

Her feckless son pointed to the TV, where some kind of reality-style panel show was playing out on one of the lesser channels. Gloria grimaced at the sight of a woman with badly bleached platinum blonde hair and a décolletage like the Grand Canyon. She wore flip-flops and had crispy ankles. A non-believer, without a doubt. 'She looks like a good scrub would kill her. Where's Jay?'

'At Tiff's.'

'You're happy for him to be around that little strumpet?' Gloria snatched up the remote control and switched the TV off. Rearranged the magazines on the coffee table into a neat pile. Collected the spent cups, observing with some disgust that her son had not used the coasters. She hit him over the head with the remote control.

'Ow! What was that for?'

'Cup rings.'

He rubbed his scalp. 'Solicitor says I have to give her one supervised hour a week. She's got a social worker there with her. Aw, come on, Mam! Give us back the remote. I was watching that!'

A whine in his voice. Pleading in his weak, teary eyes. Poor quality mirrors to a soul that lacked moral fibre. Just like his father. 'I've been working all day,' she said. 'Do you know how many board meetings I had on top of my tithe collection?'

Lev sucked his teeth and scowled. 'You mean robbing protection money with a shopping wagon like Mrs Brady, Old Lady on meth?'

Gloria pointed to her trolley, still stuffed full of more than one hundred thousand pounds. Perhaps a quarter of a million. She hadn't counted it yet. 'That's my chariot of fire, that is. And it was just a touch of light extortion from sinners who get what's coming to them.' She folded her arms tightly over her bosom. 'Anyway. Call it what you will. *I* take pride in a job well done, young man.'

'You wanna watch your back, Mam. Seriously. You were the one always lecturing me, "Lay with dogs, you get fleas."

116

Well, you're rubbing some dyed-in-the-wool, dangerous bastards up the wrong way, now. Don't be surprised if it all comes back to bite you on the arse. Jesus won't save you, then. What if someone opens their mouth? Eh?'

She opened the shutters, ignoring Lev's melodramatic squinting, unwelcome advice and general complaint. Threw open the living room window, wafting her hand in front of her face in protest at the stale smell of testosterone and unwashed twenty-something-year-old. Thought wistfully of her own home in Chorlton, which was currently being rented out by the sister of one of the members of the congregation. How she hankered after her own space and no parental responsibilities. Just a dim memory now. 'You should have been at the farm today. Especially if the boy was with his harlot of a mother.'

'There's something wrong with me,' Lev said, lying back on the sofa, arms thrown high above his head. He had the body of a fully grown, athletically built man but still adopted the same pose he had as a little boy when he had been feeling poorly. 'I feel rough when I go out. Dizzy, like. I think I've come down with—'

'You've gone down with a touch of sloth!' Gloria said, marching through to the kitchen and flicking the kettle on. Shouting so that he could hear her. 'One of the seven deadly sins, Leviticus.'

'And you've come down with avarice and pride! See? I'm not that thick, am I?'

She was just about to lecture her layabout son further on the extent of his ignorance, as far as the seven deadly sins were concerned, when her phone rang. Peering at the screen, she didn't recognise the number. Was about to send it to voicemail, lest it was some disgruntled O'Brien land-lord, deciding that he would, after all, like to ram something unpleasant into one of her lady-regions. But picking up was a useful means of sidetracking Leviticus from a conversation which was not going entirely to her satisfaction.

'Yes?'

'Is that gorgeous Gloria?'

'Who is this?' She already knew who it was. She hid her grin from her son.

Chapter 15

Sheila

'Jesus, that's a lot of cash,' Sheila said as she and Gloria finished counting the last pile. Stacks of twenties and tens rose in teetering piles all over the kitchen's island worktop. Two hours' worth of work to check and re-check.

'Nearly three hundred thousand,' Gloria said, her face lit up with obvious pride. 'There were a lot of nasty types owed you some very large sums. It's a long time since Paddy died by the reckoning of your debtors. They thought you'd forget. Luckily . . .' She winked. 'I reminded them.'

Sheila counted out Gloria's percentage and gave it to her. 'Don't let onto this new admirer of yours that you're a woman of means. Let him do the wining and dining. Last thing you need after Lev's pimp of a dad is another sponger. So, keep this under your church hat.'

'Oh, don't you worry, She. I intend to,' Gloria said, ramming a wad of money down the front of her dress. She laughed hysterically as though she'd just done the funniest thing in the world. 'Only kidding.' Clasping Sheila by the arm playfully, she moved the money from her cleavage to her handbag. 'Bob, the love-king of speed-dating, is taking me for lunch later. He can stuff off if he thinks I'm buying so much as a breadstick!'

The sun was only just coming up. With Gloria gone, Sheila sat at a bar stool, sipping her early morning coffee thoughtfully and contemplating the cash. A king's ransom, here. Two more rubble sacks that Paddy had left stashed beneath the tiles in the guest en-suite shower. So fat with dirty money that they'd caused a leak into the master bedroom below. She started to shake her head slowly.

'I can't have this in the house,' she told the hosts of the breakfast television show who spoke without sound on the muted TV, sunk into the far wall. She rubbed at the goose-bumps that sprang up beneath the skin of her forearms. Shivered. 'Come on, Sheila. Get your act together.'

Downstairs, in the quiet of the garage, Sheila heaved the last of the sacks into the boot of her Porsche Panamera and shut the lid. *Get it out. Get it somewhere safe.* She acknowledged the sweat rolling down her back on that cold September morning. *Jesus. Is this perimenopause or nerves?* But she realised it was well-placed anxiety. Even with Paddy gone, Ellis James and Ruth Darley had eyes everywhere. The police and HMRC were foes not to be underestimated, and their weapons were search warrants and audits. Retribution from Bancroft was sure to come at some point soon too. No saying trouble wouldn't come knocking on her front door. She had to move fast.

Hastening back up to the bedroom, she pulled on a pair of jeans and a cashmere jumper. Kissed Conky's forehead as he started to stir from his slumber.

His shovel of a left hand appeared from under the duvet. He grabbed the digital clock that sat beside his hairpiece. Squinted at the display with his bulging thyroid eyes. 'Jesus,

She. Where you off to so early?' Setting the clock down, he reached for her, but she had already started to retreat to the door.

'I've been up for ages. I'll not be more than an hour. Get some coffee on. I'll explain later.' She blew him a kiss, feeling dizzy with adrenalin, watching Conky's sleepy morning unfold at a pace entirely unrelated to that of her own frenetic adventure.

The gravel crunched beneath her tyres as she navigated the long drive. The heavy wooden gates started to move aside on their automated tracks, receding into the mature shrubbery. It was six-thirty now. At a glance, only the squirrels, the birds and the odd jogger were on the move on Bramshott's sleepy, leafy boulevards. But Sheila was now so keenly alert that she almost smelled the stale aroma of Ellis James before she saw him, sitting in his unmarked car some one hundred metres from her mansion.

'Sneaky, persistent little arsehole. Why you on my case all the bloody time?'

His beady eyes weren't immediately visible. His head lolled on his driver's side window. She chewed harder on her gum, wondering if the dog-eared detective was even awake. In a private no-through-road with impassable bollards crossing the midpoint, she had no option but to drive past him. Should she floor it and hope to evade detection through sheer speed, or crawl quietly, lowering the risk of rousing the sleeping policeman?

Too late. It didn't matter how fast she drove, Ellis James had sat up in his seat and was looking straight at her. Shit.

Sheila waved. 'Morning, wanker!' She forced a smile onto her face, rapidly assessing from his frown and the fact that he was belting himself in that he was going to follow her. Or was he?

As she swung her car into the road and up to the junction, sure enough, through her rear-view mirror, she spied James' old grey Mondeo pull away from the kerb.

'Come on, come on, She,' she counselled herself. 'You've got to shake the bastard off. How the hell are you going to do it?'

If she went above the speed limit, he could stop and search her. Maybe. Or at least stop her and issue a ticket. Damn! It wasn't far to the motorway and then it would be a straight journey into town. That early in the morning, however, the motorway would be empty, but for the odd taxi, taking someone to the airport or heavy goods vehicles, rumbling on to their destinations. No traffic to lose him in.

'Bugger!' Sheila smacked the dashboard in frustration, her breath coming in short gasps. She looked up at the grey Mancunian skies above leafy trees that were only just on the turn. Prayed for an act of divine providence that would do away with the determined detective on her tail; feeling the weight of half a million in rubble sacks almost draw the boot of her Panamera backwards to the bonnet of the grey Mondeo, as if bad gravity were somehow in action.

But her prayers went unanswered. Ellis James was still in pursuit, doing a steady twenty-nine about a hundred yards behind her.

Conspiracy to commit fraud.

Tax evasion.

Harbouring illegal and immoral earnings or some shit.

Sheila wasn't certain of what she would be charged with, should James find the money, but it wouldn't bode well for her. 'You're a twat, Sheila O'Brien!' she shouted as she passed the yellow box of a speed camera. 'You should have left it where it was. You panicked and now you've screwed it up for yourself.'

Then, inspiration came in the form of a large church that stood by the roadside on her right. A relief carving in white marble above the portico of the Virgin Mary, clutching the dead body of a crucified Jesus.

'Gloria!'

She brought up Gloria's number on the car phone. Her business partner answered on the third ring, still sounding positively perky. The coo and gurgle of a toddler in the background.

'I've got that shitbag detective on my tail right now, and half a mill in cash in the boot of my car. I need to shake the bastard off. I'm heading for the motorway. We're about to pass by your street. Do us a favour, will you? Get in your car and act as a decoy or something.'

On the other end of the phone, Gloria yawned. 'It's your cash. I've got my cash. I'm busy with our Jay's breakfast and then I'm getting ready for my date. Why should I abandon that to help you squirrel away—?'

'Gloria! Stop being an arsehole. We're in this together. He's in a grey Mondeo. 61 plate. You can't miss him. If he was any closer, he'd be sitting on my back seat.'

But inglorious Gloria hung up.

'Bitch!'

Sheila's molars were almost fused together with tension by the time she approached Moss Side. Only a few men and women sheltered against the autumnal bluster in bus stops. Otherwise the empty pavements and the locked-up Afro-hairdressers, international money transfer and imported reggae record shops gave the place the feel of a down-at-heel seaside town, abandoned in winter months.

Sheila wondered if she should merely turn around at the Parson's Croft roundabout and go home. Inside the electronic gates of her mansion, she was safe . . . as long as

James couldn't produce a search warrant. Or perhaps she could shake him off at this next set of lights.

'Change! Change, goddamit!'

They changed to amber. But she wasn't close enough. If she ran the lights, James could do her for a traffic offence.

'Shitting Nora!' she cried, bringing the car to a standstill.

Checking her rear-view mirror, she saw the detective was sitting directly behind her now, smiling and waving at her through the windscreen. Sheila whimpered in frustration and fear. She was going to get caught.

Onto the city, and hope surged anew. With so many roadworks having sprung up, there were traffic lights aplenty and sudden turns that would surely give her an opportunity to shake the creep off. She could not let him see where she was going.

She hung a right onto Whitworth Street East. Not where she wanted to go, but she could disappear beneath one of the railway arches perhaps and gun the car along the warren of backstreets that led up to Manchester Metropolitan University. Holding her breath, she checked the rear-view mirror.

'No! No! Piss off, you shabby little tag-nut!'

James was still on her. She hung a left. Pelted across Oxford Road towards Princess Street, swinging hastily right through the lights as she passed the Lass O'Gowrie pub on her left. Still behind her. Not good! And now, she was going in the opposite direction to her chosen destination. Worse still, she turned into a one-way street, driving in the wrong direction.

A flash of headlamps. James was indicating that she should pull over.

'Shit! Shit! Shit!' Sheila's breath came short. Tears started to leak unbidden from the corners of her eyes. Why the hell hadn't she taken Conky with her? Damn!

Starting to slow, she indicated that she was pulling over. Swallowing down a cold lump of fear.

Except her surrender was interrupted by the persistent honk of a horn and the squealing sound of a car's tyres. In her wing mirror, she caught sight of a Mazda MX-5, pulling in front of James's car at an untenable angle. A familiar-looking black woman in the driver's seat.

'Gloria!'

Sheila could see her partner, grim-faced and hunched over the steering wheel. Blocking the detective's path.

'Good on you, Glo. I owe you one.'

Hitting the gas, Sheila squealed away from the side street and arrived at her destination within minutes. She parked right in front of the safety deposit facility. Lugged the bags downstairs in two hasty journeys, once the security guys had buzzed her through three sets of barred, iron gates. Down, down, down, beneath Manchester's street level, she descended to vaults that hid the city's dirtiest and costliest secrets.

'Can I access my box please?' she asked the wan-faced security guard, who looked as though he was more than ready to get off the night shift.

'Of course, Mrs. O'Brien.' He gave her a weak smile.

Together, they unlocked the box she had recently rented – more of a vault, really, given its size. She waited for the man to leave. Shoved the rubble sacks inside. Called him back. Locked up. Done.

Finally allowing herself to breathe normally, Sheila emerged from the subterranean complex onto the deserted street. She leaned forward, gripping her knees and wondering if she was going to vomit.

'I did it,' she whispered to the chewing-gum-splattered paving slabs. 'Thank Christ.'

Sheila O'Brien kept smiling as she unlocked her car. Right until she looked up and noticed a council-owned CCTV camera, trained on the entrance to the safety deposit facility. Manchester had eyes, and she'd been spotted. How come she'd never noticed that before? She was certain it was new. And how come Ellis James had known to follow her like a greyhound with coney in its nostrils on the one day she was driving with a boot full of dirty money? Was he being fed information? Or had it just been a lucky hunch?

She was so blinded by paranoia at the CCTV and shaking, thanks to the toxic fallout of a deadly chase through the city's streets, that she almost didn't notice that one of the large new office blocks, diagonally opposite to where she had parked, sported a logo she recognised. She blinked hard at the red double 'B' flanked by wings that almost resembled the Bentley logo, positioned prominently outside the main entrance to the office block. Sheila was familiar with the signage because she had googled it ahead of a meeting by the Lowry theatre that had changed everything.

'Nigel bleeding Bancroft?'

Chapter 16

Gloria

'Is this a good idea?' Lev asked, helping Jay to spoon mashed up baked beans and potato into his mouth. 'Didn't you tell me you weren't sure about him?'

Her son didn't even bother to look at her when he was speaking to her, so obsessed was he with the boy. And the boy was making a mess of the rental's living room carpet, even though he was in a high chair with its own integral table.

'Good Lord, Leviticus,' Gloria said, stooping to pick up a glob of mush with her bare hand. She shuddered and grimaced before hurling it into the bin. Proceeded to wash her hands in very hot soapy water at the sink. 'Don't let Jay throw his food around. I don't want Sheila coming to me, moaning that she didn't get her full deposit back when we eventually leave this place.'

'You're having a laugh, aren't you? Unless they cart us off to prison, we're never getting out of this boring shithole. Not at this rate,' Lev said, pretending the blue plastic spoon was an aeroplane, hurtling towards Jay's messy mouth with a carb-laden payload. 'And if you keep getting up in the grille of that Ellis James, like you did this morning, that's gonna happen sooner than you reckon.'

'He called me a black cow,' Gloria said, poking at her carefully set hair. 'Can you believe it? A black cow! What a nasty, racist ne'er-do-well of a man. There's clearly not a single Christian bone in his shabby, flabby body.' Her minor triumph registered in her chest like a small, inflating balloon of deliciously warm air. A soupçon of pride that the Lord would surely allow her. She glanced over at little Jay, trying to grab the spoon; picking a baked bean off the high chair's plastic table. She was pleased to see that his fine motor skills were starting to improve after the brain tumour had been removed. She offered a silent prayer towards the grey sky, thanking Jesus for his many small mercies. Escaping the clutches of Ellis James had been the least of them.

'Did he *really* call you a black cow?' Lev asked.

Gloria grinned. Allowed the laughter that tickled the back of her throat to push its way up and out, like Noah releasing a white dove following the biblical storm. 'Well, *his* version of events would be that I'd swung in front of him on purpose so Sheila could get away. Then, he'd say he tried to arrest me for dangerous driving and obstructing the law.' She replayed the confrontation in her mind's eye, recalling how fervently she had prayed to the good Lord for assistance and how she had willed herself to keep standing, though her legs had been threatening to buckle with fear. '*My* version of events involves my car stalling, *him* racially abusing me for something I've got absolutely no control over, and then he tries to manhandle me. I have no memory of being read my rights, *obviously*, so I'm finding the word "assault" tripping off my tongue. And I think I might have also mentioned harassment. I don't think he was very keen for me to go to the station and register a complaint. So, now, we'll never know if he really called me a black cow or not, will we?'

Lev shook his head and sucked the air sharply through his teeth.

'Sheila needed my help and I obliged, Leviticus. That's called professional loyalty. And I'm a middle-aged black woman, living in the twenty-first century. I don't need to put up with police haranguing me at seven in the morning just because my car's steering occasionally acts up. It sets a bad precedent for your generation. Better to die on my feet than to live on my knees. There's a pearl of wisdom for you!'

Fixing her with a slack-mouthed look of disbelief, Lev paused midway between spoonfuls – the drippy, orange-tinged mash threatening to drop onto the carpet in a fat, gloopy teardrop. 'You never made that up! That's some Bible quote.'

'Actually, young man, if you had any understanding of your heritage, you'd realise it's inspired by a lyric from a very important James Brown song.'

'Bollocks. I'm gonna google it when you've gone. You're full of it! And you're playing with fire. You shouldn't be putting yourself under the nose of a copper that's hot on your trail, just to save Sheila's bloody arse.'

Her son screwed up his face. Was he angry? No. Frustrated, Gloria assessed. Did his words mean that he cared for her?

'Anyway, don't fob us off,' he continued, shovelling the mash into Jay's expectant mouth. 'You told me this property developer feller made you uncomfy. But now you're off on a date with him?'

Wiping her hands a little too roughly on the bleach-white hand towel, Gloria peered out of the kitchen's rear window at the semi-neglected garden. Fixed her gaze on some late-flowering nasturtiums that were the approximate hue of her new admirer's skin. 'Do you have to suck all the joy out of the day, Leviticus? Is it so unbearable for you to get your head round a man wanting to date your mother?'

'I didn't say that.'

'You didn't have to.' She wracked her brains for some Bible quotation that would put the cynical young upstart in his place. Smiled when she happened upon the perfect passage. *'If I speak in the tongues of men and of angels, but have not love, I am a noisy gong or a clanging cymbal.'*

'Gong? Frigging gongs? That's not a Bible quote!' Lev started to wheeze with laughter, finally turning round to face her with true amusement in his insolent face. 'You're making all this shit up as you go along, man!'

'It happens to be 1 Corinthians 13:1, Leviticus. I did not make it up!'

'Yeah, bollocks.'

He was insufferable this morning! She needed a put-down, but what? Cupping her hand to her ear, she smiled as she took out her wine-coloured lipstick from her handbag. 'Oh, sorry, Leviticus, but I can't understand you for the racket of clanging cymbals coming out of your disrespectful mouth. I reckon you could do with taking a leaf out of my book, sunbeam, because that Tiffany has got you right where she wants you. You're nothing more than a turkey voting for Christmas. *You* are certainly not one to lecture *me* about love and romance.'

Boom. Wasn't that what the young people said? What else did they say when they'd delivered the perfect retort? She could see the pain in her son's anguished face. Not so cocky now.

'I think you'll find you've just been severed, young man.'

'It's served, Mam. You *got* served.'

'Precisely!'

*   *   *

130

Driving into Bramshott village for her lunch appointment with the terribly chivalrous, if slightly creepy Bob, Gloria acknowledged that she was exposing her vulnerable core to this man, like Abraham baring his son Isaac's breast so that he might drive a sacrificial knife through his tender heart.

Reversing into a parking space in front of the Italian restaurant where they had arranged to meet was a struggle that took several manoeuvres. She hit the dashboard in frustration, mindful of the Audi-driver who was now trying to pull out behind her, flashing her headlamps in irritation.

'Flip off, sinner!' Gloria shouted through the rear-view mirror, jabbing her index finger into the air in insult.

Her throat felt tight. Her finger shook. Gloria took a deep breath. Edged forwards, finally satisfied that her parking was acceptable. *It's just a daytime date. A spot of pasta. Nothing more. Calm down, for heaven's sake.*

The maître d' opened the heavy door for her with a sycophantic smile. 'Signora.' Definitely a fake Italian accent. Gloria examined the man's shoes. At least they were clean.

'I'm meeting a gentleman here,' she said, glancing around the eatery. 'Perhaps he's reserved a table. Bob's his name.'

The maître d' checked a ledger of bookings. Gloria half-expected him to shake his head apologetically and show her the door. But then she remembered that she was a woman of substance and she was wearing her best new day dress from Hobbs. Seventy quid in the sale at Kendals, but it had been worth it.

'Follow me, bella! Per favore! Your friend, he is not yet here. Someone will bring you a drink, si?'

Buffoon, Gloria thought. 'Lovely.'

The interior of the restaurant was all leather booths and marble tables. It was surprisingly full considering how early in the day it was, but then the wealthy residents of Bramshott probably thought nothing of squandering ten pounds or more on a bottle of wine and probably the same again on some risotto. Gloria took a seat, perched her reading glasses on the end of her nose and looked at the wine list that was handed to her.

'*Thirty quid* for the house white?!' she said, looking askance at the wine waiter.

'Si, signora,' the boy said, looking bored.

'I'll have tap water for now.'

If Mr Big Shot Property Developer wanted to meet her in a place like this, he could pay for the privilege. Sheila had always been the one to pick up restaurant tabs and Gloria was not about to start indulging in uncharacteristic profligacy as well as taking a ludicrous emotional risk at one in the afternoon on a damp, grey Wednesday.

When he arrived, Bob appeared marginally less dayglo than he had at the speed-dating. Or perhaps it was a flattering light. He wore a pale grey suit that complemented his white spiked hair, though his shoes, with their pointed toes, were more than a tad on the ostentatious side. Gloria was glad his feet would be concealed beneath the table.

'Gloria,' he said, holding his arms out as he approached the table. He took her hands into his and kissed her knuckles with a satisfactorily dry mouth. Produced from his inside pocket a somewhat flattened corsage of an amber rose and a cluster of St John's Wort berries. 'May I?' He pinned it carefully to her dress.

'Oh, what a lovely, lovely gesture,' Gloria said, willing herself not to complain that he would leave pin marks in the fabric of her new prized purchase that she was hoping to wear to church on Sunday. 'Aren't you quite the gentleman?' The pastor had never bought her a corsage. Leviticus' beast of a father had certainly never bought her so much as petrol station flowers on Mother's Day. His sole floral offering had been a free undersized red rose from a curry house on Valentine's Day in the mid-nineties.

As she perused the menu and made polite conversation with this stranger called Bob, Gloria started to feel that he was looking at her in a peculiar way. There was calculation behind his eyes, but, of course, it was difficult to really read a man whose skin was so perplexingly tight; she could hardly read his facial movements as pleasure, displeasure or complete indifference. He was a little visibly sweaty on his smooth forehead, however. And he was blinking rather a lot. Perhaps he was nervous too.

'Are you driving?' he asked.

'I am, as it happens.' She found herself giggling but couldn't explain why. 'Although you'd think I'd already been at the sherry, the amount of goes it took me to get parked.' *Stop babbling, woman!*

'Not drinking, then. Good. Are you all right to stick with the water?'

Gloria stifled a frown. 'Actually, I'd like a Diet Coke, if you don't mind.'

'Two fifty,' Bob muttered under his breath. 'Bloody Nora.' He glanced at the food menu, ignoring her fizzy drink demands. 'You don't want a starter, do you? No. Good. Neither do I!'

She hadn't even had the opportunity to answer. And yes, actually, she had been looking forward to some nice garlic bread or bruschetta. *Come on, Gloria. Cut him some slack. There's a certain virtue in thriftiness. And gluttony's a mortal sin.* 'Fine.'

The chit-chat came easy enough, as they discussed the

pandemonium they had fled at M1 House. Gloria gave her usual speech about the 'youth of today', which seemed to go down well enough. Then, the food arrived.

'Where do you live then?' he asked, halfway through her pappardelle.

It seemed a terribly direct question and he kept looking at her neck. Strange and disconcerting. Gloria giggled. 'Oh, you are forward! I'm not telling you where I live!'

'Go on. I bet you live in one of those big houses, a classy chassis like you.' When he grinned, she realised his whiter-than-white teeth were capped. There was the ghost of a rotten stump beneath each one, just visible when he turned a certain way.

'I live near but not in Bramshott. And that's all I'm telling you, for now. A lady has to retain a little mystery, Robert.' Change the subject. 'What about your latest building project? Tell me about that. Or tell me about your kids. Come on! Something about you.'

Forking a piece of steak into his mouth, he chewed a little too noisily. Sipped from his Peroni, which he'd had no compunction in ordering for himself. 'It's a lickle estate in Sale,' he said. 'Seventeen houses.' More masticating. Clack, clack, clack. 'Planning department were a nightmare. Like they had a wasp up their arse from the minute I submitted for permission. *You can't do this. You can't do that.*' He wasn't meeting her gaze. He kept staring at her neck and her breasts. He forked the last piece of steak into his mouth. 'Are you and your partner cleaning the trains at Piccadilly? Or did you say the trams? Does Sheila O'Brien own that dating agency, *True Love Dates*, then? Didn't you say you had a son? Does he live with you?'

So many questions. Too many questions all at once. Gloria put it down to dating nerves. She sidestepped all of his probing save for the subject of the cleaning agency. 'Oh, me and Sheila don't do any cleaning. We've got women for that. Very good workers.' She carefully wrapped the pappardelle around her fork and shovelled the pile onto a spoon. 'We work out of the back of a builders' merchants at the moment.' She wrinkled her nose. 'One day, we'll get a fancy business address that lives up to our reputation.' Spooned the pasta into her mouth, savouring the fantasy of being able to sit behind a gleaming rosewood desk in an office that wasn't freezing cold and at the back of a smelly Portakabin. 'Amen to that!' she said aloud.

'To what?'

'Nothing.' She felt herself blush.

Perhaps Bob sensed her embarrassment and mistook it for amorousness. She wasn't sure. But suddenly, he placed a clammy palm over her hand. 'You're a very attractive woman, you know. Do you fancy . . . going to a hotel room, Gloria?'

Gloria set down her cutlery, feeling her cheeks really buzz with heat. The pastor was the only man she had imagined naked in years. 'This is un-unexpected.'

'How do you fancy it? Eh? Me and you in a nice airport hotel. Crisp sheets. A bit of slap and tickle.'

She was about to quote Colossians at him, but Gloria was suddenly aware that her body was overriding her mind. Despite the strange shine of his skin. Despite the ostentatious pointed toes of his shoes and the absence of wine and a starter – and clearly also a dessert – from the lunch menu, she felt stirrings in her best M&S panties. Animal desires. She fanned herself with a leaflet that told her to book her office Christmas party early to save disappointment.

'Oh, Bob. You are a one! I don't think—'

'Go on! I want to make sweet love to you, Gloria.'

Gloria's mind tried desperately to fight the lust that was taking over her body. Her lust won.

'All right then.'

Mulling over this indecent proposal, Gloria was so breathless from excitement as Bob settled the modest bill that she barely registered that his steak knife seemed to be missing both from his plate and his place setting. She also almost entirely failed to notice that he omitted to leave a tip for the full ten per cent. It was too late. By then, she was already committed to this terrible tryst. May God have mercy on her soul.

In her Mazda, she followed Bob's four-wheel drive to a three-star airport hotel that was sadly closer to Northenden than the more sophisticated, five-star offerings that were scattered around the airport complex itself. Still, it didn't matter.

Wordlessly, they rose in the lift to the fifth floor. Scurried like furtive teenagers to their room, where Bob unlocked the door with the slightly dodgy key card.

Once inside, Gloria started to panic that her body might not work after so many years of disuse.

'Oh, I want you, Gloria Bell,' Bob said.

He bent down, manhandling her full bosom and kissing her chest. She found herself pushed up against the closed door. Felt his member, stiff against her stomach. He was undoing his fly with one hand and already had the clammy fingers of the other inside her knickers.

You're a hussy, Gloria. A wanton woman, she thought. But all she could manage to say was, 'Ooh, Robert.'

Freeing her breasts, he led her to the bed.

'You've got magic tits.'

He tore off his shirt and trousers as though he were up

against the clock. She failed to notice the steak knife sliding out of his trouser pocket.

'I'm going to fuck seven shades of shit out of you, love. And not in a racist way.'

His erection was red and angry. Full of lustful intent. Finding herself overcome by anticipation, Gloria kicked her dress and panties to the floor, opened her legs and let him enter her.

'Go easy. It's been a while,' she said, as he started to ride her.

'I will.' His eyes were closed. His taut face almost smiling. 'And when I've finished, I've got a special surprise for you.'

Chapter 17

Conky

Whistling the Motown classic 'My Girl' to himself as he prepared his first coffee of the day, Conky McFadden considered how lucky he was on that Tuesday morning. The marble tiles beneath his feet were warmed by under-floor heating, mitigating the Reynaud's in his toes and almost compensating for the pains in his calves thanks to his thyroid being out of whack, yet again. He had traded in the cold, empty bed of a confirmed bachelor for the hottest king-size of all: Paddy O'Brien's, occupied by Paddy O'Brien's widow. Sheila. Ah, magnificent Sheila. Conky's lover; his employer; his Queen.

In the kitchen of Sheila's Bramshott mansion, Conky sung about having sunshine on that cloudy day, substituting his Northern Irish accent for a dodgy stab at American. He frothed the hot milk. Looked down at the grey veined tiles, imagining his toasty feet were attributable to Paddy, stoking the flames of hell in a fit of unbridled jealousy. 'Sorry, Pad. Life is for the living, pal.'

His moment of inner peace, savouring the fine place that the twists and turns of life had brought him to, was fractured by the front door slamming.

'Conky? Conky!' Sheila's voice. Shrill, with a worrying tinge of desperation.

'In here, love,' he called back.

When Sheila marched into the kitchen, ashen-faced, and continued onto the utility room without stopping to embrace him, he realised something was amiss.

'I thought you'd gone to yoga or out for a jog,' he said, following her to the adjacent room. It smelled of fresh washing in there, but he sensed she was more interested in the filing cabinet that was concealed in the corner behind the industrial-sized tumble dryer than in him or the laundry.

Clanging drawers open and shut, Sheila rummaged through hanging files with trembling fingers.

Conky embraced her from behind. 'Jesus! You're shaking. What the hell's going on?'

Sheila shrugged him off. 'Bancroft's buying up Manchester. He's putting the moves on me, Conk.'

'What do you mean?'

'Offices. He owns and redevelops property legitimately, right?' She related the tale of having spotted the Bancroft logo plastered all over the gleaming new block in central Manchester. 'So, he's getting his feet under the table. You think if he's buying up commercial real estate that he's not giving some city-council official somewhere a back-hander? I bet he's got local coppers on the payroll too. If me and the Boddlingtons are doing it, do you think Bancroft won't? This bastard means business. This is more than just trying to nick our drug-dealing turf.' Rummaging, rummaging through the files, like stones fired from a slingshot, she pelted her theories at Conky without so much as casting a glance at him. 'I've screwed up, Conks. Really screwed up. Bloody Paddy. This is all Paddy's fault. What a bleeding legacy.'

Conky reached out to touch a shining lock of her blonde hair but thought better of it as Sheila pulled a document from one of the hanging files. An official-looking thing with tiny print on the back. A contract, maybe.

'Bingo. This is what I'm after.' Finally, she made eye contact with him, glancing only fleetingly at his undisguised bald pate. 'Pour us some of that coffee, will you, love? I've got a mouth like a mink coat.' She finally treated him to a peck on his cheek.

Touching the place where her kiss had lingered, Conky prepared her a coffee in silence, watching her take a seat at the island in the centre of the kitchen. She started to pore over the small print on the back of the official-looking document.

'What's got you so flustered?' he asked, setting the cup on a coaster in front of her.

Her eyes darted to and fro, following the lines of the text. 'I couldn't believe Gloria's take. We counted it at the crack of dawn. This worktop was covered. Covered, Conks! Piles of cash.'

'The protection back-pay?' He sipped his own espresso. Chuckled. 'I never thought Gloria would have it in her.'

'There was so much money, I had to get it out the house. Policeman-frigging-Plod was on my back all the way into town. He's like a dog with a bone, that one. I don't like it, Conks. Why's he still hanging around like a wet fart unless someone's got it in for me and telling the little shit my business? Paddy's been dead for months! As far as Ellis James knows, I'm just the grieving widow.' She hadn't taken her eyes off the small print on the document. 'Anyway, I shake him off thanks to Gloria coming out of nowhere and doing a Stig in her Mazda, but then I spot this CCTV camera . . . Oh, shit! What have I done?' Her voice suddenly became thin and high, like nails scratching down a blackboard. The bulging vein in her forehead told Conky she was still in a state of fight or flight. The delicate features of her face – already harried-looking – had frozen suddenly, as if the wind had blown, setting Sheila's expression in horror-mode indefinitely. Finally locking eyes with Conky, she opened her mouth to speak. No words came. Her colour had drained away.

'What? What is it?' he asked, taking the document from her. Speed-reading it rapidly. 'This is your contract with the safety deposit people.' He shook his head, dumbfounded. 'I don't get it.' Enveloping her cold, slender fingers in his own, he tried to pass on some comfort through touch alone. 'For Christ's sakes, She, tell me what's going on.'

Sheila started to cry in earnest, spitting out words in angry, desperate gobs, punctuated by heaving, gasping hiccoughs. 'I thought the money would be safe in the vaults. They said it was a discreet, confidential service. I reckoned it was better than having a safe in the house that the police could force me to open. Right? But-but . . .' Her chin dimpled. Teardrops spilled onto the granite of the island worktop like salty diamonds. 'I'm caught on camera with big rubble sacks. And now *this*!' She snatched the contract up and waved it in the air. 'The safety deposit company are entitled to give your details to any "enforcement agencies that may demand them". A load of bullshit in this small print about their duty to disclose suspected money launderers.' Sniffing hard, she gulped the air like a drowning fish. 'How could I be so naïve? I've buggered it up for myself, Conk. I thought I could just stash the money and slowly . . . I dunno . . . get rid of it on the quiet. But that bastard, James, can do me at any time for it. He's watching. He's been watching. The coppers are closing in. Bancroft's closing in. There's gonna be payback for what we did to Brummie Kev. I'm telling you. It's all gonna kick off.'

Conky patted her hand, wanting more than anything to embrace Sheila like a vulnerable child and to soothe her worries, as a doting parent would. But he saw the rigidity in her shoulders and thought better of it. Sheila was best left to come out of these downward spirals of her own accord. Years of being bullied by Paddy had made her a tricky customer in love, perched on her own little island made of eggshells.

'Aw, come on now, She. You're leaping several steps too far ahead there. What the hell do these safety deposit box people know about what you've got in your vault? Nothing. You're a rich woman and much of it is legit. Paddy wasn't entirely stupid, else you wouldn't be living in a palace like this.' With his shovel of a hand, he described in the perfumed air an arc that took in the trappings of her wealth – from the precision-built German kitchen units, to the contemporary crystal chandeliers that lit the place. 'Why shouldn't you stash things under lock and key, like everyone else? Are you less entitled to use those facilities than restaurant owners from the Curry Golden Mile or solicitors from fecking Spinningfields? That's second-place behaviour, Sheila O'Brien. And you're a queen. There's no need for it, my love. And Bancroft? Well, he's entitled to do what he likes in his legitimate business. There's not a thing we can do to stop him, there. But I've personally kicked his men out of M1 House and sent him a message he'll be chewing over very seriously indeed. Sure, I don't think there'll be retribution for you to worry about, darling.

'I've been the O'Brien's Loss Adjuster for decades now, She. I know this business back to front and I've got enough experience under my big old belt to know what sort of a

142

reaction sending a head in a fried chicken bucket will elicit in a cheeky fucking aggressor. Bancroft was trying it on with you. That's all. He'll back down, so he will.'

Her shoulders moved fractionally towards their normal position. 'You're right, Conks.' She smiled weakly, the lines beside her mouth in that pretty but lean face seeming deeper than usual. Hopping off her bar stool, she buried her head in his chest, allowing him to enfold her slender frame in a protective embrace. 'I'm so on edge. But is it any wonder with all that's going on? And that Ellis James. It's like he hasn't got a frigging home to go to. He's determined to put me away, Conk.'

Conky pressed his nose into her hair, drinking in the scent of her expensive shampoo; acknowledging how strange it was to be in love with a woman who was like a doll made from sugar, spice and Semtex. She had always seemed too fragile and good for his stinking, filthy world of crime, violence and dark secrets.

'He's got nothing, She. If he had, he would have arrested both of us by now.'

She looked up at him, searching his thyroid eyes for fuck-knew-what. 'We can't go on like this, Conks.'

Those ominous words rang in his ears. *We can't go on like this.* It was his turn to be paranoid. He held his breath. Was she about to end it? He had been anticipating that moment coming as soon as they had shared their first kiss. Shite.

'In what way?'

'Running stuff the way Paddy ran it. All this cash that can't be put through the books. The old-school rackets. Me and Gloria's cleaning business – it's easy to make that legit and get away with it. It's profitable, it's almost moral, it's within my comfort zone. Know what I mean? The dating thing, too. I can get my head round it. But the bully-boy bullshit . . .' She disengaged from the warmth of his body, perching on her bar stool once more.

Conky exhaled heavily, his frown transforming to a delighted smile. She hadn't been talking about their relationship, after all. He was merely fast-forwarding to the apocalypse, as had always been his go-to behaviour in the few previous romances he had buggered up. *Have some bloody confidence, man. You and Sheila are good.*

'I just don't know what to do,' she said. 'I don't want to give it away to the likes of Bancroft, but I can't keep getting my hands dirty with it, either. Amy and Dahlia aren't going to thank me if I get slung in prison and they lose all their inheritance. Who'll pay Amy's university fees then? And what about the deposit for Dahlia's flat in London?'

Conky tutted and shook his head. 'Really, if I'm honest, darling, this is no business for a woman. I'd advise you to sell to the Boddlingtons,' he suggested. 'Paddy had already agreed terms. I reckon a phone call would get that back on track.'

When Sheila gave him a stinging slap across the face, a bewildered Conky reassessed that his pessimistic instincts had been correct. He didn't know how Sheila ticked at all. It was surely only a matter of time before the love of his life broke his heart.

Chapter 18

Paddy

Shadow Hunter: How did you get on with the bent accountant and the hair suppliers?

Paddy waited until the two ticks at the end of his sentence lit up in blue, reassuring him that his WhatsApp communiqué had been safely delivered. Noted when Ellis James had last checked his account. An hour earlier, judging by the time that popped up on the header. The bastard had been online and yet still hadn't given him an update as to whether he'd done anything about Paddy's latest chunk of information, sent days ago under his moniker of Shadow Hunter.

'Piss-taker,' Paddy said under his breath. He flung his phone angrily onto Brenda's old-fashioned Draylon sofa, debating what his next move should be. 'Who the hell does he think he is, little fucking Hitler with his badge and handcuffs?' Sighing, he acknowledged that the detective had no idea who his new, pseudonymous grass was or how he'd come about the information regarding Maureen Kaplan, accountant to the criminal stars, or the news that the Boddlingtons ran back-street brothels in run-down

Sweeney Hall terraces. As far as Ellis James was concerned, Shadow Hunter was just some fantasist, armchair-vigilante, wannabe-copper, spouting hot air about all the wrong-doings that took place in the city. As far as Greater Manchester Police was concerned, Paddy O'Brien was a dim memory of a crime lord, now pushing up daisies in Southern Cemetery.

'Who's taking the piss?' A skinny, short-arsed frame perched on the arm of the sofa, sucking the air and the light out of the room. Kyle, of course. Always hanging around like the bad smell that he was, earwigging whatever Paddy had to say.

The kid flicked through the channels on the silent TV, taking the mute off when he came across some black birds in hot pants, twerking to that hip-hop shite that Paddy couldn't abide. Cranking the volume of his chosen music channel up to ear-splitting level. There was some ponce on the screen, sitting on the bonnet of a car somewhere like downtown LA, legs akimbo, as though he owned the world. Dressed like a bloody clown in bright yellow tracksuit bottoms, his ripped torso on show – a status symbol made from flesh. A gangsta. It served as a visual reminder to Paddy that he and his ilk were dinosaurs on the brink of extinction. Kyle grinned at the screen, lapping it up.

Pocketing his phone, Paddy stood, clipping the boy on the head with his elbow as he walked past. 'None of your business, pal. Button your lip. If your Mam hears you using language like that . . .'

As he was leaving the cramped front room for the kitchen, where Brenda was applying her make-up, he heard Kyle mutter, 'Fuck off' under his breath.

Paddy turned back and grabbed the boy by the chin. Examined his malnourished, underdeveloped face – all crooked teeth and skin stretched too tight over cheekbones that certainly weren't from Brenda. The kid still looked about nine. Not unlike his brother, Frank, as a boy. 'What did you just say to me?'

'Nowt.'

Paddy gripped harder on the boy's jaw. Knew he must be hurting him. 'I hear you eff and jeff in front of me again, I'll lamp you one. Right?'

Kyle shook himself loose from Paddy's grip. Slunk off the arm of the sofa and backed away. A full six inches shorter than Paddy, who wasn't a tall man to begin with. 'You're not my dad. I don't have to do what you say.' The kid balled his bony fists. All arms and legs, hanging like Woodbines out of his baggy T and ill-fitting, hand-me-down FUBU jeans.

Poised to thump the overinflated ego out of the plucky little shit, Paddy paused, realising that Brenda might tolerate that kind of tough love herself but wouldn't look so kindly on him using her son as a punchbag. He poked the boy hard in the ribs instead. 'Watch your fucking mouth, son. Just you remember who's thirteen and who's sixty.'

But Kyle had grabbed his jacket in an urgent blur. 'Shove it up your arse, you old bastard. I've seen the way you treat my Mam. I'm watching you!'

Narrowed, keen-sighted eyes and a mouth twisted with hatred were all that lingered in Paddy's mind once the front door had slammed behind the boy.

'Prick.' He ran to the door and thumped one of the panels until the skin broke on his knuckles. Blood smeared on the cheap and nasty gloss job. Streaky red on streaky white.

'What's all that banging, love?' Brenda shouted from the kitchen. Flump, flump, flump, flump, as she shuffled in her slippers through to the lounge. One eye half made-up. One eye still partially naked. A false eyelash, poorly applied and hanging down onto her cheek. 'You wasn't having a barney with our Kyle again, was you?'

Paddy breathed heavily through his nostrils, trying to expel the hatred for another man's son from his chest. He could feel pressure building up beneath his ribs. Katrina had warned him to look after his stress levels, but mounting frustration at being trapped inside somebody else's identity had taken a hold of him of late.

'He's a mouthy shit, that lad of yours,' he said, trying to remember if he'd taken his heart tablets that morning. The hangovers were fogging his memory. 'You need to teach him some respect. What kind of a mother are you, to let a snot-nosed kid like that backchat your feller?' He raised the palm of his hand to slap Brenda hard but stopped short of her cheek as he saw the sudden disappointment in her face.

She ducked. Held her hands up defensively. 'I'm sorry. I'm sorry, Ken! I'll have a word with him.' She shouted up to the ceiling. 'Kyle! Get down here!' No answer. 'Is he in his room?'

'Forget it,' Paddy said, grabbing his anorak from the sofa. He knew of a better way to punish her than slapping her around. Today of all days. 'The little arsehole legged it. He had the right idea. I'm out of here, and all. I need some frigging space, me.' Peering around the room with a sneer on his face. 'This dump and yous two are getting me down.'

Brenda had planned on dragging him along to lunchtime karaoke at the local labour club, where she would parade him, as per, to her old has-been mates. He was Kenneth Wainwright, the shining example of manhood that she – a saggy, clapped-out shelf stacker who happened to have the greatest tits Paddy had ever seen – had bagged, despite her fat arse. Ordinarily she liked to sit in a corner, her arm linked in his, sipping half a mild and blathering on about all the songs she'd love to sing but didn't dare. Not today, though. It was her birthday. If he ducked out now, the rejection would sting more than any slap.

Reaching out to him with blue-painted nails, there was desperation in her voice. 'Come on, Ken. I'll make you a bacon buttie before we go. With brown sauce – how you like it. Cheer you up. Save you buying me lunch. I'll stick on a pan of chips, if you like.'

But he was already closing the door behind him. He had switched Brenda's mewling voice off. His thoughts turned to calling Hank to see what the latest developments were.

Moseying down the street, marking the grubby bounds of this one-star-rated exile as his territory, he dialled the number. He didn't have to wait to be answered. He was the one paying, after all, although greasing the wanker's palm was leaving Paddy cash-strapped in all other areas of his life.

'It's me,' he said.

'Hiya, mate.' Hank's chirpy voice at the other end. 'I was just thinking of you.'

'I bet you were. I shouldn't have to chase you for an update. What have you got?'

Kicking at the discarded chip-shop plates and empty lager cans that nestled by the kerbside, Paddy had reached the end of Brenda's street. Where to go next? The last place he wanted to be was that shitty hovel he called a home. The Irwell flowed noisily by, some twenty or thirty feet below on the other side of the Victorian stone retaining wall, providing a foil for his clandestine call.

He walked to the river's edge, listening to his sole employee fill him in with the latest. At this time of year, the giant hogweeds on the riverbanks were just starting to turn brown and wither, exposing the fly-tipped refuse that sat at the base of these almost Jurassic plants. An upturned Asda trolley in the middle of the low-tidal flow.

'Chopped his head off, I heard,' Hank said.

Paddy looked up at the low-lying blanket of cement-grey clouds. 'Get away! You're having a laugh.'

'Nope. Word on the grapevine says Nigel Bancroft's got his knickers in a right twist over it. The young lad that Conky topped was playing a dangerous game though. Pillock. Not like me. He was asking to get copped. I'm playing it cool, like.'

Mulling over this information, Paddy was secretly impressed by Sheila's audacity. She had taken on the Midlands and won . . . for now. Who'd have thought it? All those years, he'd assumed his wife was a pushover. Turned out, she had balls of steel – enough to send him to the grave and see a rival crime boss off. Obviously, she owed it all to decades spent learning from the master.

If Paddy was going to take Sheila down, he realised he'd have to operate with stealth.

'What about Bell?' he asked, watching a flock of Canadian geese take flight from the slag heaps of long-forgotten trash that had turned the river's low-tide flow into rapids. 'Any news on where the little shitehawk's holed up?'

Excitement in his man's voice. 'Actually, I've had a brain-wave as far as the Bells are concerned.'

'Go on. Impress me.'

'I'm drawing a blank with Lev, so I might try getting to him through Gloria Bell instead.'

'What do you mean?'

'She's a woman who likes routine, is Gloria. She goes to certain places at certain times on certain days of the week without fail. I seen this thing on telly about the FBI watching for patterns in people's behaviour. Persons of interest and that. Apparently, it always gives them away.'

'What the fuck are you on about?'

'You wanna meet in person? I'm just round the corner from you, laying a driveway. I'm due on my dinner. I'll pick you up. We can go to a caff.'

Paddy frowned. He was in the mood for a pub. Not a meet with his paid help in a café. 'Where? I've got to be really careful if I'm out in public. I can't be seen in O'Brien or Boddlington territory.'

'Bury?'

'Boddlingtons have got their fingers in Bury's pies.'

'Who the hell is going to recognise you in a Tories' paradise full of Pakis and pensioners?'

The Canadian geese soared up into the grey skies, freeing themselves of the shitty shackles of that downtrodden, long-forgotten minor mill-town. Paddy gazed wistfully at them. They were honking in delight at their great escape. Would a change of scenery for him be such a bad thing? Just for an hour? 'You've got a point.'

Standing by the river's edge, awaiting his lift, Paddy looked down into the muddy waters, wondering if he should just throw himself in. Eventually, he would be washed out to the Irish Sea if he was lucky. He would be free like those geese, instead of incarcerated in this inescapable maze – one mile in radius – of red-brick terraces, blackened by age and neglect as if even the houses had given up on beauty. Why did his idiot of a do-gooding sister have to exchange his life of a multi-millionaire for the half-life of a down-and-out? No money. No Sheila. No future.

'You meant to do this to me, didn't you, Kat, you hatchet-faced bitch?' Paddy heaved a foamy gob of phlegm onto the silty bank, watching the Irwell lick upwards and whip it downstream. 'Sister bleeding Benedicta screwed her brother over with church bells on.'

Rain started to pit the ground suddenly and with gusto. Paddy looked around but there was no place to shelter.

Contemplating seeking sanctuary from the weather in the pub, he had only walked twenty metres or so when the diesel rumble of a van's engine heralded the arrival of his man.

The white Transit rounded the corner. There he was, glowing in the cab. Hank the Wank. Club Tropicana in white overalls. Beeping.

'All right, Pad?' Hank shouted through the open passenger window. He opened the door. 'Get in, mate!'

Paddy was aware of red mist gathering in the periphery of his vision. Threatening to descend all the faster in the rain. The Rage was all that was keeping him warm. 'Keep your voice down, dickhead.'

Clambering in, Paddy listened to his oldest school friend wax lyrical about the highs and lows of the building trade, the weather, the recent closure of the Mancunian Way and how Tony Foley from school had carked it from cancer only last week.

'How do you like?' Hank said. 'Poor bastard was given weeks. Weeks, Pad! They opened him up, took one look and sent him home. He was riddled with it.'

Thinking of the scar tissue that was a constant, aching reminder of his own mortality, thanks to Leviticus Bell, Paddy grabbed Hank's hand as he changed gear.

'Ow! What you doing? Get off!'

Between gritted teeth, he let a little of The Rage speak. 'I don't pay you to gossip like a frigging bird. I pay you to be my eyes and my ears. Right? So stop giving me earache about Tony sodding Foley. He was always a loser. I didn't give a shit about him at school, and I don't give a shit about him now he's dead.' He released his pincer-grip on Hank's hand. Caught sight of the undulating Pennines in the distance as they gunned from Radcliffe New Road onto Bury New Road. The hills were studded with giant wind turbines. A rare sight for a man who had spent most of his adult life on the flatter south side of town. 'What I give a shit about is information on my business interests and my slag of a widow. Tell me what that bug-eyed bastard Conky McFadden has been doing with Sheila.'

They walked through the rain-soaked bustle of Bury market, past the rainbow-coloured palettes of the fruit and veg stalls, the tarp-covered offerings of M&S seconds; distracted by bold flashes of red inside portable chiller cabinets where florid slabs of locally reared meat had been laid out with artistry, clashing with cheese wheels and yoghurt that was displayed on viper-green synthetic grass; almost bumping into fat garlands of black pudding that hung from the supporting beams of stalls that drip-dripped with residual rainwater. It was dizzying and overwhelming for Paddy, whose new life was perpetually grey and limited.

Hank spoke of Conky, staying over at Sheila's, night after night.

'I seen them kissing in that Rolls of hers,' he said. 'Like a couple of teenagers.'

The rain stung Paddy's reddened skin. He punched a black pudding hard, sending it flying into the queue of meat-shoppers, waiting to place their orders for a Sunday joint.

'All right,' he said. 'Enough. I get the picture. What about this Bancroft business? If she's not farmed out the protection and drugs, who's doing collections? Conky and Degsy?'

Hastening into the mid-century arched halls of the indoor market, they found a café and sat at a battered Formica table for two, surrounded by unwitting, damp shoppers who guzzled strong tea, beans on toast and ham butties. Paddy's careful eyes were everywhere, sizing up the clientele to check for Boddlington crew. His attentions flicked dismissively over the two Asian pensioners at the next table who were deep in conversation, rattling on in some foreign language. One of them put him in mind of that ponce, Tariq Khan, if he had a white beard and wore one of those astrakhan hats and a pair of brown pyjamas under his coat. But they all looked the same to Paddy. This old feller was all 'blah, blah, blah' at his mate, whose chest rattled with an ungodly cough.

Nobody of any interest to him. Good.

'Not Conky,' Hank said, slurping his tea. Rubbing his drum-tight skin with a rugged hand that was at odds with the rest of him. Clean fingernails, though. 'She's got Gloria Bell doing her dirty work.'

'You're having me on!' Paddy threw his head back and guffawed with laughter. 'What's she threatening them with? Hellfire and damnation?'

Hank shrugged. Smiled. Looked smug. 'I'll get the full story soon enough. No danger. Wanna know why?'

Leaning in to hear Hank's daft revelation – no doubt inspired by some FBI conspiracy bullshit he'd read about on the web – something was playing out on the periphery of Paddy's vision. Or was it? Did he simply need a whisky and chaser, rather than the strong tea? He blinked repeatedly, processing the information. Could have sworn that the old Asian at the next table had just taken out his phone and snapped a hasty photo of him.

'Woah! Woah! Hang on!' he said, holding a hand up in front of Hank's flushed face. Turned to study the elderly men.

But there was no sign of any phone or even an indication that either of the two old men had given him so much as a second glance. They were still deep in conversation – animated chatter; waving their hands. Eyes on each other and their coffees.

Paddy took a slurp of his tea and frowned. Shook his head like a wet dog. Back to matters in hand. Abruptly, he grabbed Hank by the straps of his overalls.

'Listen, Sherlock. Keep tabs on Sheila. I wanna know if she farts out of line. I'm gonna bring that disloyal cow down, if it's the last thing I do. And find me the address of Lev Bell or you're dead.'

Chapter 19

Sheila

'We've still got five outstanding payments,' Gloria said, scanning a hand-written list through her purple-framed glasses. Her eyes were twice their normal size through the thick lenses. Mascara on those eyelashes. She counted the names on her fingers. Painted nails, today, for some reason. All very unlike Gloria. 'The Nun's Head, Bayswater Brasserie, Saffy's Wine Bar, Pizzeria Pancetta and Pete's Pint & Pie Emporium.' She removed her glasses, leaving them to hang on the chain around her neck. They sat low on her chest, threatening to disappear down her uncharacteristically low-cut top.

'Are you feeling all right?' Sheila asked, scrutinising her business partner for signs of illness.

Gloria beamed at her. 'Oh, yes. Never better.' Her breath steamed on the air of the builders' merchant's back office. She seemed unperturbed by the cold. Also unusual. Turning her attention back to her notes, she peered through her granny's jam-jar-bottom reading specs. 'I managed to get what was due from all the others, *and* I have their assurances that they'll not be late again.' Looked up at Sheila with those giant googly gobstoppers. Except there was more than optometry in play here. There was unbridled excitement in Gloria's eyes.

'Out with it,' Sheila said. 'I know you're dying to tell me.'

Giggling like an embarrassed schoolgirl, Gloria dug into her neck with one of those painted nails. 'No. I mustn't bore you with my little stories of romantic triumph.' Hands flapping dismissively.

'Please yourself,' Sheila said, looking around the freezing, spartan back office and wondering whether this was still a sensible location in which to conduct her business. Just because Paddy had always used it didn't mean she had to. It was surely a safety risk to be holed up in a shitty area in the back of beyond, sandwiched between the isolation of a nature reserve and the impenetrable concrete whirl of the M60. 'I've been thinking about what you said about leasing an office in town . . .'

But Gloria wasn't listening. She had already leaned in with a conspiratorial air and was chewing on one of the arms of her glasses. 'So, you know I went on that lunchtime date with Bob from speed-dating, right?'

Sighing, Sheila sat back in the threadbare desk chair. Nodding occasionally to make it look like she was listening to her business partner.

'I never, ever thought all that nonsense would be for me, Sheila.' Hand on her chest again like she was some two-bit actress in B Movie of the week, confessing to scandalous behaviour. 'I mean, honestly! Courting when you're young is one thing. But dating at my age is such a forward thing to do. I'd almost class it as the pastime of wanton hussies. You know? Those sorts that do vajazzles.' She whispered 'vajazzles' as though the word might burn her tongue. 'But I'm glad you talked me into it because . . .'

When is the hammer gonna fall? Sheila replayed the

scene of Brummie Kev's beheading over and over in her mind's eye. A scene of horror she wished she could forget. Wished she could dispel the rotten realisation that her lover had coolly despatched the young grass as though he had been simply preparing meat for dinner. And the very suggestion she should sell out to the Boddlingtons! *Conky thinks I'm nothing more than a little woman who should sell out and stick to dolling myself up. And he's a damned psychopath, same as Paddy. What the hell have I got myself into?*

But Gloria was unaware that her captive audience of one was anything but in thrall to this tale of being wooed and seduced. 'And he said to me that I had the nicest timbre to my voice that he'd ever heard. I mean, how about that for charming? Timbre's such a sophisticated word for a man who works in property development. Don't you reckon?'

Sheila nodded, without having absorbed a single word about timbre or property development. *Nigel Bancroft's not the sort of man to take a statement like a head in a tub lying down,* she thought. The more time had elapsed since Lev had delivered her message, the larger the paranoia loomed. *Or did I really scare Bancroft off? Am I safe?*

'You know,' Gloria continued, taking her phone from her handbag. 'He's not my usual type at all. He steals cutlery from restaurants! He nicked a steak knife from where we had lunch. Can you get over it? Said it was his little foible. But he's so flattering and so persistent. And considerate too. He's asked for another rendezvous. Look at the flowers he sent afterwards! I wouldn't give him my home address, of course. But he sent them to the church. Fancy that!'

Sheila was dimly aware of a photo of lilies and roses in shades of pink being thrust in her face. She pushed the phone down, smiling encouragingly, though the fear was really starting to kick in in earnest. Perhaps she'd drunk too much coffee. 'That's really nice, Glo.'

Flick flick through Gloria's gallery, past photographs of happy-looking, smartly dressed black women outside the church that Gloria went to. A couple of snaps of Jay, pushing a brick cart around the living room of the rented semi. Then, an unfamiliar dayglo face, topped with white hair, gelled into ridiculous spikes and bisected by an almost ultraviolet grin.

'This is him. Bob. He's a bit . . . But obviously takes pride in his appearance.' Gloria chewed on her lip. 'I mean, he's got hair and clearly looks after his teeth, which is not bad, is it? At our age! He's not the pastor, but '

When the firebomb hit the office, the entire Portakabin structure shook. Sheila was lifted off her feet and hurled to the opposite side of the office, as though a giant had picked the flimsy building up and flung it to the ground in anger. Shards of glass and splintered wood were flying everywhere. All she could feel was the searing heat and blinding light of a fireball that quickly started to gobble up the sticks of cheap furniture in the room.

Nigel Bancroft. It could only be.

But where was Gloria? Whimpering as she scrambled to her knees, wafting the acrid, roiling funnels of black smoke away, Sheila spied her business partner stretched out on the ground with arms akimbo like some ragdoll thrown away in temper by a spoiled child. Crawling over to her, dodging the terrifying fury of the flames, she grabbed the unconscious Gloria by the upper arm. Dragged her beneath a desk, just as there was a secondary explosion. Sunspot hot. A plume of fire and a deafening blast that made her ears ring.

Get Conks.

On the other side of the flimsy plasterboard wall, Sheila could hear men shouting. The lads who ran the shop. She tried to call out to them but the thick smoke snuffed out the words in her throat. Reaching for her phone, she realised she had missed calls. Conky. She dialled him.

He picked up on the first ring.

'She. I've heard. I'm on my way. Nearly there. Are you safe?'

She screamed in response, part of the ceiling collapsing on the desktop above. 'Help! Help! I can't breathe.'

'Get out of there, for Christ's sake. You'll die of smoke inhalation.'

Fire raging in front of the window. No escape there.

Leaving the phone on Gloria's stomach with the call still running, Sheila crawled to the door. Grabbed the handle but was forced to let go of the scaldingly hot metal as it hissed and started to weld itself to her delicate skin. Kicked at it to attract attention.

'Help! Help us!'

No answer. She guessed that the sales lads were outside, scratching their arses and waiting for the fire brigade.

Sirens in the distance, heralding half-hope. Providing they were quick enough . . .

Retreating to the phone, feeling woozy and barely aware of the tears that rolled onto her cheeks, she shouted to Conky. 'We're trapped! There's no way out. We're gonna die!'

She dropped her lifeline to the outside world, feeling suddenly sleepy and overwhelmed. Imagined picking up a chair and hurling it through the wall but realised it was mere fantasy of an overheated mind that was becoming rapidly oxygen-starved. She took Gloria's limp hand into hers. She closed her eyes, wondering if death by asphyxiation would hurt. Felt regret at being too weak after all. Certain that Paddy would have found a way out. At least the girls were well provided for, as long as Ellis James and that tax bitch kept their noses out of her business.

This was it. Salient thought had all but left her. All was black.

This was the end.

Chapter 20

Youssuf

'Dad, I think you should just stay home and watch some telly,' Tariq said, absently flicking through the morning paper. '*Cash in the Attic*'s on later. You like that.'

Youssuf eyed his son's youthful clothing – a lumberjack shirt and jeans with too many zips and pockets. Tariq dressed like a teenager. It wasn't befitting of a middle-aged law graduate. None of it was. 'All the sacrifices me and your mother made . . .' He shook his head, examined the myriad of tablets in the egg cup that Anjum had doled out for him. Emptied the medication onto his tongue and downed the lot with a mouthful of bitter black coffee.

Tariq looked up at him, finally. So much like his mother, in some ways. The same large, brown almond-shaped eyes, fringed with thick black lashes that Saffiya had had. But the thick eyebrows that bunched together quizzically were Youssuf's genes coming through. 'What's that got to do with *Cash in the Attic*?'

Saffiya. Youssuf acknowledged the ache in his heart as he thought about his wife. He felt the larger capsules lodge uncomfortably in his throat. Another sip of coffee would push them down, along with perhaps a bite of the toast he couldn't quite face.

'It's a good job your mother isn't alive to see what you've become, Tariq Khan. A hoodlum. A liar. A husband with a discontented wife. Don't think I haven't noticed there's bad feeling between you and Anjum. She knows, doesn't she? That you're a criminal!'

'Oh, this again?' Tariq closed and folded the newspaper into a perfect, tight rectangle. Checked over his shoulder, presumably to ensure that Anjum wasn't within earshot. 'I thought we'd dropped the subject of what I do for a living when you had a little think about the prospect of going into some grotty NHS nursing home in Cheetham because I've gone straight and have to get rid of all my assets. That's the alternative, Dad!' He lowered his voice. 'And *my* relationship with *my* wife is nothing for you to concern yourself with. In fact, Anjum's the last of my worries. I'm more bothered about Jonny. He's not pulling his weight. He's too busy feeling sorry for himself.' He drew breath to reel off yet more excuses for his shameful activities.

'Do you think it's acceptable to be brawling in public with petty criminals?' Youssuf asked.

'The guys at the car wash, again? They were going to kidnap you, Dad. The other day, you were congratulating yourself for having had a go at one of them with your stick!'

'If you led a clean life, you wouldn't need to threaten thugs from a rival gang in the street. Nobody would be trying to bundle me into a van.'

'Eat your toast, Dad. You shouldn't take your pills on an empty stomach.'

'I don't want my toast.' Youssuf pushed the plate away

and levered himself gingerly off the kitchen bar stool. 'You can help me get dressed and then I'm going out.'

Rising from his own seat, Tariq reached out to steady him, passing him his stick. 'You're not going out. It's dangerous. I thought we'd agreed.'

Sticking his chin out in defiance, Youssuf snatched the walking stick. The confrontation had set his pulse racing. His lungs struggled to keep up. 'I didn't agree to anything. I went to Bury the other day with a friend, if you must know. And I was fine. I don't have to hide myself away, watching rubbish on the television. I'm an honest man. A god-fearing man.'

As his son took him gently by the elbow, steering him towards his own downstairs bathroom, Youssuf tried repeatedly to shake him off.

'Please just stay in for a bit, Dad. Until things calm down. My business rival died in the spring. There's lots of bad types running around and new people trying to flex their muscles. Manchester's like a volcano waiting to erupt. It's all just a bit—'

'I don't want to hear it!' Youssuf said, wondering whether he should mention the photograph he had taken of the unpleasant-looking character in the café, who had cursed too much and spilled his tea in anger before storming out on his companion. Youssuf was certain he had read the man's obituary in the newspaper earlier in the year. Hadn't he been referred to as a suspected crime boss? Hadn't Tariq said he had gone to the funeral, no less? No. He would keep this little nugget to himself for now and do a little investigation. He wasn't in his dotage just yet. 'I just want things to be the way they were. I want my freedom back. I want my health. I want to show my face at the mosque and not feel shame. You don't even listen to me, Tariq.' He stopped just outside the bathroom, fixing his son with an accusatory stare. 'It's like I'm invisible just because I'm old. When was the last time you took my wishes into consideration? Eh?'

Tariq opened and closed his mouth. Seemingly chewing over an appropriate answer. 'I'm coming with you to Mecca. I'm trying.'

'If a donkey goes to Mecca, when he comes back, he's the same donkey! You need to give your dodgy business up, son. Turn your face to virtue and your back to vice. Set a good example for your children!'

But his son may as well have stuck his fingers in his ears. 'Let's get you ready. I'll wipe down one of the sun loungers so you can get some fresh air in the back garden, if you like.'

Tariq smiled and tried anew to steer him into the bathroom.

It was like talking to a brick wall, Youssuf mused. Stubborn. The boy was like his mother in that respect too.

'It comes to something when the only person who listens to me is Colin Chang.'

'Your pharmacist? You're not still going on about him, are you? You said he'd gone away.'

'Not gone away. Gone missing. I think he's got into trouble with the wrong sort.'

'Is that what you want, Dad? Do you want to go missing? Because that's the kind of thing that could happen to you. Someone, like those scumbags in the black van, is going to get a grip of you so they can get at me. You need to be careful, Dad. No wandering the streets. Not in your condition.'

As Tariq turned on the taps of the shower and laid out a clean towel, a plan started to formulate in Youssuf's mind.

His son was unyielding and controlling, forgetting who was the elder and wiser. That much was clear. Some subterfuge and a little light rebellion was therefore in order if Youssuf were to reclaim any of his lost dignity.

'Okay. You win,' he said. 'You go to work. Anjum's back from the school run soon. She's working from home today, isn't she? She'll make me a nice lunch. I'll watch the TV. Satisfied?'

The brilliant smile lit up his son's handsome face. 'Great, Dad. Thanks.'

Grunting softly as he alighted from the bus, Youssuf bid the driver a friendly farewell and turned towards his planned destination. Leaning on his stick, he gave himself a few moments to catch his breath. Enjoyed the feel of the weak Mancunian sun on his face – such a rarity in this almost perpetually grey place, where the damp crept into his bones. Thought wistfully of the blue skies back home; vivid green palms and the flame-coloured flowers of the Gul Mohr trees providing a bright foil to bleached-out streets. Cheering himself with the thought of their planned trip during Hajj. At least it would be nice and hot in Saudi Arabia, though he wasn't looking forward to the long flight. Or going with Tariq, for that matter, which rendered the pilgrimage a sham. That boy needed reining in.

Youssuf sighed. Then started the trek along the cracked slabbed pavement – heavy going in his sandals. He had told Anjum he was merely going for a walk in Boddlington Park. But there was no need for either his son or his daughter-in-law to keep tabs on him now that he was returning to better health.

He straightened himself up, ignoring the dragging ache of the scar tissue. *Grit your teeth and get on with it, Youssuf.*

The man with a white beard and toothless gums must still attend to worldly affairs. His family was under threat; under surveillance by a detective who had slipped him his business card. His favourite pharmacist was missing. A crime boss claiming to be dead was not dead. Here were mysteries that needed solving, and Youssuf had nothing but time on his hands and zero interest in daytime TV.

When he arrived outside the pharmacy, his heart leaped at the sight of the raised shutters. The sign on the door said it was open for trading. He smiled. Pleased with himself, as though he had caused this about-turn in Colin Chang's fortunes, whatever they might be. Delighting in the prospect of being able to sit and chat amiably to the nice young man while his assistant prepared his medications.

'Morning!' Youssuf said to the girl behind the counter. He drank in the familiar smell of cardboard packaging and pine disinfectant. Toiletries on display in glass cabinets. An array of over-the-counter medication on the shelves and children's colourful novelty hairgrips on the carousel. He approved of the old-fashioned feel. Here was a place where he was listened to and taken seriously. 'I'm pleased to see Colin is back. How are you, my dear?'

The harried-looking assistant put a pile of prescriptions into a toothpaste-green plastic basket. 'Colin's not here,' she said. 'We've got a temporary pharmacist. He's in the back. Do you want to see him?'

'No,' Youssuf said, the smile evaporating and leaving only a residue of disappointment on his lips. 'I hoped to catch up with Mr Chang. I had things I wanted to tell him. About a loft extension I'm designing for a young couple. He was interested.'

'Can *I* get you anything?' she asked, pushing her glasses up her nose. Chewing gum like a masticating cow.

Way too young. Way too pushy.

'Where is Colin?' Youssuf took a seat and sat expectantly with his walking stick between his knees. Feeling his warfarin-thin blood succumb to the cold in the shady shop, despite the thick cardigan, slacks and woollen socks he had put on. Shouldn't have worn the sandals.

'I can't say where Mr Chang is, I'm afraid,' she said, focusing studiously on the basket. 'He's still away.'

'Away where?'

'Further away.'

'Has he gone on one of his nice trips to Hong Kong? I like to hear about those. He shows me the photos when he gets back.' Youssuf tried to read the girl's expression and suddenly realised she was hiding the truth. The bad feeling he had had when the shutters had been down during the summer returned. 'Tell me where I can find him. I'd like to send him a letter.'

The girl scowled and looked him up and down like a security guard at the airport, suspecting every brown man of hiding plastic explosives in his pants. 'Why would you want to do that?'

'Young lady,' he said, levering himself out of the chair and pointing his stick towards her, 'I've been coming here for over ten years. Just because I'm a customer doesn't mean Colin Chang and I don't like each other as people. A man can become friends with a professional associate over that length of time. But you wouldn't know, because you've only been serving here for two years and have never so much as asked me how I am.'

The girl looked crestfallen and duly admonished. Youssuf knew he had wedged his sandaled foot in the door of her guilty conscience.

After half an hour of ingratiating himself with the

temporary pharmacist and chivvying on the assistant, she had let slip that Colin Chang was in 'a spot of bother with some unsavoury types'.

He walked out of the old-fashioned chemist clutching a piece of paper with an address on it.

Chapter 21

Sheila

The din of something heavy being hurled against the Portakabin wall roused Sheila. How long had she been out for? She had no clue. Pure daylight flooded in where all had previously been engulfed in smoke and hellfire. She was dimly aware of a tall figure, clad in black, discarding a lump hammer; running through the flames towards her. Realised she was being hoisted onto one of Conky's shoulders, Gloria over the other. Then all was dark until she woke to find a paramedic placing an oxygen mask over her face.

'Get this sodding thing off me,' she cried, wrenching it off her head. 'I'm fine.'

Woozy and confused, the sense of urgency percolated through the smoke damage to her brain almost immediately. She realised her hand was encased inside Conky's. Shook him away.

'I don't need saving!' she shouted. Easy to say, now she was free of the burning wreckage. Kicking out at the male paramedic who was trying to get a blood pressure cuff around her arm. 'Where's Glo? Where's my business partner?'

She expected to hear Gloria, perhaps only some feet away, strapped to an ambulance gurney, just as she had been, spouting the Bible.

'Gloria's gone off to hospital,' Conky said, stroking her brow.

'What do you mean? Where is she? I want to see her!' Sheila coughed and spluttered her demands.

Soft fingers through her hair. Trailing gently over her chin. Conky had taken off his glasses and was gazing into her eyes with evident adoration. 'She was out cold, darling, but they said her vital signs were fine. They've got to give her a brain scan and some oxygen. They're going to keep her in for observation. Don't worry yourself, my love.' Conky's voice was soothing and placatory like a father trying to calm a fraught toddler.

'Sod it, Conky! Get off me, will you?' Pushing his hand away, she registered the disappointment in the way that his smiling, craggy, smoke-smudged face fell. But sitting up, trying to unbuckle herself with clumsy fingers amid wracking coughing, there was only space in her mind for thoughts of home. Get behind those tall gates. Gather her composure. Call Bancroft. Confront the bastard. Sort this nonsense out.

'Sheila!' the paramedic said, placing his hand on hers in an attempt to stop her escape. 'Sheila! I need you to rest and put the mask back on. Come on, love. Let's get you checked out.'

She peered at his neck, trying to focus on the red patch where he had been overzealous with a razor. 'It's Mrs O'Brien to you, pal, and I'm not your love.' Finally, the buckle came loose. She swung her legs over the side of the gurney and stood up. Dizzy. Her ears rang with tinnitus from the blast. But there was no need for these men to see

171

her weakness. Plunging her hand into her jacket pocket, she felt for her car keys. Still there. But no phone. She reasoned she must have dropped it when she passed out. She'd have to get a new one. Shit. No way of calling anyone until she was home, anyway.

'Where do you think you're going?' Conky said, trying to take her arm.

'Leave me alone, for Christ's sake!'

Fending off his overbearing attentions by shaking him loose, she drank in the extent of the damage. Paddy's builders' merchants had had it. The shopfront was a jumble of smashed glass, buckled window frames and stud walls that had been reduced to a pile of firewood. All that remained of the back office were some supporting beams, charred and smouldering. Fat jets of water from the firemen's hoses blasted what was left of the Portakabin, smothering the final daring coils of thick, black smoke that belched from within. Sheila privately acknowledged she had had a near miss. Next time, she realised, she might not be so lucky.

When a Police squad car pulled in behind the fire engines, she galvanised herself into action. Time to go. Sharpish.

She grabbed Conky's arm in a placatory gesture. 'My Mam's expecting me to turn up to her ladies' darts tournament tonight. I'm not letting her down.'

'You can't drive, Sheila. It's dangerous. You passed out.'

He made a grab for the car fob in her hand but she weaved out of his reach.

Focus on getting in the car, She. Don't let Conky tell you what to do. Just crawl back to Bramshott. You can pull into a layby if you feel weird. You don't need saving. 'I'm going home to ring Lev and sort my head out. As soon as you can, try and get in that back office and find my phone. I

172

can't have the coppers getting hold of it. It's got all sorts on the SIM card. Conversations between you and me. Offshore banking information for "Scrubbers". Correspondence from that Bancroft. Contacts for every single player in the O'Brien firm. That phone could have us all chucked in clink. And we're gonna have to give the police a statement for the insurance. I can't face it. You stay and speak to them.'

'But—'

'That's an order, Conky. Sort this crap out. That's what I pay you for.'

She took the M60 back in Paddy's diminutive million-pound Bugatti, sandwiched between two heavy goods vehicles, crawling at a snail's pace the super-car had never been intended to endure. Checking her mirrors, she prayed she wouldn't be spotted in the heavy traffic of the slow lane should Conky come after her. No phone meant no inter-ruptions. No chance for the police to quiz her.

Get home. Check everything's okay. Call the girls. Come on! Come on!

She imagined the damage Bancroft and his firebombs might do to her precious home. Found she was holding her breath and was then rewarded with a coughing fit that almost made her swerve from her lane. The driver of the HGV behind her honked his horn angrily.

'Cock off, pal!' she told his reflection in her mirror.

Got to ring the girls. Got to see they're safe.

Finally, the Trafford Centre was within sight. Though her lungs felt like they had been filled with cement, her ears buzzed and her head throbbed, she was almost home. With careful negotiation of the M56, she made it back to Bramshott, steering the Bugatti carefully through the secu-rity gates. No sign of any sabotage.

'Thank you,' she whispered to the shards of jagged crystal in the contemporary chandelier that cascaded down from the first floor.

But she had been inside for no more than five minutes when the buzzer sounded. Somebody at the gates. Feeling the blood drain from her prickling lips, she padded across the oak floor to check the CCTV, wondering if she'd need to head for the panic room that had been installed just before Paddy's death. On the screen was a man in dark clothing with a neat beard. Youngish. Didn't look like one of Bancroft's. In his hand, she could see an envelope. Could he be a bailiff of the court? Was it some kind of a trap? The light-headedness was back, threatening to knock her to the ground.

'Yes?' she said via the intercom.

'Delivery for Mrs O'Brien. Needs a signature.'

His voice was steady. He looked straight into the camera's lens. Nothing to hide?

'Show us your ID.'

The card that he held up to the screen was attached to a lanyard around his neck. It seemed legit. He was a courier. She buzzed him in, noting the baseball bat that was in the umbrella stand by the door.

Having snatched the envelope from him, the man started to rub his hands together. 'Getting parky, isn't it?'

She said nothing, signed his hand-held device and slammed the door in his face. Watched him disappear down the path and through the gates. But what was in the bloody envelope? Some deadly chemical that spies killed each other off with? Ricin or anthrax, maybe?

'Oh, get on with it, Sheila. Open the sodding thing.'

Tearing at the seal, she whimpered as she withdrew a photograph of her two daughters, Amy and Dahlia, clearly taken at their father's funeral. Amy, with her strawberry blonde hair peeping from beneath her hat. That smattering of freckles across her nose. Reminiscent of her father, but all Sheila in temperament. Dahlia in her lawyer's suit, all dark hair and eyes like Sheila's Dad. Her girls. Her precious girls.

'Oh, Jesus. No!'

Dropping the photograph to the floor, she ran to the landline on the kitchen island. Amy's number was on speed dial. No answer. But she had the mobile number of her neighbour in the student halls where she lived. She dialled. Waited for what seemed like an age.

'Yeah?' A boy, trying to sound nonchalant but polite. 'Can I help you?'

'Hiya. I'm trying to get hold of my daughter, Amy O'Brien. Have you seen her, lovey? Please?'

'She's in the kitchen, I think. Hang on.'

Agonising moments as the boy shuffled off to find her daughter. The pitter-patter and squeak of someone running down the corridor in trainers.

'Mum?'

Sheila bit back the tears when she heard Amy's voice. 'Are you okay, love?'

'Yeah. Why?'

But there was little time to explain. Sheila gave a swift, believable excuse, told her daughter to be watchful and to stay close to her pals at all times. Nigel Bancroft would have trouble getting to Amy, with all the locks and key-coded systems in halls. There was safety in numbers, and communal living would be Amy's saviour, should anybody try to harm her. Of that, Sheila was certain.

She hung up, dialling Dahlia. Would her eldest be in a meeting or in court?

Mercifully, she was put through to her immediately by her secretary. 'Please tell me you're okay.'

'Of course! Why? Listen, Mum. I'm knee-deep in reading through a contract. Are you all right?'

Dahlia's rich, calm, educated voice made Sheila's heart slow a little. Of course Dahlia was fine. She was capable and intelligent, ensconced in the high-security offices of a City of London law firm. Nigel Bancroft couldn't touch her at work. But her living arrangements were a different proposition altogether. Dahlia had always cherished her independence.

'I'm fine, love. Just fine. I guess I wanted to hear your voice.'

'Well, er, now you have.'

'Listen, Dahlia, love. Watch your back.'

'What's wrong?'

'Nothing.'

'Mum?'

'I'm just having a spot of bother with the business. You know how it is. Rich people attract enemies. I don't want my girls getting tangled up with my crap. I think you should go and stay at a friend's for a couple of nights, though. Or book into a hotel. I'll pay.'

'Why the hell should I do that?'

'It's important, Dahlia. Please. Promise me you'll do it. Just a few days. Please.'

'No. I don't want to. I've got people coming for dinner tonight. I'm certainly not shipping out if you won't tell me why.'

'I can't tell you why. Just do it, will you? *Please*. For me.'

Couldn't Dahlia hear the urgency in her mother's voice? She always had had Paddy's headstrong streak.

There was a pause.

'Oh, all right then.'

Satisfied that the toxic reach of the firebomb had remained within the perimeter fence of the builders' merchants, Sheila ended the call. Made enquiries after Gloria and briefed Lev that his mother was fine and might be discharged the following day, after a night of being under observation.

Ignoring her home phone that rang and rang with Conky, the police, the fire brigade, various builders' merchants staff, Frank and the insurance company – all leaving fraught messages – she determined to wash away the horror of the afternoon in a deep foam bath. Over and over, she rehearsed what she planned to say to Bancroft.

'You mess with me, you're messing with the wrong one,' she told the television screen that was sunk into the stacked-stone slate of the bathroom wall. *The Real Housewives of Beverley Hills* was showing on a lesser ITV channel with the sound on mute. Sadly, they had no advice to offer her. 'I'm going to end you, Nigel.'

No. That didn't sound right.

'I'm the Queen of Manchester, you Brummie bastard, and you've committed treason.'

Better.

By the time she was dressed and climbing into the Roller for her mother's darts tournament, she was feeling calmer. A cheeky vodka and tonic and a shot from some old Ventolin inhaler that had been left in the medicine cupboard from the last time Amy had visited served both to calm her nerves and ease the congestion on her chest. Confronting Nigel Bancroft could wait for the morning. She wasn't Paddy, steaming in with his Smith & Wessons blazing if another man so much as looked at him askance. She would take time overnight to cogitate on what had happened and what her next move might be. She needed to put out feelers to check it was, indeed, Bancroft. The enemies of a woman like her were many and varied, after all.

At the community centre in Chorlton, her mother wasted no time in parading her to the other women on the team.

'Come and meet our Sheila, Doreen!' she said, dragging some pensioner with a tight perm and matching hatchet face over to inspect her long-lost daughter. 'She drives a Rolls Royce. What do you think of that?'

Doreen, swathed in so much nine-carat gold that she stooped, reached out and touched one of the oversized diamond studs in Sheila's ears with a nicotine-stained finger. 'Are them cubics?'

'Pardon?' Sheila limboed away from the woman's touch.

'Cubic zirconia. Only, my Janet got a pair just like them the other week for her birthday. Argos catalogue, wasn't it? Gorgeous stuff in there. Her Billy blew his giro on her. They were two carat. Bleeding lovely, they are.'

Sheila's mother pulled her darts top over her ample bosom, revealing her team's logo of a parrot wearing a helmet, clutching a dart in its beak, though Sheila didn't dare ask what helmet-wearing parrots had to do with darts or a Chorlton community centre or a gaggle of elderly bingo-goers. 'Two carats in what, precisely?'

'Cubic bleeding zirconia, of course!'

As the almost surreal argument escalated, Sheila registered a humdinger of a hangover after the explosion, manifesting itself as dizziness and worsening tinnitus. She took a seat, idly observing the bickering women, allowing the warmth and novelty of the place to seep into her stiff muscles; she was successfully anaesthetising herself against the horror of the attack with the laughter and banality of lesser lives. Being away from Conky and the business for an evening was just the ticket.

Her mother had just thrown a bullseye, causing consternation with the opposing team, when somebody's elderly husband came in from the fire exit, bringing with him the stale odour of cigarettes. Sheila's stomach contracted as the man made eye contact with her, marching straight over until his wizened face was inches from hers..

'There's a feller in the car park wants a word with you,' he said.

'Me?'

He nodded. 'That's right. Feller in a posh car. Said it was urgent. A matter of life and death, he said.'

Grabbing her bag that contained her snub-nosed pistol, Sheila tottered outside, gripping the handrail as the descended the steps to the carpark, wondering if death had changed his mind and had opted to pay her a second visit in one day. There, parked next to her Rolls Royce, was a gleaming Mercedes CLS. Its tail lights glowed red, but in the darkness she had no way of discerning who was in the driver's seat.

Clutching her gun with her hand concealed inside her bag, fighting her exhaustion, she approached. The passenger door opened and she heard a familiar voice from within. A voice she really did not want to hear. Taut. Fraught. Constricted with fury.

'Get in. I want a word with you.'

Chapter 22

Conky

'Batter you? I'm gonna rip your bloody head off and use your neck as a vase, you big Irish bastard!'

As the fist of the enemy gang-member sped towards his jaw, Conky considered the prospect of flowers in a vase. Coolly grabbed the man's wrist and twisted it backwards so that it snapped with a brittle cracking sound reminiscent of breaking bamboo.

'They say imitation is the sincerest form of flattery, so I'll thank you for that,' he said, pressing his face close to his now-yelping opponent. 'See, I already tried that with your wee man, Brummie Kevin. And I have to say . . .' He looked over and winked at Frank, whose face was contorted with apparent horror. 'The gullet is a less than ideal receptacle for a nice rose or two. Very narrow.'

Wrestling his rival combatant to the floor, Conky considered the flowers he'd sent to Sheila only an hour earlier. Had she received them yet? So far, she had ignored every call he'd placed to the home phone, checking she was okay. There was a tightness in his chest at the thought she might be lying in some hospital somewhere, having crashed on the motorway journey home. If only he'd been able to find her damned mobile phone in the wreckage before the authorities had had the opportunity to get their mitts on it.

How would he break that news to Sheila?

The fire-fighter hadn't wanted to let Conky dig through the dripping, charred wreckage of the builders' merchants. 'Site's unsafe, mate! The investigators haven't examined it yet. Don't make me get one of the police officers over to deal with you.'

Tempted to grab him by the scruff of his neck, Conky had desisted, realising the guy had simply been doing his job. He had removed his glasses to reveal his protruding eyes in all their terrifying glory. 'Catch yourself on, big lad. Some eejit has firebombed this place in an act of sabotage against a poor wee widow. It sickens my pish.' He had eyeballed him to ensure he knew no backing down had been about to take place. 'Mrs O'Brien asked me to look for something of sentimental value that she dropped when she passed out. Now, step aside and let me do my job. Then I'll let you do yours.'

There was youth and some trepidation in the fireman's eyes. He couldn't have been more than late twenties. 'Ten minutes, then. Watch your step.'

Raking through the steaming remains with a stick, Conky had not been able to spot the phone. Could it have melted?

'Ah, Mr McFadden. Fancy seeing you here.'

Conky had frozen, mid-search. He had recognised the smug tones immediately.

'Ellis James. What a surprise!'

Turning around, the sight of the dumpy detective with his dull blond buzz cut and perpetually greasy-looking coat had made Conky's heart sink. A grilling would be inevitable.

'In my car please, Mr McFadden. I'd like to take a statement.'

He had to fob James off; get rid of him so he could have another look for Sheila's phone. All those decades, he had hankered after her. He'd be damned if he'd lose the love of his life over an incriminating SIM card.

In the foetid Mondeo, which had reeked of stale chippy dinners, cheesy feet and the funk of unwashed hair, Conky had relayed a tale of a sudden explosion.

'Oh, you know how the wee bastards round here are, Detective James,' he had said, looking prosaically through the windscreen at the chaotic scene of uniforms, firemen, slightly chargrilled O'Brien's Builders' Merchants workers and fire investigators in their black uniforms. Police tape had already been fluttering around the site, holding back the rubber-necking neighbours from the budget tyre-fitters next door and the neighbouring estate.

'Do I?' Ellis James narrowed his eyes at Conky. 'How do I know this wasn't some insurance scam?'

'Sure, that's for the insurance guys and the fire investigators to ascertain,' Conky had said, sighing. 'Forensics. The indisputable purity of science. I think you'll find my version of events a fair and accurate representation of what's gone on.' Ellis James had had diddly shit on them. Of that, he had been certain. 'There are five witnesses will tell you the same. We were in the office one minute. A firebomb came through the window and the next thing . . . boom! Nothing more to add. And I'd offer you a coffee but the machine's melted, so it has.' He had forced himself to smile amiably.

'My friend Ruth Darley and I had a very interesting trip out the other evening.' James's eyes had narrowed.

'Oh.' Conky had glanced pointedly at his watch. Had been careful not to allow any concern to register on his face. 'And? Did she let you cop a feel?'

Ellis James's mouth had twisted into a sneer. 'We had a tip-off about Maureen Kaplan's illicit stash of accounts.'

Don't react. Don't raise so much as an eyebrow. Genghis Khan would give him the cold face. Channel Genghis. 'Illicit? Surely not! I'll bet you didn't find anything interesting, did you, detective? Go on! You can tell me!'

That James's sneer sagged into a scowl told Conky everything he needed to know. The hapless detective and his ballbreaker of an HMRC squeeze had been fed good information too late, yet again. Maureen was circumspect and experienced – no match for those low-level chumps.

'I'm sorry your date turned out to be a disappointment,' he had said, nudging James and grinning. 'Next time, eh? Now if you don't mind . . .'

Finally, he had watched with a degree of levity as Ellis James had driven away in that shitty cesspit of a car. Time to look anew for Sheila's phone. Except, the fire investigator had been standing close to the spot where Sheila had been sprawled, unconscious. Frowning, he had been examining a black, flat lozenge shape in his hand. How had Conky missed it? Damn his shitty eyesight to hell!

Too late to stem the tidal flow of crap that would surely now come the O'Briens' way.

Several hours later, long after the light had failed and Conky had spent an age reporting the sabotage to the insurers from the non-comfort of the nearest dingy council estate pub, when his phone had started to ring, he had answered hastily, without checking the screen. Praying it would be Sheila.

'Conks! You've got to come quick!' Frank on the other end. His voice had been stringy and high-pitched. The sound of men shouting and crashing in the background. Smashing glass.

'What in God's name is going on there?'

Frank had yelped in answer and hung up.

Striding out to his car, Conky had guessed this was Bancroft, following up an almighty right hook with a series of jabs below the belt.

Two Range Rovers had been parked outside an otherwise silent M1 House. No sign of the bouncers so early in the evening. Frank's wheels had to have been around the back. Conky had calculated how many of Bancroft's lackeys might have rocked up, ready for a fight in two seven-seater cars. Fourteen? Jesus. *Where's Degsy, Lev and Pulp Friction when you need them?* Ignoring the aches in his legs, he had reached into the secret compartment beneath the glovebox of his car. Empty. What the hell had he done with his SIG Sauer?

Plunging his hand inside his coat, patting the pocket and looking up quizzically at the M1 House neon sign above the door to the club, he had felt his pulse quicken. Nothing. Not in his waistband. Not on his person. He had to have dropped the fecking thing in amongst the firebomb fallout.

No sign yet of Lev or Degsy, though he had left messages for them. Should he go in solo? It could be certain death. But leave that hapless twat Frank to fend for himself? No way. That was not how the Loss Adjuster rolled.

Steeling himself to walk in there alone, he had entered the club and happened upon some ten men. They had been smashing the hell out of the beer fridges behind the main bar with crowbars. The cold air, not yet warmed by the bodies of dancing young revellers, had tasted of fear and violence; had reeked of spilled alcohol. Not good. One of them – the black guy with the dreads who had accompanied Bancroft to Salford Quays – had had a hand around Frank's neck, leaning the poor bastard backwards over the bar, screaming something barely intelligible into his terror-stricken face.

'Get your hands off him!' Conky had grabbed a stool from one of the seating areas that surrounded the empty expanse of the dance floor. His speech had been thick and clumsy with adrenalin and aggression.

Bancroft's man had released his grip on Frank and had sprinted towards Conky, wielding a knife. 'This is a message from Bancroft,' he had yelled, jabbing at Conky. 'Manchester is the new Birmingham. Surrender or—'

'An empty vessel makes the most noise, so it does. Shut your bake, dickhead!' Bancroft's guy had taken a blow to the arm from the base of the stool, knocking the knife across the polished concrete of the club's floor. A swift blow to his head with another swing of the stool and he had been out cold.

Panting, feeling the skin on his face stinging and uncomfortably hot, Conky had just had enough respite to register two of the other attackers rounding on him with their crowbars to give him a shot at grabbing the dreadlocked guy's knife. There it had been, glinting on the ground beneath the club's spotlights like treasure waiting to be found. Conky had abandoned the stool, flinging it in the approaching aggressors' path. Had propelled himself towards the knife. Gasping as his fingers closed around it. *Unfit bastard. You should cut down on the sneaky burgers when Sheila isn't looking. You're meant to be a professional.* Had brandished it at the men, who had goaded him with threats of how they had been just waiting to batter his head to a pulp.

But Conky, like the seasoned predator he was, had smelled the anxiety oozing from their every pore. He knew at that point that both of them had seen Brummie Kev's severed head.

Removing his Ray-Bans with his left gloved hand, sliding them into his pocket, he had drawn himself up to his full height. One of the men had faltered; had taken a half-step backwards. Conky had wrenched the crowbar from his uncertain grip and had brought the weight of it crashing down onto the man's shoulder, knocking him to his knees.

Two down. Eight to go.

With the knife in his right hand, he had lunged for the other prick. But Conky had found himself stunned by a swing from another crowbar to his ear. The pain had been intense, accompanied by a high-pitched squeak as something within the delicate bone structure of his middle ear had failed catastrophically.

Suddenly, the bloodythirsty Brummie had cast aside his weapon with a clatter. Had put his fists up like some excitable sparring newbie in a boxing ring for the first time.

'You squaring up to me, big lad?' Conky had said, trying his damnedest to ignore the squealing in his ear. 'Are you planning to batter me?'

'Batter you? I'm gonna rip your bloody head off and use your neck as a vase, you big Irish bastard!'

And so, despite reminding the wee shite of how Brummie Kev had recklessly lost his head and despite snapping his wrist into the bargain, Conky had been surprised by his opponent falling upon him in an incensed frenzy of spittle, sweat and testosterone. A younger man. A hungrier man. Focused. Raining punch after punch down on his head with his good hand, so that Conky's careful hair arrangement was sent scudding across the dance floor, along with his pride.

The agony in his ear raged on and Conky's vision begun to blur – he was barely registering Frank's feeble efforts to come to his aid, clutching a bottle of Newcastle Brown as a makeshift bludgeon. Within moments, the battle became nothing more than an execution waiting to happen, with odds that Conky recognised to be on the terminal side of badly stacked against them.

Now, the Brummie thug's fist made contact with Conky's jaw anew, sending his head backwards onto the unyielding ground. Bancroft's side had triumph within reach. How was it that such a bad day could take a turn for the even worse? And yet, there was apparently more to come, as M1 House shook with the deafening sound of a gunshot fired . . .

Chapter 23

Sheila

'You?!' Sheila said, peering at the man in the driver's seat of the Mercedes in disbelief. Her enemy.

She gripped the open passenger door, steadying herself, though the charms on her Tiffany bracelet betrayed her as they jingle-jangled in time with her thudding heart. No intention of getting in. '*You* firebombed me, you bastard?! But I didn't die, so now, you've come to finish the job? Is that it?'

The car park was deserted. If she screamed now, she doubted the rabble inside the community centre would hear her above their raucous laughter and arguments over who had scored double top and who was a lying cheat.

She locked eyes with her opposite number in the dark and damp of that chill Mancunian evening. All after-effects of the bomb now washed away in a wave of adrenalin.

'Firebomb? What are you on about?' Tariq Khan asked, a bemused expression on his handsome face.

'And some creepy picture of my kids, delivered to my door in a sodding envelope by a courier. Trying to kill me wasn't enough so now you're trying to spook me and all, are you?'

'No! Look . . .' He glanced around the car park, one hand on the steering wheel, one on his lap. Reached over and patted the passenger seat. 'Get in. Please. We need to talk. I'm not armed, I swear. I'm here about my dad.' Held his hands up and offered a weak smile as corroborating evidence.

Sheila knew she had a decision to make. 'Why should I trust you, of all people?'

The smile slid from Tariq's face, to be replaced by a scowl. His shoulders seemed to rise an inch. Anger licked like flames along the silky-smooth edges of his cultured, Oxford-graduate's speech. 'Listen. I know you've kidnapped my dad. Your men tried and failed to drag him off a car-wash fore-court, didn't they? Well, now they've succeeded. By rights, I should have just steamed in on you, guns blazing. But I thought we could talk and sort this, like human beings. Grown-ups.' The ferocity in his tone wavered. 'My dad's a sick man.' He blinked hard, the Adam's apple in his neck bobbing up and down.

Looking back at the fire exit of the community centre, Sheila wondered if she should just run. Get back to her mother and hide among the feisty, fun-loving pensioners of south Manchester. If nothing else, they could dart Tariq Khan to death like some lost tribe of South America that had wound up confused but deadly in the mizzle of Chorlton.

'Please, Sheila! We've got to sort this out! Have a heart!'

She could see the solitary track of a tear, shining on Tariq's cheek in the moonlight.

'I must be sodding mental.' Exhaling hard through pursed lips, with her breath steaming on the air, Sheila swung herself into his car and closed the door. 'Don't you dare lock it or try to drive away with me.'

'I won't.'

'Or Conky's coming after you and your family.'

'I *won't*. All right?'

The Boddlington boss shook his head in silence. Tears standing in those soulful brown eyes. She had never seen him anything but controlled, suave and quietly terrifying from a distance. Close up, he was a real looker. Smelled good, too. Sheila kept these thoughts to herself, eyeing his thatch of black hair, streaked with silver. Maybe it was just a flattering light and being in close quarters inside his car. She felt her skin pucker up into goosebumps.

'Now do you promise it wasn't your lot that firebombed my builders' merchants today?' she asked. Studying his expression for the subtle tells of a bullshitter. God knows, she knew what those looked like after half a lifetime spent with Paddy O'Brien.

Tariq took a perfectly folded white cloth handkerchief from his jacket pocket. Unfolded it with care and precision. Dabbed at his eyes, then seemed to give up and merely wiped them with the back of his hand. Pleasantly hairy. Sheila liked that.

'I swear on my children's lives. I haven't come near your lot since before Paddy's funeral. We've seen enough bloodshed.'

'But Jonny Margulies is still after Lev Bell. Or so I've heard.'

He shook his head. 'Jonny's gone rogue. He's out of his mind with grief and depression. I've got no jurisdiction over what he does outside of the business. Sorry. But Lev . . . I've still got a lot of respect for the boy. He's not working for you now, is he? I'd hoped he'd show more loyalty than that. I've been texting and texting him.'

'And the Fish Man? I've heard the Fish Man's still out there.'

'I'm barely using the Fish Man,' Tariq said. He swallowed but held her gaze. 'He's too hot after the shooting at M1 House. If Jonny's contracted him to hit Lev, that's on Jonny. I'm not my business partner's keeper.' He looked down at Sheila's miniskirt. At her knees. Back up to her face. His eyebrows arced in supplication. 'What have you done with my dad, Sheila? Seriously! Taking out my brothel keepers was one thing, but an innocent, ailing—'

Sheila had heard enough. 'Have you finished laying into me? Why the bloody hell should I know the first thing about your old man?'

'A pair of thugs in a black van,' he simply said.

'Who?'

'One had dreadlocks. The other's hair was cropped. They tried to bundle my dad into a VW van the other week in broad daylight. Now Dad's gone missing. I haven't seen him since breakfast yesterday.'

'They don't sound like anyone working for me, and I certainly didn't order any of my lot to kidnap your dad. Go to the police, for Christ's sake!'

He laughed mirthlessly. 'Are you kidding me?'

Chewing on the inside of her mouth, Sheila sized up the line of Tariq's shapely lips, framed by the neat black beard. Perfectly straight teeth and the skin of a man at least ten years younger than his forty-something years. She was dimly aware of licking her own lips. What was this crap? Some life-affirming nonsense after having survived the firebombing? She felt her breathing come short, gathering pace.

'The last time me and Jon heard anything directly from you,' he said, his nostrils flaring and that edge to his voice reappearing, 'was the wreath of lilies you sent to Jonny's home, saying RIP on the card or something like that. It was in poor taste and it was hardly a bloody olive branch, was it? Then, attempted kidnapping, and now, this!'

'I don't know a single thing about your dad. Honest. I swear to God. I've had my hands full with some dick called Nigel Bancroft.'

'The Birmingham boss?' She saw concern flit across his face as if a deeper shadow had fallen on the interior of his Mercedes.

'Yep. He seems to think I'm easy meat.'

'And you're not?' Tariq was looking at her quizzically. Almost confrontational, now, as he leaned in towards her.

What the hell did he mean by that? Sheila couldn't work it out. Had it been intended as an insult? She could feel his breath on her collarbone, he was so close. Beneath his leather jacket, the top three buttons of his black shirt were open. She caught sight of dark chest hair climbing its way up to his neck. The suggestion of a honed body beneath the tight-fitting fabric. The opposite of Conky.

The thrill of sexual anticipation welled up from somewhere deep within her. Perhaps, the natural conclusion to a day from hell. Sheila stroked Tariq's beard and leaned in to kiss him.

At first, he backed away, startled. 'What the hell are you doing?'

But she found herself grinning. Registered the spread of anticipation in her knickers. She took his hand into hers and placed it gently on her breast. Leaned in to kiss him again. The chemistry was incendiary. It felt as though the car and its aircon system were powered by the electricity that crackled invisibly between them. Their tongues intertwined. His hair felt luxuriant between her fingertips. Her touch wandered down to the exposed skin of his chest and on towards his abs. Through the shirt fabric, she sought out the happy trail that led along his naval down to his groin.

'Oh aye?! Here we go.' She ran her fingertips over the bulge in his jeans. 'Somebody's feeling a bit more chipper.'

Tariq broke away, frowning, as though he were surprised by what had come to pass. There was something reminiscent of a spooked deer in his eyes. He took her hand off his penis, placing it on her knee. 'We shouldn't be doing this. This is not what I came here for. My dad's out there somewhere. He could be lying dead in an alleyway. And I'm married. I'm not like . . .'

Desire, however, was already coursing around every vessel and along every synapse in Sheila's body. Whatever pheromones Tariq Khan was unwittingly discharging into the car's interior were doing their work. And they told a very different story to the one coming out of his shapely mouth. Sheila placed a finger coquettishly on his lips.

'Shhhh. It can be our secret.' She leaned in for another kiss, stroking the insides of his thighs.

He pushed her away again, blinking hard. Then the apparent confusion on his face seemed suddenly to subside, as though he had mulled a conundrum over and found a solution he could live with. 'Actually, I've separated from my missus.' Six words that seemed to absolve him from guilt.

'Well then.'

'But my dad . . .'

'Come on, Tariq. I know you can feel it. This chemistry.' Sheila peeled off her jacket and unbuttoned her blouse with hasty fingers. Unhooked her bra and allowed her breasts to fall free.

He reached over to touch her, caressing each bosom gently as though feeling his way along the curves of a valuable sculpture. Leaned over and took her nipple into his mouth, his tongue circling softly and with skill.

Needing this conquest, showing no such finesse, she undid his belt with anticipatory, fumbling fingers. Yanked his shirt open, busting the buttons to run her hands over that torso. The antithesis of men like Paddy and Conky. Here was a man who looked after himself. A dish Sheila couldn't wait to devour.

With some tricky manoeuvring, they managed to do what perhaps millions of clandestine lovers had done throughout the years. Clambered through to the back seat. Sheila mounted Tariq with little preamble, excited by the union and the prospect of straddling a well-proportioned cock that was unencumbered by an oversized gut. His fingers knew where to go as she rode him in that cramped space. She savoured the feel of his soft beard as she kissed him – no sandpapery five-o'clock shadow to take her skin off – and felt every cell in her body charged with erotic adventure as she gripped him inside her. Here Sheila O'Brien was, riding her enemy like a damned choo-choo train. It was the biggest turn-on of her life.

They screwed with urgency. Sheila's body convulsed with pleasure as she came; wave after wave of ecstasy washing away the residue of the day's disasters. She tried and failed to stifle a yelp. Felt Tariq buck upwards, grunting long and low. His eyes rolled back into his head. His eyebrows bunched together in desperate joy and loss of control as he thrust his last. The heat of his orgasm spreading inside her and the sheer delight in his expression made her come a second time. Her knees were wrecked and her knickers torn. It was messy. It was bloody fantastic.

'Jesus,' she said, panting. Climbing off. A ligament in her knee twinged, heralding a week of pain from an old running injury. Not that that mattered. It was a more than fair trade-off for such fun. She fell to the side, giggling. Breathless. 'That was incredible. I feel alive.'

With his erection starting to subside, Tariq wiped the sweat from his brow. Lolled on the back seat. Defeated. Smiling. 'I never would have thought in a million years . . .' He shook his head. Stroked the inside of her naked thigh as she pulled her bra back on.

She flinched. Pushed him away. 'Give over, will you! God, you've made bits of me ticklish that have never even been ticklish before.'

'Does that mean I've got the magic touch?' His fingers wandered upwards to her breasts. Further up, to stroke her cheek and smooth her hair away from her face. He stole a fleeting, tender kiss on the cheek that had more emotional intent to it than any of the sex. 'You're beautiful.'

Pleased that the shadows inside the car wouldn't allow him to see her blush, not wanting him to think that she was game for more than an opportunistic encounter, Sheila moved to the far side of the back seat. 'Let me get my clobber back on before somebody sees us and has us arrested.'

'That would make front page news.'

Like a pair of furtive teenagers, they dressed, knowing they might be caught at any moment, though every window in the car had steamed up.

'I've got to go,' Sheila said, sighing. 'My Mam's inside. She'll be wondering where I've got to.' She planted a passionate kiss on Tariq's mouth. Pushed him away when he tried to prolong the contact. 'Look. I hope you find your dad. I promise it wasn't me. If you like, I'll ask my people to keep an eye out for him. I'm sure he'll turn up.'

'Please god, he will,' Tariq said, all his relaxed demeanour gone now as he ran his index finger up and down the piping on the side of the driver's seat in front. He sighed. 'Can we do this again?'

Sheila thought about Conky with his flowers, his platitudes and his cloying over-protectiveness. She had exchanged a narcissistic monster for a psychopathic gentleman, and neither had hit the spot. 'Yeah. Why not?' She traced a line from Tariq's Adam's apple to his chest.

'We could join forces, me and you.' His eyes shone with earnest fervour. Thick lashes batting as he blinked. Flick, flick.

She laughed. 'Don't talk shit. We're enemies, remember?'

Tariq cleared his throat, fastening the cuffs of his shirt with precision. Frowning. 'We don't have to be that way, though, do we? Paddy's gone. Jonny's lost the plot. You're in trouble with Bancroft.'

'I am *not*.'

'Really? Okay. Whatever you say. Think of it, though! Twice the turf. Twice the money. Half the overheads. Pool our staff – because I bet you've got personnel shortages same as me, thanks to Paddy and Jonny's little dick-swinging competition.'

Feeling uncomfortable with the way this conversation was going, Sheila grabbed her handbag from the front seat. 'Give me a shout when you want to hook up again, Tariq.' She scribbled her phone number on a piece of paper. Pressed it into his shirt pocket. 'Seriously. Best of luck with your dad. Let me know how you get on.'

She opened the rear door to the Mercedes and shrieked when she saw Lev standing over her. Waiting. Eyebrow raised.

'Hiya, Sheila.' Lev's arms were folded over his parka. Was that a grimace on his face or the beginnings of a knowing grin?

'What the bloody hell are you doing, standing there like a weirdo?' she asked. She scrambled out of the car, glancing back at Tariq apprehensively. Faced Lev with her chin jutting in defiance. 'Are you stalking me?'

'I came looking for you to give you the latest on Mam, seeing as you're not picking up your calls and haven't even been to see her in hospital.' Lev ducked and stared blankly at Tariq, who was holding his shirt closed. 'Long time, no see, Tariq.'

Both men appeared to be wary of one another, Sheila noted.

'You've been missed, Lev,' Tariq said, climbing out of the back seat behind Sheila. Clearly dishevelled and with the remnants of an erection and a small dark stain visible even in that dim light on the crotch of his jeans.

Lev sniffed, his breath steaming on the air. 'What? By the Fish Man? Yeah, cos I'm really queuing up to get my throat cut by that mental dick.'

Tariq focused on his sneakers. 'I'm sorry about—'

'Forget it, man.' Lev sucked his teeth. 'Lots has changed since the spring.' He inclined his head towards Sheila. Winked. 'More than what I thought, anyhow.'

Feeling the blood chill in her veins, trapped between the man she had presumed to be her enemy and the man she had thought was in her debt, Sheila realised that during those few minutes she had spent in Tariq's car, covertly observed at some point during the proceedings by Lev, power had shifted away from her. *Shit. Not good, Sheila. Not good at all.*

'I'm going to go and see your Mam in the morning,' she told Lev. 'I felt rough, myself. It really shook me up. And I couldn't get out of this.' She jerked her thumb back towards the community centre. 'Anyway, how is she? Your Mam.'

Lev shrugged. 'She's alive. She's awake. She's driving everyone pissing mad. Same old, same old.'

'What do you want, then?'

Sizing her up through narrowed eyes, Lev treated her to a wry, calculating smile. 'I'll bob round tomorrow. We can have a chat.' He nodded at Tariq. Turned back to Sheila. 'Oh, and don't be expecting me at the weed farm.'

Here we bloody go. Mutiny. She could sense it with every fibre of her being. Like so many women before her, she had been undone by daring to satisfy her own basic needs and indulge her heart's desires.

'You what?' She took a step towards Lev, drawing herself up to her full height in those heels, though she still fell short of him by an inch or two. 'I need you. Bancroft's trying to bring us to our knees.'

'No, Sheila,' Lev said. 'He's trying to bring *you* to your knees.'

'Cheeky little shit! If I say, you're working at the farm, you're working at the farm.'

'I don't think so.' Lev buried his hands deeper into the pockets of his parka. He appeared larger than usual, with that fur hood stretched out behind his head. 'See you at the hospital in the morning.' Glanced at Tariq, then fixed her with hard eyes. 'Oh, and I saved Conky's life today. Give him my best.' He winked.

Chapter 24

Gloria

'Ooh, these are lovely! Are these for me?' Gloria ran her fingers over the grosgrain ribbon of the box, all wrapped up in gold paper. Felt the weight in her hand. Checked the label attached. 'Belgian. Yummy. I haven't been given nice chocolate in years. Thanks.'

Sizing up the visitor who was sitting on the edge of her hospital bed, she reasoned that the good Lord must be smiling on her at long last. Yesterday, she had been at death's door. Today, here was Bob: a well-presented man – her very own admirer – showering her with mid-priced Belgian chocolates and an only slightly poorly written and misspelled 'Get Well Soon' card.

'*Every good gift and every perfect gift is from above,*' she said quietly, contemplating the calorific value of the white chocolate ones. 'James 1:17.'

Bob leaned forward, taking her hand. Kissed her knuckles gently. 'My pleasure, cherie. It was the least I could do, seeing you were too poorly last night to make it to our lickle airport love-nest.'

Gloria looked up at Bob's orange face, wondering again why his skin was so very shiny and why his facial muscles didn't move when he smiled. The pastor's face crinkled up in a wholly pleasing way when that philandering false prophet smiled her way. Still. Where was the pastor when she was lying on her near-deathbed? Nowhere to be found. But this orange admirer was here, bearing gifts.

'How did you find out I was in here?' she asked. 'Did my son call you?'

'How about we go for a lovely pizza when you're back on your feet?' he asked. 'Round my way. I know this lovely lickle place on the way to Heywood. They do cracking meatballs too and the manager's a friend of mine. Always calls me signor when I go in. I get a sparkler in my tiramisu on my birthday. Cheaper than that Bramshott place. You'll love it!'

Lickle. The lickle was beginning to pall. At the speed-dating, Frank's house fizz had dulled her ears. In the not-near-the-airport airport hotel, she had been distracted by Bob's sexual advances. But now . . . And pizza? In Heywood? Was that the limit of his sophistication? A weekend millionaire, smoking cheap cigarillos in wine bars and eating spaghetti incorrectly in the only eatery in his small town that wasn't a chippy. *Everyone who is arrogant in heart is an abomination to the Lord, Gloria Bell*, she reminded herself.

'Sounds smashing. So did Lev call you?'

Bob picked up another of her 'Get Well' cards, studying the message inside; moving his lips as though he were absorbing the syllables one at a time. 'It must have been a nightmare. Fancy being in an explosion!' He set the card down. Picked up another, scanning it with similar undis-guised curiosity. 'It's like something out of a film. You're like a dusky Jason Bourne, aren't you?'

Dusky? Had he seriously called her dusky? *Be nice, Gloria.*

This is the first man in decades to show an interest in you. This is the new you. The fresh start. He polishes his shoes, so he must be decent! 'Ha. Jason Bourne wouldn't have ended up in Hope Hospital, miles from home.'

'And where is home?' he asked, resting the card on his lap.

Above the pain of her persistent headache and the strange sensation of her chest having been compressed beneath a great weight, some other gnawing sensation rang out in Gloria's body. She couldn't put a finger on it exactly, but it was something akin to wariness.

'I told you on the speed-dating and I told you at lunch,' she said. 'South Manchester.'

'The posh side of town, eh?' Bob chuckled, though his taut face refused to match the apparent amusement. 'Tell you what, why don't you give me your address? You can trust me. I won't stalk you. But I might send you something lovely to cheer you up, when you get out of here.'

'Oh! How considerate of you. What a gent!' Gloria looked up at the clock. Visiting time was coming to an end. Still no sign of Sheila or Lev, and she had had enough of her admirer's attentions. Wonderful though they were, they felt like too much white chocolate in one hit. She yawned dramatically. Closed her eyes. 'I'm feeling so sleepy.' More yawning. She let her head loll to the side, facing away from him. 'Such lovely chocolates. I bet the pralines are . . .' Closing her eyes tightly, she allowed her words to drift away.

He's bound to go in a minute, she thought. *Keep your eyes shut, Gloria. You don't want him to think you're a pushover. Leave him hankering for more.* The hard-headed cynic within her acknowledged that the reason she wanted him gone was his over-familiarity. It made her feel more than a little uncomfortable. Though it was nice. Very nice, to think that a man desired her in real life, rather than in the confines of her imagination. She was torn.

The bed rose as he stood. She heard him clear his throat. The squeak of hinges made her wonder if he was opening her bedside cabinet. There was a shuffling of papers and moving around of her personal effects, perhaps?

Gloria cleared her throat. Started to cough, though she kept her eyes steadfastly shut. The shuffling ceased and was followed by the sound of footsteps click-clacking away. Then more footsteps, growing closer. Coming towards the bed.

Opening her eyes, Gloria rolled over quickly, determining to confront him for rummaging through her things. But it wasn't her new beau who was standing over her bed.

'Sheila!' She started to cough violently, the sooty particles from the smoke rattling in her chest, as though she'd been on thirty a day for her entire adult life. 'At last!'

Her business partner pulled up a plastic chair beside the bed. Opened her camel coat to reveal a dress that was too short and tight for a woman of her years. All knees and thighs, as usual. Flung a Mulberry handbag onto the floor, pulling out some fashion magazines and dropping them onto the bed. 'Jesus, Gloria! You're acting like I buggered off on you for a month and left you like a dog in a manger. I brought you these.' She examined her nails. 'Anyway, I felt rough myself. Obviously. I did pass out, you know!'

Gloria pushed the magazines onto the floor. *Vogue* and *Cosmopolitan*, indeed! Eyeing the rosy glow in Sheila's cheeks, Gloria snorted with derision. 'You look like you've had a week on a health farm, you do. And here's me, coughing chunks up in a hospital bed in Salford – *Salford*, I ask you! Why on earth couldn't they have taken me to Wythenshawe?' She glanced over at the kidney dish full of blackened sputum. Grimaced.

'They had a bed for you here, I suppose. Or maybe it was nearer. I dunno. But you're getting the care you need.'

'I bet *you'd* have gone to the Alex in Cheadle. It's like a hotel there. Your own room and three course meals on tap.' Gloria couldn't quite keep the antagonism out of her voice, thinking of the gulf in personal circumstances that lay between them. She reminded herself that the good Lord wouldn't take kindly to coveting Sheila's private health care plan, however understandable it seemed under the circumstances. 'Anyway, how come you're all pink-cheeked and shiny-eyed?'

'Never mind that,' Sheila said, dropping her voice to a whisper, seemingly avoiding making eye contact with Gloria. 'Conky reckons the fire investigators have got my phone. If that's true and Ellis James gets hold of it, we're stuffed. I've got everything on there, proving every last shitty bit of business I conduct. Access to email. Texts connecting me to all sorts of people, including Bancroft. Phone logs to people-traffickers. Facebook messaging with wholesale coke suppliers. WhatsApp with Conky about beatings, dog fights, debt-collection, executions, stolen art. The lot!' She rubbed her face. 'What are we gonna do?'

'You mean, what are *you* going to do?'

Sheila picked up the magazines and slammed them back onto Gloria's lap. 'We're in this together. We've always been in this together. I know you think you're holier and godlier than me, and you're not wrong. You'll definitely get through the pearly gates before I ever do. But just remember who's on the receiving end of a good chunk of my texts and emails!'

Swallowing hard, Gloria swung her legs out of bed. 'We've got to get it back. Don't you have people on the inside?'

'Not in the fire service. No. Only the cops.'

'Won't they pass it onto the police?' Gloria could visualise the scene of her downfall now – standing in the dock with the other elders of the church looking on from the viewing gallery. All of them, judging and moralising. Aghast, as a magistrate or some such issued a harsh sentence. The pastor would turn his back on her for good, with Kitty Fried Chicken grinning smugly as her love rival was sent down. She would be an outcast. She would be reduced to even less than the Gloria of old, who had married a heart-breaking wastrel and who had lived a shameful life of the dirt-poor and blasphemous. Smoking and drinking in Sweeney Hall pubs. Taking her clothes off for money, which all went in The Wastrel's back pocket. Occasionally pleasuring men behind the bins at the back of the local cinema for twenty pounds here and twenty pounds there, when Leviticus needed nappies and The Wastrel wouldn't provide. No. It couldn't happen. 'You've *got* to get it back!'

Sheila patted her hand, exhaling heavily and closing her eyes, as if she realised the buck stopped with her. 'Don't worry. I'll see to it. Money talks, right? And everyone's got a price. There'll be a way.'

'What's your price, Sheila?'

The man's voice permeating the women's ward made Gloria jump. She looked up to see her son standing by the lavender curtain that afforded her some privacy from her immediate neighbour in the next bed.

'Leviticus,' she said. 'And my little Jay.'

Stretching out her arms, she encouraged the child to come to her, hoping to put on a grandmotherly show that might make Sheila envy something that money couldn't buy: her family, within arm's reach.

'Are your girls coming up for a visit, Sheila, to check you're all right?' She savoured the sight of Sheila's lean, heavily made-up features visibly sinking into an expression that was positively sullen.

'I told them not to bother. I'm fine.' Thinned lips said she was anything but fine. That rosy glow had subsided quickly.

Gloria beckoned her grandson to her, but Jay started to protest. He clung to Lev's hip, burying his head in his father's chest.

'His bandages are off,' she said, annoyed at the slight.

'I took them off last night,' Lev said. 'It was time. And it's also time I got full custody of him from that cow, Tiffany.' He looked at Sheila pointedly. 'All I need is some cash for a good solicitor and a place I can call my own that's not in some damp high-rise in Sweeney Hall where the lifts are always broken and stink of piss.'

Why was he looking at Sheila in that way? Gloria wondered. She could sense that something unspoken was passing between them as they glared at each other.

'So, come on, Sheila,' he said. 'What's your price?' His words seemed loaded.

'You've got a cheek,' Sheila said, picking up her oversized bag and holding it in front of her with whitened knuckles. 'I already pay the rent on you and your Mam's place.'

'But I'm not fifteen and I don't want to live with my Mam. And the only reason we're down the road from you, cooped up in a shitty, boring semi, is the Fish Man. And the only reason he's after *me* is because of the favour *I* did for *you*.' He was pointing. Gloria had never seen her son this riled since he had been a perpetually angry teen.

Sheila stood abruptly, rounding on Lev. 'You didn't do me no favours, you cheeky sod. You did a well-paid job for a good bleeding cause. You want a round of applause for earning your money?'

The nurses on the desk in the centre of the ward were beginning to watch this conflict unfolding. Exchanging knowing glances and whispering to one another. Nudging. Nodding.

'You're attracting attention to us!' Gloria said, whispering too loudly.

Sweeping the curtains around Gloria's bed defiantly shut, Sheila trapped them all inside the makeshift lavender cocoon. She reached past Jay and poked Lev hard in the shoulder with a manicured red fingernail.

'Ow,' he said.

'Don't you blackmail me, young man.' The ferocity in her voice and the lavender glow gave her a demonic air. 'Now, what the hell do you want?'

Lev kissed Jay on his blond curl-covered head. Held the child close so that their cheeks were pressed together. 'I want out.' He looked at the boy with undisguised love emanating from his every pore. 'And if I'm getting out, I need money to take Tiff to court. I need money to buy a little house in a nice place, far, far away from Manchester, where everyone will leave me alone.'

Gloria opened her mouth at the mention of his moving away. She was just about to protest when the sister of the ward whipped the curtain aside. Hers was a formidable presence in that dark blue uniform with that wide bottom that spoke of too many shifts sitting at the desk, eating the tubs of Roses that thankful relatives brought in. She wore a dour expression, exacerbated by a utilitarian haircut with a blunt fringe.

'Is everything all right in here?' The sister treated Gloria to an accusatory stare.

'Fine,' Gloria said. 'But you can shut that curtain, dear. We're having a family conference.'

Sheila wrenched the curtain from the disgruntled-looking sister and drew it brusquely, shutting her outside. 'Nosey bitch!'

'And while you're at it, tell the doctor I want discharging!' Gloria shouted through the fabric. She turned to her son. 'You're not moving anywhere, Leviticus. Not with my grandson.'

Lev sat on the end of the bed, allowing Jay to play with the remote control that manoeuvred the bed up and down. The boy started to press the buttons, giggling with glee as he threw Gloria into varying states of collapse; raised her by a foot or more, then dropped her back down abruptly.

'Control him, Leviticus! He's going to injure me. He's feral!'

'See? You're full of shit, Mam.' He grabbed the remote from Jay's chubby little hands. 'You don't give a monkey's flying arsehole about him or me. In fact, you didn't give a stuff about either of us until I came to you, asking for help.'

'That's not true.'

'What's his birthday then? Eh?' A pregnant silence permeated the space. 'See? You haven't got a clue. You're only ever interested in what's in it for you. Jay makes you a bit more popular at church, doesn't he?'

Gloria breathed in heavily and looked to Sheila for support. When none was forthcoming, she merely gathered the honeycomb blanket to her chin.

'And that's why I want out.' Lev grabbed at Sheila's slender wrist. Lowered his voice. 'I've done stuff that will stick with me forever. My boy deserves a better chance than I had.'

'Cheek!' Gloria yelped.

But Sheila was studying his face. Biting the inside of her cheek in a contemplative manner. 'Tell you what,' she whispered. 'Get my SIM card out of my phone for me and you've got a deal. I'll pay your legal fees. I'll give you a hundred thou in cash. It's dirty money, mind. How you get it clean so you can buy a house is your responsibility, not mine. But you get me the SIM card and you keep your gob bleeding well shut about what you've seen.' She nodded and winked. Raised an eyebrow.

'*Judas, would you betray the Son of Man with a kiss?*' Gloria said. 'Luke 22:48.'

'Shut it, Glo. You've got a car. You can drive to see him. I need that damned phone or we're all screwed.'

'Why can't Conky do your dirty work?' Gloria asked.

'No.' Sheila's lips thinned. 'This is a job for Lev. His last job. And he's got to do it tonight or the deal's off.'

Chapter 25

Youssuf

Swaying in the toilet cubicle of the coach, Youssuf had tried desperately to urinate but was annoyed to find he couldn't. Where was Tariq when he needed him? With a broken lock on the door and the facilities covered in the waste of other careless, selfish travellers, he couldn't even sit down. Tariq would have sorted something out for him.

'Pee, will you?!' Youssuf chided himself in Urdu.

There was a rap-rap on the door.

'Anyone in there?' The door was pushed ajar by several inches.

Turning around, Youssuf spied a young black man's inquisitive face through the crack. His hair was tucked into a knitted hat of the same style worn by that oik that had tried to abduct him.

He yelped, feeling the urine in his bladder turn to ice. 'Go away!' he shouted. He slammed the door shut in the intruder's face, realising with relief that it wasn't Dreadlocks from the car wash but just some hapless boy who happened to have a similar hat.

Darn it. Now he really couldn't pee! It was no use.

Unsuccessful and with a stabbing pain in his bladder

that didn't bode well for the rest of the journey, he returned to his seat. The feeling of unease was intense, though he didn't spot any obviously hostile faces among his bored-looking fellow travellers. The woman that clutched at a squalling, snotty baby at his side flashed him a look of utter hatred when he asked to access his place by the window.

'So sorry,' he said.

'It's fine.' Her thin-lipped half-smile told another story.

By now, as the flat plains of Cheshire gave way to the furred arteries of Birmingham's industrial heartland, Youssuf could only worry that he had forgotten his medication. With nobody to pack his bag for him, he had been at a loss to remember the sort of things one might take on a long journey. Nothing to read. No change of pants. And with the food he had snaffled from Anjum's Tupperware stash of pre-cooked nibbles in the fridge already eaten by the time they had pulled onto the M60, not a single thing left to eat. He still wrestled with a queasy feeling that somehow, he was being observed, though he'd already spent two nights at an old friend's in Levenshulme to allow his trail to go cold. *Stop it, you old fool. There's nobody there. Just normal people on a coach like you.*

'You visiting family?' the woman asked once the baby had finally passed out with its red-cheeked head on her bosom.

'Sightseeing,' Youssuf said.

'Oh yeah? Where are you planning on going, then?' the young mother asked. She stroked the fluff of her baby's golden hair.

'Buckingham palace. Changing of the guard.' Youssuf panned for a nugget or two of tourist gold among the dust of his many memories. He happened upon the recollection of him and Saffiya, having taken Tariq and their two younger daughters, Zeeba and Aisha, to London in the late 1970s. A quicksilver sliver of a memory that tried to wriggle away from him like a glittering anchovy in the fast-disintegrating bait-ball of his past. It was one of the only times he could recall when they had all been together. 'A musical. I'm going to see a musical.'

'Nice. Which one?'

'*Jesus Christ, Superstar*,' he said, enjoying the obvious and flagrant fib.

The miles passed by slowly with burgeoning queues of traffic and diesel stink from the juggernauts that flanked the coach on all sides. By the time he reached Victoria, Youssuf's body had almost moulded itself into the shape of his seat. He could no longer feel anything below the waist and the lurching motion of the coach, as it had woven its way through central London in rush-hour, had left him feeling beyond nauseous.

Jostled on all sides by Londoners and bewildered tourists barging their way across the busy concourse at Victoria station, Youssuf found himself careening away from the Underground sign he had planned to make for. No idea where the toilets might be.

Anxiety sent a blur of colours and abstract lines whizzing around him in go-faster stripes made from people and neon signs. He glimpsed Tariq's kindly, patient face everywhere and nowhere in every dark-skinned, black-haired man. The pressure in his bladder had gone beyond simple discomfort now. Tariq. He needed Tariq. But his boy was not in that unfamiliar, hostile place full of impatient strangers, hurrying hither and thither, always looking down at their feet or up at the giant electronic timetable, never looking at one another. Youssuf was alone.

Taking slow, deep breaths, he spotted the toilets; reminded

himself that he was not a lost, defenceless child but a grown adult with a reasonable bill of health for a man with his dubious medical history.

The relief at being able to pee in a cubicle that was locked and unmoving was intense.

'Colin Chang,' he said in the mirror as he washed his hands among travelling businessmen and Spanish backpackers. He remembered the point of his mission: salvation beckoned.

The Underground network ran at too fast a pace for Youssuf. He struggled to negotiate the ticket turnstiles, finding himself trapped on the wrong side of the unyielding gates with a queue of impatient passengers stacking up behind him.

'Come on, old man!' he heard some youth say.

Youssuf turned around, ready to give the youngster what-for with a shake of his walking stick but baulked when he spotted a tall man with dreadlocks and terrible acne scarring, some hundred yards away at the mouth of the large, subterranean concourse. He was making straight for him.

Calm down, you old duffer. Youssuf jabbed his ticket into the machine yet again, praying it would be accepted this time. It was spat out the other end. The gates remained shut. He chanced another look round at the dreadlocked man, willing himself to accept that it was just a coincidence that the bowels of London contained a man who simply looked similar to his attacker. *It's just that the lad from the coach has followed you down here.*

But it wasn't. They locked eyes. Youssuf realised this time that it *was* the dreadlocked black man that had tried to kidnap him. His instincts had been correct.

'Let me through!' he shouted to the attendant. 'Quickly!'

Barrelling past the disgruntled passengers, pushing them out of the way with his stick if they wouldn't yield, Youssuf shuffled in his sandals at some pace towards the wide gates that allowed access for those bearing bulky luggage and pushchairs. His attacker was gaining on him.

'Hurry!' he told the attendant. Should he ask for help? But then he would have some explaining to do to the police and he wasn't ready yet. He had to give this fellow the slip somehow. 'I'm late!'

Finally, he was through. He squashed himself in through the bottleneck of people at the top of the escalator. Realised, when he saw the vertiginous drop, that he would never be able to trot down the left side of the steep moving stairs with his stiff old legs. He clung to the rubber banister on his right, peering upwards. There he was! Dreadlocks was scanning the ranks of people descending to the Victoria Line. Starting to make his way down. Youssuf kept his head down. He'd have to think fast.

'Oi!' his pursuer shouted. 'Khan!'

Chapter 26

Lev

Lev pulled the black tracksuit bottoms and polo neck on. The balaclava was tight and itchy but did the job. He would have to stuff that into his parka pocket on the way there. And he'd have to leave the coat in a bush somewhere until after the job was done. It was too bulky for a task that demanded stealth.

Looking in the mirror, he puffed air out through his cheeks. Rolled the balaclava back up so it was perched on his head like a black, knitted johnny. *What a tool.*

'Come on. Do it for the boy.'

Except there was still the issue of what to do with a sleeping toddler at 3 a.m.

With his mother still in hospital, Lev realised with some regret that he didn't have a soul in the world he could rely on. He had begged Sheila O'Brien to take Jay, but had been met with a frosty, 'What do you think my house is? A bloody crèche?'

Even with his new-found knowledge of her liaison with Tariq, Sheila had cunningly manoeuvred him into a position where he would be in her debt. Yet again. Everyone had a sodding price tag, including him. Now, he was faced with a tough choice: decline to do the job and miss out on the money to buy a new life for him and Jay, or plonk his precious son onto his skank of a babymother with whom he was at war. *Some damned choice!*

'Jay-Jay!' he said in soft, sing-song tones. 'Come on, Jay. It's a new day. Time to get up! Time to get up!' An instruction dressed up as a gentle homespun nursery rhyme.

The boy's eyes fluttered open. A smile, followed by a piercing shriek as Jay caught sight of the strange black headgear. Flashbacks to when he had cried incessantly during his illness. Lev shuddered at the memory of being stuck in a godforsaken A&E side room with a dying child, screaming so much he had vomited himself dry.

'Come on, lad,' he said, smoothing the skin on Jay's velvety forehead. 'Just a bit longer and you and your old dad will be home and dry.'

The taxi sped off into the black of night. This was not the sort of place where the mainly Asian drivers liked to hang around, even during daylight hours. Too many pissheads ready to stagger up to the driver's side window, leaning in and telling them to get back to wherever they came from, with booze-fume breath that could take out an elephant. Now, as they stood by the kerbside, Lev's lifeline was reduced to two red pinpricks in the distance, disappearing round a corner towards Cheetham Hill, leaving the two of them stranded.

'Mam!' Jay said, pointing up at the double-height block of maisonettes. 'Mam, mam, mam!'

This particular corner of the Sweeney Hall estate had been thrown up in the late seventies. Long Battenberg-slabs of dwellings, sandwiched one on top of the other, above a row of garages that were now all burnt out, kicked in or had been sealed off by the coppers after some nefarious drama had played out in the shadows. Two or three security lights sputtered over the open brick stairwell and the odd one still shone on the galleried landing.

Above where Lev now stood, clutching Jay to his chest, only one or two lights shone in the windows of the maisonettes on the upper level. The dull thud of drum and bass told him it was more likely to be a dealer's pad than the sign of some hospital porter just returned home.

Ascending the stairwell, Lev knew he was on Boddlington turf. Clutching Jay's head beneath his chin with a protective hand, he held his breath as he rounded a corner on the piss-soaked stairs, his synapses flaring with anticipation.

Above him on the next flight, there was a pungent stink of marijuana and the glow of a spliff being inhaled. Footsteps as the smoker came down to meet him.

'Wanna buy some gear?'

Lev sized the lanky kid up in his flashy designer streetwear. Assessed him to be no more than fourteen. Fifteen, at a push, with high-top clad feet that seemed too large for such a puny body.

'Get out the way, son.' He pushed the boy aside, letting him hear from his disparaging tone that he didn't have time for playing soldiers on the stairs.

But the boy was all ganja-gobshite, getting up in his grill. Poking. Gesticulating. All, 'Who d'you think you pushing, you fucking knob? This be my staircase, innit?'

The young dealer reached inside his puffa.

Lev grabbed the dealer's scrawny hand inside his own, squeezing hard, forcing the kid to drop the semi-automatic pistol he'd started to withdraw. He kicked the piece through a sizeable hole at the base of the stairwell's wall where floodwater was designed to run during heavy rains.

'Ow! You broke me hand! You bastard.' The dealer was doubled up.

Lev grabbed him by the collar. Stared into his washed-out face. Smelled the weed on his breath. 'Know who I am?' He pulled the hood of his parka down to reveal the lightning bolt, shaved into his buzz cut.

The boy merely shot him a pained look as Lev released him.

Lev continued on his climb, grinding the spliff out beneath his foot on the damp brick step. 'That's right. So, show some fucking respect or I'll have to give Tariq a call. Dozy little twat.'

Leaving the Boddlington pretender behind to lick his wounds, he arrived at the door to Tiffany's mother's place. It was unlocked, as usual. A light was on in the kitchen. From his vantage point in the dark, he could see Tiffany, sitting at the kitchen table, chugging on a can of lager. Her mother was stood at the stove, frying chips with a cigarette hanging out of the corner of her pruned mouth. Even at 3 a.m., here was a side to the city that never slept.

'It's only me,' Lev shouted from the hall. The smells of cigarette smoke, beer and stale lard curled out from the kitchen to greet him immediately.

'You've got a cheek,' Tiffany said, not moving from where she sat. She lit a cigarette and blew the smoke towards Lev. Failing to look at her child, as if he were merely a figment of Lev's imagination. 'What the hell do you want? You said you'd see me in court!'

'Mam! Mam!' Jay held his arms out, straining to reach his mother. Saw the lack of response in her eyes and instinctively turned towards the older woman. 'Nanananana!'

'Does our Jay-Jay want a plate of chips off his nana?' Maria asked, smiling with her eyes as she dragged on her

L&B. Seemingly oblivious to the war of attrition that raged between her daughter and her grandson's babyfather.

Lev eyed the half-empty bottle of Scotch among the culinary detritus on the worktop and realised why. *This is a mistake. Just leave. You can't let these stupid, pissed-up cows look after baby Jay.*

His common sense told him to backtrack, but, as ever, the prospect of a better future loomed large like the first grey light of dawn on an otherwise dark horizon. A future not eked out in some damp, council shithole like this.

'I need you to watch him for an hour,' he told Maria, turning his back on the once bodacious but now emaciated frame of Tiffany. 'Just an hour, and I'll be back. I've got work to do and there's nowhere else. My mam's in dock. It's a long story. Can you take him?' He spoke fast, knowing his desperation would be audible, even to a brain-dead old boozer like Maria. At least Maria could hold her drink.

He glanced back at the staircase, noting that Tiffany still hadn't asked her mother to install stair-gates. The social worker would have a field day when he fed that little nugget back.

'Not a problem, Lev, cocker.' Maria started to coo and fuss over Jay. 'Give this lovely baby boy to his nana.'

'You're a cheeky bastard!' Tiffany said, standing abruptly and scraping her chair on the vinyl tiles.

'Take no notice of her!' Maria said, winking at Lev; abandoning her chip pan to blow a raspberry on Jay's stomach. She was rewarded by a squeal of delight.

'Ta.' *It's fine. It's an hour. Get in. Get the phone. Get back. He can survive an hour.*

Taking a kitchen chair, Lev placed it at the foot of the stairs. 'Keep an eye on him. Don't let him past the stairs and keep the front door locked!'

He released the latch and pulled the door behind him, praying he was doing the right thing.

The fire station where the call to the firebombed builders' merchants had come from was a short black cab journey away. Twenty minutes, tops, across the border from Boddlington turf into the O'Brien heartlands. Lev was careful to have the cabbie drop him two streets away in front of an anonymous-looking 1930s house in a side street, away from the main road.

Would the fire station be occupied? He had got Sheila's computer-student whizz to take time out of developing her world-class online-dating site to hack into the local council's town planning office. For a nerdy little shite like that, sourcing the fire station's blueprints had been child's play. More to the point, Lev had been able to work out that the secure room containing the evidence locker was upstairs, at the back of the building.

With the fire station in sight – the sole source of light in an otherwise still-slumbering area – Lev took the burner out of his parka. Dialled 999 and asked for the fire service. Gave the details of a blaze two miles away. Hung up, when the operator asked for his name.

It was a gamble.

His heart bounced inside his chest like a ball being slammed against a wall. The probability that his little plan would backfire was high. Wasn't there another fire station on the far side of this postcode?

'Please let this work, for God's sake!' He looked up into the velvet blackness of a fine, cold night's sky, wondering that the stars glittered like diamonds above this run-down area of south Manchester just as they glittered above the legends of Hollywood or the Himalayas or the pyramids and their eternally sleeping royalty entombed within. 'Please God!' He intoned to his mother's sweet Jesus – a god he wasn't sure about at all.

The solitary light that shone in the first floor of the station spread throughout the building. The giant doors to the garaging lifted to reveal the big red trucks. Lights flashing. Men in their full regalia, clambering aboard. No sirens at 3.30 a.m., but the trucks pulled away and roared up the hill into the distance.

Now, Lev had his chance.

Leaving his parka in the bushes, he jogged over to the fire station with his balaclava pulled down over his head. Skulking in the shadows. It was likely there were some staff members left behind.

I can't believe I'm doing this. I must be mad. If I get copped, I'm going away.

Lev crept around to the rear, looking for a way into the building. He spied the giant wheelie bins against the back wall. Felt for the crowbar he had stashed in his waistband. *You can do this, man. Think of getting that skank out of Jay's life for good and getting as far away from the O'Briens and the Boddlington bullshit as you can. Fresh start. Do it for the boy.*

Pulling himself onto the wheelie bins was easy. Back here, he surely couldn't be seen. There was a high-rise block some three hundred yards away, but just beyond the fire station fence, there was only a poorly lit car park. Above the bin was a small obscured-glazed window. Almost certainly a toilet. Producing the crowbar, Lev levered the old wooden frame open enough to slide his gloved fingers inside and lift the latch. Glad of his brutal regime at the gym, he pulled himself up and through the small aperture with relative ease. Dropped down, as expected, onto a cistern that

220

smelled of freezing cold, backed-up shit from lacklustre plumbing and possibly a trace of cheeky cigarette smoke.

Outside of the cubicle, Lev could hear a television playing low. He peered cautiously through a crack in the door. Heard the sound of whistling and the clanking of cups. A tap running. Whoever had been left behind was washing up. Good.

Lev visualised the blueprints. Found his bearings. Padded off to his left. Tugging the irritating balaclava eyeholes to the side, he looked up at a door, expecting to see a sign for evidence. But the locked room was not there. It was merely a store.

Wrong direction, silly arse. You're remembering the plans back to front!

Retreating in near silence, hardly daring to breathe, he bore right. Found himself in full view of the person in the main area – an older man, thankfully with his back to Lev. He was indeed washing up, now singing some old 80s song at full tilt. *Shit.* Lev froze. Despite willing his feet to move, he found himself rooted to the spot, just staring at the back of this man who might turn around at any moment, spot him and blow the whistle.

Move it, you tit. You're no use to Jay-Jay in Strangeways.

Slinking along the wall and back out of sight, Lev finally found the door he sought. Tried the handle. It was locked. He took two specialist picks from the pocket of his jogging bottoms – tools of the trade that he'd borrowed from one of the lads who worked in the cannabis farm with him – and inserted them into the lock. Sweat was seeping from every pore in his face into the itchy acrylic of the balaclava. He willed his hands not to tremble.

The clanking in the kitchen had stopped. Lev held his breath as something inside the lock's mechanism gave way and clicked. He turned the handle. Good. He let himself inside, pushing the door to behind him. Took out a pocket torch. Shone it onto the shelves. *Quickly, for god's sake! Before they all come back.* Looking for something that might be labelled *O'Brien Construction* or *O'Brien Builders' Merchants.*

The evidence seemed to be arranged in date order. Lev looked for the date on which the firebombing had taken place. Found a Perspex box, labelled with the details he sought. Bingo. Opened the box, praying he would find the phone. *Please be there. Please, god. Please.*

But there were only the fragmentary remnants of a home-made explosive by the looks of it. Some wires. That was it. No phone.

'Hey! Who the hell are you?'

The light went on, rendering Lev momentarily blind. Holding his hand before his eyes, he could make out the old guy from the kitchen. Adrenalin took over. Lev pulled the crowbar from his trousers, brandishing it before the man.

The man screamed. Calling for help. He backed out of the doorway with his hand aloft.

'Don't hurt me!'

Catching sight in his peripheral vision of the fast getaway he so needed, Lev elbowed the man aside and sprinted to the fireman's pole. Dropping the crowbar, he grabbed it, wrapping his legs around it and slid to the bottom.

'Come back here, you bastard!' the man shouted after him.

But Lev was fast. He sprinted across the unattended garaging, out of the fire station lights and away into the darkness. Only once the adrenalin had subsided did he realise with a heavy heart that he would not be receiving a penny of this mission's handsome pay.

When he eventually made it back to the Sweeney Hall maisonette, strutting in his parka as though he had merely been for a stroll, it was already 4.45 a.m. The suggestion of the sun coming up brightened the sky. But when Lev reached the door to Tiffany's mother's place, he was alarmed to find it ajar.

'Jesus! What did I say about leaving the frigging door open?'

With a thundering heart and a throbbing head, wondering if his infant son might be lying dead at the bottom of the stairwell at the far end of the block, Lev pushed the door open.

'Maria? Maria! Jay! Tiff!'

No sign of Maria.

Striding through to the living room, however, he frowned at the scene that lay before him. Tiffany was sitting in the middle of the floor with a screaming Jay.

'Me Mam went to the offy for fags,' was all she said.

Lev ran to his son, lifting him from the carpet.

'What the bloody hell is going on? Why's he crying? He stinks of shit. Didn't you change him, you lazy bitch?'

His attention was drawn to the glowing embers of a cigarette in the ashtray beside Tiffany, who merely contorted herself into the lotus position and started toying with her lank hair with her left hand.

Jay was screaming, clutching at his arm. Tiffany held a cigarette butt. Click.

Holding his son's arm out, Lev spied the red welt on Jay's delicate skin. Speechless. Nauseous. Angry. Questioning. Crippled by guilt. There was not enough oxygen in that squalid lounge to service the array of emotions that coursed through Lev's tired body.

He reached out to hit Tiffany. His hand was stayed only

by a swift calculation that Jay would remember his father hitting his mother. Not good. Tiffany must have sensed his reticence. She backed away, scrambling to her feet.

'Aw, look at what you just did to Jay-Jay's arm,' she cooed. Clearly pissed and stoned, but the clarity of thought was there, all right.

'What do you mean, what *I* just did? I didn't do nowt! I've not been here, have I? *You* burned him, you evil cow!'

'Ah, the social worker and my solicitor are going to love it when I tell them what Jay's mean Daddy did to him with a ciggy.'

'You stone-cold bitch. You wouldn't!'

'Who wouldn't? Fucking watch me!'

Chapter 27

Conky

'I know it's here somewhere,' he muttered to himself. Conky grunted as he sifted through the rain-sodden wreckage of the builders' merchants yet again. His head still throbbed from where he had been knocked to the ground in Frank's club. His heart ached, succumbing as it was to Sheila's worsening frost. But mainly it was his back and legs that were giving him tremendous grief that morning. 'Keep looking, Degsy! Maybe it's been knocked under a pile of wood. It looks like a doll's house has been smashed to smithereens with a wrecking ball, so it does.'

Degsy stood in the freezing downpour, water dripping from the end of that nose that looked too big for his gaunt junkie's face. Hand on hip. 'Come on, man! You taking the piss? In this bleeding weather!'

With the standing water seeping upwards into his black tailored trousers, making the hems cold and heavy, Conky took large strides over to his acolyte. He grabbed Degsy by the neck.

'Are you questioning my authority, Derek? Is your fecking head cut?' With his left hand, he pushed his Ray-Bans onto his forehead. They were a pain in the arse in any case in this torrential downpour. All drippy and steamed up.

Staring steadfastly at his cheek, rather than his bulging thyroid eyes, Degsy's reddening face was a picture of contrition. Conky released his grip, leaving the fool to run exploratory fingers over the places where it would later bruise. 'Sorry, Conks.' The rain had flattened his greasy hair, showing the threat of a bald pate within the next couple of years.

Conky thought of his own artfully constructed hair-confection and felt a degree of sympathy at the sight of Degsy's pink scalp. He softened his voice. Patted the eejit on the sodden shoulder awkwardly. 'I need you to hoak through this mess again! My piece has to be here somewhere. I know I dropped it. We can't afford for the kids from the local estate to be pissing about with a loaded SIG Sauer. And if the peelers find it . . .'

As Conky bent over, poking at the flotsam and jetsam left behind by the firebomb with a length of timber, he screwed his eyes shut, trying to push the pain away. Should have got the head injury checked out, really. But had it not been for Degsy and Lev Bell stepping in at an opportune moment with a pump-action shotgun and an Uzi, Conky realised he would have left M1 House in a body bag – of that, he was certain. Perhaps the Loss Adjuster was losing his edge.

'What's the next move on the Brummies?' Degsy shouted from the other side of the wreckage, as if reading his thoughts.

Straightening himself up with an unpleasant cracking sound in his lower back, Conky belched quietly. 'I don't know. I need to speak to Sheila but she's in and out at the moment, choosing city-centre premises for her and Gloria.

And I've spent hours and hours pissing about with insurers for this shit-tip.'

What he didn't want to admit to Degsy was that the O'Briens were faced with a run on reliable staff that would make any attempt at open war a suicide mission.

Stepping into a boomerang of soggy dog shit, he cursed aloud. 'I don't believe this. I bet Genghis Khan never trod in shite in his new Italian loafers. Two hundred quid these cost me in Selfridges.' He examined the ruined soles. Felt the runny solution seep through the stitching to his socks. 'God give me strength.' He looked up at the leaden sky that rained without respite as though a disgruntled God was squeezing out a celestial sponge full of scummy water from the earth's dirty washing. Sighing, he considered how poor a career choice being a gun for hire at his age had turned out to be. As a cocky young man, he had thought he'd be retired to the Costa del Sol or the South of France by now. Not picking through the wreckage of somebody else's life in the rain, with lumbago, aching legs and a shitty shoe.

'Conks! Over here, man! I've only gone and found it.'

Degsy sounded jubilant. Held a large black object in the air. Aimed it playfully at Conky.

'Thank fuck for that,' Conky said, catching Degsy on the jaw with the sights as he snatched the handgun from him. 'Never point a loaded gun at a man, even in jest, you wee bollocks.'

Conky stuck his index finger through the trigger guard and allowed the gun to hang only inches from his face. Squatted amid the mayhem, finally exhaling heavily with relief. Allowed himself a satisfied smile. 'Hello, darling. Daddy's missed you.'

He was just about to check the magazine of bullets was unsullied, when he noticed Degsy's face fall.

'Mr McFadden. How good of you to drop by. Is that for me?'

Standing, he turned around to see Ellis James behind him, hand held out expectantly. *Shit, shit, shit. How could I have been so stupid?* His headache suddenly changed up a gear, feeling like his skull was being gripped inside a vice.

'What? This?' He held the gun out to the dog-eared detective. Chuckled nervously. *Come on. You're the bloody Loss Adjuster for Christ's sakes. Think, man! Think!* 'Aye. Take it. Young Derek and I were just assessing the damage, weren't we, Derek?' He looked to Degsy for a nod of approval. 'You know, in a shitey area like this, you can expect all sorts of skulduggery going on after dark, so you can. So, we thought we'd better come over and check for signs of drug misuse and illicit love trysts in the wreckage. And lo and behold, I'm having a wee shufty for one of Mrs O'Brien's earrings, which she lost in the explosion, and I find this bad boy. Who'da thunk it, eh?' He slid his Ray-Bans over his eyes, the fogged, wet lenses making his nose tickle like he was going to sneeze. Ensuring he wiped the prints surreptitiously with his leather gloves, he pushed the gun into James's hands, as though he were himself allergic to it. 'Foul things, aren't they? And the USA wonders why it has over twenty thousand deaths per year from firearms.' He shuddered for effect.

But Ellis James's stony expression did not soften one iota. He took out his cuffs. Read Conky his rights.

'What on earth are you arresting me for, Mr James?' Jesus. This was not a turn he had expected the day to take, given he had already woken next to an empty space instead of Sheila's warm, comely body – surely a zenith of crap in itself, worthy of the worst of days.

'Do I really need to explain the illegalities of being copped with an unregistered firearm in your possession, Mr McFadden?'

With his arms yanked painfully behind his back, Conky marched glumly to the detective's car. Today, it smelled of Stilton that had passed its best and cheap antiperspirant, masking the musky tang of athlete's foot and neglected BO.

'Good God, man! Didn't they teach you at school that cleanliness is next to godliness?'

'I'm not a religious man, Mr McFadden, and you smell rather like dog shit to me.'

Peering through the foggy rear windscreen of Ellis James's car, Conky watched Degsy's dumbfounded face disappear into the distance, until his head was just a pink blob atop an ill-considered lime green tracksuit.

'What are you hoping to get out of me?' Conky asked. 'I demand to speak to my solicitor! You've placed me under unlawful arrest. You haven't got a shred of hard evidence, tying me to some gun that was clearly dropped in among the wreckage by some local 50 Cent wannabe hardnut. Young Derek and I found used condoms! The place has been a convenient stage set for a modern recreation of Sodom and Gomorrah, so it has. Kids will be kids.'

'On the contrary, Conky,' James said, eyeing him through the rear-view mirror, 'I've got an impressive array of evidence and witness statements against Mrs O'Brien and her minions – and that includes you, big boy . . .' He winked. 'Enough to launch a lovely new investigation. And this time, the good guys *will* win. No wriggling out of what I've got.'

'Fancy yourself as some sort of James Bond figure, do you, detective? Stalking a respectable woman for weeks on end outside her own house? Building your pathetic wee case file? Your investigation will almost certainly fall to bits like that cheap shirt you're wearing once Mrs O'Brien's solicitors get a hold of whatever cock and bull prejudicial hearsay you've come across.'

'You sound very confident for a man who hasn't got a damned clue what he's up against. In fact, you're nothing but a big, clueless Northern Irish twat, Conky McFadden.'

'I beg your pardon! That's racist!'

'Where's Sheila O'Brien right now? C'mon, Conky. You can tell me. Where's the luscious Mrs O'B?'

'Choosing new office space for her cleaning company. And then, I believe there might be an appointment at the hairdresser's. I'm lucky enough to be accompanying her to a charity function tonight. And I'll thank you to refer to her with a little respect.'

'Oh, yeah?' Ellis James nodded. Pulled off the slip road for the turn-off that led to the Greater Manchester Police HQ. 'And where does Tariq Khan fit into her hectic schedule? Eh?'

Conky frowned. Processing that which was implicit. Tariq Khan. And Sheila? 'I don't understand.'

Another wink in the rear-view mirror as he nosed the car out of a line of traffic. Cocky wee bastard. 'You're not the only one with guns, Conky. Have you seen Tariq Khan's? His are brown. Not in bad shape for a man in his forties. And that Oxbridge-educated accent too. No wonder Sheila finds him irresistible.'

Leaning forward, suppressing the urge to nut the impertinent fecker from behind, Conky willed himself to breathe. *Don't rise to his bait. Whatever he's suggesting . . . it must be a misunderstanding or a bullshit concoction designed to get you to talk.* 'You wouldn't be trying the old divide and rule tactic on me, would you, detective? Because I think you'll find I'm too old and wise to fall for such rudimentary child psychology.'

'Inseparable. That's the word I'd use. I'd say they looked inseparable when I clocked them checking into a furnished apartment at the back of Piccadilly Station. All very sneaky. But I can report that they were holding hands.' James was assessing him with those cold blue eyes.

Turn the tables on the bastard. He's just playing you. It's nonsense. 'I've been reading an interesting book called *The Mandibles*,' Conky said, gazing out of the window at some rain-soaked trading estate that whizzed by. Trying to appear too cool for school and blithely disinterested in this non-gossip. 'It's about how a leading nation can fall apart when there's a shortage of something – money, gold . . . confidence in the dollar. You get a run on anything, suddenly you end up with anarchy.' He considered the shortage of trustworthy muscle sending the relative peace in Manchester spiralling into yet more turmoil. He raised an eyebrow, keeping his concerns to himself. 'What happens when you good guys have rounded up all the bad guys, detective? Do you think that's even possible? In the book I'm reading at the moment, the dollar is replaced by currency called the bancor. People find a way to trade. People come up with solutions to drought and shortage. Do you think if you expunge all illicit activity and all aspiring emperors from within this damp little basin, surrounded by its seven magnificent hills, that the city will hold together?'

'Shut it, McFadden. You lot are going down for good.'

'The streets will run red, Mr James. You deny free citizens

of their recreational pursuits and poison of choice, there will be anarchy. A shortage of that which is in demand will usher in the end of days. You're only expediting your own demise and the death of this great city. A city of twenty-four-hour party people.'

'Are you threatening me, you windbag?'

Conky grinned enigmatically, though his heart was slowly breaking. Could it be true? Sheila and Tariq? No. He didn't believe it. Perhaps they had met to discuss the threat of Bancroft. That was infinitely more plausible. And now, as James's car was pulling up in front of GMP HQ, he was faced by an even worse predicament.

'I want my phone call,' he said. If he dialled Sheila's number, would he catch her breathless and excited in the midst of a tryst with that Boddlington bastard?

'All in good time.'

Inside, he was faced with the indignity of being booked in amongst a gaggle of wet-behind-the-ears lads, done for shoplifting in Ashton shopping centre. They stank of too much cheap deodorant and stale clothes. Trying too hard to impress the little slags who bunked school to trail in their wake, hoping for a handout of some cheap jewellery or fake Uggs. Their noise was drowned out by the lurid slurring of some old boozers who had been caught pissing in a bus shelter near to a nursery school, by all accounts. The drunks, god bless them, seemed harmless enough.

'Jesus, look at this 'un, Jimmy. Roy Orbison.' One of them swayed to and fro as his fingerprints were taken, pointing with his filthy free hand at Conky. He looked seventy, though he could have been as young as fifty. The booze had not been kind. 'He's got a neb on him like a pissing anteater.'

Conky smiled. 'That's right, sir. God was generous in the nose department with my family. You know what they say about men with big noses.' He wrinkled his nose, causing his Ray-Bans to shimmy halfway down.

The drunken feckers started talking about the craic and the hard stuff. The same tropes Conky had heard a million times before. Calling him big feller, like the second-generation pseuds they were. But they provided a welcome foil for the anxiety that was building up inside him, gathering pace like an avalanche that would consume him entirely if he wasn't careful. He hated getting arrested. The bird he had done with Paddy O'Brien was enough to last him a lifetime. Day after day, cooped up in a confined space with somebody else's farts and opinions. Trapped: his imagination the only space where he was truly free to roam. An hour a day of walking around the yard in the drizzle didn't count. Within the confines of his handcuffs, Conky clenched his fists repeatedly, digging his nails into his palms until it hurt. *Control yourself. Channel Genghis. Give these bastards in here the cold face, Temujin.*

'Okay. Make your call,' Ellis James finally said, treating Conky to a full-on yellow-toothed smile that put Conky in mind of his father's dentures, grinning overnight from the jam jar on the corner of the bath. The shabby little prick even raised his arm to slap Conky on the back, but seemed to think better of it when Conky growled at him.

Ringing, ringing. Six rings in, and Sheila still hadn't picked up. The sensation of his heart collapsing in on itself like an imploding star made Conky feel like someone had punctured the battery that fuelled his soul, draining him until he was flat. Devoid of any light or sparkle. Powerless.

'Hiya. It's Sheila. I'm busy. Leave a message!'

He opened his mouth to answer the jaunty voice on the end of the phone, but realised it was merely her voicemail recording. Sheila O'Brien was otherwise engaged – he shuddered to ponder how – and Conky didn't want to waste his call.

Who else was there? Paddy was dead. Degsy was a pillock of the highest order and not to be trusted. Gloria was laid up. Lev . . . He still wasn't sure about Lev. His only remaining options were Frank or Katrina. The idiot savant or Sister Benedicta. He hadn't spoken to Katrina since Paddy's funeral. For someone who had been all over the biblical scenes of family grief like a paschal outbreak of boils, she had been strangely quiet ever since. In fact, judging by Sheila's sour expression whenever Katrina was mentioned in conversation, he suspected the two women had engaged in some kind of territorial conflict. An O'Brien women's pissing competition. But still. Katrina was a grown-up where Frank would tremble like jelly at a kids' party if tasked with the responsibility of instructing the solicitor.

The phone connected, with a well-meaning Irishwoman on the other end.

'Holy Trinity Nursing Home, can I help you?' The sound of companionable laughter in the background and a dementia-stricken resident wailing in desperation over *Jeremy Kyle* on the TV or pie for lunch, no doubt.

'Can you put me through to Sister Benedicta, please? It's urgent.'

There was a delay; Conky was forced to listen to some ecclesiastical hold music. He remembered Paddy's last days in the overly floral and brightly coloured room – a grim but functional place, just along from the convent's chapel. *Jesus. What a place to end your days in.* The choir in the recording continued to insist otherwise. All *Hosanna* this and *Hosanna* that. Then the heavenly vibe was rent apart by Katrina's sharp, clipped, no-nonsense voice.

'Conky. What in heaven's name do *you* want?'

'I'm in trouble, Katrina. If I'm honest, we're all in trouble. And I need your help.'

Chapter 28

Youssuf

'Checking out, sir?' the girl asked, treating him to a disingenuous smile with lipstick on her teeth.

'I'm surprised I haven't already,' he said, chuckling to himself as he considered the close shave he'd had on the Victoria line escalator upon arrival in London.

With Dreadlocks only steps above him, Youssuf had been certain that he was going to be caught yet again by that thug and manhandled back up to street level and into some van or else pushed beneath a tube train and killed. Reaching the bottom of the seemingly never-ending tube escalator, he'd escaped the clutches of his dreadlocked pursuer by pushing past a group of shrieking Italian school children. He had spotted the sign to loop back up to the District and Circle lines and had headed for it, hoping to become lost in the crowd, which had stood six people deep along the platform, waiting for the train whose arrival had been heralded by a warm wind and sense of stiff competition as to who would succeed in boarding an already packed carriage.

Dreadlocks had been scuppered by the sheer volume of people. Youssuf had slipped through an opening on the concourse as the train had arrived. He'd shaken Dreadlocks off. Temporarily, at least. Shaking and struggling to breathe, he'd had no option but to shelve his aspirations to head straight for Colin Chang and had instead made for a budget hotel in Covent Garden, simply by following a gaggle of backpackers from some Spanish-speaking country and hoping for the best.

Now, having blown most of his emergency cash, he stood at the reception desk. He handed in his key card to the bemused-looking receptionist, determined that today, he would confront the pharmacist that had fallen from grace.

Taking the packed and stuffy tube, he clutched his stick and the Disney rucksack he'd taken from Zahid's wardrobe, alighting at Leicester Square. Late-morning, and already the smell of Peking duck pervaded the streets of China Town – a sweet/savoury welcome for an old Asian adventurer who planned to free one man with a view to locking up another.

'I'm looking for Colin Chang,' he told the disgruntled-looking waitress in the restaurant. He had never been inside a noodle bar before. While he waited, he was transfixed by the fat little bottles of soy and chilli oil; the canisters full of paper-wrapped bamboo chopsticks; the small type of the menus that sat beneath the glass of all the easy-wipe tables. Photos of numbered dishes were backlit in lightboxes on the walls. Cantonese conversation rang out from the kitchens.

His old heart clippety-clopped inside his chest. Would Colin show? What if this trip had been nothing more than an old fool's final indulgence? With no warfarin and heart pills and some criminal, hell-bent on kidnapping him in order to get to Tariq, it was entirely feasible he wouldn't make the return journey to Manchester at all.

But then, he felt eyes on him for the third time that trip. Glancing over to the back stairs, he caught sight of the familiar face of the man who had dispensed his myriad lotions and potions for over ten years. Youssuf shuffled towards him.

'I found you. At last!' He beamed at the sight of his favourite pharmacist, though Colin Chang appeared shorter and thinner than he'd remembered, dressed in washed-out clothes that looked borrowed and were too big for him. Certainly, the shadows beneath his eyes and the haunted expression on his face told Youssuf this was a man dogged by a guilty conscience or else fear.

'Youssuf? What the heck are you doing here?'

They engaged in an awkward fumble of an embrace.

'I've come to check you're all right,' Youssuf said, bidding him to sit with a nonchalant wave. 'You haven't been around for months. I was worried, you follow? One minute you're there. Next, you're gone and the shutters are down on your pharmacy. Nobody could tell me where you'd got to.' He clicked his fingers, ignoring the sting of the arthritis in the joints. 'But Youssuf Khan is determined, if nothing else.' Took his hat off and held it on his lap. Ran a shaking hand over his trim white beard and slurped the green tea that one of the waitresses had brought him. It was the first drink he'd had all day, since he hadn't been able to afford breakfast at the hotel. 'I heard you were in trouble with bad men.'

'I've been . . .' Colin dabbed at his top lip with a napkin. 'Visiting family. I thought I was overdue a break. A sabbatical of sorts.'

'Working in a restaurant?' Youssuf looked up at the oversized photos of stir-fries, crispy duck and noodle dishes on the wall. His stomach growled, though the meat in this place would be haram and inedible for a good Muslim. He inclined his body stiffly towards the window, where bronzed ducks turned on a rotisserie to entice passing customers inside. He sniffed. 'You're a man of more talents than I gave you credit for.'

'Look, Mr Khan—'

'Please. Youssuf, after all these years.'

'Youssuf, it's very nice of you to come. It's really kind of you to care.' Colin's eyes swam suddenly with tears that didn't fall. 'But honestly, if I'd wanted people to know where I was, I'd have put up a note in the pharmacy or called my favourite customers. I just needed to get away.'

'There, there.' Youssuf gripped his walking stick, hoisting himself out of his seat. He patted him on the shoulder. 'There's no need to get upset.'

Colin shrugged his touch away. 'I'm fine. I'm not upset. I've got an eye infection.'

'Yes. Okay.'

'I have!' Colin folded his arms tightly across his chest. Those tears had gone now. 'You've not told your son where I am, have you?' He shot a surreptitious glance at the door, as if he expected Tariq to walk through it at any moment. Clearly, this unassuming pharmacist knew about the nefarious doings behind the respectable front of T&J Trading, too.

Youssuf took his seat again. Started to cough and chuckle, his lungs wheezing and groaning like a pair of overworked vintage bellows. 'My boy doesn't even know where I am. I've gone rogue!' He threw his head back, laughing heartily at his own daring. 'Isn't that what they call it?'

'Where are you staying?'

'Last night, I blew most of my money on a hotel. Today? I don't know!' More laughter as Youssuf contemplated the lunacy of what he'd done. 'I've got some relations in Southall but thought I could maybe stay with you.'

Colin swallowed hard and looked down at his hands. The skin was wrinkled and red, as though he spent his days washing up. Was that the truth of it? Had this educated man run away to London to wash up in a restaurant rather than face the wrath of a Manchester crime lord? 'No, I'm sorry. It's not possible. I bed down in here and I'm not supposed to. If my cousin found out . . .'

'So you *are* in trouble?' Youssuf studied his body language carefully to see what it revealed.

Shaking his head, Colin pulled at the grimy, stained fabric of his tank top. He looked again at the red-raw skin of his hands. 'Maybe a bit.'

'You can trust me,' Youssuf said. He took up a pair of pristine chopsticks. Removed them from their paper wrapping with trembling fingers and snapped them apart, making Colin jump. 'Everybody has a breaking point. Well, I've reached mine. I've had enough and I'm here to put an end to it all.'

A sweat had broken out on Colin's forehead. 'What do you mean? An end to what?'

'The illegal and immoral goings-on. My son. The O'Briens. I know what you're all caught up in. I overheard my daughter-in-law, Anjum, telling Tariq that you'd been into her offices, trying to help some young Chinese girl to seek asylum.'

Colin blanched. Shrank back in his seat, clasping his arms around him. He rose abruptly. 'I've got to go, Youssuf. You shouldn't have come here. I'm sorry.'

But feeling frustration and disappointment mushroom inside him, Youssuf banged his walking stick on the floor, causing one of the waitresses to glare at him. He glared at

Colin. Pointed in accusatory fashion, though the small outburst exhausted him. 'We can put everything right. I know you have a good heart.' He stood with some effort, leaned over the table and poked Colin in his pigeon chest. 'I can see it. I've always known it. You're in debt. Am I right? Gambling? Yes? You think you travel entire continents and live a life of poverty in a country where you can't even speak the language and bring up children and get to my age and *still* can't read the truth in people's faces? Think again! I see the story in your face, Colin Chang, pharmacist. I see your conflict. The more you stir up filth, the more it smells. And I can smell it! Now, man up! Isn't that what the youngsters say?'

'What do you want from me?' Colin shouted.

'The truth. What were you doing for the O'Brien scum?'

Silence between them seemed to make the time slow. The air thickened.

'Free yourself, Colin,' Youssuf said, retrieving Ellis James's business card from his pocket. 'I intend to.'

Opening and closing his mouth, Colin glanced down at the card, reading the detective's handwritten note, saying that Youssuf should call when it all got too much. He shook his head vehemently. 'I can't.'

'I came all this way. I know you're involved. Tell me!' Youssuf had to convince him. The restaurant staff were watching and trying to eavesdrop. Could he change Colin's mind before they forcibly threw him out on the street? 'You must. You can trust me.' He softened his voice deliberately now, taking on the tone of an encouraging father.

'You're right,' Colin finally said, flattening his palms on the table top. 'I got into bad gambling debts. Over quarter of a million in illegal poker games. I think O'Brien had rigged the cards on purpose.' Blushing, he stared blankly at the menu beneath the glass table top. 'I owed him. He had me running a cannabis farm. More of a factory, really, in an old disused warehouse on a semi-derelict industrial estate. I advised on the production of crystal methamphet-amine. You know what that is?'

Youssuf tutted. Shook his head.

'I never did a thing to help any of the trafficked kids there. Not a thing, and I should have. The way they were treated . . . starved, abused, exposed to toxic chemicals. I was weak. I was scared.' He wiped a tear away. 'But how does this help me? How does my telling you undo all the bad things that happened to those kids? They're dead. That's it for them. And this is my punishment. I made it out alive. My pharmacy will bring me in money that maybe one day I'll get my hands on.'

Youssuf cleared his throat. 'My son thinks I can't work a computer. But he's an ass. We have computers at the day centre. So, I looked up this O'Brien man. There was a two page obituary in the *Manchester Evening News*. Two pages!'

Colin's thin eyebrows shot upwards towards his receding hairline. 'O'Brien's dead?'

'Apparently.' Youssuf considered showing Colin the photo he had taken in Bury's indoor market of a man he could have sworn was Paddy O'Brien. Running his tongue over the palate of his false teeth, he opted to keep quiet. It wouldn't do to spook this reluctant refugee. 'But the funny business and illegal doings are still going on. His wife's in charge now, I believe. And my Tariq is . . .' He sighed. 'We can stop all of them. For good. The net's tightening, Colin, and we hold the strings.'

He was certain he could see wistful longing in Colin's eyes. He held his hand out. 'Come back with me to Manchester. Ellis James will be pleased to hear from you.

He can offer you protection in return for giving evidence in court. I've already broached the subject with him . . . in secret, of course.'

'You'd grass on your own son?'

Youssuf nodded. 'If it means my grandchildren escape the ill effects of this immoral mess and grow up to be good people. Yes.'

He closed his eyes for at least a minute, waiting for his encouraging words to sink in. When he opened them again, he smiled. 'Well? Will you come with me to the police?'

Chapter 29

Paddy

'Guess who I had a call from, begging me to fish him out of the clink?' Katrina said, walking at a pace Paddy wasn't entirely comfortable with. She climbed upwards in those ugly flats she wore, pausing only to regard the satellite tower rising out of the golden and orange-clad trees that surrounded them. 'You'll never guess!' She turned back to him, grinning. Beckoning him to hurry.

Paddy almost lost his footing entirely as he trod on a giant fallen horse chestnut casing. His ankle turned painfully. 'Ow! Slow down, Kat. It's not a sodding race. I haven't got the shoes for this. And I can't catch my breath.'

'That's why I've brought you out for a walk, Patrick. You need to keep in some kind of shape. Look after your heart, and your heart will look after you.' She was already advancing on the border fence that surrounded the Heaton Park Reservoir. Was the crazy bitch going to climb over it and go for a bracing dip? Paddy wouldn't put it past her.

'It's only a couple of months since I was on life support. Christ's sake, Katrina!'

'Blasphemy!'

'Slow down! Or did you save me just to kill me . . .?' He came to a standstill. Grabbed at his knees, wiping his sweaty hands on the crappy acrylic fabric of Kenneth Wainwright's trousers. Gasped for air and stood, grimacing. '. . . when it suits you, your worshitfulness?'

'Your mouth always was like a sewer.'

The ground was damp and muddy, crunchy in places where it was covered with a blanket of fallen acorns and hazelnuts. Paddy spied a horse chestnut and grunted as he picked it up. Running his thumb over the smooth, shiny umber and chocolate stripes that ran through it. Remembered playing conkers with Frank as a kid. Never brilliant with his hand-eye co-ordination, he had always ended up giving Frank a pasting with his conker in frustration at not being able to win the game. He tossed the nut away. A life lost. Memories that were now worth nothing.

'Come on, Patrick!' Katrina grabbed the arm of his anorak and pulled him along like he was some docile resident in her nursing home. Her cheeks had coloured up in the fresh autumnal air. She looked as though she'd been at the whisky. 'Put your best foot forward, man. Don't you want to hear my gossip? Come on. It's not like we meet in person that often.'

'Go on, then.'

'Conky.' She turned to face him, clearly waiting for a reaction.

'That cheeky Irish bastard?' Paddy considered all the information Hank had passed on about Conky and Sheila. 'My corpse isn't even cold. He's in my bed, and here I am, living hand to mouth, no chance of seeing my girls. My house. My wife. My life.'

Katrina had steamed ahead yet again. Her stout nun's

legs could move some when she tried. Thick black stockings spattered with mud hung beneath the A-line hem of her navy skirt. Her short veil flapped in the gentle breeze.

'Hold your horses, Jolly Fucking Hockey-sticks,' Paddy muttered begrudgingly beneath his breath.

His elder sister was only a pack of beagles and a celestial horn short of her own hunt. 'Don't you want to know why he called?'

'Go on, then. Please tell me they've got him for double murder and they're gonna throw the book at him.'

'Apparently, the builders' merchants was blown up.' Katrina stopped dead and appraised Paddy with a degree of suspicion. 'That wasn't anything to do with you and Hank, the Henchman of Heywood, was it?' A wry smile played at the corner of her mouth. The skin on her lips was chapped, cracking as the smile deepened.

Paddy shook his head. 'My builders' yard? You're shitting me.'

'Well, it's just a pile of rubble now. Only, Conky had dropped his handgun in the ruins and got copped red-handed by Ellis James, fishing it out from under a pile of wood.'

'Get out!' Paddy threw his head back and wheezed with laughter.

'Well, he's a free man again, thanks to me. Sister Benedicta to the rescue, once again.'

Paddy's laughter stopped abruptly. Anger and resentment curdled inside him, along with his medication. Sheila couldn't hold it together. The O'Brien empire was under attack. Everything he had amassed over decades from a mere fifty-pound investment in some super-strong hash from Morocco that he'd flogged to students, undercutting the Jamaican dealers who had operated in Moss Side's bullrings. All he'd built up was being systematically dismantled because of that dozy, weak bitch and her clueless bug-eyed muscle. He punched the perimeter fence, breaking the skin on his knuckles.

'Was that really necessary, Patrick?' Katrina asked, raising an eyebrow disparagingly. She pushed through a loose piece in the fence and climbed over crowns of thorns in the grass, up the steep slope to the reservoir's edge.

Huffing and puffing, Paddy followed reluctantly. He clutched his bloody hand, savouring the sting as a dim reminder of the old days. He didn't like it up here. Felt exposed. Behind them, the forested area of the park fell away in a glorious autumnal riot of colour. But those pretty pinks, oranges and yellows could be concealing any nosey arsehole that might conceivably, in this neck of the woods, have links to the Boddlington gang.

'This is a bad idea. I might get spotted.' He peered down at the water. The gunmetal surface was choppy, thanks to the gusts of cold wind. 'I've got to get my life back,' he said, feeling the dense skies bearing down on the scene – suffocating him. End of the world cloud formations in a dour monochrome palette of deepest sludge grey. 'All yous lot have ever done is steamroller me into doing what you want. Just cos you think you're cleverer than me. Brenda does it. Sheila did it. And you do it . . . Women! You all reckon you know what I need, don't you? "Take your medicine, Paddy, like a good lad." And I just swallow it. *You* decided to take my life away from me, you inter-fering god-botherer.'

His sister rounded on him, fists balled. Ever the alpha O'Brien, whether she was wearing a crucifix around her neck or a knuckleduster on her hand. 'What a load of stuff and nonsense, Patrick! You? At the mercy of women?

Is that how you see it? Paddy the King who ruled by divine right. The Despot! You're about as hard done by as Kim Jong-un or Donald Trump. Good Lord! And how dare you accuse me of taking your life? I saved you from certain death. Or did you forget that you were left to bleed your last at the side of your own swimming pool? Do you think another willing hitman wouldn't have come after you to finish what you insist Leviticus Bell started? Really?'

'I'll never know now, will I?!' Paddy yelled, his voice echoed across the flat expanse of the reservoir. 'Maybe I shouldn't kill Lev Bell. Maybe I should just prove he tried to kill me and tell Ellis James that I hid in self-defence. Or tell him how you bullied me into this fresh start, false identity rubbish. I want my life back. I want—'

'You start revealing your true identity and you know who'll get it in the neck?' Katrina yelled. 'Me! I committed the sort of fraud that will ruin my good reputation, get me excommunicated and put me in prison for life. And they'll lock you up and throw away the key. Have no doubt about it.'

'Me? What the bloody hell have I done?'

'You're guilty of benefit fraud, for a start.'

His sister rounded on him, her hard, well-scrubbed face mere inches away. She poked him in the shoulder. Strong fingers belonging to a woman who was no stranger to hard domestic work. '*Are* you Kenneth Wainwright? Really? Are you entitled to his disability benefits? His council tax benefit? His rent rebate? Do you really think the police and the tax man will take a kindly view on any of this? You open your mouth, and we're both in it up to our eyeballs, Patrick.'

Staring into the middle distance, he monitored the

laboured pounding of his heart. Breathing shallow and fast. Was that pain he felt in his left side or just wind from Brenda's breakfast fry-up? Trying to slow everything down, inhaling and exhaling slowly, he patted Katrina's arm in a gesture of fragile truce. No point dying in the midst of an argument with the only person remaining who gave anything approaching a shit about the old Paddy O'Brien.

But as he contemplated facing down death yet again, he thought he spotted someone familiar through the wider spaced trunks of a copse of oaks. A big Asian man, walking an aggressive-looking dog.

'Stop feeling sorry for yourself and let's get going,' Katrina said, pushing his hand away. Peeling her veil back, where the wind had stuck it to her chin.

'Shush!' Paddy held his hand up. Studying the man, who was facing in their direction but whose attentions lay elsewhere as he waited for the Staffordshire bull terrier to retrieve the stick he had thrown. And then it clicked. Paddy gasped. 'Get down!' he cried, motioning that his sister should duck. Here they both were, on the crest of a hill, with the water on one side and the man the other – the last person he needed to see.

'What on earth is wrong with you?' Katrina yelped as Paddy pulled her down the stone slope that dropped steeply to the bleak water's edge.

'Nadeem or Nasim or something. It's Tariq Khan's bloody lad! His second cousin or some crap, I heard.'

Katrina shook him loose. 'What of it?'

'He works with Asaf Smolensky. The Fish Man. The Boddlington's muscle. If he spots me, I'm a goner.'

They crept along some five or ten metres, when a stick hurtled over the lip of the reservoir and down the slope to where they crouched. There was excitable barking and a man's whistle from the other side. But then, scampering and the heavy panting of a muscle-bound dog on a mission.

'Damn it! The bleeding dog's gonna come and get the stick. It'll lead him right to me.'

'Rubbish.' Sister Benedicta's morning constitutional was apparently not about to be disrupted by a dog. 'It will never find its way through the fence.'

Except it had. The stocky terrier bounded into view at the top of the hill. Scudded down the stone side at full pelt, suddenly more interested in the lingering smell of Brenda's bacon on Paddy's trousers than the stick. It snarled, latching onto the ankle of his trousers with barred teeth.

'Help! Jesus, Kat. Get it off me!'

On the other side, getting closer, he could hear Tariq's man calling out. 'Rihanna!'

'Rihanna?!' Paddy glared in disbelief at the rabid dog.

Nasim or Nadeem or whatever the hell he was called was getting closer. 'Rihanna. Come to Daddy!'

Paddy looked at his sister, all pleading eyes, as he had often done when they had been little. Katrina placed a well-aimed kick up Rihanna's behind. The dog whimpered and howled. Its owner appeared on the rim above them.

'Turn away!' Katrina whispered.

Paddy dropped to the ground, facing the water. Pretended to wipe mud from his shoe.

Cowed, the dog picked the stick up in its mouth and skulked back up to the top. Reunited with its owner, the two lingered on the crest of the hill for a moment too long.

'Don't look,' Katrina muttered.

Paddy could hear the man fussing over his dog, but steadfastly kept his head down.

'They're gone,' Katrina said.

Clutching at his chest, Paddy heaved himself back to standing. 'Do you think he saw me?'

'No way of telling.'

'I told you this walk was a terrible bleeding idea.'

When Katrina had pulled her battered old Volvo estate up alongside the kerb of a quiet side street, some hundred yards from Kenneth Wainwright's house, he had taken the envelope containing the extra money he had begged her to give him. She had delivered some patronising bloody sermon or other, of course, about not blowing it all down the pub but spending it on healthy food. He had yeah-yeah'd her and clambered out, his legs throbbing from overuse. The adrenalin of almost having been spotted by a Boddlington, of all people, had made him feel as though razor wire were being dragged through every blood vessel in his body. The old bitch had wanted to put him through the wringer. He had been certain of it. Sister Benedicta liked the ungodly to sample purgatory while they were still living.

As he stood over Brenda's prone body in a corner of her dingy bedroom, with his fist raised in readiness for another revitalising punch, the small part of Paddy that hadn't been absorbed in the hellfire of the rage mulled over his situation. Katrina and Sheila had stolen everything from him and had left him castrated. Conky had betrayed his memory by sleeping with his widow before the marital bed was even cold. Lev Bell had not been made to pay and proved more elusive than a marauding nocturnal slug that left only a silver trail as a clue it had ever been there. Frustrated and angry, he wanted to hurt them all.

As Paddy kicked Brenda in the kidneys, failing to notice her son, Kyle observing through the crack in the bedroom door, he knew what to do. Where Paddy had had his daughters stolen from him, Leviticus Bell would have his mother snatched away and Sheila would have her beloved old slag of a business partner wiped off the face of the earth.

'I'm sorry, Kenneth! I'm sorry. I didn't mean to insult you, love,' Brenda said, holding her hands defensively over her head and middle. Weeping like the weak puddle of piss Paddy knew she was.

Abandoning her in that shitty bedroom that stank of sex, dust and stale bedding, Paddy pulled on his clothes, pushed past Kyle on the landing. The boy was giving him evils.

'What you staring at, you sneaky little shite? Go and make your Mam a brew.'

He clipped the kid around the ear just to show him who was boss. Spotty runt. Descended, grabbed his coat and left, feeling almost like a new man. As soon as he had slammed the door to Brenda's terrace behind him, he dialled Hank. Chirpy, dim arsehole was full of bonhomie on the other end, like it was a fresh summer's morning instead of a dank early evening, barely scraping ten degrees. Perhaps he was boning some bird.

'Paddy! I was just thinking about you.'

'Oh yeah. Listen. The job's changed.'

'How do you mean?' Uncertainty in his voice.

'I'll pay you extra, but you've got to go through with it like a man. No cop-outs.' Paddy picked up his pace, positively swaggering down the street now, feeling so much better for clawing a little control back over his life and the destinies of others. 'Get close to Gloria. Do her odd jobs or summat. Let her trust you, and pump her for everything you can about what Sheila's up to. Right? Then . . .' He had reached his front door and withdrawn his key, poised to insert it into the scratched and battered Yale. Spotted the pub at the end of the street in his peripheral vision. Felt the call of a nice pint of strong lager. A couple of bevvies wouldn't hurt.

'What? What do I have to go through with?'

'I want you to top her.'

Chapter 30

Sheila

'As you can see, Mrs O'Brien,' the letting agent said, stalking in her cheap heels and tight skirt over to the aluminium windows and tapping on the glass. 'The views from up here are cracking. You can see all of town. Spinningfields from the smaller office. The courts from this one.' She started to giggle. 'You can even see if there's any nice-looking fellers in the bar down there! Save you a job going, if they're all a bit rough!' Her eyes shone with the naivety of the young, single and hopeful. No ring.

'Fellers don't look at me anymore, love. And I'm in a relationship.' The blemish-free girl, with her mane of tumbling blonde locks made Sheila feel old. Damn her. Why couldn't they have lined her up with an agent who was a bloke or an older woman? 'The rent's a bit pricey. I understand you've got quite a few units up for grabs.' There was a deal to be done, here. There was always a deal to be done in a city that was still on one bended knee, post-recession.

The girl shook her head. Her full cheeks flushed pink beneath her foundation. 'Oh, you'd be surprised. We've just let the entire penthouse suite.'

Sheila peered down at the shining damp pavements

below, watching the umbrellas unfurl and swirl in discs of bright colour as the rain started to fall anew. She checked her watch. Twenty minutes into the appointment and still Gloria hadn't arrived, though she'd been given a clean bill of health and discharged by the hospital. It was most unlike Jesus's favourite sunbeam to be tardy. Pain in the arse. And her blackmailing dipshit of a son still hadn't been in touch about the SIM card. 'Who to?'

'Well, it's the developer that refurbished the block actually. One of his subsidiary companies. He's doing a lot in the city.'

'Bruntwood?'

'No. This isn't a Bruntwood block. It's a Bancroft building. The boss's head offices are in Birmingham but he wanted a Manchester base for his subsidiary, seeing as he's starting to expand up here.'

Sheila swung around to face the letting agent. The air-con vent in the office was suddenly blasting out icy air. The grey partition walls seemed to be moving further and further in towards her. 'Come again.'

'Bancroft. Didn't you see the sign as you walked in?'

'I thought this was Hardacre Tower.'

'Yeah.' The girl rolled her eyes in a way Sheila didn't entirely appreciate. Cheeky cow. 'But it's owned by Nigel Bancroft. All his properties are Bancroft buildings. Didn't you see the logo in reception with the big BB and the wings? He's got a block up near Piccadilly too. You want to see that? We've got a lovely suite going there for a lot less than this. My agency does all his lettings.'

Sheila had to get out of there. Fast. Had to warn Gloria. There was shitting on your own doorstep and there was this. There wasn't even a phrase for this level of lunacy. 'Has Bancroft moved in?

255

'Oh yes. Last week. Why? Have you heard of him?'

Marching to the lifts, Sheila pressed the button impatiently. Pressed it again. Tapping her Louboutins on the marble tiled floor. She held her Chanel tote as close to her body as possible, wondering if she could just upend the entire bloody thing onto her head if Bancroft turned out to be in the lift on the way down. *Shit, shit, shit.*

'Is there a problem?' the letting agent asked. 'Have I offended you?' She looked as though she was about to cry. Pink blotching starting to crawl its way up her pale neck.

Pulling out her oversized Prada shades, Sheila shook her head. 'No, love. I just need air. These modern offices . . . you know.'

But she noticed the lift was still on an upper floor. Double digits showing on the digital display.

'What number is the penthouse?'

'Fifteen,' the girl said.

The lift was on fifteen, according to the poison-green glowing numbers that shone brightly on that display. It was coming from the penthouse.

'I'll walk. I need the exercise,' she said, beckoning the girl to follow. Turning her ankle in haste. 'Come on. Let's go straight to the Victorian conversion near Albert Square.' She pushed open the door to the stairwell. Turned to the girl. 'That's not a Bancroft place, is it?'

'No.'

'Right, then. Let's go. You got a car? You can give me a lift. The vibes are all wrong here, I'm afraid.'

Climbing into the girl's cramped Fiat that was adorned with the letting agency's livery, Sheila whipped out her phone, turned it off silent and thumbed a text to Gloria.

Where the hell are you? Do NOT go to Hardacre Tower.

Meet me at Pankhurst Mansions near Spring Gardens/Albert Square.

Bloody Gloria and her new-found lovesick, lackadaisical bullshit.

As the girl hung a sharp left onto Quay Street, Sheila's phone pinged.

'At last!'

Unlocking the screen, she expected to see a message from Gloria. She was yearning to tell her about Bancroft's legitimate expansion into Manchester, creeping like a mutating virus into the fibre of the city's upper echelons as well as trying to infiltrate and infect its underbelly. But it wasn't Gloria, contrite that she was running late.

Still no sign of my dad. Been in town, handing out missing person flyers at the station. Are you around? Meet me at The Midland Hotel in half an hour? Tariq.

Stop, start. Stop, start. The Fiat was making poor progress in the mid-afternoon traffic. At her side, the letting agent waxed lyrical about the glorious, almost ecclesiastical interior of Pankhurst Mansions. The windscreen wipers swept left and right, left and right with a hee-haw sound that grated. Bancroft was in town. Lev still hadn't got her SIM card. Conky was calling her constantly to ask why she was behaving coolly towards him; why he'd had to rely on Katrina to sort his legal representation and get the charge of firearms possession dropped.

Sighing, she texted Tariq back, dimly aware of a white van that had been two cars behind since they had left the girl's parking spot near the Opera House.

OK. Make it 40 mins. Book the room under Mr Boddlington. I'll find you. S.

Now, she felt almost cheery at the prospect of their fourth meeting inside a week. Tariq Khan couldn't get enough of her, nor could she of him. She pictured his pleasantly hairy, toned forearms and almost gasped. This was more like it. This was an excellent antidote to the shitty stress of being south Manchester's crime boss.

Suppressing a smirk, she climbed out of the Fiat and looked up at the beautiful sandstone Victorian building.

'It used to be a bank,' the letting agent said, juggling her clipboard and slinging her PVC bag over her shoulder as she locked the car. 'It's got a lovely oak staircase. I think you'll like this.'

The place was elegant and had been beautifully divided up into multiple office spaces, all with arched, mullioned windows. High ceilings made it feel more spacious and Sheila loved the original cast-iron fireplace that was in the office she would be claiming for herself. Better than that shithole of a builders' merchants, any day of the week. There was parking, ample enough to accommodate her Rolls Royce in a basement car park, accessed from a one-way street at the back. Shuttered. High security on reception. Preferential rents, as it was away from the financial district. Close enough to China Town to get one of the visiting cleaners to nip out and get Chinese as the occasional lunch-time treat. Gloriously close to King Street and St Anne's Square for a spot of shopping when the mood took her.

Looking out onto the Georgian building opposite, she watched all the office bods – the women, in their beige, Next shift-dresses and the men, in their white shirts and blue ties – beavering away at their desks beneath glaring strip-lighting, hunched over their computers. It was an old, cramped Mancunian street on the slightly wrong side of town. A street lined with double parking. A yellow VW Beetle with a female driver, applying mascara in her rear-view mirror. An empty Ford Focus, covered in birdshit. A white Transit van, containing a middle-aged man, wearing a stupid baseball cap the wrong way round, who glanced up at her and hastily backed away from his window. This was Every Street. Anonymous as hell. As the offices for a bent cleaning agency that was staffed with trafficked women from Africa and Asia and those whose visas had simply run out, it was perfect.

'I'll take it. Where do I sign?'

The girl beamed at her. 'Magic. What about your business partner though?'

Chapter 31

Gloria

'Bob! Bob, where are you?' Gloria turned on the spot, wondering where her boyfriend had disappeared to now. But the maize towered densely all around her – its leafy tops, sun-scorched and past their best, reaching far above her head.

Why had they had to spend the morning in a maize maze in the middle of Cumbria?

'What kind of blasted date is this?' Gloria asked herself as she ran to the end of the row, turning left, only to find a dead end. Her heartbeat quickened yet again; her chest was screaming after the battering it had taken from the smoke of the explosion. 'Why on earth couldn't we have just gone for a drive round the local churches like I wanted?' she muttered angrily as she probed the passage to the right. Coughing. Feeling disappointment acutely, she imitated Bob's voice – a strange mix of nasal rapid-fire Mancunian and Lancashire-borders country drawl. *I'm tekkin you to the maize maze, Gloria. You'll love it. It's reet good fun.* 'Reet good fun, indeed! I'll give him reet good fun when I find him.' More coughing.

'Boo!'

Gloria yelped and took a step backwards as Bob appeared from between the giant stalks. 'Good Lord, Robert! There's no need to startle me like that.' She clasped her hand to her chest, annoyed by the way in which her paramour had been laughing at her, as though she was providing him with a good morning's entertainment like some life-sized doll.

'Your face! It's a picture.' Bob bent over, his delight seeming overdone like a clown's slapstick in a pantomime.

There was something beyond the laughter in his eyes, Gloria assessed. She reasoned that it was, in all likelihood, hurt. Perhaps he'd overheard her mocking him. But there was a cynical part of Gloria that wondered if a little predatory calculation wasn't behind those blue, blue eyes. Cruelty, too.

'Are you getting a kick out of me being . . . discombobulated by this?' she said, anger, disappointment and an unnerving sense of foreboding laying heavy on top of her early morning coffee.

He reached out. Grabbed her gently by the neck and kissed her on the cheek.

'Don't do that,' she said. 'I don't like that.' She batted his hand away, shivering involuntarily. Coughing painfully.

'Catch me if you can!' Bob darted back into the maize, disappearing within one or two long strides.

Gloria was alone again. Perhaps. Turning on her heel, she scanned the tall stalks. No sign of any other explorers this early in the morning. No sign of Bob, though she sensed him studying her every move, nevertheless, from behind the wall of leaves.

Checking her watch, she was dismayed to see that the time had passed more quickly than she had anticipated. Ideally, she should have left an hour or so ago to make her meeting with Sheila and the letting agent in central

Manchester. Why, oh why had she allowed Bob to talk her into this spontaneous lunacy?

They had met outside their usual airport hotel at 8 a.m. Given it had been the first time she'd seen him since being discharged from hospital, she'd anticipated a morning of lascivious doings between the poly-cotton sheets. But Bob had had other ideas and an air of mischief about him.

'Why would I want to trek round a maze with you, Robert? I've got business to attend to.'

He had seemed evasive in his response, trotting out 'Because' several times before he had resorted to, 'It's dead romantic.'

Torn between wanting to put her orthopaedic-shoe-clad foot down and not wanting to alienate a man who seemed to be falling in love with her, she had agreed reluctantly. Hours later, she was lost beneath Cumbria's rain-heavy grey skies, swamped by dank-smelling crops past their best.

'Oh, Gloriaaaa!' Bob's voice rang out from somewhere to her left. A few paces up ahead.

She jogged towards him – or so she thought. A hand thrust out from the stalks on her right and Bob snatched her in amongst the maize.

'C'mere!' he said, encircling her waist with a strong arm and dragging her further into the thicket.

'Get off me!' she shouted, pushing him away.

'I want you. Like this. In here.' He reached for her again but Gloria didn't feel comfortable. What the tight skin of his face kept secret, his eyes revealed in terrifying detail. Bob had a bloodthirsty look to him that set her internal alarm blaring. She was not about to offer herself as easy meat to this suddenly carnivorous man.

Sprinting along the corridor cut into the tall maize, she determined to get away from him and get back to her car at all costs. Perhaps once they got out of that claustrophobic hell-hole, he might calm down. Panting, she listened to the rustle as he dashed alongside her through the crop. He dived out in front of her, blocking her path.

'Here's Bobby!'

'What are you doing, for heaven's sake? Stop it, Robert!'

Doubling back, she ducked down another path. Pounding the ground beneath her, her handbag felt cumbersome, jostling against her hip as she ran. Her chest screamed in complaint.

'Oh, Gloriaaaaa!' His call travelled across the leafy tops to find her. Where had it been coming from?

Running, running, Gloria was barely able to catch her breath, feeling the burn of lactic acid in her legs and the thump of her heart against her ribs. Coughing. Coughing up blackened sputum still. She came to an abrupt halt. Listening. But all she was able to hear was the sound of the dried foliage crackling on the wind. The odd, giant cob that had been overlooked during harvest, swaying above her like jack-in-the-boxes, nodding; tipping her the wink that Bob was lying in wait, ready to snatch her and put his hand around her throat again. Was it some kind of kinky foreplay? Or were his intentions sinister?

After a wait of some minutes where Gloria tiptoed in the general direction she had guessed the exit lay, she heard a phone ringing some way off. Hearing Bob's voice, indistinct and serious-sounding on the breeze, she checked her own phone. No bars. Her network had no signal here. Darn it! What was Bob saying and to whom was he talking? Was he talking about her? She was certain she had heard him say, 'Gloria'.

All fell silent. Perhaps an hour passed since the call. Maybe longer. Despite shouting at the top of her voice in that vast field of rustling maize, Gloria could not be heard. She was trapped. She had missed her meeting with Sheila and the letting agent. Nobody knew where she was. More to the point, she had no idea where Bob might be.

Chapter 32

Sheila

'I thought you were never coming,' Tariq said, pulling the covers back for her. He patted the sheet. 'Let's have red-hot sex in the middle of the afternoon.'

Feeling her instantly ignited desire burn away the grime and the greasy cold of the city, Sheila undressed slowly and provocatively, dropping her garments to the floor one by one. Enjoying the grin on her lover's face as she theatrically twisted and turned in some silent approximation of a striptease. 'You're a naughty boy, Mr Khan. You've got a sad widow very, very wet.' She flicked a fingernail over one of her erect nipples. Traced her index finger downwards to stroke her pussy provocatively. 'What have you got for me?'

Tariq revealed his nakedness, all taut abs and trim, muscular thighs. He was already aroused. 'I really need you, Sheila. I really need this. I'm so stressed about Dad. It's the only thing keeping me going.'

With the sinuous movements of a stalking wild cat, she mounted the bed. Put her finger on his lips. 'Shhhh.' Kissed him gently. Kissed him harder. Straddled him and rubbed the heat of her body along his, feeling him hard against the inside of her thigh. 'Come on, then. Screw me. That's what you want, isn't it?'

She felt him slide inside her, thrusting upwards. The thrill of the knowledge that she was cheating on Conky made her arousal all the more intense. It was wrong. It was dirty. And that was precisely why it was terrific. Gripping her upper thighs for balance, she bounced up and down on him, savouring his hands on her breasts, and the sight of their coupling reflected in the full-length cheval mirror. Just what the doctor ordered. At that moment, despite all the trials and tribulations of her professional life, Sheila felt like a woman in her prime. Wise. Wicked. Sexy as hell. She had forgotten all about her burgeoning wrinkles, the sagging of her neck, her droopy tits and the split veins that had begun to appear around her nose and on her cheeks.

'Faster. I'm gonna come,' she said.

But the build-up of intense pleasure and urgency was interrupted by Tariq's phone reverberating its way across the bedside table.

'Ignore it,' she said, trying to focus on the task in hand.

'I thought I'd put it on silent,' Tariq said, rolling her onto her back and stretching his arm out to retrieve the phone.

'Leave it, for Christ's sake! I'm nearly there.'

He squinted at the screen, bringing it closer to his face. Baulking visibly when he saw who had messaged him.

'Anjum! Oh no.' Still inside Sheila, he pulled his glasses on, propped himself on his elbows and balanced the phone on her sternum. 'Dad's been spotted in the day centre, safe and well, she says.' He grinned. Withdrew his fast-deflating manhood. 'Oh, man. Thank you. Thank you, God. I don't believe it.' He looked at Sheila, his eyes shining as if they were backlit by pure joy. A flurry of tickly beard as he kissed Sheila on the lips. 'I'm going to have to go. I'm so sorry.

I've got to get back up to Cheetham as quickly as possible before the old bugger decides to go walkabout again.'

Five minutes later and with her lover gone, Sheila lay in the emperor-sized bed staring up at the gold curtains. She rolled over to revel in the heady scent of Tariq's lingering aftershave on the pillow, hugging it to her; surprised by the plethora of emotions that, all at once, supplanted her simple mid-afternoon lust. She raised her knee to feel the place on the sheet that was still warm from his body. Felt tears prickle at the backs of her eyes. Her period was only six days late. And at her age, she was well aware it could merely be the dreaded onset of perimenopause, screwing with her cycle. And yet . . .

'You're such a silly bitch, Sheila O'Brien. You and your sodding hormones. Why are you doing this?'

Wiping her rogue tears away on the counterpane, Sheila pushed the spectre of a possible pregnancy out of her mind and started to dress. She was the Queen. Once a victim, she was now one of life's winners, on her own terms. She was in control!

But taking her phone out, she saw that there was still no news from Gloria or Lev. Felt her shoulders stiffen up at the prospect of that SIM card still being out there, some-where. Not so in control, after all.

Dialling Lev's number, he picked up straight away.

'Well?'

'I told you, Sheila. I think the coppers must have it.'

'So get it.' She examined her red nail extensions, flicking one off in temper.

'Look. I need that money,' Lev said. 'My ex burned my boy with a ciggy. It was a threat. She's playing dirty. She says she's gonna get social services on my back.'

'And that's my problem because . . .'

267

'Come on, now! I did what you asked. It wasn't in the fire station. I can't exactly walk into the cop shop and nick something the size of a one-pence piece without getting collared. I wouldn't even know where to look. It could be anywhere. Manchester's a big place. Lots of criminals. Lots of cop shops.'

Sheila sat down heavily on one of the burgundy plush armchairs, rolling her eyes at the tall windows. 'Ellis James will have it. He's the one who's got a stiffy for the O'Briens and the Boddlingtons. Maureen Kaplan and my Paddy made a tit of him. I thought I'd get different treatment once Paddy died, but . . . James is not daft and his reputation's riding on bringing the whole shebang down. And if he's got my SIM, it'll have gone to HQ.' She exhaled heavily. Felt suddenly nauseous. Morning sickness?! Maybe it was just the power of suggestion. She'd read about that in a *Vogue* article about losing weight. 'Listen, I'll speak to my man on the inside. If it's there, he'll be able to lay his hands on it. But I can't be seen with him. I need you to be the go-between. You get it from him and give to me. Then, we'll talk about your money.'

On the other end of the phone, Lev paused. Sheila could hear the sound of tiny children chattering and screaming with delight. The whine of swings moving backwards and forwards, she imagined. He was in the park with his son. Could she do another round of broken nights and play-grounds? On her own? Or maybe a second chance with Tariq. Could she wake up next to him every day for the rest of her life? She didn't know the first thing about Tariq Khan as a person. Not really. Was it conceivable that she could bear a healthy child in her mid-forties and continue to be a successful businesswoman? A crime boss with a crib. *Can it, She! That's crazy talk. Tariq would want a slice of your action, anyway. Men are all the same. Controlling wankers. And you're just late because you're bloody well over the hill.*

Finally, Lev spoke. 'I want ten thou up front, or I'm telling Conky about you and Tariq. I mean it, Sheila. I've got to get my kid away from his shitbag of a Mam. I can't do that unless I can pay a top-notch solicitor. Have a heart. She's using him as an ashtray to get to me! What kind of a dad does that make me, if I can't keep my baby out of danger? I need to get a fresh start, away from all this. I've had enough.'

Aware that she could merely have Lev discreetly killed, rather than pay out or risk Conky discovering her treacherous tryst with the Boddlington boss, Sheila decided she was better than that. She wanted to be everything Paddy wasn't. Lucid, savvy, borderline-ethical. 'Go on then. I'll drop it round later. But I want you to get this done today. I'm gonna phone my bent copper now and set it up. Between yous, I want that SIM card back in my hands before midnight tonight. Right?' Strangely, she felt a lump in her throat yet again. Jesus. What was wrong with her? She tried to keep the sorrow out of her voice. 'Do yourself a favour, Lev.'

'What?'

'Get yourself a proper bloody babysitter with childcare credentials, you dozy arse!'

'But I can't let anyone know where I'm at, in case Fish Man finds out, can I?'

'Think it through! And tell your Mam I'm not very happy with her. She'll know why.'

Dumbfounded by Lev's stupidity, Sheila made the call to her man on the inside of the force, who reported that Ellis James had been walking around with a grin on his face for several days. Not good. But her contact did, at least, sound confident that he could gain access to the evidence room. If the SIM was there, he'd find it. Money always made the impossible possible.

As she took the lift down to the lobby, calculating whether she could walk in her heels to the car park where she had left the Rolls or whether she'd have to take a cab, her mind was everywhere but on her immediate surroundings. She barely noticed the glorious, oversized flower arrangement on a table, in the centre of the checkerboard marble floor. She paid no heed to the drab Mancunian daylight that leeched through the giant glazed lanterns, set into the ceiling. She absolutely did not notice Conky until he strode up to her – a phalanx of black – and placed a hand on her shoulder.

Startled, Sheila let out a squeak. 'Christ on a bike!'

'Sheila,' Conky said, a half-smile on his lips, though with those shades on, she had no way of knowing if the smile reached his eyes. 'Fancy seeing you here.'

Chapter 33

Youssuf

'Look. You have to stop worrying,' Youssuf had said, patting Colin on the arm. 'Nobody will recognise you in that outfit.'

He had surveyed his handiwork. A quick foray to his distant cousin Ahmed's in Southall had ensured that Colin Chang had been able to travel incognito. Provided nobody had been looking carefully, the middle-aged Chinese pharmacist could have easily been mistaken for any Asian man of pensionable age. Heavy woollen overcoat on top of a beige salwar kameez – long tunic; baggy trousers. Thick woollen socks. Leather sandals. All topped off with a flat brown Pashtun hat. His cousin had even given him an old pair of half-framed tortoiseshell glasses with scratched but handily weak lenses. The transformation had been convincing enough to persuade Colin to board the Virgin West Coast Pendolino train from Euston to Manchester – a celebratory upgrade from the crippling coach journey on the way down that had wrought havoc with Youssuf's aching bones and weak bladder. Youssuf had been more than happy to blow the last of his pilfered cash from Anjum's just-in-case-cash-tin on that.

Colin had dabbed at his clean-shaven upper lip with a

large white handkerchief, visibly sweating, though the Manchester Piccadilly concourse had been freezing cold and draughty as they had woven their way through the late-morning crowds. 'I hope you're right about this. I do really, really want my old life back.' His eyes had been everywhere, perhaps expecting every face to be an unsavoury type from his recent past. 'But now I'm here, this feels silly. Anyone could spot me.'

'Slow down!' Youssuf had said, tapping Colin between the shoulder blades with his walking stick. Wheezing slightly as he had tried to keep pace with the younger man. 'Nobody will be looking for you after all these months. And even if they are, they're looking for Colin Chang and a young Chinese girl called Mae Ling, escaped from a gangster's cannabis farm. They're not looking for two old Asian men. You follow?'

They had descended the escalator to the tram station in silence, listening to the nasal tannoy announcements of delayed journeys to Huddersfield and Manchester Airport. Wrong leaves on the line. Wrong drizzle in the air. Malfunctioning heating. Please keep an eye out for unattended baggage.

'We want the tram to Bury,' Youssuf had said, shepherding his charge towards the platform with a wave of his stick. He had allowed Colin to carry the Disney rucksack for him, feeling the fatigue from his adventures in earnest after nights away from home, sleeping first in an unfamiliar bed in a budget hotel and then on a lumpy guest bed mattress in Ahmed's cramped terrace. 'In my heart, I feel thirty again,' he had said, checking in his wallet for his pensioner's travel pass. 'But my body . . .? I'll be paying the price for this for weeks with sore feet and an aching back.'

'*You* will?' Colin had said. 'I might be paying the price for this with my life.'

'Oh, stop being melodramatic. You sound like my son! Look, it's going to be easy. We get to the day centre – I'm among friends there. Nobody's going to give us any bother, and we'll be in time for lunch.' The thought of sitting in the massage chair in the sun-room, enjoying a plate of hot pakoras and samosas followed by a nice helping of dhal, had momentarily seemed to banish the chill from the air. What tales he had imagined regaling his friends with! Though clearly, he would never be able to give them the full story. Merely that he, Youssuf Khan, had absconded on a road trip to London. Alone! Those were the actions of a hero for a man of his age. 'Then, we go to the rendezvous point and just sit tight for Ellis James to come and meet us. He told me on the phone he'd picked a safe place to take our statements.'

But Colin had been so jumpy that Youssuf had started to worry that he would attract the wrong kind of attention to them. Every time a passenger had joined the ranks of sombre-faced travellers, waiting patiently on the platform for their onward connection, Colin had covered the lower part of his face with his hand. Had looked down at his borrowed sandals, two sizes too big. Had started nagging in a high-pitched, stringy voice that this fellow over there had looked like Degsy; that that scraggy-looking girl over here had looked like Maggie.

'Ya-allah! Will you keep calm? Please! We've come all this way to do very important work. Your soul depends on it. Your conscience demands it.'

On that journey to Cheetham, Youssuf had sat in silence, peering out of the window as the hustle and bustle of Piccadilly Gardens and Victoria Station had given way to

273

the litter-strewn sidings of Collyhurst, punctuated only by 1970s tower blocks where the poor white trash lived. This had given way in turn to Abraham Moss – an area Youssuf had always felt more comfortable with and where he had spent some of his earliest years in Manchester, scratching a living in the garment factories of Strangeways, whilst living in a damp, run-down house with two other recently arrived Pakistani families on the Cheetham/Crumpsall border. Decades on, Youssuf contemplated how he had progressed, mainly thanks to his son's efforts, from those humble beginnings in a cold, damp new homeland, to the easy life in Boddlington Park.

The enormity of what he had been about to do had started to nibble away at his bravado at having run away from home. He had been about to ruin his son's life in a bid to save his soul: swapping a mansion built on corruption for prison and purifying penitence.

'Are you okay?' Colin had asked.

'Miles away,' he had said. 'It's our stop next.'

Walking through the backstreets up towards the day centre had been a cause for concern. Youssuf had been blighted by his slow, heavy legs and the laboured breathing of a sick man who had not taken his medication for three days. Furthermore, he had realised that Tariq would almost certainly have had every man, woman and child in the Asian community keeping their eyes peeled for him. Only the rain that had begun to fall in earnest had offered the hope of evading discovery – just long enough to meet with the detective.

'Why couldn't we have just met this Ellis James in town, where it was safer?' Colin had asked, linking him in a bid to speed up their progress.

The question had been a good one. Youssuf had frowned,

considering his answer. He'd stealthily observed two women in billowing black burkas, making their way up the hill towards the main road, wheeling shopping wagons. Had they recognised him? Unlikely, given how they had been engaged in womanly chatter. 'This is my turf,' he had said. 'If we're going to do something daring and defiant, it should be on familiar ground.' Had that been a good enough answer?

Colin hadn't seemed convinced. 'It's not my turf.'

'I don't know, then! I guess I just wanted to come home.' There it had been. In the pit of his empty, growling stomach, Youssuf had acknowledged an ache – a combined malady that couldn't be cured with tablets: homesickness and doubt. Now that his need for a quiet rebellion had been sated, he had been left with the very real and fairly unpalatable prospect of handing his only son over to the authorities. He had reflected on his cherished memories of his long-dead wife. What would Saffiya have counselled him to do?

'Is this it?' Colin had asked, shaking him out of his reverie.

Youssuf had smiled and exhaled deeply. Had looked up at the battered old signage, written in English, with subtitles beneath in Urdu, Punjabi, Hindi and Gujarati explaining that this was the day centre for North Manchester's elderly Asian community. He was back. And he had brought Colin with him. To avoid Tariq getting wind of his return, he'd better act fast. 'Yes.'

Inside, Colin had immediately aroused suspicion amongst the regulars. Youssuf had found himself beset by questions from his buddies, all shouting above the limits of their hearing aids in Urdu or Mirpur Punjabi.

'I heard you were missing, Youssuf. Your boy has been nagging everyone. Handing out leaflets. Where were you?'

'Who's the Chinese, dressed up like one of us? What's going on?'

'He's not Chinese,' Youssuf had said, avoiding the steely-eyed gaze of his arch-rival, Ibrahim. 'He's . . . from Kashmir. Yes. This is Mohammed from Kashmir, right near the Chinese border. He's a family friend. He's come for lunch, then we have business matters to discuss. Private business.'

Ibrahim, still enjoying the posture of a man half his age, had towered over Youssuf imperiously, snorting with derision. 'If he's Kashmiri, I'll eat my flip-flops. Does your wide-boy son, Tariq, know you're here?'

'Asalaam,' Colin had said, squinting through the borrowed glasses, trying to tug Youssuf away.

Youssuf had nudged him sharply in the ribs, shushing him and ushering him into the day room. But the massage chairs had already been taken, and though the smell of cooking had wafted through the day centre like narcotic gas, the food had not yet been ready. His stomach had growled in protest. 'We're going to have to get this over with quickly.'

They had sat together at the back of the packed arts and crafts room, hoping to take cover among the canvases – art of the arthritic, daubed in bright colours with shaky brushes. Youssuf had discreetly placed the call to Ellis James, explaining that they had arrived back in town and that they had better meet sharpish, lest Tariq get wind of his return.

'So, what's the plan?' Colin had said, pushing the half-framed glasses that were too big for his face back up his nose. Scratching at his flattened, black hair beneath the Pashtun hat.

'We wait.'

Now, Youssuf found himself staring blankly at the wonky-eyed portrait of a Bollywood starlet – Pooja Hegde – that one of the women had been painting as a gift for her granddaughter. But his mind was not on poorly proportioned Pooja. He realised that once he began the process of revealing all to Ellis James, he would be stepping over a threshold to a new, harsher world from which there would be no return. The Boddlington Park family home would be seized as an asset by the authorities, no doubt. Tariq's bank accounts would be frozen, rendering him reliant on Anjum's significantly lesser, legitimately earned income. Where would they stay? And if Tariq and Jonny were sent to prison – which undoubtedly, they would be – what would happen to Tariq inside? Were there other Asian men in Strangeways? Would he be ostracised for his cultured accent or revered by the other criminals as North Manchester's co-ruler?

He regarded Colin Chang, who presumably had nothing whatsoever to lose by giving evidence against the O'Briens, as long as he was guaranteed protection by the police. Colin had the chance of a clean slate. But the well-being of the Khans . . .? Now he was faced with the day of reckoning, Youssuf was wondering if his dogged pursuit of spiritual unimpeachability was actually just an act of self-indulgence.

Checking his watch, he saw he had fifteen minutes before they were due at the café rendezvous, just five minutes' walk away. Fifteen minutes to decide. To tell. Or not to tell.

'Hey, Mr Khan!' one of the young men who volunteered at the day centre said, placing a hand on his shoulder. The boy looked over at Colin, his eyebrows knitted together in an expression of puzzlement.

Youssuf looked up and patted his hand. 'Is it lunchtime?' He grabbed his stick, wondering if he could snaffle some pakoras before they headed out to meet the detective.

'No. But I called your family to tell them you're here. I hope you don't mind. Only, I've had your son dropping in three or four times a day, looking for you. It was your daughter-in-law I spoke to on the phone. She says Tariq will be round in five.'

'Round where?' Feeling the griping pain in his empty stomach move to his chest, Youssuf hoisted himself out of the seat, legs almost giving way beneath him. He dropped his stick. Cursed himself for his clumsiness.

Colin had also leaped to his feet, scooping the walking stick from the ground. Offering it to him. No need to communicate. They both realised that their window of opportunity to do the right thing was closing fast.

'Here,' the boy said, smiling, as if he had said something clever, the interfering donkey.

Glancing through the succession of doorways from the art room to the front of the building, Youssuf glimpsed the street beyond and the parking spaces out front. Was that Tariq's Mercedes, swinging into the space right beneath the window of the main day room?

'Out the back,' he told Colin, pushing the pharmacist towards the patio doors that led out to the communal gardens, certainly devoid of day centre members on a squally day like today.

Get going! He'll see you! But why am I running away from my boy? Why am I doing this? The din of conflicting voices was deafening. But Youssuf felt a compulsion to put distance between Tariq, Colin and himself. To buy those extra five minutes in which to consider this devilish conundrum.

Slipping through the side gate back onto the street as Tariq entered the day centre, wearing a smile of triumph and relief, Youssuf led Colin down a dark, desolate and drenched backstreet that led to the rendezvous point.

When a tall man stepped out from the shadowy recesses of a doorway, Youssuf yelped.

'Hello, Mr Khan. And Mr Chang. What a surprise! Going anywhere interesting, gentlemen?' The man's accent was identifiably Israeli. His appearance was distinctive too. A wide-brimmed black hat, a long black satin coat and the bushy beard and immaculate ringletted sidelocks of a Hassidic Jew.

This was the man who worked for Tariq at the factory. Youssuf was sure of it. He greeted him with a bemused smile, but at his side, Colin Chang baulked and started to crumple downwards to the floor.

'Smolensky, isn't it? Asaf Smolensky!' Youssuf said, feeling somehow this scene was all wrong but trying to keep the friendliness in his voice.

No answer.

The smile slid swiftly from his face when Tariq's taciturn employee withdrew a long, thin knife that in the murk of the alley seemed to draw all light to it. It shone now with lethal menace.

Chapter 34

Lev

'You took your time,' the DCI said, stepping out from behind a giant roll of felt-backed office carpet.

The sheer volume of the floor covering absorbed almost entirely any echo his voice might have had in that lofty space. Sales assistants were nearby, talking to some Asian man about a Berber in his native language. But their voices were reassuringly muffled.

'Fifteen bloody minutes, I've been waiting here like a berk! There's only so much browsing for cheap shit carpet you can do before you start to attract attention.'

'It was hard to find,' Lev said.

'Your type can't find your arse with both hands.' The DCI's breath was visible in the freezing *Carpet It Quick* warehouse air.

Lev could see why this destination had been chosen. Not far from the police HQ, on a quiet trading estate. No CCTV whatsoever, by the looks. Row after row of roll-ends stretching from the concreted floor to the corrugated iron ceiling and a veritable, double-height maze of off-the-roll bales to hide behind. It was a place you could get lost in.

The DCI looked Lev up and down; eyeing the pushchair and Jay, who was teething on a plastic ring, with clear disgust. 'Why've you brought a snotty-nosed kid to a meet?'

'Because he's *my* snotty-nosed kid.' Lev sized up Sheila's man-on-the-inside. The older detectives often seemed to let themselves go. This one had a round, shaved head and a fat neck like a Buddha. All red cheeks and wheezy, like his blood pressure was high. Too many years eating chippy in the car during a stakeout. 'Why you an ugly fat bastard?'

'Wind your neck in, son,' the copper said. 'It wouldn't take much to get you banged up. I know who you are, Leviticus Bell.' He took a step forwards and poked Lev in the chest with a chipolata digit.

'Yeah, I'm really scared,' Lev said, quietly praying that he would get this exchange over and done with as quickly as possible, securing his exit route from this purgatorial life. 'Cos being a bent Chief Inspector who takes handouts from South Manchester's crime boss makes you untouchable, doesn't it? The local Sunday schools are gonna be sending the little kids round to bottle everything that comes out of your gob, like you're spouting the word of God or some shit.'

'Shut your trap, smart-arse.'

Lev didn't much like the sneer that had set in like bad weather on the DCI's oversized face. This was not a cool guy. 'You're like one of them fishes what feeds on a shark's underbelly,' he said, pleased with the comparison. 'Anyway, I'm not standing here flirting with you. You got the SIM or what?'

The bent copper nodded and handed over a tiny baggie containing the small gold square.

'Money,' he said.

Lev took the robust brown envelope out of the inside pocket of his parka, wondering how much Sheila had put in there in return for this 'favour'. He was surprised that the DCI didn't check it but merely squeezed the envelope, trousering it with the deft hands of a man who regularly stashed illicit things of value in a hurry.

'Tell her I swapped that SIM for an identical one. Ellis James only got it from the fire service the other afternoon and I've made sure he's been a busy boy, investigating an attempted armed robbery that turned out to be owt and nowt.' The DCI winked. 'Far as I know, he didn't even get a chance to look at the original SIM, so I doubt he'd have made a copy.'

'You *doubt*?'

'That's as good as it gets, son. If she doesn't like it, she can give me her SIM back and see how that works for her. But the sweetener's non-refundable.' He patted his pocket and manoeuvred his heavy features into a half-grin.

Only too glad to be away from the freezing-cold claustrophobia and fibrous, asthma-inducing air of *Carpet It Quick*, Lev hastened away from the trading estate as fast as Jay's pushchair would allow him. He zig-zagged through the East Manchester backstreets, past almost identical run-down Victorian terraces, certain he could hear the call to prayer from a mosque, amplified to the faithful masses by the wind, though he couldn't spy a minaret from his vantage point. With every step he took, he felt a weight lifting incrementally, allowing the corners of his mouth to curve upwards.

Soon, he reached the place where Sheila O'Brien was parked in an anonymous-looking Nissan four-wheel drive. A rental, no doubt.

'Well?' she asked, leaning out of the driver's side window.

He popped the boot, collapsed Jay's pushchair, ramming it sideways into the space. Installed his son in the car seat at the back.

'Jesus! You know how to keep the sodding tension going, don't you?' she said, as he clambered into the passenger seat, blowing kisses back at Jay.

'Got it!' He withdrew the baggie, waving it beneath her nose. Snatched it away when she reached out to grab it from him. 'I want paying first. A deal's a deal. I've got a future to fork out for.' He held his hand out, expecting his palm to be crossed with rather more than silver.

The delight in Sheila's face – brilliant enough to light up the interior of the car and that dank street – was quickly extinguished. 'You're getting nothing til you've done another job for me.'

That sensation of lightness that had buoyed him from *Carpet It Quick* to the car was replaced by a leaden feeling in the pit of his stomach. Thoughts of the judgemental social worker suddenly started to nibble away at the rosy mental image of him and Jay, spending their first night together in a new home, far, far away from shitty, gritty Manchester and its godforsaken satellite towns. 'You said. You said you'd pay me when I got the SIM card back. Well, I have. You're safe. And as long as you pay me, I won't be telling no one about you and Tariq. A promise is a promise. I wouldn't mess about with Jay's future like that.'

Sheila glanced back at the tiny boy in his car seat, babbling away happily to himself, pointing to the sky, the tree across the road, and the white van, parked some hundred yards away, naming them all in some language that clearly made sense to him. 'Why did you bring him with you on a job, for Christ's sakes? Why couldn't you have left him with Gloria?'

'Me Mam? She's got her head stuffed up her arse since she met this new feller. She trashed the house getting ready this morning and disappeared off, saying she had to go out and get something for a date. Lipstick, new knickers, fluffy bloody handcuffs . . . Who knows? It's like having teenager in the house as well as a toddler. She got stuck in a bloody maze near the Lakes! A maze. What the fuck's that about? He buggered off and left her to be rescued by some German tourists. I don't think she even likes him, but she keeps going back for more.'

Tutting, Sheila shook her head. 'She's shag-happy. That's what's going on with her. I'll deal with her later. But in the meantime, I need you to get some heavy bags for me from the safety deposit place.'

Lev exhaled so hard that the windscreen of the Nissan steamed up. 'Aw, man! You're not on.'

'It's just some heavy lifting. Five rubble bags. You get to keep one if you bring them up to the car for me and help me get them stashed. I can't lift them and they've got to come out, like yesterday. That DCI you just got the SIM card off gave me a hot tip. He says the tax are gonna raid me.' With a broken red nail, she tapped the giant, glittering solitaire engagement ring and the diamond-encrusted eternity rings on her tanned, slender fingers. 'They can piss off if they think they're getting my money! But I can't be dragging bags and they weigh a bloody tonne.'

'Why not?' Lev ran through all the reasons why Sheila might feasibly entrust him with what was obviously a huge sum of cash. A sporting injury? Concern for her nails? He smiled, wiping the steamy windscreen with his forearm. 'You're up the duff, aren't you?'

She pushed him hard in the shoulder, her over-made-up face looking pinched. Dark under the eyes, beneath that concealer. Something was troubling Sheila O'Brien. 'I am not up the duff!' Started the engine, revving it for all it was worth as if to make some kind of a point. They squealed away from the kerb, unaware that the white van had started to follow them.

'Nope. Whatever you say.' He grimaced. 'A little Conky, running round, eh? Will it inherit his eyes and nose? Ouch.'

Glancing to the side, Lev was surprised to see Sheila had fat, shining tears standing in her eyes.

'I'm giving you a big bloody bag of cash, Leviticus Bell,' she said, blinking fast, as though she could will the tears back inside her. 'Enough for you to stop shooting your mouth off.'

Tariq's baby, then. He opted to hold his tongue.

They pulled up close to the safety deposit facility in town, among the hubbub of workers scurrying from their places of work to cheap eateries, emerging minutes later with cardboard coffee cups in their hands. Outside the office block where Sheila had found a parking space, men and women stood, muffled up in anoraks or shivering in inadequate woollen coats, dragging on vaping sticks and cigarettes, their complexions almost the same shade of grey as the sky that hung limply above them.

'It's a pity there's no spaces outside,' Sheila said, scouting the busy street ahead. 'But it's probably best we don't park where that bloody camera can catch us.' She pointed to a CCTV unit that was strapped high on a lamp post, angled down towards the entrance to the vaults. 'I reckon that damned thing is why HMRC is about to pounce. I reckon it's caught me going in and out of the safety deposit place once too often with big bags.'

Lev squinted up at the camera, following its trajectory downwards to the anonymous-looking entrance. 'How we gonna do this? They're not going to let me take your shit out, are they? Not unless you give them permission.'

Glancing at Jay in the back seat, Sheila's red-rimmed eyes narrowed. 'Bring Jay and the pushchair. There's a massive golf bag in the boot. Use that and all. Follow me in after a minute. Act natural.'

Uncomfortable with the notion of using his son to aid and abet the movement of unlaundered drug money, Lev shook his head in silence. Rolled his eyes. What option did he have? How much cash would be in a rubble sack, stuffed to the brim? Certainly the hundred grand she'd promised him. 'Bugger it. Let's go.'

Idling on the street corner, he watched Sheila drape her handbag over her arm and trot into the facility as though she owned the place.

'Look at that, Jay,' he said to his son. 'All the confidence in the world. That's how I want you to be when you grow up, love.' The boy clapped his hands together, pointing at a 'nee-naw' that drove past with sirens blaring. 'Losers like your dad just can't strut like that. Even if one day I win a million on the lottery . . .' He continued his train of thought in silence, certain the sickly stink of poverty would always cleave to him, even if he were clad head to toe in the very finest of designer togs. The cumbersome chip on his shoulder that was part of his genetic inheritance from Gloria *and* his father would always prevent him from flying. But he was determined that for Jay, it wouldn't be so.

Full of purpose, he followed Sheila a minute later, carrying the trolley and the golf bag, slung across his body, carefully navigating his way down a winding stone staircase. He passed through one iron-barred gate after another as the buzzer entry system bade him down, down, down to Manchester's discretely guarded hoards. Finally, he and Sheila met at the bottom.

'I've squared it,' she said, nodding and smiling at what appeared to be a dour-faced jailor, carrying the largest bunch of keys Lev had ever seen. 'They know you're helping me because of my back problem.' She smiled. Two rows of radiant whitened teeth like strip lighting being switched on in that gloomy subterranean place.

Alone among the safety deposit boxes, Sheila led Lev to a box that was more the size of a large cupboard. 'In here. Just get it all stacked in the golf bag and on the trolley. No looking at what's here and no questions asked. Right? Act natural.'

'Yeah, you keep saying that. Easier said than done!'

Jay had started to cry, presumably freaked by being in such an enclosed space. Perhaps he sensed that they were deep below the city, on a par with the remnants of the secret, subterranean old Manchester – a now long-forgotten network of tunnels, abandoned shops and even a disused tube station that had been buried beneath the relatively new layout above. Perhaps Jay was sensitive to the city's artifice, with the grit and grime of the truth lying just beneath a shiny surface. Either way, he was making a right racket, pressing his hands to his ears as though the pressure of the air at that depth was too much for his delicate little lugholes.

'Don't worry, Jay-Jay. We'll be out of here in a minute.' Lev could feel the sweat rolling down his back as he hoisted the rubble sacks from the vault, stashing one in the basket beneath the pushchair and one beneath Jay's bottom, meaning the boy was perched uncomfortably too high in his seat, reminiscent of some scene from the *Princess and the Pea*. He shoved another two into the golf bag. 'There's no room for the last one,' he told Sheila.

Sheila tugged on the waistband of his jogging bottoms. 'In there.'

'A rubble sack full of cash?' His whisper was more of a shout.

'Do it. Zip your coat up over it. Come on, for Christ's sake! Earn your keep.'

His muscles screamed in complaint as he lugged the golf bag and the heavily laden pushchair back up the stairs to street level. All those years of bench-pressing in the gym had nothing on this.

With Sheila already waiting in the car, Lev was careful to pull his hood over his face and to put up Jay's rain hood on exiting the vaults. The last thing he needed was Ellis James on his case, asking why a part-time cleaner and suspected gang member had showed up on the council's CCTV footage, leaving a place where the legitimately rich stashed their goodies.

'Let us in!' he said, knocking on the passenger door of the Nissan.

Odd that Sheila got out and opened the boot but hadn't unlocked the passenger side for him.

'In there,' she said, indicating where the golf bag and the bag down his jogging bottoms should go. 'And the one that Jay's sitting on.' Smiling encouragingly.

'I thought that sack was gonna slice my bollocks off, getting up them stairs.' He chuckled whilst quietly acknowledging the unsettled feeling in his stomach, realising it had nothing to do with the well-being of his tackle. Something was off.

With four bags stashed in the boot, he started to undo the clip on the straps of Jay's pushchair.

'Not so fast,' Sheila said.

Her face was set hard. All deadly serious, now.

'Eh?'

'You can get the tram.'

'You're kidding.'

'If you think I'm driving you to my new hidey-hole, you're having a laugh with yourself. I've got help at the other end. You can get the tram or bus or a taxi, even. You've got a hundred K in the basket of that pushchair. You can afford a black cab!'

'Tight cow,' Lev said to himself, manoeuvring the sluggish pushchair along a quiet backstreet towards the rebuilt St. Peter's Square, where the trams were finally stopping again. Thankfully, the rubble sack was completely hidden from view in the cleverly constructed basket beneath the push-chair. He hoped it would hold the weight of all that paper. The last thing he needed was a sack of twenties and fifties blowing across town.

He was just about to tell Jay what Daddy had decided to make for tea when he registered a white van pulling up behind him, depicted in the reflection of a plate glass window on the office block up ahead. At first, he thought nothing of it. Vans like that were everywhere. Jay threw his beaker onto the ground and started to cry.

When Lev stooped to pick the beaker up, the muscular, hairy arms that grabbed him from behind took him by surprise. One arm around his torso. One over his mouth. Kicking out, unable to yell, he found himself dragged back-wards into the deep shadows of a secluded office block loading bay. Jay, strapped in his pushchair, lay within sight but beyond reach. Brakes off, slowly rolling backwards down the backstreet's incline towards the dual carriageway. But Lev could do nothing.

The stinging blow to his head stopped his thoughts dead at 'Jay!'

Chapter 35

Sheila

Sorry bout the maze. Let me tek you to Blackpool on nice date. Mek day of it n see the lights. Luv Bob. x

Gloria held the phone up, encouraging Sheila to re-read the message for the fourth time in ten minutes.

'Go on. What do you think? Good, eh?' Grinning from ear to ear and with a glow that exceeded the wattage of the kitchen chandelier, Gloria looked like a woman who was getting laid regularly for the first time in decades.

'Yeah, yeah. I already said. I'm really glad for you.'

'What on earth is up with you, Sheila? You're being really nowty and you seem out of breath.'

Avoiding her business partner's scrutiny, Sheila retreated to the other side of the kitchen, putting the kettle on and rummaging through the cupboards to find the ginger biscuits. Good for nausea, it had said online. 'Nothing. I'm fine. Except you were on my case the minute I got home. I wish you'd been that enthusiastic when we were supposed to be viewing office space.'

On Sheila's return home, after the swift drop-off at her mother's where she had stowed the rubble sacks of cash in the old coal-hole and swapped cars, leaving the Nissan for her mother to return to the car-hire place, Gloria had been waiting at the gates. She had been parked up in her Mazda, itching to show her this declaration of enthusiasm and Bob's possibly significant use of the word 'luv'.

'*Rejoice in hope, be patient in tribulation, be constant in prayer.* Romans 12:12,' Gloria said, beaming at the screen of her phone. 'After a lifetime of tribulation and prayer, I think, I'm finally going through my "hope phase", Sheila.'

'Lev told me Bob left you in a field and buggered off.'

Gloria closed her eyes melodramatically, spreading her newly manicured fingers on the worktop. 'That was a misunderstanding. He had a sudden work commitment.'

'Oh, and you didn't?'

'Please don't ruin it.'

Sheila was about to launch into a rebuke about Gloria's new-found rebelliousness when the buzzer went. She frowned. Conky, who was currently giving the O'Brien dealers a briefing on what to do if they spotted Bancroft's interlopers on their turf, wasn't expected home for another couple of hours. Was this it? Was this the HMRC crackdown? Had she been fed wrong information by her man on the inside about the raid? Her breath coming short, she made her way to the hall and checked the screen to see who was at the gate.

'Lev?!' And he looked in a bad way. Doubled up. Throwing up, from what she could see. Behind him was a cab. It sped off, leaving Lev alone.

Calling Gloria to her aid, Sheila pressed the button to open the gates. Pulled her thickest cardigan from the coat stand and crunched her way briskly down the drive, wrapping the twenty-ply cashmere tightly around her against the chill.

Lev was on all fours at the end of the drive, dry-heaving. Beside him, Jay was trying to climb out of his pushchair, unsecured. When Lev looked up, Sheila saw that the left side of his head had been bleeding heavily. The flow had covered his scalp, face, neck and shoulders in claret-coloured blood.

'Jesus! What the hell happened?'

Gloria was right behind her, hands flapping. 'Oh good Lord. Good Lord. Oh dear. Good Lord.' She reached out towards her son but withdrew her hand. Reached in. Withdrew, grimacing at the blood.

'Help,' Lev said, heaving anew and bringing up bile onto Gloria's chunky court shoes.

'Oh, really!' Gloria took a step backwards, staring at the mess. Holding her nose.

With her left hand, Sheila grabbed Jay by the upper arm and coaxed him back into his pushchair. With her right, she took out her new phone and dialled Conky's number. He picked up after only two rings.

'Sheila. Are you—?'

'Get round here straight away. And get Fitzpatrick. It's urgent.'

'The doc?'

'Yep. Lev's in a bad way. Head injury. But we don't need paramedics and 999 knowing our business.'

Sinking to her knees, she held Lev by the shoulders. 'A private doctor's on his way, Lev.' She raised her voice, wondering if he could hear her or make sense of what she said. Tried to make eye contact.

'Man hit,' he said. His speech was slurred. He started to gag. 'Hit head.'

'Help me get him inside,' she told Gloria.

But Gloria seemed to be in shock, a puzzled expression

on her face as she studied the splatter pattern of bile on her shoes.

'Gloria!' Sheila yelled. 'Bring Jay in. Now!'

Wondering if the fledgling life in her belly would cope with the exertion, Sheila somehow managed to strong-arm Lev up the drive and into the house. Counting the minutes until Conky and Fitzpatrick showed – only moments between them. Their respective cars crunched and skidded up the long gravel driveway.

'Is he gonna be all right?' she asked, as the discreet private practitioner cleaned Lev's head wound.

'He needs a CT scan to check for a bleed on the brain.' Fitzpatrick's breath smelled of stale coffee. His clothes had a whiff of hospital corridors and medicinal alcohol about them. He fitted a blood pressure cuff around Lev's arm. Pumped it up and stood for several seconds in sombre silence while he took Lev's pulse. 'His blood pressure's in his boots. He needs fluids.' He shone a penlight into his eyes. 'Pupils are dilating fine, though. We should get him over to the hospital as soon as—'

'This needs handling with sensitivity,' Conky said – a commanding presence, as he stood, legs astride, filling the doorway to the guest bedroom. 'The lad's been attacked, possibly by a business rival. We don't need the authorities sticking their oar in. That's why Mrs O'Brien pays you through the nose, so she does.'

Fitzpatrick nodded, rubbing his eyes – prematurely haggard, but not for a heart surgeon who burned the candle at both ends, juggling NHS clinics and private practice with removing the odd bullet or stitching the odd head wound on the side for Manchester's bad boys. 'Bring him to my private rooms. We've got a scanner on-site. I'll get him scanned tonight and we'll see what's what.' A nod and a wink and his palm was greased with a cool couple of grand. 'But in the meantime, if his condition deteriorates and he gets drowsy or starts vomiting again, get him to A&E immediately.'

After some thirty minutes, Lev had started to pull round in earnest. His speech was gaining clarity. Gloria had finally calmed down. She was sitting in the easy chair in the corner of the guest room, bouncing Jay on her knee, feeding him ice cream to ease the boy's teething pain. But still, Gloria was pointedly looking anywhere but at her own son, seemingly unable to process her own feelings about Lev's head wound, Sheila assessed. Or perhaps just being a cold-hearted bitch.

'Did you see who did it?' Sheila asked, perching on the edge of the bed.

Lev fixed her with hazy eyes. 'Nah. Whoever it was came at me from behind.' He spoke slowly, as if considering every word were an effort. 'But I did clock a white van pull up, reflected in a window. And now I think of it, there was the same kind of van parked in that street, when you picked us up after the meet with the copper.'

A white van. Sheila mentally hit 'control F' to find all incidences of a white van in her memory's files. Hadn't she seen a white van knocking around town in almost every office-to-let she had visited? Hadn't there been a white van outside M1 House? Could she remember its driver? No. And white vans were everywhere. But hadn't she regularly seen one hanging around outside the house?

'I'm being followed,' she pronounced.

'White vans are ubiquitous, She,' Conky said, advancing into the room. Leaning against the dressing table with his arms folded and his glasses perched on his forehead.

'Even my boyfriend, Bob, drives a white van when he's

working, Sheila,' Gloria said, beaming at the very mention of the word 'boyfriend'. 'It's just a coincidence.'

'I don't believe in coincidences,' Sheila said. She turned to Conky. Realised that what she was about to ask of him would scupper her blissful indulgences with Tariq for at least a week. But then, perhaps if Conky suspected anything of her affair, this would allay his suspicions. 'I want you to trail me for the next few days. Me and Gloria, if you can. Get one of the other lads on her.'

'But the feller came after me,' Lev said. 'He left me for dead and all. The only reason I'm still here and Jay-Jay's pushchair didn't roll into traffic was a couple of smokers outside the next office block. They heard Jay crying and ran out to help. In the nick of time! He was just about to go under a frigging bus.'

'Could this feller have been after the . . . *thing* I'd given you?' Sheila asked, sensing that Conky and Gloria had pricked up their ears. But the nosey sods could whistle if they thought she was about to clarify her financial arrangements with Lev.

Lev closed his eyes. 'It's all still there.'

Sheila could feel Conky's eyes boring into the back of her head. 'Listen, if your ex-scrubber had been savvy enough to put a hit out on you, she would have taken Jay.'

'That strumpet's too slothful and money-grubbing to hire a hit man!' Gloria said. '*The desire of the sluggard kills him, for his hands refuse to labour. All day long he craves and craves, but the righteous gives and does not hold back.* Proverbs 21:25–26.'

'Shut it, Mam,' Lev said. 'Just take a fucking day off, will you?'

Patting Lev's hand, Sheila continued. 'I reckon it's more likely this van driver has been after either me or your mother. I'm not sure why they've gone after you today, but I'm pretty certain I *have* been followed. For months. And I didn't think anything of it. He's got to be one of Bancroft's.'

'I'll happily trail you, Sheila,' Conky said. 'I wouldn't want to jeopardise the safety of the woman I love for a nano-second.' Suddenly he was standing right next to her with a hot, territorial hand on her shoulder. 'But catch yourself on! I'll be finding out all your lady secrets, won't I? He he.' Wink, wink.

There was jocularity in his voice but Sheila could detect uncertainty and hurt beneath the faux chuckle. He'd seen Tariq leaving that hotel. She was sure of it.

Later, with the house finally empty of guests and Conky away to M1 House to staffing issues with the O'Brien dealers and Frank – the riotous noise of the three Bells now merely experienced as tinnitus – Sheila ascended to the en suite in the guest room at the top of the house, where she knew she would be undisturbed. She took out the pregnancy test she had bought earlier.

'Who am I kidding?' she asked her reflection in the mirror above the sink. She already had that pinched look that she had acquired at the start of all her previous pregnancies. Five in total. Paddy had thumped three out of her. She winced at the memories, feeling his erstwhile wrath ricochet across her already bloated abdomen. The two pregnancies that had endured had grown into Amy and Dahlia, of course. But Sheila was experienced enough to know the signs. 'I already know the result.'

She peed on the stick, feeling a rush of unexpected euphoria. Now, she had to wait.

Sitting on that guest toilet, Sheila considered her situation. She had been careful. She had been cunning. She had taken the reins of Paddy's business and had steered them down a better-hewn path that was more suited to the modern, digital age and an economy that relied on the service industries.

'Why the hell have I still got Ellis James and Tax Bitch on my back?' she asked the spotlights, sunk into the gabled ceiling.

Toying with the silken panties that hung around her ankles, staring blankly at her painted toenails, she shook her head. Someone was stoking up the obsessed Ellis James like a bear agitating a beehive, hoping to bag a golden honey pot. And where James went, that frumpy cow Ruth Darley followed.

'Bancroft?'

Except Bancroft had a vested interest in keeping South Manchester running smoothly. He wanted to swoop in and absorb her going concerns as his own. The Boddlingtons wouldn't sabotage her in this way either, because their priority was covering their own arses and keeping as far from Ellis James and HMRC as possible. And now she knew Tariq biblically, at least, she was certain he wasn't the kind to go running to the police with tales. The Boddlingtons took by force or through negotiation.

No. Somebody was trying to ruin her. But who? Could Katrina, in some fit of jealousy and need to avenge her brother's death, be stirring the shit? Yes. Katrina.

'I wouldn't put it past that sneaky, hard-faced cow.'

Two minutes were up. Squeezing her eyes shut and swallowing down the dyspepsia that roiled around her gut, Sheila took the pregnancy test up from the lip of the adjacent bidet. Took a deep breath.

Here she was, standing at the edge of the precipice. A woman in her mid-forties; a woman being chased down a reproductive cul-de-sac by the passage of time and physical decay; a woman trying, after years of being nothing more than a high-end masturbatory aid to a bullying man, to make it in a world of men. Slavishly she had pandered to the last glorious sputter of her youthful hormones as they prepared to abandon her for good – had she screwed it all up when she screwed her business rival knowingly without using protection?

'Please God,' she said, though she wasn't certain what she was asking God for.

Looked down at the test. Two blue lines. Bold. Perfectly visible. No room for doubt.

Sheila O'Brien was carrying Tariq Khan's baby.

Chapter 36

Conky

'I'm losing you,' Conky muttered beneath his breath as he trailed some twenty metres behind Sheila. He wove his way in and out of the throng of pedestrians, all hurrying and scurrying to their places of work before the clock struck nine. 'I can feel it in my bones. Tariq Khan with his hair and his abs. Bastard.'

Sheila was wearing flats today. Unusual. She was dressed in uncharacteristically loose clothing too. Sensibly attired for the freezing damp. Not like Sheila at all.

Concentrate on the job in hand, for God's sake! Stop feeling fecking sorry for yourself, man.

Glancing across the road, he could still see the van driver, shadowing Sheila's movements. He had followed the sneaky bastard from the car park by the MEN arena, on the flattened site of Manchester's oldest, most iconic brewery, where the white van had cunningly sandwiched itself between two long-wheel-based Sprinters in an elevated section of the car park. Had Conky not been looking out for this bollocks, he would never have spotted him from the main car park below. The guy – a man in his fifties with a bad fake tan wearing a baseball cap at a ridiculous angle over what appeared to be white hair, dressed in grubby workman's cargo trousers and work boots, all covered by an anonymous anorak – knew his stuff.

Now, he slid into a café while Sheila disappeared into the building opposite – the one where she had just leased office space. How long was the mysterious workman going to sit there? Conky debated whether he too should venture into the café to wait it out until his next move. Would the man recognise him if he sat a few tables away? Possibly. With his distinctive appearance, every criminal north of London and south of Glasgow would spot him a mile off.

Hanging back, browsing in a man's boutique from which he had a good view of the workman, Conky avoided catching glimpses of himself in the mirror.

'Can I help you?' some trendy young shop assistant asked. The lad had a head full of glorious, gelled hair. He was staring at Conky's confection of glued-on hairpiece with an expression that walked the border between admiration and disbelief.

Unsure of what to say to a boy like that in a young feller's shop like this, Conky opted to stare at the assistant's footwear. 'Your guddies are beezer. Can I try them in a size thirteen?'

'My trainers?'

'Well, I'm not talking about your fecking underpants, am I?'

Positioning himself by the window, pretending to admire a suit, Conky noticed that the workman buried his head inside his tabloid newspaper when Gloria walked by. Interesting. Gloria could clearly ID this chump.

It had been agreed beforehand that Sheila and Gloria would move about as frequently as possible in a bid to flush this guy out conclusively. Before the shop assistant had had the opportunity to bring the trainers out for him to try, Conky was on the move again, following the man who was following the two women.

Down the cobbled King Street they walked until they reached a natural pause thanks to the traffic of Deansgate. Outside Kendals, the two parted company. Conky expected the man to follow Sheila but was surprised when he tailed Gloria. Odd. Popping in and out of various shops, the trail went cold when Gloria shook both of them off, disappearing somewhere in the pedestrianised St Anne's Square. Dead end.

The following day, Conky began his labour of love anew, this time picking up the white van man back on the trail of Sheila, who was also being followed by Ellis James. Again, Conky was forced to spend another few uncomfortable hours ducking and diving out of sight of both the van man and the shabby detective.

'I wonder if this guy's a cop,' he mused aloud to Sheila on the phone. 'Could be working for Ellis James.'

'Not if he battered the living daylights out of Lev,' she said.

Fair point. Even the bent cops didn't play dirty like that unless they got a nonce in the cells and thought they could get away with it.

'Try to follow him home when he's finished with me,' Sheila said. 'See where he lives or if he meets up with anyone.'

Hanging up, Conky sensed from the brisk efficiency in Sheila's tone that it wouldn't be long before it was only business between them. He could feel their intimacy evaporating and with it, his hopes of living out his remaining years beside his dream woman. The woman he had always yearned to share his triumphs, failures and favourite novels with. Deep within him, there was a part of Conky willing to acknowledge that he and Sheila actually had very little in common at all, apart from history and an employer/employee bond. There had been chemistry. A spark of sorts had definitely ignited after Paddy's funeral, when she had had him teetering on the edge of death in a hired apartment in Beetham Tower. But if Sheila had indeed embarked on a sordid affair with her opposite number, the quiet domesticity that followed a day's toil at the coalface of the O'Brien criminal empire was clearly not something Sheila wanted to pursue longer term. The novelty of loving a devoted but ugly man had clearly worn off for her, though Conky's abiding adoration of Sheila would never, ever wane. Of that he was certain. He would carry his love for her to the grave.

Caught up in his thoughts of the inevitable grieving he must do for this enduring love-lost, Conky was surprised when the paths of Ellis James and the white van man diverged. Lev's suspected attacker led Conky back to the Bramshott mansion.

'Oh, now this is interesting. Let's see what happens here.'

The white van pulled up directly outside the house. Conky was careful to hang back outside the neighbours' some four doors down to observe as the cheeky wee bastard removed ladders from the roof of his vehicle and hopped over the fence.

'Come on. Turn round, you shifty fecker so I can get a good look at your bake.'

Pondering what his next move was, Conky scurried over from the cover of his car to watch the man's movements through a miserly gap in the dense laurel hedging. The wide Bramshott boulevard was the sort of exclusive place where all the households had the ominous black CCTV orbs hanging from poles in several locations on the periphery of their properties, which meant they could see the road as well as inside the manicured boundary. He'd be lucky if some nosey do-gooder didn't call the police on him. Their kind certainly wouldn't recognise a neighbour if one slapped them in the face with a proverbial wet kipper. Though they might ask if it had been responsibly sourced.

Whistling. The van man was whistling something jaunty by Wham. Clambering up the ladder, carrying a mix of something in a bucket and a toolkit hanging around his thick waist. Conky's lower legs screamed with discomfort as he crouched, watching what appeared to be a workman carrying out a simple repair job. Odd.

The van man hung his bucket from the top of the ladder. Started to gouge out mortar in the brickwork just beneath the master bedroom where Sheila and Conky slept.

Pointing? Was this lunatic actually fixing pointing that wasn't in need of repair? The house had only been built a few years earlier. It was a state-of-the-art, contemporary mansion, with stylish grey oversized windows, a soupçon of dressed stone and red cedar cladding. *The place would give Huf Haus an inferiority complex, so why's this eejit fixing it?*

Barking and a woman's voice made Conky jump.

'You! What are you doing?'

Conky turned around to find an elderly woman crossing the street. She was dressed in expensive-looking hot-pink gym gear: the kind that looked good on Sheila – a woman twenty years this old bag's junior. Not wanting to alert the van man to his presence, he strode over to head Mrs Nosey Tits off.

'Oh, good morning,' he said. 'I'm your neighbour. I'm just checking that your man there is doing the job he's been paid to do for my partner, Mrs O'Brien.'

The woman's taut face barely moved. Too many face uplifts on this one, and Conky noted the type of boob job that looked preposterous on the young, let alone the elderly. 'You're not Mr O'Brien.'

'Mr O'Brien sadly passed away in the spring. Or did the sizeable funeral cortège fail to pique your interest in the same way that a well-dressed man squatting by a bush did?' He removed his glasses and treated her to The Eyes.

As she baulked and started to come out with some clap-trap about the Neighbourhood Watch scheme, Conky heard drilling on the other side of the hedge. What was that trespassing bastard up to?

With Nosey Tits fobbed off, Conky returned to the gap. Whatever the man had done, he was now merely applying mortar neatly to the spaces between the bricks. The scraping noise as he took the excess mix off set Conky's teeth on edge. He had had enough. Surreptitiously, he made his way to the gates and used his fob to open them. Noiselessly, they swished open. The man was still busy about his task. Good.

Sprinting the fifty metres to the ladder, Conky shouted. 'You! What the hell are you doing, you trespassing, stalking fecker?'

Finally, the man turned to him. Like the nosey neighbour, he looked like an old man who couldn't bear to give up on his youth. He still wore the baseball cap at a jaunty angle. Shiny faced and perma-tanned – the approximate shade of a cheesy puff. Not like any builder Conky had ever met. There was surprise in those wide eyes. 'Oh,' he simply said.

Conky grabbed the bottom of the ladder and started to shake it.

'Get off, you nutcase!' the van man shouted.

'I'll get off when you tell me what the hell you're doing up there.'

'Pointing!'

'The pointing doesn't need doing, you shyster. And you've been following Mrs O'Brien, who owns this place.' He started to shake the ladder from left to right.

'Stop! Stop! I'm going to bleeding fall and break my neck.' Clinging onto the top of the ladder with a white-knuckled grip, the man seemed sufficiently rattled. His cap fell off, revealing white hair beneath, impressively gelled into spikes that his headgear had not flattened.

'Get down from there and speak to me, you lying arsehole.' Flashing the man the stock of his gun, holstered against his body, Conky finally let go of the ladder, allowing the trespasser to descend.

When he set foot on the ground, he came up short on Conky, though most men did. His breath was rasping. His hands shook. Whoever this guy was, he was an amateur. A pro didn't show fear. Ever.

Conky gripped him by the shoulder. Took his phone out of his coat pocket.

'Say, "cheese!"'

'What?'

He snapped the guy's photo and pinged it immediately in a text to Sheila, Gloria and Lev, asking if they recognised the man.

'Now, why are you tampering with brickwork that hasn't got a damned thing wrong with it? Why are you skulking around Sheila O'Brien's garden and why did you beat Leviticus Bell over the head and leave him for dead? Who are you?'

The man held his trembling hands up as a gesture of surrender. 'My name's Bob. I'm doing property maintenance. Honest.'

'What's with the stalking routine?'

'I don't know what you're on about.'

'I've been following you, following Mrs O'Brien and Mrs Bell. Tell me what your beef is with Lev Bell.'

'I haven't been following a soul. I swear. If it looks like I have, it's complete coincidence, mate.'

To punch, or not to punch? It was hard to tell, studying the man's clearly Botoxed face, whether he was lying or not. No discernible expression at all. Very perplexing for Conky, who preferred to leave nuance to the literature he read and to deal in absolutes when it came to his job.

'Are you gonna let go of my shoulder, you big Irish ranch-pot?'

Punch.

Battering his fist against the trespasser's jaw, Conky paused only to reiterate the question, 'Why did you attack Leviticus Bell?' He held the man tightly by the bib of his overalls, preventing any chance of escape.

'I didn't!'

'I don't believe you.' A kick in the bollocks and a knee to the stomach had Bob, the uninvited maintenance man, spitting blood into the paling autumnal hydrangeas.

'Please yourself, pal. But it's the truth.'

Conky hauled him up against the wall by his straps so that they were face to face. He pushed his glasses up so he could eyeball this stubborn ponce.

'If you're a builder with all that botulism filling out your wrinkles and those idiotic plucked eyebrows, I'll eat my superior-quality hairpiece.' He glanced down at Bob's hands. 'I've never met a manual labourer that had such clean fingernails for a start. You're full of more shite than the sewerage works at Trafford Park. Who are you working for, you duplicitous fuck-trumpet?'

'Myself. I've got a lickle property development company.

Honest. And I look after my hands. Clean fingernails are very—'

'Bancroft? Is that it?'

Conky administered another blow to Bob's belly when only silence ensued. He was about to do something unkind to the prick's ears with a pair of pliers that he'd spotted in his tool belt when his phone pinged multiple times in his pocket. Dropping Bob to the ground, Conky read the response from Sheila.

Never seen him before. Why? Is e'thing OK?

Then from Lev.

Can't tell. Never got a look at twat's face.

Finally, the response from Gloria.

That's my boyfriend, Bob. Don't touch him. I'm on my way.

'You're Gloria Bell's feller?' Conky frowned, wishing he'd paid more attention to the stream of consciousness, Bible quotes and other verbal diarrhoea that came out of Gloria's mouth. 'Gloria? Gloria Bell? She doesn't have a feller.'

'Yes she does,' Bob said, dusting himself down. The bruising on his jaw was already starting to show purple. Swelling beneath the skin made his face appear even more stretched tight than before. 'We met at speed-dating.'

Taking a step back, Conky thumbed the gun in its holster beneath his coat. 'Where?'

'The big night club. You know? The famous one.'

'M1 House?'

'Yep. That's it.'

This unlikely turn of events felt like the intellectual equivalent of bad maths to Conky. A builder with a Botoxed face dating Pulp Friction, of all people. An apparent stalker and possible attacker of an O'Brien employee. A man too old for clubbing, who had been inside M1 House but who claimed not to be in the employ of Bancroft. None of it stacked up. There was an important part of the equation missing but Conky couldn't put his finger on what that might feasibly be.

Pinching Bob's unpleasant button nose between his forefinger and thumb, Conky pushed him to his knees. 'You expect me to swallow this crap? Mrs O'Brien doesn't recognise your photo. So, how come you're working on her house if she doesn't know you from Adam?'

With eyes clenched shut, Bob opened his mouth to respond. But his words were drowned out by the beeping of a car horn and the revving of an engine. The sound of squealing tyres in the street and more impatient horn-blowing heralded the arrival of Gloria. Conky opened the gate with a flick of the fob and watched with curiosity as her Mazda swished up the gravel drive, swerving just short of the grand entrance.

'What in the Lord's name are you doing, Conky McFadden?' Gloria yelled, climbing out of her car. 'Put Robert down.'

Releasing his grip on the builder's nose, Conky wiped his fingers on his overalls. 'So he *is* called Bob.'

'And he *is* my boyfriend!' Gloria said, hands on hips.

'Well, what's he doing repairing an almost new house, then, when Sheila's never clapped eyes on him before?'

Bob rubbed his nose and shot a wounded look in Conky's direction. 'I told you. I do property maintenance. The pointing wanted a bit of TLC.'

'You sidestep questions like a politician, Robert the Property Developer,' Conky said. Glancing up at the wet mortar beneath Sheila's bedroom window, he contemplated climbing the ladder to see exactly what this shifty son of a bitch had been up to up there. But then Conky remembered that he hated ladders with a passion and that his legs were playing merry hell with him because he kept forgetting to take his thyroxine. 'This is the chump that was tailing Sheila,' he told Gloria. 'I'd put money on it that he bashed in your son's head. What do you have to say to that?'

Clasping her hand to her chest, Gloria looked as though she were caught in a private maelstrom of conflicting emotions and loyalties. 'Did you hurt my boy?' she asked, taking several steps towards Bob in those schoolmarm shoes she wore. 'My Leviticus, who had to have a brain scan? Did you? Tell me honestly, Bob. *There are six things that the Lord hates, seven that are an abomination to him: haughty eyes . . .'* Another step towards him and Bob's face was beginning to buckle like an empty Tango can. '. . . *a lying tongue, and hands that shed innocent blood, a heart that devises wicked plans . . .'* Ever closer she moved. The volume of her voice rose until she stood only inches away from Bob, shouting at the top of her voice. '. . . *feet that make haste to run to evil, a false witness who breathes out lies . . .'* She treated Conky to a withering glance. '. . . *and one who sows discord among brothers.* Proverbs 6:16–19!'

Bob shook his head vehemently, crossing his heart with his index finger. 'God's honest truth, Gloria, lovey. I don't know anything about your son. I couldn't even tell you what he looks like, could I?' All smiles now. 'But I'd love to meet him, if you ever fancy cooking me a nice home-made dinner round yours. I bet you're a cracking lickle home-maker.'

Gloria folded her arms over her prissy silk dress. Conky could see from the triumphant way she held herself that Bob had won her over. 'Maybe when we get back from Blackpool.'

'Tell you what. Get your glad rags on. I'll clean myself up and we'll go.'

Gloria smiled cautiously, all outward signs of antagonism now gone. 'When?'

'Now! See the illuminations.'

'You're on, honey bunny.' She winked. Pulp Friction actually fecking winked.

Polishing his sunglasses on his shirt tails as the two love birds disappeared off for an evening session of Bible study and heavy petting by the sea, Conky sighed deeply and studied the drying mortar from below.

Ignoring the pain in his calf muscles and the sensation of his knees turning to jelly merely at the thought of climbing a ladder, Conky made his way round to the garaging. Inside, beyond the five gleaming super-cars, he located a long ladder that might just do the job. Carried it to the place where Bob had been 'working' and set it against the wall.

'I must be completely mental.' His bulk forced the bottom of the ladder deep into the soft earth of the flower beds, but setting his feet on the lower rungs, the thing wobbled ominously; barely enough room for his size thirteens. 'This is precarious activity, Conky McFadden. She doesn't even love you. I don't know why you're doing this.'

But loyalty and curiosity are strong motivators. Conky knew this much as he climbed higher and higher. The ladder didn't quite stretch to the sill of the master bedroom window. He found himself balancing on an upper rung, far beyond a level where he could safely grab onto the rails. Flattened against the wall like an overweight, mortal rendition of Spiderman, he felt his way up and over to the wet mortar. Scraped the mortar out from between the brickwork with his index finger, steeling himself not to look down. Beneath his fingertip, he felt something smooth and thin. Cabling. The ladder wobbled beneath him as he gouged at the cable with his short fingernails, trying to prise it free. Juddering and wobbling, his calf muscles screamed in complaint. His sensitive thyroid eyes streamed as the wind changed direction and blasted into his face. He could barely see.

In the split second that Conky realised he had stretched too far over to his left and that the ladder was beginning to tip, he pulled the cable free. Recognised it immediately as a fibre-optic camera, destined to poke through to the bedroom at the place where the landline telephone cable entered the house.

Crafty bastard's Bancroft's spy, Conky thought as he plunged some twenty or thirty feet at frightening speed onto the unforgiving paving below.

Chapter 37

Tariq

'What do you want me to do with him?' Asaf Smolensky asked, pointing to the Chinese pharmacist who was currently sitting in the hot seat in the hole – the windowless place where punishment was meted out on grasses, turncoats, thieves and anyone else who foolishly failed to walk in step with the Boddlington bosses. He had been strapped multiple times with duct tape to the chair that was bolted to the floor. The silvery tape covered his mouth as well, of course, though there were no other outward signs of abuse. Not yet.

Smolensky had removed his hat and his yarmulke, revealing the dark clippered hair beneath. He was standing behind a petrified-looking Colin Chang, sharpening boning knifes. Like fingernails being scratched down a blackboard, the sound set Tariq's teeth on edge.

'You want me to cut him?' Smolensky asked.

Pulling up a chair so that he was facing Chang, Tariq sat in silence, studying the puffy-eyed face of his father's favourite pharmacist. Wondering what to do with this curious find.

'No. That won't be necessary. Take the tape off his mouth. I want to speak to him.'

Smolensky ripped the duct tape quickly off Chang's mouth. Tariq winced at the noise. It brought back memories of his father whipping plasters off his scabbed knees as a little boy. He had yelped, just like Chang.

'Why are you keeping me here?' Chang asked, whimpering. He craned his neck to stare accusingly at the Fish Man. 'What is he going to do with me?'

'Well, that rather depends on you,' Tariq said in a soft voice. Smiling deliberately to put the man at his ease. Educated guys like Chang scared easily enough without the need for unrelenting violence or the threat of it. Especially a submissive beta-type like this. 'You and my father were going to the police, weren't you? Tell the truth.' He blinked slowly and steadily, still silently assimilating the painful revelation that his own father had been poised to tell that scabby little detective everything in return for guaranteed entry to paradise in the hereafter.

When Chang didn't respond immediately, Tariq waited. Observed the pharmacist's bloodshot eyes. The sweat stains around the yoke and the armpits of the borrowed tunic he wore were deepening, creeping ever outwards. Two days in the hole. He'd talk all right. He was clearly just finding careful words.

'I wasn't going to tell Ellis James about you,' he said. 'Obviously. I don't know anything about the Boddlingtons. My relationship to Mr Khan is coincidental. He's a good man, your dad . . .'

Examining his perfect fingernails, Tariq raised an eyebrow. 'You were going to tell the police about the O'Briens?'

Chang nodded. 'Your dad convinced me. In exchange

for my old life back. I thought I'd get police protection or something, so I could come back to Manchester. I miss my—'

'And my dad said he was going to blow the whistle on me.'

Even in the dim light of the naked bulb that buzzed above them, Tariq could see Chang blushing at the awkward truth. 'He's worried about you. About your kids. I think he meant well.'

In a soft but deadly voice, Tariq reminded the pharmacist that he didn't need a stranger to pronounce on his father's motives. It was time to step up the drama. With an almost imperceptible nod in the Fish Man's direction, the sound of knives being sharpened ricocheted around the claustrophobic room once again.

'I'm going to tell you how you can avoid being filleted and dressed with cucumber at the hand of the skilful Mr Smolensky, here,' he said, 'and served up on a man-sized platter for Sheila O'Brien's delight and delectation. Shall I tell you?'

The pharmacist's face crumpled and tears started to leak onto his cheeks, drip-dropping perfectly round, sorrowful splashes onto the concrete floor. He nodded.

Reaching forward, Tariq slapped him playfully on the shoulder, knowing he would flinch, thinking it was the end. 'You're going to come and work for us!' He grinned, knowing his plan was pure genius. 'It's serendipity really. My business partner and I need to get in on the pharma side of things. We Boddlingtons normally play to slightly different strengths, you see. We've always brought our ecstasy and meth in from Holland and the Czech Republic. But you're going to help us expand into a new field of home-made synthetic drugs.' He pointed at his gaffer-taped guest with both index fingers as though he were selling him a top-drawer investment. Genuinely pleased with this little turn of events. 'I'm going to save you a wasted, premature trip to the cemetery by offering you the job of company chemist on a part-time basis. I'll even pay you generously, which, I heard on the grapevine, Paddy O'Brien never did. So, providing you keep your mouth shut and stay away from the boys in blue and that carbuncle in a bad wig from the tax office, you get to live *and* my dear old dad gets to keep his favourite pharmacist. What do you say?'

'Do I have a choice?' Chang asked. His eyes were dead now. Resigned to his fate of continuing bondage.

'Of course you have a choice! Of course you do!' Tariq said, standing. Patting his shoulder in a chummy fashion. 'We're not totally amoral.' Giving the Fish Man the nod.

Smolensky grabbed Chang by the hair, yanking his head to the side. He took one of his long, thin boning knives and pressed it against the pharmacist's carotid artery.

'You work for me or you die right now. Not one, but *two* choices. Which is it to be?'

With that bit of business satisfactorily concluded, Tariq left the unlisted, anonymous-looking Boddlington factory with its hustle and bustle of trafficked workers and the grind of the conveyor belts feeding a production line for counterfeit goods. He walked through the potholed back-streets, sidestepping mud-splattered packaging from the wholesalers inside the old Victorian warehouses that squatted in the shadows of Strangeways' gothic splendour. It was a place where all the shit nobody would ever need was bought and sold for a handsome profit. It was Tariq Khan's spiritual homeland. He had swapped the spires of Oxford for the lesser, steepled peaks of HMP Manchester and its surrounding brick-strewn field of broken dreams.

Bidding familiar faces a jaunty, 'Assalamualaikum' as he passed his favourite snack bar, he was careful to check he wasn't followed back to his legitimate premises of T&J Trading. Inside his office, his father was sitting with his feet up on the leather sofa, reading a copy of *Architectural Digest* and sipping tea.

'How long are you going to keep me a prisoner here, Tariq?' the old man asked, looking at him pointedly over the tops of his glasses.

Tariq squeezed some antibacterial gel onto his hands and rubbed it in a little too thoroughly. 'You're hardly being held prisoner. I'm just—'

'Keeping your beady eye on me!' His father threw the magazine onto a side table and swung his feet onto the floor. 'Treating me like I'm a wayward child and a liability.'

'Dad, you were on your way to tell the police everything. If I hadn't been on the ball and arranged for the Fish Man the keep a lookout for you, I'd be on remand, awaiting trial now. And where would you be? Relying on people's charity?' He was raising his voice. He felt guilty for being disrespectful, but the tension and resentment that had been building over the past week felt like a vice clamped around him. Tightening, tightening, it had finally pushed vitriol up and out with some force. 'Do you really think anyone in the community would have taken pity on you, Anjum and the kids if I'd gone down?' He could feel his eyes threatening to water, unwilling to break eye contact with his father. 'You would have been shunned. Untouchable. Have you never heard of guilt by association? Nobody would opt to be seen with the family of Boddlington Park's most-wanted.'

Finally, his father heaved himself off the sofa and walked

stiffly to the window. He gazed out at the rooftops of the neglected buildings opposite from which buddleia sprouted optimistically. His posture curved submissively towards the view, rendering the old man some three or four inches shorter than he had been a decade ago. Tariq felt so protective of him; so angered and frustrated by him.

'I already told you. I'd had a change of heart anyway.' He sighed, placing a gnarled hand on his paunch. Shook his head. 'I would never have gone through with it. I couldn't betray my only boy.'

'Anjum still might.'

'I doubt it. Make amends with her, Tariq. And try to fix this broken life you've burdened yourself with. It's not too late. You're not safe, son. None of us are safe while you're playing these dangerous games. You have enemies everywhere and you've forgotten what true friends look like.'

Arranging some paperwork into a neat pile, Tariq considered Sheila O'Brien's welcoming curves. What they had together . . . was that friendship? Or was she still his enemy, offering the white flag during a vulnerable truce? 'I know what I'm doing. I know what's best for my family.'

'Do you? Oh really? What about Paddy O'Brien?' the old man suddenly said, turning round and beaming at him, as though he'd had a revelatory thought.

'What about him?'

'He was your arch-enemy, wasn't he?'

Did his father know about the clandestine affair with Paddy O'Brien's widow? No! Surely not. It wasn't possible.

'Why are you bringing Paddy O'Brien up, Dad? What's he got to do with my fall and redemption? He's been dead for months.'

'Ha! Shows how much you know.'

His father looked suddenly smug. There was no other word for it.

He took his phone out of his cardigan pocket and shuffled over to Tariq's desk. Thumbed through several screens with an arthritic thumb. 'How do you explain this, then, know-it-all?!'

Tariq closed his eyes and shook his head. Opened them again to look closer at the photo his father was holding before him. Taken by an old man with shaky hands and a basic smartphone, it was a little blurred and grainy. The lighting was appalling. But it undoubtedly appeared to be a photo of Paddy O'Brien, sitting at a table in a café.

Swallowing hard, Tariq felt light-headed. Ringing in his ears. A cold sweat spanned his back from one shoulder blade to another. His lips prickled. 'When was that taken?'

'Two weeks ago. In Bury.'

'No. It's not possible.'

'I recognised him from the *Manchester Evening News*. The obituaries. I like those.'

'Send that photo to me, Dad. Please. There's somebody needs to see this straight away.'

Tariq typed the briefest of messages to Sheila, knowing the photo said everything. It was the worst news he could ever deliver. But she needed to know. And they all needed to take cover.

Chapter 38

Gloria

'I can't believe we're doing this,' Gloria said, ignoring the insistent reverberations from her buzzing phone inside her handbag. She held Bob's hand tightly, gazing up at his only slightly sagging jawline. In the twilight of the late afternoon, in the glow of the illuminations, her new boyfriend looked handsome. 'Just downing tools like that! I don't think I've ever done anything so footloose and fancy-free in all my born days. You're a bad influence, you are!'

Bob stopped short outside the spectral glow of the giant skull of Coral Island. The Blackpool Tower – a pocket-sized imitation Eiffel – glittered in the background, pointing to the same darkening celestial canopy that covered Blackpool's better-heeled twin of Vegas.

Clamping his hands onto her freezing cheeks, he kissed her passionately on the mouth. She could taste the salt and vinegar with a fishy aftertaste on his lips.

'Only the best for you, honey bunny. I wanted to be romantic and spontananous.'

Gloria giggled coquettishly, holding her hand over her mouth as she smiled. Awash with lustful hormones that told her she was in love. Still mindful of the nagging,

320

doubting Thomas in her head that was desperately trying to override the giddy passion with cold reason. Bob was a strange-coloured man who couldn't pronounce, 'spontaneous'. And this Golden Mile was little more than fools' gold, rendered resplendent only by the gleam of a million bulbs, paid for by the council and tourist revenue.

'A trip to Vegas might have done the job better.' The words tripped out of her mouth gaily. Doubting Thomas had shouted his unwelcome truths above the buzz of electricity and pounding music coming from inside the arcades and bars.

Bob's already tight face set hard. 'Sorry I'm a disappointment,' he said, walking ahead.

'No! No! I didn't mean it. *I'm* sorry,' Gloria shouted, trotting after him. She struggled against the flow of the crowds heading towards the Tower or else the North Pier, where the giant Ferris wheel beckoned like a blazing beacon. Above her, brightly coloured mermaids and sea turtles hanging from the lamp posts leered down at her, silently berating her for lacking backbone. Or were they screaming that she was shallow and unappreciative? Either way, she couldn't win. 'Come back, Bob!'

The chill wind whipped in from the Irish Sea, blowing the smell of burnt onions, cheap burgers and candy floss towards her. Her eyes streamed. Her phone was still buzzing incessantly but she had made the decision to cut reality loose, just for one evening.

'Wait!'

Her new-found beau was swallowed up by the thronging stag-parties that spilled out of every venue onto the pavement.

'No! Don't leave me!' Somewhere deep within her, Gloria was aware of a gnawing sensation that told her to get on the first coach, bus or train out of there, back to Manchester. Why had Bob acted so strangely in the maize maze? Where had he disappeared to so suddenly, abandoning her like that? Why had he been working on Sheila's house? Why had he been stalking them? And had Lev sustained a near-lethal head injury at the hand of this man of few charms? The Doubting Thomas inside her wanted answers to these questions. But the part of her that was a desperately lonely middle-aged woman couldn't bear the thought of losing the suitor who plugged the gaping chasm that her love-disinterest, the pastor, and before him, Leviticus' father had left. 'Get out of the way, you foul beasts!' she yelled at the drunken young white men who lolled in her path, clutching plastic pint glasses full of lager, tilted at rakish angles.

There was Bob, already some way up ahead! Hurrying along the promenade, Gloria finally caught up with him and entwined her arm with his. 'I didn't mean to insult you. I'm sorry. Blackpool's . . .' *Not the Bahamas. Not the Maldives. Not Tokyo or Hong Kong or even London.* '. . . smashing. This is very thoughtful, honey bunny.' She stretched upwards on her tiptoes to kiss him on the cheek. Her pride stuck in her craw along with a piece of wayward, indigestible fish batter as she tried to swallow it.

'Tell you what,' he said, touching her carefully styled hair that had so far withstood even the stiff seaside wind. 'Let's go to the Pleasure Beach.'

Gloria took a step backwards, patting her straightened fringe. There was an enigmatic glint in Bob's eye. 'Ooh, I'm not sure I—'

'You're not scared of having fun, are you?'

The brightly lit old tram rattled along the golden mile promenade, scudding past glorious gaudy illuminations that spanned the street in a cat's cradle of twinkling lights, until they reached the Pleasure Beach. Under normal circumstances, Gloria would have been able to think of nothing less pleasurable, but she had downed two stiff sweet sherries en route. Darkness had fallen, giving a normally god-forsaken place a certain showbiz glamour.

'How about that ride?' Bob said, pointing to what appeared to be airplane fuselages spinning slowly round above them.

'I get dizzy.'

'Try it! There's blinking kids on there. Look! Lickle kids. If they can do it, you can.'

She allowed herself to be corralled into boarding the gateway ride. Found herself laughing as the rudimentary fuselages spun faster and faster. There was the blackness of the sea. There was the Pleasure Beach, all spangled and sparkling and riotous. There was the sea. There were the lights. There was Bob, with his arm around her. Gloria felt like she was in a centrifuge with all her pent-up inhibitions spinning away from her, leaving a happy woman behind as the true nucleus.

'My word. That was some kind of fun!' she said, staggering down the ramp, giggling, once the ride had ended. 'What's next?'

They tried the Ghost Train, charmed and appalled in equal measure by its tackiness and terrible ghouls, daubed in UV paint inside the two-tier ride. Gloria screamed as their cart plunged abruptly from high to low on the outside, only to disappear back in, where they were greeted by a horrible half-dressed skeleton that looked like it needed a good dusting.

'Big Dipper!' Bob suggested next.

Ignoring the persistent buzzing of her phone, she allowed

herself to be yanked along to a rickety old rollercoaster. 'Oh, I couldn't,' she said, eyeing the sharp turns and steep curves of a wooden frame that looked as though it had been built in the Victorian era, or at least not long after it. A packed car of thrill-seekers hurtled up and down towards their vantage point on a pedestrian bridge. They shrieked with a mixture of fear and pure unadulterated adrenalin as they shot past.

'It's flipping child's play compared to the Big One.' Bob pointed to the giant metal structure beyond that dwarfed the iconic old ride.

'No.'

'Aw! Spoilsport. And to think I had you down as a bit of a risk-taker!'

He nudged her playfully. A grin sliced into his too-tight face. Those small teeth shone blue-white in the glare from the surrounding attractions, putting her in mind of an electric eel. Again, that nagging feeling that she should turn on her heel and just go home frayed the edges of her warm, sherry-fuelled sense of well-being. But like the unpopular girl in the class, Gloria shrank away from the implicit criticism that she was cowardly or boring in any way.

'Go on, then.'

Grabbing the safety lap-bar in the carriage, with the wind biting through the fabric of her woollen coat and into her stockinged legs, she caught Bob studying her. He rattled her bar.

'Just checking. Ha ha.' He smiled and blew her a kiss, tugging at his own bar, almost as if he were testing its strength.

'Maybe *you're* the bundle of nerves,' Gloria said, batting her eyelashes at him. Trying to appear alluring and unfazed by this dreadful excuse for entertainment.

As the carriage started to climb its first tall slope, Gloria saw the park fall away from her. Up here, she felt exposed. The whole structure felt flimsy in that biting Irish Sea gust. And Bob kept testing the bar, though they were about to hurtle into the abyss.

'Give over, rattling the bar, will you?' she said.

But her words were snatched away as the carriage plummeted downwards. The scream that tore itself free of her lungs felt primal and liberating. Gloria's hair was flattened against her forehead. Spray splashed her from the log flume as they swooped low and soared high, coinciding with other rides in the illuminated dark of an autumn night, full of possibly ill-portent in a Lancashire seaside town. Twisting and turning precariously, the carriage rocked into the bends and almost flung her from her seat.

Bob leaned into her. It felt like he might knock her from the carriage.

Gloria tried to shout 'Move!' but her words were swallowed as the carriage nose-dived into a pitch-black tunnel. All she had seen before entering this black hole was a sign warning the carriage's occupants not to stand. Screaming in the dark, she was sure she could feel Bob trying to push her out.

Chapter 39

Sheila

'Jesus, no!' Sheila's phone slipped from her fingers, dropping onto the top step of the grand oak staircase of her new business premises. It bounced. Dropped to the next step down and the next, gaining momentum until it came to rest on the landing below. 'This can't be happening.' Nausea hit her in waves, causing her to dry-heave. She gripped the banister to steady herself.

There was click-clacking above her, as somebody was hastening down the stairs.

'You all right, love?' A frowsy-looking woman – a secretary, judging by the polyester suit – from one of the offices above stopped short on the stairs when she saw Sheila gasping for air, grasping at the sudden cramps in her stomach.

Sheila nodded. 'Yep. Fine, thanks. Dicky tummy. Steer clear if I were you. Think it's norovirus.'

The woman's smile faltered. Nodding with feigned sympathy, she hastened down the stairs, leaving Sheila to absorb the information: Youssuf thought he had seen Paddy, alive and sipping tea in some shitty café in Bury's indoor market. Paddy O'Brien. Alive. The blurry photo of her supposedly dead husband would be forever more singed into her neural pathways. A phantom bad memory. A harbinger of her own personal end of days.

Gingerly descending the staircase, though she felt she might lose her footing at any moment, she retrieved her phone. Sitting on the step, she traced her finger over the intricate spider's web of cracked glass. It was still working, thankfully.

With a protective hand over her abdomen, she started to dial Conky. Instinctively wanting to tell him the earth-shattering news but regretting the call the minute the phone started to ring.

'Sheila. Are you okay?' His voice was thick with concern but echoed as though he were in a lofty space. The cannabis farm, perhaps. Or maybe the spa of her house. 'Any news from Gloria? I've been ringing and ringing her but—'

'Bollocks to Gloria,' she said, waves of nausea threatening to drown her. 'I think Paddy's still alive.' Already several steps ahead, she knew he'd ask where she had got such outlandish information. 'I've seen a photo. I'm sure it's him, Conk.'

There was a beat of silence between them. 'Send me the photo.'

With slippery, cumbersome fingers, she forwarded the image. Locking the fearful tears inside as she closed her eyes. 'It's on its way.'

'Are you crying, darling?'

She wiped her eyes on the sleeve of her silk blouse. 'No. Conky, if it's true and he's still out there . . .'

'I've got it now, She.' His voice flattened to a sombre monotone. 'Oh, shite. It bloody well looks like him, doesn't it? I mean . . . how? Just fucking *how*? And where did you get this?'

There it was. The question she didn't want to answer. 'That doesn't matter. I need to find him, Conk. I buried the bastard. You carried his coffin from the church and helped lower the damned thing into the ground. For Christ's sake! I saw him. Dead. I saw his dead body in Katrina's nursing home, Conk. With my own eyes! This doesn't make sense. I need . . .' The sob erupted from deep within her without warning. She ended the call, not wanting to hear Conky's suspicion masked by words of manly comfort.

The stairwell started to spin in a vortex of claustrophobia; every dust mote on the air threatening to snuff the life out of her. She had to get outside. But first, there was someone she needed to call.

'Sister Benedicta, please,' she told the woman at the other end of the line.

The hold music – some religious aria that grated on her nerves – seemed to go on for an age. Finally, her sister-in-law picked up.

'Sheila. This is a surprise.' Katrina's voice was devoid of warmth. It rang with the brisk efficiency of a nun that ran a convent and its attached nursing home like some South American autocrat. Hail Sister Benevolent Dictator Benedicta, full of grace and grit. 'How are you? How are the girls keeping?'

'He's alive, isn't he?' Sheila said, gripping the banister and pulling herself up. Fearing for the baby inside her. 'Meet me in an hour.'

'*What?* What nonsense is—'

'Jodrell Bank. Under the big dish.'

'Who's alive? I can't possibly—'

'I'll be waiting. One hour. You don't turn up, I'm going to the police.'

She had an hour to pull herself together. An hour to

decide what to say. She'd never needed a vodka and tonic so much in her life.

When she pulled up at the site of the giant Lovell radio telescope that was today pointing straight up to the heavens, her hands were shaking violently. The interior of the Panamera was pungent, not with the smell of fine leather but with the smell of vomit, mercifully caught in a Waitrose bag at the traffic lights on the main dual carriageway that cut through Parsons Croft.

'Take a deep breath, Sheila,' she counselled herself. 'You can face this old bitch. You're strong.'

Negotiating the pathways of the sprawling rural discovery site was tricky in the heels she had deliberately changed into to give her a physical advantage over Katrina. She turned her ankle twice. Kept her eyes peeled for a stout nun, dressed in navy. But it was hard to see past the armies of children who walked hand in hand, wearing brightly coloured anoraks, screaming with delight on their school day trip.

The white structure of the big dish, which sat on a criss-crossed rotating base resembling an old rollercoaster that had somehow missed the point, dwarfed everything around it for miles. Sheila was out of her jurisdiction, but Katrina, an unknown quantity now that Paddy was ostensibly gone, would never try anything on with so many children around. It was in the middle of nowhere. It was the perfect spot.

'Where are you, you lying old bag?' she muttered, holding her coat tightly closed against the wind that whipped across the flat Cheshire plains.

There she was. Rubbing her hands together by the fence that lined the telescope's circular track. Same anorak. Same flat walking shoes. Same A-line skirt. She was wearing a short navy veil that lent softness to her otherwise flinty O'Brien face.

Sheila felt anger surging through her, heating her freezing extremities and thawing the frosty words she had planned.

'Where's Paddy?' she said, strutting towards her sister-in-law.

Katrina didn't bother to smile. Not now. 'In the cemetery. What on earth is wrong with you, Sheila?' Her sharp blue eyes spoke to early nights and clean-living. They cut through Sheila's bluff like lasers. 'Are you mentally ill?'

Suppressing the urge to punch a nun, Sheila took out her phone and showed her Youssuf's photo. 'Explain that, you scheming old bag. How the hell did you do it, Katrina? Tell me who we buried if it wasn't Paddy? And where is my lying snake of a husband?'

Touching her crucifix with a short-nailed finger, Katrina's brow furrowed. She finally smiled in that pitying, sarcastic way she normally reserved for Frank. 'That's not Paddy, you silly woman!' Handed the phone back. 'How can you possibly think that? And how could you think that of me? I'm a Bride of Christ, Sheila O'Brien. After all I did for you and—'

'Save me the bullshit, Katrina,' Sheila said, snatching the phone back. Glancing down at the photo yet again and questioning what she saw clearly. 'That's Paddy. Taken two weeks ago in Bury. Do I have to get his grave exhumed?'

But Katrina had already started to walk away. Shook her head and raised her hand dismissively. Shouting merrily over her shoulder. 'I'll see you at Christmas for Midnight Mass. Bring the girls. Give them my love, won't you?'

Stumbling over the patchy grass, made muddy by the trampling feet of visiting hordes, Sheila gained on her.

Grabbed her by the shoulder. 'It's him! He was dead and now he's alive and you're in on it. I want the truth.'

Katrina came to a standstill. With an iron grip that was clearly bolstered by hatred, she picked Sheila's hand off her shoulder. Turned around slowly. But for the red rash of split veins on her cheeks, her face was as drained of colour and thunderous as the oppressive steely canopy of rain-clouds above them. She stepped towards Sheila, uncomfortably close now. Speaking with clipped conso-nants in a deadly quiet voice that was almost whisked away on the breeze.

'How dare you, you disloyal strumpet? Do you have no shame?' She raised an eyebrow in challenge. 'Do you have no *fear?*'

'Are you bleeding threatening me?' Sheila asked, steeling herself to stand her ground. Had she completely under-estimated the O'Brien blood that ran through the veins of this woman of the cloth?

Sheila noticed Katrina's hand sliding into a bulging pocket of her navy anorak. A dangerous shine to the nun's eyes. A shine she'd seen time and again in Paddy's eyes, right before he'd punched, kicked or forced himself upon her. Her first thought was of Tariq's baby, growing in her womb and of the bright future she instinctively felt was about to evaporate at the hand of Sister Benedicta.

'Am I threatening you?' Katrina said. 'Oh, I don't deal with threats, my dear. I only deal in promises.'

Katrina started to withdraw her hand slowly from her pocket. Sheila baulked, stumbling backwards in those damned heels. Falling, falling to the ground . . .

Chapter 40

Gloria

'No, I really don't want to go on anything else,' Gloria said, shaking her arm free of Bob's. 'I need to sit down. I'm all of a dither.' She walked briskly ahead of him, keen to put as much distance between her and the Big Dipper as possible.

'Don't tell me you didn't enjoy that,' he said, jogging to catch up with her. He put his arm around her and squeezed her tightly. Planted an uninvited kiss on her cheek. 'You were laughing your head off!'

Gloria felt suddenly like a small girl, overwhelmed by all the glare and the noise; the tattooed louts and their pierced girlfriends; the smell of frying and sugar and low-grade processed meat on the sizzle; the infernal peer-pressure to enjoy this kitsch-fest. 'I'm not an adrenalin-junkie like you, Bob,' she said, annoyed by the tears that welled in her eyes. She missed the now-familiar presence of her son and grandson. Even Sheila and Conky or the women from church would do. She felt alone. 'I wasn't laughing my head off. I was screaming. And I felt like I was going to fall out of that dratted carriage.'

'There's no point going now!' Bob said, rubbing her upper arm.

'Well, I'm sorry. I want to go.'

'One more ride. Please. Then we'll head off.' He took her hand and kissed it. 'Please.'

Her body felt sluggish and old in that place for youngsters. The strength she gleaned from Jesus had never eluded her so completely as in that den of slot machines and cheap thrills. But she was relying on Bob for a lift home and, in truth, didn't fancy a two-hour drive back through snail's pace, snarled traffic sitting beside a sulking man whom she desperately wanted to love her.

'Go on, then. One last ride.'

'It'll definitely be the last. I promise.'

Bob stared at her in silence, as though he were evaluating her. Neither smiling nor frowning. She felt like she had been placed on a slide beneath the lens of a microscope. That gnawing feeling was amplified.

'Wild Mouse,' he said. Nodding. 'Yep. Just the ticket.'

The rickety-looking ride looked like something from a 1970s horror flick. It was another wooden structure, by the looks. Gloria had never seen such steep drops and tight turns.

'Oh, this makes the Big Dipper look like a kid's ride. I'm really not happy about this, Robert,' she said. 'My hair will be completely ruined.'

The tiny carriages that appeared to seat only two – one in front of the other – ricocheted around a track that had been tightly packed into a space the size of the average bungalow plot. It was ludicrous. It looked more than precarious. She doubted even prayers would keep her safe in something designed to look like a mouse but which was clearly just a death trap.

'Your hair's fine! You're gorgeous.' Bob patted her bottom. Winked. Pointed to the revellers who were already hastening around the hairpin-bends. 'Listen to them! They're loving it. I adored this ride when I was a young lad. It's a cracker. One of the best lickle rollercoasters in the world. Honest.'

A baby pink cart, empty of its previous occupants, rattled towards them. With a quailing heart, Gloria stepped forward, taking her place between Bob's legs.

'Good Lord!' she cried. 'It's just a normal seat belt, like what you get in a car! This can't be safe.' She looked questioningly at the lad who manned the queue.

'You're all right, love,' the lad said. 'Safe as houses. Put your hands in.'

It was too late to protest. The car jolted forwards and they were off. She could feel Bob's knees gripping her; his fingers digging like pincers into her shoulders. The cart lurched upwards in a steep climb. Gloria was already regretting having said yes to this ride. And as they reached the summit, she was plagued with doubt as to why Bob had been fiddling about with Sheila's brickwork. He had said he'd coincidentally been working on next door and had spotted a fault in her mortar. Sheila's side to the story . . . she had yet to hear.

'Here we go!' Bob shouted. 'Hold on tight.'

The car dropped almost vertically, picking up speed with every millimetre that it fell. Gloria felt her bottom lift out of her seat. Her whole body pressed painfully against the flimsy seat belt. She screamed. Tensed up every muscle. Braced herself for the inevitable crash. But it didn't come. Instead the car whipped back upwards, sending her reeling back into Bob's lap. She hated each second. She wanted out.

So concerned was she with the potential for spinal injury and the sheer horror of being tossed around in mid-air, just as a cat plays with a mouse, that the cold steel pressing against her temple took her by surprise.

'Tell me where Lev lives or you're dead,' Bob yelled.

'What?'

She had a split second in which to understand her situation. She was strapped into a rollercoaster car with a gun to her head, held there by her lover.

'Lev. Tell me his address or I'll shoot.'

Unable to turn around to face her interrogator, Gloria could only stare ahead as the cart tracked left and right, swinging into a neck-breaker of a turn.

'Bob! No.' Fear kicked in suddenly. She started to scream.

'Not Bob. Hank. My name's Hank. And if you're not going to tell me where to find your son, I've got orders to kill you. Goodbye, Gloria. I'm sorry,' the renamed Hank said, just loud enough for her to hear above her own din.

The bullet left the gun just as the car shot downwards yet again. Time seemed to slow in that deafening last moment on earth. The ground hurtled up to meet her and Gloria considered the words of John 11:26.

And everyone who lives and believes in me shall never die.

Closing her eyes, she waited for heaven and prayed death would not hurt. Remembered Leviticus as a small boy and her grandson, Jay, recovering post-op in a Baltimore hospital. Remembered the pastor and her futile unrequited love for him. At least now, she would find peace.

'Shit!' Hank cursed behind her.

Except she was not dead, apparently.

The rapid descent had thrown his aim off and he had missed. With her survival instinct on high alert, Gloria grabbed his hand and rammed it repeatedly up against the side of the car in an attempt to liberate the gun.

'You sh— scoundrel!' she yelled. In truth, 'shithouse' had been on the tip of her tongue, but the near-death situation didn't give her carte blanche to drop her standards.

'Agh, my hand, you bitch! You broke my fucking hand.'

The gun went off a second time, the thunderclap close to her ear, almost masked by the incessant rattling of the car as it pinged like a bagatelle ball up, down, from side to side.

Hank squeezed her ribs so hard with his knees, Gloria wondered if he would puncture her lungs. One more shot might finish her. She had to kill or be killed. Grabbing his gun hand again, she bit down hard into the sinewy flesh. He punched her in the neck with his right fist but her cleaner's stamina stood her in good stead. Her bite was so unrelenting that she tasted blood. With all the strength she could muster, she smashed his hand into the side of the car one last time. The gun went spinning into the air, clattering and bouncing down through the intricate lattice structure of the rollercoaster.

But his right hand was around her throat, squeezing hard.

She tried to shout 'Stop!' but a hoarse gurgle was all she could manage. Why was this happening? How had her love soured so quickly? Was he Bancroft's man? Her consciousness was ebbing away. Soon, the ride would be over and she would be dead.

Kicking out, flailing in a bid to take a breath, Gloria's hand hit the fastening for the flimsy seat belt. Though her mind was sluggish, she knew what to do. With her last drop of energy, she depressed the button, freeing them both.

As the car plummeted into its final steep nosedive, Gloria clung onto the bar in front for all she was worth, though she lifted clean out of her seat. Behind her, she felt Hank dislodge with the force of their descent.

He shrieked as he flew from the car. Propelled through the Blackpool night sky like a human cannonball from the circus attractions of old. Gloria's last sight of Hank was the glimpse she caught of his body breaking against the unforgiving ground below.

As the cart came to a standstill, a bloodied Gloria launched herself back onto solid ground, patting her hair back into place and smoothing her dishevelled clothing. She spoke to the lad in a tremulous voice that quickly gathered strength.

'*And the great dragon was thrown down, that ancient serpent, who is called the devil and Satan, the deceiver of the whole world – he was thrown down to the earth, and his angels were thrown down with him.* Revelation 12:9.'

Flushed with a grim euphoria, Gloria fled from the Wild Mouse as the first screams at the discovery of Hank's body pierced the fateful night.

Chapter 41

Lev

'No. I still don't know where my Mam is and I still haven't heard from her. How many times do I have to tell you?' Lev said, ending the call from Conky. 'I'm sending the next fucking call straight to voicemail,' he told Jay, who merely chewed on his teething ring in response, strings of drool stretching all the way to his lap like gossamer rice noodles.

'You shouldn't be using language like that in front of the boy,' an old woman on the seat opposite said. She clutched her shopping wagon for balance as the tram leaned to the left, making its agonisingly slow progress from Piccadilly Gardens southwards past the City Art Gallery. 'It sets a bad example.'

'Piss off, grandma,' Lev said, immediately feeling a prize shitbag for treating the nosey old cow with such flagrant disrespect. He knew better than that. 'Soz. I'm having a bad day.'

Her wizened face didn't soften. She merely glanced at the dressing on his temple where he had been struck with the crowbar and turned with a sour, judgemental expression to look out of the window.

Sod her. Lev's breath was still coming in short, shallow

338

gasps. He felt transparent and weak like a piss-water cup of tea. Taking Jay's warm little hands into his for comfort, he shot furtive glances around the tram, dreading the next stop. Would the police get on? Would they be coming for him after what had gone on? Undoubtedly caught on CCTV.

With a whine and a hiss, the tram pulled up against the concourse at St Peter's Square. Might there be a spy at every window in the town hall and the surrounding office blocks, peering out in the city-wide manhunt for Leviticus Bell – hardened criminal turned fugitive?

'Hurry up! Hurry up! Jesus.'

Willing the passengers to get on and sit down so that they could leave the city in haste, Lev saw Tiffany in every glum face that boarded.

'Daddy!' Jay shouted joyfully, blowing him a clumsy dribble-kiss.

But he felt undeserving of his son's love. He had pushed Tiffany down an escalator. An accident, almost certainly. He wasn't even sure how it had come about. But he was now shafted beyond redemption nonetheless. That accusatory face of hers, as she had levered herself up from the bottom, surrounded by horrified, shrieking women and concerned men . . . that embittered, underweight face, covered in fire-engine red blood. Red for danger.

Why had it had to happen at a time when he desperately needed to keep Tiffany sweet?

It had been a chance meeting. He had been wheeling Jay through the Arndale Centre, blithely looking in the shoe shops at mid-season reductions on trainers. With his new-found wealth and his clean bill of health after the clear CT scan, he had been feeling chipper. The new, high-end solicitor, paid for with Sheila O'Brien's money, had said his chances of getting full custody of Jay were excellent, providing he kept his nose clean and they moved fast. The social worker's visit to the rented house had gone particularly well. So, he had already treated Jay-Jay to a celebratory new outfit from Selfridges, because the boy deserved labels, man. Hadn't it been his plan to bag himself some fine new Nikes?

But on the way through the upper mall from TK Maxx towards the bright main section with its temple to Apple and the double-height Next cathedral, he had to bump into Tiffany, didn't he?

'Oh, here he comes. Captain fucking Catwalk with his posh bags.'

His babymother had looked even more washed out than usual under the bright Arndale Centre lights which forgave nobody and which paid no heed to the darkening early evening sky outside. Her hair, scraped into a high ponytail, had been thin enough to reveal the scalp beneath.

'Look,' Lev had said. 'I'm not gonna do this in here. My solicitor told us not to talk to you. I don't want bother. I'll see you in court.'

Notably, Jay had not even stretched out his arms to his mother. He had merely sat contentedly in his pushchair, singing a toddler's garbled rendition of 'Baa Baa Black Sheep'. Lev had started to walk away, recognising his increasingly frenzied heartbeat as an anxiety marker – the sort that had led to his being cooped up in the house for what felt like an age after the head-in-a-Fried-Chicken-Family-Bucket debacle. Anxiety was not good. Tiffany was worse.

'Hey! Don't you bleeding well walk off on me, you ignorant knob-end! I wanna talk to you about custody, without all this bleeding legal-eagle shit. I want my frigging baby back. He's mine.'

She had tugged at his parka. He had shaken her off. But

hand on hip, Tiffany had rounded on them. She had latched onto their little father-son outing like a frenzied, bloody-minded wasp buzzing around beleaguered picnickers.

'Leave it, Tiff. People are staring, and it's not nice for the boy.'

Shouting and acting out like a cornered shoplifter, Tiffany had been all bony hands flailing and hooked fingers jabbing at him. 'It's not nice? Who the fuck do you think you are, Leviticus Bell?'

Perhaps inadvertently, though in hindsight, Lev reasoned that it had more likely been intentionally, she had manoeuvred them near to the top of the escalators. Perilously close, in fact, so that they were partially blocking the access.

'I'm not having this, Tiff. I'm really sorry, the way things worked out between us, yeah? But you screwed it all up for yourself the day you stubbed a ciggy out on my son's arm. You're a conniving witch.' He had rapped his index finger against his forehead. 'You're tapped and I'm not having you poisoning my boy with your bullshit.'

Standing on her tiptoes, she had taken a swipe at Lev. Had made contact with his jaw with a bony junkie's fist. Fingers that had once caressed him. Knuckles he had once kissed. The sad decline of their relationship had not been lost on him. But the Arndale Centre at the witching hour of 5 p.m. had been no theatre in which to play out their personal drama – especially not in front of Jay, who had started to observe their antics.

He had grabbed her hand. Making physical contact. The biggest mistake, he now realised.

'Pack it in,' he had said in a calm voice, trying and failing to move away from the escalators. Sensitive to the tutting of passers-by, who had been forced to edge past the cringe-worthy contretemps.

Tiffany had somehow wheeled him around so that the two of them had formed a stopper at the summit of the escalator.

'Get off me, you big bullying bastard!' she had shouted, eyeballing the shoppers, as though she had been performing for their benefit.

Lev had wheeled Jay's pushchair clear of the descending steps. Baulking at the sight of all that metal, throwing up memories of him being five or six, screaming for help as the hem of his jeans had caught in the jagged teeth.

'I'm out of here. You're fucking fruit loops.'

He had tried to back away, but she had grabbed hold of the pushchair, trying to prise Jay free of his straps. Lev had yet again gripped her arm to free Jay of her. And then, whatever had happened next was still a mystery to him, as he raked over the sequence of events on the tram to Altrincham.

Somebody had barrelled into him from behind. There had been a struggle with Tiffany. He didn't even remember having a hold of her arm at that point, but she had fallen headlong down the escalators. The world had come to a standstill. His babymother lay sprawled at the bottom of the long, steep staircase. Somebody had hit the alarm, bringing the escalator to a halt, but Lev had been convinced at that moment that Tiffany – a broken woman whom he had once adored – had been killed. Blood on the ground beneath her: a gleaming deadly puddle of dark red, pooling outwards. How could she have survived such a fall? And he had been unable to run to her aid. His primary instinct had been to stay by the pushchair with his son. Slowly backing away from the scene.

At the bottom, a crowd of rush-hour homeward-bound workers had already started to gather. People had been dialling for help on their phones or else taking photos of the ragdoll of a woman who had been lying motionless, face down on the floor.

With his flight instinct and blind panic kicking in with gusto, just as he had been about to turn around and walk away, Lev had noticed Tiffany start to move. Like some zombie in a shoot-em-up Xbox game who refused to lay down and die, she had raised her bloodied head. Had craned her neck to stare up at him with sheer menace in those medicated eyes.

'You're fucked, Lev Bell.'

Had those been her words? From that distance, he'd had to lip-read. But yes. As he replayed the chain of events in his fevered mind, he was certain she had threatened him. And from that moment, he had known that she intended to get him for attempted manslaughter.

Now, he was watching a twilit South Manchester speed by as he headed back to the rental, expecting at every stop that the police would board the tram with handcuffs and batons at the ready for Lev Bell – a domestic abuser of the worst kind; an attempted woman-slaughterer. Accusatory faces on the passengers that lined the platform of Trafford Bar, Old Trafford, with its stadium bearing down on him, Stretford, Sale . . . Every stop held peril. Every time the tram slowed, he expected some conversation to be taking place at Timperley, perhaps, between Transport police and the track operatives. They were all conspiring to root him out and bring him down.

With the world spinning around him, he finally boarded the bus at Altrincham interchange, suspecting every pedestrian of being a plain-clothes policeman. But they passed through Hale, veering out towards Bramshott. The golden-leafed oaks and sunburst-coloured beeches – grey in the evening murk, save for where the street lamps shone a light on their brilliance – replaced the ungainly 70s office blocks and cramped streets of overpriced Victorian terraces. Lev's breathing eased. The spinning slowed, like a merry-go-round running out of steam.

'Right,' he said, disembarking with his son in the push-chair. 'Daddy and Jay are going on a little adventure, son. All right?'

Packing was easy. What he couldn't fit into a single case, he would buy when he got to the other end. As long as he could fit in the rubble sack of money and a few nappies, that was all that mattered.

With Jay burbling at the television from the safety of his playpen, he hastily threw together ham sandwiches to eat on the hoof. Caught up in thoughts of Tiffany and her threat. *You're fucked.* She knew she had won through one simple, life-threatening act of self-sabotage. Tiffany, Tiffany, his mind was full of blood-soaked, nightmarish Tiffany. When he heard the front door slam, he jumped. Ran through to the hall, armed with a breadknife and a thundering heartbeat.

'Mam!'

Bedraggled and spattered with dried blood, as though she were carrying Tiffany's torch as an Olympic-standard drama queen, Gloria stood in the hallway, trembling. He could hear a car's engine running outside.

'What's up with you, for Christ's sake?'

Gloria hugged herself tightly. Kicked off her shoes, looking a good deal smaller and somehow childlike in her stockinged feet. 'Don't blaspheme,' she said in a quiet voice. 'Bob's dead. He tried to kill me. Bob wasn't even his real name. He was called Hank!' She opened her arms, clearly expecting a hug from her son like any normal mother would. But Gloria wasn't a normal mother.

'Did you kill him?' Lev asked, lowering the knife but ignoring her outstretched arms. 'You topped your boyfriend. Am I guessing right?'

She shrugged. 'It was an accident. Self-defence. He tried to shoot me.'

'So, you *did* kill him.'

Tears rolled onto Gloria's cheeks. '*Blessed be the Lord, my rock, who trains my hands for war, and my fingers for battle*; Psalm 144:1.'

If Bob or Hank or whatever he was bloody called had tried to kill Gloria, chances were he was one of Bancroft's men, Lev calculated. And if Gloria had killed Hank, Bancroft's men would be coming for Lev, in addition to that psycho, the Fish Man and whatever other loons had it in for him, including the coppers.

'That your taxi outside?' he asked.

His mother nodded.

Running to the door, he flagged the Skoda estate car down just as it was engaged in a three-point turn, ready to pull away. A Blackpool cabbie, unwilling to take another job that left him at the wrong end of the M61. Until Lev showed him a wad of twenties . . .

'You can't leave!' Gloria yelled, as Lev carried the heavy case to the cab. She followed him outside in her bare feet. The rain had started to fall and the dried blood washed into the fabric of her dress like a stain of guilt.

'I can and I will. I've had it up to here . . .' – he poked the top of his forehead – '. . . with the bullshit.' He walked back inside to retrieve Jay in his car seat and all the bulky regalia that was essential to life with a toddler.

'Where are you going?'

She reached out to touch Jay's cheek but he swung the car seat out of reach.

'Somewhere safe. Somewhere we can't be found. I'm starting again, Mam.' He looked down to see her tugging at his forearm. 'Let us go.'

As he slammed the car door, he glanced at his rain-soaked, bloodstained mother, shivering in her stockinged feet. Felt like a weight was lifting and that somewhere, the sun was coming out.

'You can't take my grandson away like this.' The ferocity in her voice cut through the closed windows of the car.

'Get going,' Lev told the taxi driver.

'I'll find you! I mean it!'

In answer, Lev shook his head and waved dismissively. The taxi pulled away, leaving Gloria Bell standing alone in the middle of the quiet, suburban street, quoting a Bible passage at the top of her voice.

Chapter 42

Sheila

'You ready for this?' Sheila asked Gloria.

'I've got nothing left other than what I started with – me, you and the church. What have I got to lose?' Gloria's smile was one of wistful resignation.

Sheila nodded sympathetically. 'You got everything?'

Gloria patted the tartan shopping trolley that was wedged in the rear footwell of the Mercedes GLE, driven by a twitchy, overexcited Degsy. 'Shotgun. Spare cartridges. Baseball bats and a handy spade that I found in the garden shed. Oh, and some nasty-looking aphid killer. I'm sure a dash of that in the eyes won't be very pleasant.'

Sheila nodded, staring at the plaster on her business partner's head. An incongruous fawn colour against mid-brown skin. She felt anger surge through her, enlivening her sluggish, bloated, newly pregnant body like a cheeky vodka and tonic. 'Great. Good. Let's do this.'

Degsy pulled up outside the office block in Spinningfields where Sheila had only recently viewed space to let for their own enterprise.

'Stay there,' she told the scabby-faced arse-clown, using the same tone as she'd use on a dog. Degsy was a liability, but with Lev gone, what choice had she had? Not Conky, that was for sure. Conky was too busy getting his thyroid checked at the sodding doctor's.

'No worries, Mrs O'B,' Degsy said. He produced a fake disabled badge and slapped it onto the dash. 'We're good all day, now.'

'Keep the engine running. And if Conky calls, you don't know where I am.'

Degsy failed to make eye contact with her, smiling unconvincingly.

'I mean it, Degsy. Remember who pays your bloody wages. And it's *not* Conky.'

Together, she and Gloria stood before the entrance to the refurbished block, staring up at its many floors. Like a northern Tower of Babel, it stretched towards the brooding, bruised skies, housing inhabitants who spoke in the languages of accountancy, advertising, marketing and law but who all understood each other and their corporate world perfectly. There, at the very top, she knew Nigel Bancroft lurked.

'Feeling biblical, Gloria?'

At her side, Gloria nodded. 'Apocalyptically so, Sheila. *The best trick Satan ever did was making the world think he did not exist.*'

'New Testament?' Sheila asked.

Gloria shook her head and started to walk forwards, wheeling her shopping trolley. '*The Usual Suspects*, if memory serves.'

The lift ascended, carrying four other people with them to the upper levels. Smartly dressed men in their fifties, by the looks, smelling of that damned aftershave that Paddy had worn; a ubiquitous stink in every smart bar and restaurant in Cheshire, since the 200-pound price tag spelled success. And there was a young lad – perhaps an office junior – with great hair that the older men could probably only remember wistfully, wearing a cheap suit and plastic shoes. Sheila wished they'd bugger off. In silence, she played through the mental footage of her past twenty-four hours.

Meeting Katrina at Jodrell Bank. Being certain that she was about to pull a gun on her. And it had turned out to be nothing more sinister than Rosary beads.

'I'm a Bride of Christ,' Katrina had said, thrusting Jesus into her face. 'Why would I lie to you about the death of my very own kid brother? Good Lord, Sheila. You've lost all perspective since he died. You're seeing white and calling it black. My faith is as solid as that big dish.' She had pointed up at the telescope, pointing to the heavens. 'Do you really think I'd risk my place in heaven and the purity of my soul to fudge Paddy's death? To what ends? Have I tried to seize O'Brien power? No! Of course not. I'm a nun! A nun, Sheila. And you're mad to think there's some kind of dodgy cover up going on! Get some flipping bereavement counselling, woman! And get to church! When was the last time you confessed?'

There had been nothing but sincerity and grief etched into Katrina's face. Sister Benedicta had seemed to be telling the truth. Conky had insisted that the blurry photo of Paddy was spurious at best. Perhaps he'd been right. Conky surely wouldn't lie. Tariq had simply got it wrong. Hearsay from his father – an old, ailing man in his dotage who had never met Paddy even once in person.

As the men stepped out on the tenth floor, she and Gloria found themselves alone in the lift.

'You sure you're ready for this?' she asked.

Gloria was admiring her pure silk white dress in the mirror like an avenging angel, checking she looked the part for this show-down. She turned to Sheila, her eyes gleaming with deadly intent. 'My son's left me. I might never see my grandson again. My boyfriend tried to kill me. The pastor doesn't love me. I've got killer PMT. Three of those things are down to Bancroft. He's going to wish he'd never been born.'

The lift doors opened at the top. It was easy for two respectable-looking, middle aged women to gain access to Bancroft's business premises. But at the reception desk, they were met with blank stares from the receptionist, who merely batted her false eyelashes at them and chewed gum noisily.

'You got an appointment?' she asked. Boredom freezing her youthful, over-made-up features into a mask of nonchalance. She smelled of market-stall perfume.

In her mind's eye, Sheila had fantasised about going in there, all guns blazing. But the message she wanted to deliver would be ineffective if she couldn't even get past the gatekeeper. She needed to get into Bancroft's inner sanctum. Had to exercise measured self-control where Paddy never had.

'Not exactly. But he'll see me.'

The idiot girl was blinking too much, looking incredulously at Gloria's shopping trolley. 'Oh yeah? Mr Bancroft doesn't see anyone without an appointment.'

'He'll want to see me.' She wanted to slap the girl into submission. Felt she was about to cry inexplicably. Hormones working overtime. Sheila touched her abdomen.

'Name?'

'Tell him Sheila O'Brien has come to discuss terms with him. And I have to see him now. Right this minute. Okay, love?'

At her side, she sensed Gloria, bristling. 'Has nobody

ever told you chewing gum is a foul habit, young lady? Show your elders some respect!'

The girl's face fell. She rolled her eyes, picking up the phone. Speaking, presumably to Bancroft at the other end. Staring at the two women. Nodding. Every second seemed to pass with slavish slowness. Then a nod.

This was it. Squeezing Gloria's hand, Sheila offered a prayer to a God she wasn't sure about that they would triumph; that the baby growing inside her would be safe; that she would prove to Conky and all her male acolytes with their swinging-dick routines and testosterone-fuelled shows of supremacy that she and she alone ruled now.

'Mr Bancroft says he's busy,' the receptionist said. Bat, bat, bat with those cheap showgirl's eyelashes. Superdrug's best.

Caustic ire – the lethal kind that only pregnant women and the PMT-afflicted will ever know – swirled within Sheila, burning away all her self-disciplined resolve. *Bugger this for a game of soldiers.*

Pulling her handgun, she leaned over the reception desk and grabbed the girl by her make-up-stained collar. Pressed the gun to her screaming head. 'Take me to his office now, cunt.'

Euphoria flushed warm through every cell in her body. At her side, Gloria had withdrawn her baseball bat from her tartan chariot of fire and was smashing up everything that came within reach. Holes in partition walls. Shattering the glass of office interior windows.

'*Behold, the day of the Lord comes, cruel, with wrath and fierce anger, to make the land a desolation and to destroy its sinners from it!*' Gloria yelled.

When Bancroft emerged from his office, clearly nonplussed, Gloria whipped out her shotgun, advancing before Sheila could even say a word.

'You!' She poked the shotgun into his belly; the baseball bat pressed against his forehead. The musculature on her forearms was that of an athlete. 'You had Hank lure me into lasciviousness and then try to murder me, you scoundrel!'

Sheila was being upstaged. Delivering a blow to the receptionist's shoulder with the stock of her gun, she forced her down onto the floor and waved her weapon at the office staff.

'Get on the floor! Hands above your head where I can see them. Any of you pricks calls the police, and I'll put a bullet in every last motherfucking one of you!' Turned out, Pulp Friction was great fun after all. Sheila had never felt so alive. She pocketed the gun. Snatched the baseball bat from Gloria, striking Bancroft on the collarbone until he backed inside his office.

'Not enough you should try to rob my business,' Sheila screamed, feeling the burn in her throat. 'But you had to grass. I've had the coppers and the tax man on my back, getting information they could only have got from someone who's in the know.' She smashed a framed portrait of Bancroft that hung on the wall above his glass-topped desk. Bancroft pressed his hands to his ears. Eyes clamped shut. 'And there I was, thinking somebody in my firm had opened their gob!'

'I didn't,' he said, shaking his head. Not so brave, now that he wasn't flanked by his two beefcakes.

'You plant one of your arse-kissing lackeys in my cannabis farm? He's feeding information to you and you're passing it onto that wanker, Ellis James? Is that it?' Pop. The glass top on the desk shattered beautifully with an almighty blow from the baseball bat. Pain ricocheted up her arms with the force, but she barely registered the ache. 'And you blow up my damned builders' merchants, nearly killing me and her!' Her ears rang as Gloria fired two shots – one into a cabinet, whose glazed doors fell to the ground in shards like a cloudburst in miniature; one into the maple board table that ran the width of the far end of the office. 'And then, you send some fat twonk to pump my business partner, in more ways than one!'

'What the—?' Bancroft was on his knees. Staring up at her now with questioning eyes. Two-faced shite was full of it. 'I don't know what you're talking about, you crazy bitch.'

'Hank. Hank the bloody Wank, trying to install fibre-optic spying equipment into *my* bleeding brickwork, so he could earwig on what me and Conky say in *my* frigging bedroom. Cheeky bastard!'

At her back, she could hear Gloria reloading her shotgun with fresh cartridges. Clicking the barrels into place. Some commotion outside, though, above the petrified din from the prone staff. Security, perhaps? Police? Surely not. They had to get out of there. Shit. Had to get back to Degsy.

But Gloria had marched forward, gun raised and pointed at Bancroft's head. 'Nobody makes Gloria Bell look like a fool and gets away with it.'

'No, Gloria. We've gotta go!'

Too late. With a deafening boom, the shotgun went off. Bancroft dropped to the floor, writhing for some seconds, then still. All that was left of his beautifully styled hair was a smoking patch of florid, bleeding scalp. Was he dead?

Backing away from the Birmingham crime boss, Sheila turned to run. They'd gone too far, but perhaps they could get away. That blissful adrenalin had been replaced by a transfusion of pure cortisol and unfettered dread. She could barely see. Panicked tears streamed freely

'Freeze!' Men's voices. Shouting at her. 'You're under citizens' arrest!'

Sheila blinked away the tears to see two security guards. Unarmed. Chancing their luck, clearly, because Sheila and Gloria were mere women. The relief was intense and instant.

'Kiss my arse!' Sheila said, drawing her handgun and waving it at them.

Their flushed faces soon drained of colour. They dropped to the floor, lacing their hands together above their heads.

Without turning to Gloria, she yelled. 'Let's go!'

Stomping through that foyer, she felt triumphant, waving the gun at anyone who dared look at her. She was better than Paddy. She had done all this without the need for Conky. Creating a minimal scene by gangsters' standards, she had delivered the message that Sheila O'Brien was not to be trifled with.

Gloria had pressed for the lift but it was already coming up, up, up.

'Nearly home and dry,' she said, patting Sheila on the back with the hand that wasn't still clutching the shotgun.

Sheila nodded. Grinning. Breathing too fast. Exhilarated. 'Bancroft picked on the wrong one.'

'Do you think I killed him?'

Shrugging, she said, 'Do you care?'

She moved to the window – a cursory glance at the world below to check that Degsy was still parked on the street. Except there were two Tactical Aid Unit vans parked out front. Two coppers had hauled Degsy over the bonnet of the car and were patting him down. A guy who looked more like military than a cop pointed a long-range rifle at his head. Could someone have feasibly sneaked a call to the police?

'We've got company,' Sheila said.

The lift kept coming, not stopping at any of the other floors.

'They're in the lift. Cob your weapons,' she said, throwing her gun out of reach to the far side of a pot plant.

Gloria followed suit just as the lift doors parted with a ding. Sheila's legs gave way as six, maybe seven armed-response police emerged. A phalanx of black Kevlar, with heavy artillery trained on the two of them.

'Hands in the air!'

Shit.

Chapter 43

Tariq, then Conky.

Tariq was struggling to get to sleep on the sofa bed in the guest room. He could feel the springs digging into his hips. The wadding in the mattress felt uncomfortable. But still, he consoled himself, his father was back, Anjum had not yet gone to the police with what she thought she knew about the Boddlingtons and he had acquired a cook to manufacture pharmaceutical drugs.

Shifting around so that he was lying on his back, he looked up at the ceiling. Imagined Sheila O'Brien on top of him, riding away with a look of pure delight on her face; her tonged hair bouncing up and down on top of her small, jiggling breasts. He reached into his shorts and felt his erection. Started to massage his penis, feeling the tension leech out of him. Conky himself had said his father's photo of Paddy O'Brien was nothing but a coincidence, captured by the shaky hand of an old man. He had a willing lover who made him feel young again; made him forget that his wife had filed for divorce and that his business partner had been sucked into the quicksand of depression.

Things were looking up. Sliding his pants down hurriedly, he lay on his side, tugging away, thinking of Sheila's pert

356

mouth around his manhood. He needed to come. Needed to lose himself in a moment of self-indulgence. Except there was a loud whumph noise downstairs.

'What the hell was that?' he muttered to himself.

He could smell smoke and petrol. Couldn't he? No! No! *Don't be daft*. Perhaps it was his overwrought imagination. It had been a hell of a few months, let alone weeks.

Continuing to masturbate, he put the strange noise out of his mind. The alarm certainly hadn't gone off, so perhaps it was just movement in the old house's joists as they contracted with cold. The heating had gone off an hour ago. It made sense.

Feeling his mojo return in a warm flush of pleasure, he pictured lovely Sheila yet again. Wished she had answered her phone earlier. Couldn't wait to arrange a new rendezvous so he could hold her in his arms.

But in the next room, the high-pitched wail that could only belong to his youngest, Zahid, struck up, cooling his ardour in an instant. He waited in the dark to see if the child would settle. The tell-tale padding of small feet on the landing and wracking sobs told him something was amiss. A temperature? A bad dream? Perhaps he would go to the master bedroom to rouse Anjum.

'Daddy!' The door to the guest room crashed open. There was Zahid in his Disney pyjamas, clutching his teddy. 'I heard a noise. It smells funny. I'm scared.'

The choking stench of smoke and petrol billowed invisibly into the room. Tariq yanked up his pants, all thoughts of escaping his life for a moment gone.

Fire. Was it possible?

'Let's go and wake Mummy, Zahid. I want you to stay with her until I've worked out what's going on.'

On the landing, he could hear the crackling of flames

downstairs. Could see the glow even from here on the first-floor landing.

'Anjum! Wake up! We're on fire.' Ushering his son into Anjum's room, he snatched his daughter Shazia out of bed, carrying her sleeping form to his wife, though she clung to him like a baby koala and wouldn't initially let go.

'Fire?' Anjum said, throwing the duvet back in haste. 'Call 999!' She started to cough as the smoke bit. The children were howling, clearly terrified at a commotion they didn't fully understand. 'Get your dad. We've got to get out. I'll carry the kids downstairs.'

'Wait!' he said, retreating to the doorway. Glancing at the orange and yellow light that flickered up the walls of the staircase. 'Let me check it's safe.' Holding his T-shirt over his mouth, he sprinted to the top of the staircase. Felt the oppressive heat and smoke rising in coils to greet him like an agitated king cobra. The ground floor was engulfed.

'Get to the fire escape in the attic!' he shouted to Anjum, just as there was an explosion beneath him. Perhaps the boiler in the utility room. It shook the whole house.

As Anjum clattered up the stairs to the suite of rooms in the attic, clutching an apoplectic Zahid under her arm and leading a weeping Shazia by the hand, Tariq ran to his father's room.

'Dad! Dad!' he cried.

The smoke was thick in here. Too thick. Somehow penetrating from the kitchen below. Tariq could barely breathe. Coughing, he forced his way in, the floor scorching hot beneath his bare feet. Could barely see the unconscious form of his father, lying on the floor on the far side of his bed. 'Dad!'

With inexorable force, the acrid black smoke clawed its way through the gaps between the old Edwardian floorboards, smothering everything it touched with its sooty, deathly embrace. Flames started to lick up, piercing the gloom with shafts of hellish light. As Tariq felt the darkness overcome him, he realised the insulation in the void between the joists had caught ablaze. Sinking to the ground beside his father, the last thing he saw before he passed out was the entire floor giving way with the screech and whine of stressed timber, collapsing into the inferno that had once been a family kitchen, engulfing the nightstand, his father's bed and—

* * *

When Conky arrived back at Sheila's Bramshott mansion, he drove the Panamera into the garaging and locked the door. Walked under a full moon and a black sky studded with stars to the end of the back garden, enjoying the crunch of gravel underfoot as he traversed the path, though his limbs were stiff from his fall from the ladder. He could still smell lavender in the air, though summer was long gone. He whistled happily as he replaced the petrol canister on the dusty, cobwebby shelf in the garden shed, savouring the inimitable aroma of rotting vegetation that came from the adjacent compost heap and the bags of ericaceous compost that the gardener had stowed inside. Emptied of its contents now, the canister wouldn't pose a threat to anybody in here. The cook's matches he returned to the knick-knacks drawer in the utility room.

Feeling hopeful that Sheila would be returned to him soon enough, once he had let her stew for a bit in a holding cell, Conky sat on the edge of his and Sheila's bed. He pulled off his socks. Took down his trousers. Congratulated himself on a job well done. There was only one obstacle that remained, steadfastly blocking the path of true love.

He sprawled across the emperor-sized bed and retrieved

the offending object that had been wrapped in toilet roll and stuffed at the back of Sheila's bedside cabinet. Took the positive pregnancy test out of its wrappings and stared dolefully at the two blue lines.

'Ah, Sheila, Sheila, Sheila.'

Perhaps she would claim the baby was his, until it popped out, decidedly darker-skinned than your average Celt and bearing none of the McFadden hallmarks of a beak of a nose and eyebrows that would scare the crows. He had never told her that he had always fired blanks.

What would Genghis and Kublai Khan do in the face of such an obstacle? Conky picked up the fifth book in Conn Iggulden's *Conqueror* series, running his calloused finger over the cover. Inhaling deeply and imagining the fabled warriors laying waste to their enemies' kingdoms in a bid to make that land Mongolian.

Setting the book aside, smiling, he snapped the pregnancy test in two and tossed it into the bin.

Chapter 44

Sheila

'Please God, let me get out of this,' Sheila muttered to the scuffed and dirty wall of the holding cell with its scratched graffiti, splattered stains from old vomit and gob-marks, where other detainees had left their desperate imprints, praying for bail and cursing the justice system. She lay on her uncomfortable bunk, curled up into a foetal position with her hand held protectively over her belly. An over-nighter in custody had served as her own personal purgatory. 'What the hell was I thinking?'

She felt the tears coming. Tried to hold them back, knowing that's exactly what Paddy had always done, presuming the hard bastard had still been capable of crying. Even at Jack's funeral, he hadn't shed a tear. He had always made a big thing about being emotionally invulnerable. Now, as he had been the King, she was the Queen. She had to be made of iron too. 'Stop bloody crying, you silly cow.' She wiped the tears away defiantly, realising that she had to keep strong for Amy, Dahlia and the baby inside her, if for no other reason.

Briefly, she wondered how Gloria was faring in the next cell. Had Gloria killed Bancroft with that final blast from the shotgun? How the hell could they explain this away? Even if they had not been found toting the weapons and had left no prints, there would surely be CCTV footage that would say otherwise. Bancroft had an entire office suite of witnesses. They had been caught red-handed.

'I'm going down,' she said to the latrine in a small voice. 'Jesus Christ. I don't believe it.'

She stood abruptly, almost knocked off her feet by the rush of blood to the opposite ends of her body. Steadied herself against the door, bashing it with her fists.

'Where's my damned solicitor? I want to see my brief. *Now!*'

Hours later, after she had reluctantly eaten the carb-laden grey mush that had been offered as an excuse for lunch, the door to her cell was flung open. A stout WPC stood expectantly in the doorway, eyeing her as though she was an infestation rather than a human being.

'Where's my solicitor?' she asked. 'I'm pregnant. You can't treat me like this. I'm innocent!'

'That's what they all say, love,' the WPC said, contorting her lumpen, well-scrubbed face into a smile that was anything but benign. 'Detective Ellis James wants to interview you. Follow me.'

Don't speak. Don't give him anything, Sheila reminded herself, wondering why the hell she hadn't heard from the outside world. Silently, she prayed that Gloria wouldn't shoot her mouth off. No, Gloria knew better than that.

In the interview room that stank of cleaning fluid and stale booze from its previous occupant, Sheila sat gingerly on a chair that had a dubious stain ingrained in the seat. Ellis James ran through the formalities. Set the tape running. Grinned at her, as though she were the centre of his universe

362

and he were the most content man in the world, hopelessly in love with her. He sighed.

'So, Mrs O'Brien. At last.' He put his hands behind his head. His faded blue shirt untucked itself from his trousers, riding up over a blond hairy navel. 'You're a guest in Her Majesty's halfway house and I feel confident we'll be enjoying your company for a good while.' He leaned forwards, pushing his smudged glasses up his nose with a grubby-looking finger. 'Smashing up the offices of a respected businessman with a baseball bat, eh?'

Sheila stared at the recording equipment. Focussed on James's unshaven face. He still had a whiff of cheap car interior and egg sandwiches about him. Sergeant Stakeout. Bloody self-righteous tosser was loving every minute of this humiliation. *Remember not to lash out. Keep your gob shut at all costs.*

'What were you doing at Bancroft's offices with Gloria Bell?'

'No comment.'

'The armed response unit found a baseball bat, a shotgun and a handgun on the premises. Where did you get the guns, Sheila?'

'No comment.' She fixed her gaze on his florid cheeks, willing herself not to cry or lean over and punch him.

'Mr Bancroft has been taken to hospital with flesh wounds.'

Oh, so he's not dead, Sheila thought, feeling hope surge inside her.

'Oddly, he's not pressing charges against you or Ms Bell. Why is that, given the amount of damage you wrought to his premises, Sheila?'

Result! 'No comment.'

'We'll still do you for the firearms possession, though.

And if the ammunition that nearly blew his head off matches your handgun or that shotgun, you're in very deep, very hot water, whether he presses charges or not. Lucky for you, he owns the building. Shame his staff aren't seeking damages.' Ellis James cocked his head to one side and scrutinised her with narrowed eyes. 'What hold have you got over Bancroft?'

Sheila folded her arms, trying her damnedest to look as confident as possible. Feeling optimistic that he couldn't do either of them for firearms possession, could he? He was surely bluffing on that front. But this was still uncharted territory. With her arms folded tightly across her chest, it was all she could do to stop her body from visibly quaking. She raised an eyebrow archly, as though she knew something James didn't.

'No comment.'

She emitted a long, bored sigh. Expended every last ounce of mental energy on this show of bravado, whilst imagining the faces of her beautiful daughters. If only Dahlia were here as her legal representative. Now, more than ever, she needed somebody close to her to tell her it was going to be okay.

James shifted in his seat. A whiff of stale armpits as he did so. 'Never mind,' he said. 'It will all come out in the wash. In the meantime, I'm having your house and business premises searched.' There was a breeziness to his voice, accompanied by a yellow-toothed grin. Good on the inside. Rotten on the out. 'Conky McFadden's having to play coffee boy to my fellow detectives and our lovely sniffer dogs.' He pursed his lips. Tutted and looked melodramatically to heaven. 'And then, of course, we've got to round up all those landlords, club owners and restauranteurs you extort protection money from.'

Sheila felt her neck tighten in the grip of burning, tense muscles. Her breath came quickly, though she was careful to keep as quiet as possible. How the hell did he know who owned an O'Brien pub? That had been the best kept secret for decades.

'No comment.'

'See, I've got this very handy informant . . .'

She was tempted to say she didn't believe him. Frank wouldn't grass. Conky was her most trusted ally. Gloria would never, ever implicate herself in a crime. She was too clever and self-interested for that. And Paddy was dead . . . wasn't he?

Her insides fizzed like a bottle of cola being violently shaken. Paddy. No! Everyone had insisted that Paddy was definitely dead and that Youssuf Khan had coincidentally snapped the wrong man in the right place at a fortuitous time. How she wished at that moment that she'd had Paddy's coffin exhumed. She now felt like a hardened smoker with a persistent cough who had opted not to have a chest X-ray. If Paddy were somehow alive, did he realise the extent of Sheila's murderous plans?

'No comment,' she said, barely able to hear her now feeble voice above the clamour of conflicting thoughts and theories in her head.

So wrapped up was she in her private nightmare that she almost didn't hear Ellis James saying, 'Ooh, terrible news about Tariq Khan, by the way.' He tutted. Shaking his head.

'What?'

James sat in silence for too long, studying her, perhaps trying to intuit what her immediate reaction had given away.

'Fatal blaze burned his house to the ground. Haven't you heard?'

She felt a griping pain in her abdomen. Gasped. Clutched her belly. *Fatal.*

James continued, rocking back on his chair as though he were telling a bedtime story with alacrity. 'Yes, the body they found had to be carried out in separate bags. It was like a well-roasted chicken apparently. Flesh just falling off the bone.'

'No,' Sheila said. 'No.'

The abdominal cramping worsened as Sheila processed the information, throwing up a wave of nausea. She felt the blood drain from her face; her lips prickling cold. *Don't puke.* A fatal blaze. Surely no accident. But who had been behind it? Bancroft? Could Hank have planted a timed explosive device in Tariq's Boddlington Park home before luring Gloria to Blackpool? Perhaps. What about Paddy?!

A cooked body in bags.

She was poised to ask whose body it had been. But the unwelcome sensation between her legs snatched away the intended words from the tip of her tongue. She looked down to see a vivid red bloodstain flowering quickly on the pale fabric of her skirt.

Chapter 45

Tariq

'My God,' Anjum said, pulling up outside what little was left of their family home. 'Look at it.'

Wincing with the effort of leaning forward to get a good view of the Edwardian house he'd bought with proceeds from his first big deal, some fifteen years earlier, Tariq choked back a sob. The glorious part-timbered façade of the three-storey detached gentleman's residence had been reduced to a single-storey ruin, barely supported by the blackened skeleton of the remaining few beams that pointed to where the first floor had been. Of the roof and upper storeys, there were no traces beyond a pile of charred rubble and scattered slates.

Anjum turned to him, tears in her eyes. She glanced back at the children. 'I'm glad they're asleep. I'm glad they can't see this.' She reached out to touch his forearm.

He breathed in sharply, though her fingers had merely brushed his bandages. 'Don't. The morphine's wearing off.'

His voice sounded muffled to him. Examining his reflection in the mirror that was embedded into the car's lowered sun visor, he felt like he was looking at an extra from the set of an old horror flick. Beneath the bandages, he knew his hair was gone and that he would be scarred for life. And yet, he had still fared better than his poor, poor father. He shut the sun visor quickly.

'I can't believe he's gone,' he said. His tears stung as they seeped into the fabric dressing. 'I loved him so much.'

Anjum nodded, wiping her eyes on her silk dupatta. 'I know. Me too. I'm so sorry, Tariq.' She took hold of the fingers of his left hand – the only place free of dressings. Stroked his wedding ring finger. 'I realise now. We've got to pull together.' Her voice was small. Defeated. She looked over at Jonny's modern mansion, diagonally opposite, where there was no sign of his business partner or his wife, Sandra, at any of the windows. 'We've only got each other, haven't we? Come on. Let's get out of here.'

As the car pulled away from the cul-de-sac that had held so many of his happy memories and so many of his and Jonny's secrets, Tariq sobbed. He sent a silent prayer skywards, hoping that his father had finally found the paradise he had so desperately hankered after and that he had been reunited with Tariq's beloved mother, after so long apart.

Deep down, Tariq was certain that the blaze had not been down to some unfortunate electrical fault or gas leak. The investigators would surely come back with a verdict of arson. And that purest of old souls, Youssuf Khan, had been caught in the crossfire of Tariq's reckless life. The shame of that knowledge bit even deeper than the agony of his burns. But in amongst the wreckage of his life, Tariq realised that something could yet be salvaged: his marriage.

Locking their dalliance in the imaginary box that contained every sinful memory Tariq had, he pushed Sheila O'Brien as anything other than a business rival out of his mind for good.

Chapter 46

Sheila

'The baby's going to be fine,' the obstetrician said, reading through her notes. She glanced down at the handcuffs that bound Sheila to the hospital bed. A slight curl of her lip evident before her gaze moved onto Sheila's abdomen. 'Your placenta's very very low. You must take it easy.' The furtive sideways look at the female police officer who was sitting by Sheila's bedside said everything. 'Difficult, given your unusual circumstances.'

Finally their eyes met.

Sheila felt her cheeks flush hot. 'My daughter's due to arrive any minute. She's a big hotshot in a London law firm, you know. She's going to sort all this nonsense out.'

She rolled her eyes at her uniformed babysitter and offered the obstetrician a weak smile, belying the fact that the last twenty-four hours had been nightmarish. Conky had failed to organise her usual legal representation, which meant he definitely knew about Tariq and was far from happy. Gloria was no use to her either, given she was still in a holding cell at the cop shop. Her eldest daughter had reluctantly agreed to get on the next train out of London and step in. By the end of the day, Dahlia would be faced with the uncomfortable prospect of finding out how her mother really made her living. Still, it was time for the family to close ranks.

The obstetrician replaced the clipboard of notes onto the end of the bed. She treated Sheila to a smile that looked begrudged. 'Well, placenta praevia can be very serious indeed and you're lucky you didn't lose this pregnancy. We'll have to hope the placenta moves out of the way of the cervix in time for labour, otherwise you'll have to have a planned caesarean ahead of delivery.' She pursed her lips. Looked again at the flint-faced copper in the day-chair. 'Have they let you inform the father?'

'It's complicated.'

'I see.'

Sheila wondered briefly what a middle-aged obstetrician, presumably with her reproductive aspirations long behind her, made of a woman like her: over the hill, up the duff and under arrest. Screw her. 'No, you don't see. You don't see at all, love.'

She swallowed a sob at the thought of Tariq. A visit to her cell from her man on the inside had revealed that her lover was still alive but badly burnt, and that his father had died in the blaze. How would Tariq react to the secondary bombshell that Sheila was carrying his child? Was there a future for them? More to the point, had Conky had anything to do with his house fire?

Sleeping fitfully for several hours, Sheila was jolted awake by the sound of Dahlia's voice. She looked up at her daughter, whose furrowed brow conveyed confusion at best, and irritation at worst.

'Mum.' Dahlia reached down and kissed her on the cheek. Her dark bobbed hair hung in tracts over a subtly made-up face that was end-of-the-day shiny. She smelled of faded expensive perfume and coffee. Still dressed in a skirt-suit and heels, it was clear she had come straight from work. 'First of all, are you okay?'

Sheila shuffled up the bed and smiled. Warmth flooding through her tired body at the thought that her child had finally rocked up in support of her. 'Oh, you're a sight for sore eyes, my love. Ooh, I've missed you. Give your mam another kiss.' She tapped her cheek in invitation. Dismayed to see Dahlia take a seat, ignoring the plea. Her daughter's body language was all business.

'This isn't a social call or a dutiful daughter thing. I'm here as your legal representative, Mum. I think you've got some explaining to do, haven't you?'

With the policewoman gone to allow them privacy, Sheila studied her daughter's earnest face. To be economical with the truth or to tell her the whole shebang? She knew what to do.

'Your dad was a liar, Dahlia. All your life, you've been living a lie without realising it. Everything you had, every privilege you've enjoyed, has been ill-gotten gains. I'm sorry. But there you have it.'

'Are you telling me—?'

Sheila held her hand up. 'Let me speak. Before I tell you what I'm gonna tell you, you need to understand, I'm not your dad. I love you and I respect you and I'm not going to lie to you like he did. I'm the Queen of South Manchester, chuck. Your mother's an organised crime boss. I rule the roost. And yes, I'm pregnant. And yes, they've caught me teaching a rival a hard lesson. And no, I'm not going to apologise for it. This is who I am and no matter how screwed up things get, I intend to win this game. And now, you're in it with me.'

Dahlia closed her eyes. Her lips were a grim, downturned

line. Would she simply get up and walk away? Tell the police everything Sheila had just confessed to? She held her breath, waiting to hear if her firstborn would set aside her solicitor's moral code and her distant demeanour to don the mantel of a loyal O'Brien. What stuff was Dahlia really made of?

Dahlia opened her eyes. Sniffed and pulled her skirt down towards her knees. She took a sheaf of notes out from her boxy lawyer's briefcase.

'So, the good news is, the case is weak. You were wearing gloves and you discarded your weapons, so there's no forensic link to either you or Gloria. The CCTV footage from the street apparently just shows two middle-aged women going into a corporate building, one wheeling a shopping wagon. No harm in that. Bancroft's security say they've got zip. This Nigel Bancroft is clearly a big fan of the no-grassing rule,' Dahlia said, as if Sheila hadn't just revealed that her daughter's life had been nothing more than a stage set of a semi-rural idyll, concealing the street-robber's paradise of a grimy parking lot behind. 'I'll bet he's also paid his staff to keep quiet too, so the old adage of "honour amongst thieves" has some substance. You seem to have won a turf war, which is no mean feat. Well done.' She reached out to touch the part of the honeycomb blanket that covered Sheila's belly. Withdrew her hand. 'A new baby in the family. Good. Saves me a job. If we're going to be frank, you may as well know I personally have absolutely zero interest in motherhood.' She locked eyes with Sheila, clearly challenging her. No hint of sentimentality in her voice.

Sheila nodded, fighting off tears of relief that she might wake from this nightmare; tears of bitter disappointment that the brisk efficiency of her daughter didn't guarantee that the girl loved her. Was she so very different from Gloria Bell, after all? 'Does this mean you're on my side?'

Hooking her hair behind her ear, Dahlia raised an eyebrow. She spoke quietly. 'Mum, I'm not going to engage in a debate about how comprehensively you've just ruined my life and my legitimate career. Right now, if you weren't pregnant, I'd walk out of here and never come back. There's no point explaining how what you do – what dad did – goes against every fibre of my being and every value I've ever held dear. I'm a fucking solicitor.' She enunciated carefully. The resentment was audible in every clipped consonant. Then, she sighed. 'But you're family, and I love you.'

Sheila smiled broadly, holding her hand out to her daughter, which Dahlia took, tutting.

'You can't put a good woman down, eh?'

Dahlia smiled, finally. 'You can't put an O'Brien woman down.'

Chapter 47

Paddy, then Kyle

'You all right, Ken, love?' Brenda shouted from the lounge.

Paddy could hear applause and laughter coming from the TV. Some shiny bloody nightly chat show she loved to watch, hosted by two birds and some smug London ponce he'd never even heard of. If he didn't feel so gruesome already, watching that crap would definitely be enough to send him over the edge. He rubbed at his stomach, wondering at the diarrhoea he'd been stricken by over the last few days. Had it been something he'd eaten in the pub? Brenda and that little sneaky shit Kyle seemed right as rain. Was he about to have another explosive episode? He grimaced at the wind that tore through his gut.

'Are you coming in, love? The next guest is coming on.' Her high-pitched voice had grown even more irritating of late. Especially since he had given her that black eye. Now, he could hear the nagging need for approval in every word she uttered. *Do you love me, Kenneth? How can I be better, Kenneth?* The harder he hit her, the more she demeaned herself. Women like Brenda couldn't live without a man. Pathetic.

'I'll be in in a minute, I said,' he shouted, satisfied that there had been sufficient irritation in his voice. He belched painfully. Felt like he had been thumped in the chest. 'Jesus Christ, Brenda. You're on my case all the frigging time. It's like I'm being policed. Let me breathe, woman.'

He knew she would be quaking on the sofa, worried and wondering exactly what she may feasibly have done to piss him off yet again. Sap.

Bloody hell. This wind was bad. He was nearly crippled with pain. And sweating. A cold sweat had broken out on his forehead and neck.

Looking at the screen and the flickering cursor at the end of the damning statement he had just typed to Ellis James under the guise of Shadow Hunter, he grimaced with satisfaction. Rubbed his hands together. Turns out, Sheila had landed herself at the bottom of a shitty, six-feet-deep hole, all of her own accord. He was merely going to knock the nails into her coffin with a little more information that would bring the whole O'Brien protection racket down and her with it. When he eventually cast his and Katrina's cover-up aside to reclaim his throne, he would be able to rebuild all that side of the business. Intimidating people to cough up cash had never been a problem for Paddy O'Brien. Better he should punish his inconstant widow and punish her right for what the scheming, lying bitch had done. Paddy O'Brien had only to clamber over one last layer of his enemies' bones to claim his position at the top of the heap once more. *That* was something to celebrate.

Flump, flump, flump. He could hear Brenda's slippers dragging against the floor. She was coming in. He switched screens abruptly to bring up an article about heart disease.

'Are you sure you're all right, Ken, love?' she said. She was carrying the evening newspaper, which she dropped onto the table beside him. Enfolded her arms around him from behind. He could feel her pillowy breasts against his back; could see, reflected in the laptop's shining screen, the rainbow of purple-green bruising all down the left side of her face where he had hit her. It was still swollen and red on her brow bone where the skin had broken beneath his knuckle.

'I was just reading up on my ticker,' he said, batting her arms away. 'All the shits might be to do with that. I'm not a well man, am I?' He silently congratulated himself on having endured most of this stomach upset in her house. Better she should clean up after him than he should have to wipe the carsey down after himself. That kind of skivvying was unbecoming for a man. Especially a man like him. 'Do us a favour, will you? Pour us a whisky. I'm parched. Anyone would think you're leaving me gasping on purpose. You trying to dry me out?' He looked round at her, engaging her in direct eye contact that she simply couldn't hold.

Obviously, she started mumbling something or other about how she only wanted to keep him happy and look after him and how she was so sorry her Kyle had said those nasty things. The kid didn't know what he was on about. It was his age. Yadda, yadda, yadda.

'And he swore blind he wouldn't touch your betting slips or your cigs again,' she said, setting the tumbler of Famous Grouse onto the kitchen table and kissing the top of his head. 'He's a good lad, really, you know.'

'Leave us the bottle.'

''Course, Ken.' She set the half-empty bottle on the table beside the laptop. 'That's your special tipple anyway. Nobody touches it but my Kenneth. Don't you worry. I've warned our Kyle. He knows.'

'He wouldn't dare.'

Once she was back in the living room, watching her

precious, crappy TV programme, Paddy flicked through the newspaper, trying to ignore the crippling spasm in his stomach. He wondered if there would be anything in there about Sheila or the Boddlingtons. Sometimes the press uncovered nuggets of gossip that otherwise failed to reach him through Hank.

'Load of cobblers,' he said, pausing briefly to read a story about a swearing parrot in Blackley that had earned its elderly owner an ASBO.

A headline pulled his attention to the opposite page.

HEYWOOD BUILDER DIES IN BLACKPOOL THRILL-RIDE SHOCKER.

Holding his breath, Paddy read on with a sense of dread, somehow knowing this tale of misadventure was connected to him.

'Hank McMahon, a fifty-nine-year-old Heywood builder, originally from Parsons Croft, was thrown from the roller-coaster's carriage . . .'

Hank. Hank the Wank. His oldest school friend and paid ally was dead. Paddy was surprised by the sudden lump in his throat. Embarrassed and irritated by his own weakness, he swallowed it down with a sip of whisky.

'Police are asking for witnesses to come forward who might know the identity of a black woman who had been with Mr McMahon shortly before his death.'

Gloria. That Bible-bashing hypocrite. Who else could it feasibly be? How could Hank have put himself in that position? Selfish, stupid, trusting dickhead had left Paddy to rot in exile.

'Shit!' Paddy rubbed his eyes and grimaced. Shook his head. 'I've had it with the Bells. Gloria's gonna pay for this.'

Wondering how he might best avenge his friend's death, with a shaking hand, Paddy downed the tumbler of whisky.

It burned as it hit the back of his throat. He gasped, hoping that the alcohol would both settle his nerves and also go some way to killing off whatever germs were making a mockery of his digestive system. An ominous gurgling sound came from his stomach. He arched his back as an agonising spasm shot through his lower intestine.

'Fucking hell. I feel like I'm dying. Again.' Stroking the scar tissue on his torso, he wondered if he'd have time to make it to the bathroom. Launched himself off the greasy pine kitchen chair.

As he lumbered upstairs, he passed Kyle. Hanging around like a bad smell in the hall, all arms and legs and shit hair. Had the snidey little twat been watching Paddy?

'What you looking at?' Paddy said.

* * *

'I don't know,' Kyle responded. Not quite loud enough for the old bastard to hear. 'They don't label shit.'

With his mam's bastard of a feller out of sight, Kyle slid into the kitchen. The TV was still going. Good. His mam was too wrapped up in *The One Show* to pay any attention to his movements. He navigated that house like a wraith. Always below the radar. Well, almost always.

'Right, you old bastard,' he muttered, withdrawing the small bottle from his trouser pocket. No label on the glass, though Kyle knew exactly what was inside because he had personally produced the perfect antidote to the poisonous Kenneth Wainwright. Who knew arsenic could be concocted so easily in a school chemistry lab, during lunch break? Had that wanker ever bothered to ask him what his best subject was? Had he actually checked the browser history on those occasions when he had borrowed Kyle's laptop without so much as a please or thank you? No! Course not. Amazing what deadly secrets the internet laid bare to a promising young chemist. And now, the evil bully would be sludge at the bottom of a barrel before he even realised why he felt like he was dying.

In the bathroom above, Kyle could hear this cuckoo in his mother's nest groaning. Flushing the toilet. Groaning again. Thumping the wall. He was in agony, Kyle knew. Good.

Squeezing the pipette in the small, unassuming-looking bottle, he withdrew the tiniest amount and administered it carefully into the neck of the Famous Grouse. A bully like that didn't deserve to die quickly, and Kyle knew just how to make his end as drawn out and dreadful as possible.

Most important of all, as any aspiring young killer worth his salt knew, Kyle had already worked out precisely how he was going to cover his tracks. A cunning cover up was always the key to murder. Nobody had come close to solving the circumstances surrounding his abusive father's disappearance. And soon, Kenneth Wainwright – or Paddy O'Brien as Kyle had recently learned was this wanker's real name – would disappear without a trace.

THE END

Acknowledgements

None of my writing would see the light of day without help, expertise and emotional sustenance from the following people:

Natalie and Adam for making me want to be a better woman and to demonstrate that a big dream, a large helping of optimism and a whole heap of graft can move mountains.

Christian for his child-wrangling when a deadline looms and for his continuing friendship and support.

Special Agent Caspian Dennis for executing his role in the drama of my life with great wit, poise and panache, offering friendship, wisdom and cast-iron loyalty without question.

The team at Abner Stein – especially Sandy Violette, Laura Baxendale and Felicity Amor. Never was there a shit-hotter literary agency.

My editor, Phoebe Morgan, who is always a pleasure to deal with, and the team at Avon – Helen H, Oli, Rachel, Victoria, Molly, Rosie, Hannah, Sabah and Elon. The energy of those guys could power the national grid!

Nigel Adams, who gave me great advice about fire investigation.

All the many bloggers who have given me their ongoing support, both for the George McKenzie series and for this

Manchester series, and the members of various book clubs, who are incredibly engaged readers. Those guys are always a pleasure to interact with.

Barry Forshaw and Jake Kerridge, who saw fit to really enjoy *Born Bad* and then write about it in the national press! Becky Want, for having me on her splendid BBC Radio Manchester show.

Angela, for helping me to find my voice.

Tammy Cohen, for sage-like advice (which I often ignore because I'm pig-headed), connoisseur-level gin preparation and a half-cow, half-dog called Doris.

The cockblankets, for the finest friendship and heartiest laughs a gal could have, and my other writing and non-writing pals, who listen to me drone on incessantly about my private life and my professional conundra. I won't name you all. I'll just dedicate a book to you at some point in the future!

The wonderful people of Manchester, for providing endless inspiration for a series that is so close to my heart.

Finally, thanks to my readers, for being the best readers in the whole wide world.

Find out how it all began in
Born Bad,
the first in the gritty
Manchester crime series

'A leading light in Mancunian noir' *Guardian*

The pulse-pounding thriller
from Marnie Riches.
For anyone who loves Jo Nesbo and
Stieg Larsson, this book is for you!

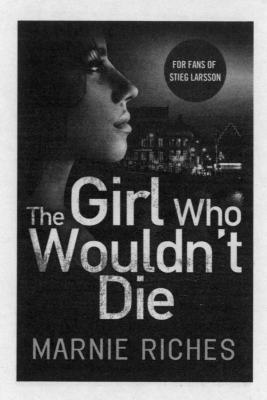

Start your journey into the world of
George McKenzie now!

The second book in the bestselling
George McKenzie series.

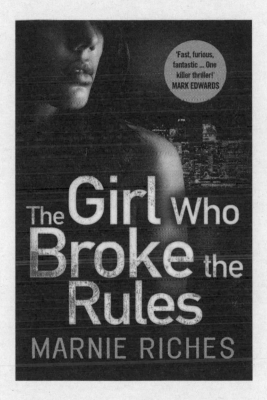

George is back – and you need to be ready.

The third edge-of-your-seat thriller
in the George McKenzie series.

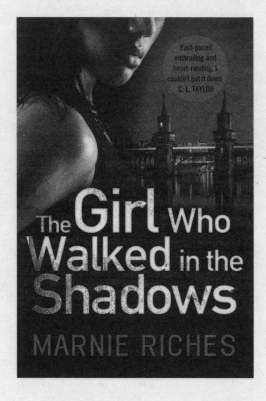

'Fast-paced,
enthralling and
heart-rending, I
couldn't put it down'
C. L. TAYLOR

The Girl Who
Walked in the
Shadows

MARNIE RICHES

Can George outrun death to shed light on two
terrible mysteries? Or has she met her match . . .?

The fourth gripping thriller in
the George McKenzie series.

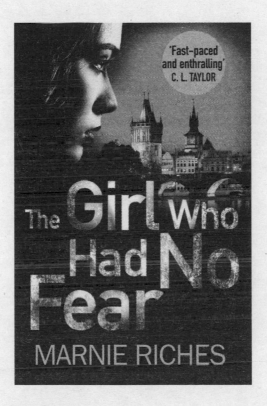

'Fast-paced
and enthralling'
C. L. TAYLOR

The Girl Who
Had No
Fear

MARNIE RICHES

**Four dead bodies have been pulled from
the canals – and that number's rising fast.
Is there a serial killer on the loose?**